Mink Elliott is a journalist who has worked on magazines in both the UK and Australia. She and her husband live happily (most of the time) with their three-year-old daughter in Sydney.

The Pi**ed-Off Parents Club

MINK ELLIOTT

sphere

SPHERE

First published in Great Britain as a paperback original
in 2010 by Sphere
Reprinted 2010

A CIP catalogue record for this book
is available from the British Library

ISBN 978-0-7515-4339-1

Typeset in Caslon by M Rules
Printed and bound in Great Britain by
Clays Ltd, St Ives plc

Papers used by Sphere are natural, renewable and
recyclable products sourced from well-managed forests and certified
in accordance with the rules of the Forest Stewardship Council.

Mixed Sources
Product group from well-managed
forests and other controlled sources
www.fsc.org   Cert no. SGS-COC-004081
© 1996 Forest Stewardship Council
FSC

Sphere
An imprint of
Little, Brown Book Group
100 Victoria Embankment
London EC4Y 0DY

An Hachette UK Company
www.hachette.co.uk

www.litttlebrown.co.uk

To Mum and Dad

It's hard because we've got kids – the house is a mess, the kids are screaming all the time . . . And the other night, [my husband] got really pissed off and stormed off to the pub. I said to him: 'What the f*** are you doing here? You're meant to be looking after the kids!'

Jo Brand
Live at the Apollo, 2008

1

'Turns on the head of a pin, my *arse*,' I say to no one in particular. The front wheels of Joey's bargain-basement, no-name buggy are stuck – again – this time in the footpath outside the Oxfam shop. I've just bought Joey a dark blue UMBRO sweatshirt (for £1 – bargain) that makes her look even more like a boy. A chubby boy in a fat suit. Thanks to her lack of hair and my refusal to dress her top-to-toe in pink and put plastic tiaras or too-cutesy-by-half hair clips on her bald, bumpy head, she often gets mistaken for a boy. But what the hell – it's chilly, she's got a rotten cold and I forgot to bring a jumper out with us. Not that she fits into any of the clothes we have for her age any more – she's into stuff for two-year-olds now and she's only ten months old.

As I push and pull the buggy, trying to get it unstuck and making Joey bounce around inside it, I think I recognise the woman pushing her buggy towards us. Yes, it was definitely her at the baby clinic yesterday. She'd had a face like a slapped arse on her then, too. We'd had our respective babies on the changing mat at the same time, taking their clothes and nappies off to get them weighed.

'What a gorgeous little boy!' I'd trilled, trying to sound as if I meant it. I mean, he was a boy, definitely, but gorgeous? No. Generic baby at best. But it's usually a great ice-breaker – most mums like to think all strangers are totally taken aback by their baby's beauty. This particular sour-looking mum didn't take the bait, though.

'What's his name?' I tried again, a little less enthusiastically.

She mumbled something, not looking up.

'Oh! How lovely!' I gushed.

Joey was the first to get weighed.

'Twenty-eight pounds,' said the weigh-in woman.

'Jeez!' I hoiked Joey off the scales and headed back to the changing mat. 'Is that a lot for a ten-month-old?'

'Well, considering that's the average weight for a two-year old ...' The weigh-in woman trailed off as she handed me our red baby record book and turned her attentions to Slapped Arse's sombre baby. Like mother, like baby, I suppose.

'No more pureed KFC for *you*, then, Butterball!' I said, laughing.

I looked around, smiling at the other mothers and babies waiting behind us and saw a sea of disapproving faces. I swear I even saw a baby shake its head and tut at me, disappointedly. I got Joey back into her clothes fast and legged it.

Joey and I have been back in Riverside for a couple of weeks, after being away for five weeks, staying at my friend Charlie's (in Bath) and my parents' (in London). We moved into a tiny Edwardian terrace in the decidedly chavvy end of Riverside – a gorgeous, picturesque, perfect-for-a-*Midsomer-Murders*-episode village in Berkshire – two months ago. And the builders have been in, 'improving' it ever since.

God, I wish we'd never left London.

I wish we'd never left our top-floor Victorian flat (with a turret, no less) in leafy Chiswick. Jack, my boyfriend (fiancé, actually, but he may well be my ex any day now), lured me away from London. I can remember word-for-word what he wrote on the back of an envelope one night in Chiswick, trying to speak to me on my level, in the only language I truly understand – *List-ese*.

WHY MOVING TO THE COUNTRY WILL BE GREAT
1. No crime
2. No sirens and double decker buses and trucks careering up and down the road
3. Birdsong to wake you up
4. No more snoring from me – fresh country air – and no more smoking!
5. Friendly locals (people, not pubs, although probably true either way)

6. Cheaper, fresher, healthier food
7. A range cooker
8. Cath Kidston aprons coming out of your wahzoo
9. Great walks, a more active, smoke-free life
10. We'll only be an hour – max – from London, so you can go and see your parents and friends all the time.

WHY LONDON IS SHIT

1. Heaps of crime
2. Heaps of noise and pollution (double deckers, sirens up and down our road)
3. No friends ever come to see us
4. They don't do take-away deliveries in the bush, so we'll be forced to abstain altogether. Or at least *WALK* (briskly) to the local chippy. Genius!
5. We can't afford to go to restaurants, the theatre, concerts, ballet or the opera. And even if we could afford it, we never go. But out in the country, we'll be able to save up for it and when we go, it'll be a real treat.

I'd bought it at the time. I mean, Jack was right. No one ever just *dropped round* to see us – we never went to the theatre, either, and the closest we ever got to opera was watching *The Sopranos* on DVD.

And even though Dad said things would be worse in the country ('You'll lose all your friends! An overland train on top of a tube trip? Forget it!') and I trotted out the old

4

'tired of London, tired of life' line, it didn't faze Jack. He was set on selling up and downshifting. I didn't put up too much of a fight – I figured Joey and I would go to London just about every other day, we'd all lose weight munching on the fruit we'd grow in our own orchard and I'd have Cath Kidston aprons and oven mitts strewn all over our huge, *Country Living*-esque kitchen. I'd have White Company wicker baskets in the loos, holding a surplus of toilet rolls; brass pots and pans hanging from an oak rack on the ceiling in the kitchen (as well as bunches of dried lavender and garlic bulbs on strings) and Joey would be apple-cheeked and healthy and sweet and vital, impeccably dressed head to toe in Mini Boden, looking like a model straight out of the catalogue.

None of it's come to pass – except for the range cooker, we do have one of them. It's half-sized and not an Aga or Rayburn or anything, and it's covered in plaster and dust and dented from the fallout from the ceiling – the floor of the en suite. But there is a range cooker under there, somewhere.

So I agreed to the move. In all honesty, though, I had no choice – there was no way we could afford our outrageous mortgage on just Jack's salary and buggered if I was going to go back to work full-time once our beautiful, blue-eyed baby girl was born.

God, did I just say that? About Joey? When I look at her these days, all I see is a big baby Benny Hill with chubby cheeks which, when she laughs, create crescent moons out of her slate-grey eyes. But maybe that's just me. Or maybe she's growing into her boy's name. I always thought girls' names you could shorten to boys' names were cool. Jo from Josephine, Sam from Samantha, Charlie from Charlotte, Frankie from Francesca, Stevie from Stephanie – they sound strong but cute; feisty and smart. So I suppose it's my fault (what isn't these days?) if she's developing gender issues.

So anyway, here we are out the front of Oxfam and I'm gurning like a moron.

'Turns on the head of a pin, ha! As if!' I snort to the mightily miffed-looking mum coming our way. She's pushing exactly the same no-make buggy as ours, so I figure she'll recognise the line they used to sell it to us on the internet, and we'll strike up a conversation. Hopefully, she'll crack a smile, stop to help me and we'll engage in some jolly mum-to-mum banter about crap buggies, crap babies, baby crap, the weather or *something*.

But no, nothing. No response, no acknowledgement. She just keeps walking, looking dead ahead, stony-faced. I can't help feeling like ostracised Dolly Parton in *Nine to Five* when she says to her husband something like 'Ah dunno, hun, Ah'm just about as friendly as Ah know hah to durn-well be in that office, but no one evah talks to me', and I wonder what you have to do to elicit some friendliness from the locals in this sinkhole.

Eventually, we get out of the pot-hole and go to Sunny Farm Stores, the local supermarket in the posh bit of

Riverside to get yellow peppers for Joey, mince and beef stock cubes for Jack and a packet of twenty Marlboro Lights for me. Jack's signature dish (for when he's hungover), Wet Dog, is made up of vegetable oil, beef mince and two beef stock cubes. No onions, no garlic, no tomatoes, not even any salt. It's a revolting concoction and smells like wet dog, hence the name. And Jack and Joey love it.

We take the long way home, down Cowslip Crescent, so I can have a cigarette without too many people seeing me. I always say to anyone who'll listen (myself, mainly), that I take Joey the long way round to avoid the fumes of the main road. But really, it's so I can have a sneaky ciggie without feeling judged by every car with a baby seat in it that goes past.

I know, I know. It looks awful, buggy in one hand, cigarette in the other – I used to give smoking mothers dirty looks when I was pregnant. The selfish cows! The poor innocents, suffocating by their own mum's nicotine-stained hands! But, well, you know – needs must when you're an addict. And anyway, I'm stopping on Monday.

Joey's feverish, miserable and crying.

'It's OK, babe,' I say in what I hope is a reassuring, soothing tone. 'We'll be home soon and then we can have something to eat and have a bath and get ready for a nice long sleep.'

She doesn't fall for it. The crying becomes wailing and I put my fag out before I've finished it, fearful that any onlookers in this small village might think she's crying because she's getting smoked like a kipper. Which, let's face it, she probably is. It starts to rain and, true to form, I didn't bring the buggy's rain cover out with us, so now my mood's gone sour, too.

'Oh, Joey, keep your hair on, will you? Not that you've *got* any.'

Joey's sitting on the floor, bawling her eyes out. I'm sitting on the couch, head in hands, doing the same. We both startle and look up at the door when we hear the key in the lock. Jack walks in and as soon as she sees his face, Joey stops crying and beams, her wet, shiny cheeks bulging up into her eyes, turning them into slits. She even giggles. I put my head back in my hands.

'Ha-lo-de-ho-de-ho!' he sings, and in one fluid movement he chucks his backpack on the floor and scoops Joey up into his arms. 'Good day, then?'

I'm in no mood for him or his sarcasm.

'Oooh! Who's a bit whiffy, then? Eh? Who-hoo-hoo-hoo's a bit of a whifter? Foo-wee, whifty! Is it you, Rox?'

I kick the nappy bag towards him and stomp upstairs.

'Oh, right,' he calls after me. 'I'll change her, then, shall I?'

I flop on the bed, creating a huge cloud of dust and stare at the lumpily-plastered ceiling and blotchy paint job, thinking about the massive hole in the kitchen ceiling and Pavel, our shyster builder.

Nobody told me it'd be like this. Well, they did, really – Charlie did and so did my brother, Alexander, when he still lived in London with his wife and then two-year-old son. I remember thinking, when he was on one of his endless rants about how your life stops for at least four years when you have a baby, that he was lucky just to *have* one. I'd recently had my second miscarriage, you see, so I thought he was a bit insensitive, too. But anyway, their son is *gorgeous*. No, really. I'm not just being a proud aunt. Alex gets stopped in the street by modelling scouts in Bondi asking about Leonardo (as in Da Vinci, not DiCaprio. Chrissie, Alex's wife, is an artist). He's ri-*di*-culously cute: long, brown, curly hair and the *hu*-gest brown doe eyes. I picked him up from his nursery once and when he saw me, he squealed 'Auntie Rock!', threw his Lego on the floor and fairly *raced* over to me, jumping up on to my chest and flinging his arms around my neck. If, in the unlikely event Joey ever showed me any affection like that, she's so heavy I'd probably be in traction for weeks.

I can hear Jack and Joey laughing downstairs as he does his dutiful dad bit. They sound so happy, so in tune with each other. Sounds like they're having fun. Which is all well and good – and I'm happy for them. No, really, I am. It's good to hear them making the most of each other's company while they're in it. Jack stays at my parents' place in Paddington two nights a week because Mum and Dad are working in Sweden, to save him the horrendous commute. Which is great . . . *for him*. Bit of a bummer for me and Joey, though – we don't get to see him all that much during the week (he leaves at 6.30 on the mornings he wakes up here) and when he does come home, at 6.45 p.m., Joey'll have his attention for a mere half an hour before she's bundled off to Bedfordshire.

When I'm feeling particularly unloved by either Joey or Jack (or both) it cheers me up a bit to think that that's why she's so demonstrably in love with Jack and so dismissive of me – because he's a rare treat and not here for the boring day-to-day stuff. And I should be happy that he's so much fun for her when he is here.

I get up off the bed (no easy feat – I still look and feel about twenty months pregnant) and lumber over to the en suite. I put the lid down and sit on the loo with my elbows on my knees, my palms pushing themselves into my eye sockets. What is *wrong* with me?

I look up at the space on the wall, above the bath, where the shower should be. The fiercely expensive, posh, boutique hotel-type shower we agonised over buying. The one the builders broke when they tried to install it.

'Rox!' Jack calls from downstairs. He needn't have yelled, though; the walls and doors in this house are so pathetically paper-thin, he could whisper softly and I'd hear him loud and clear.

What?! What *now*? No peace – not even for five bloody minutes. I don't answer, I just tut loudly and wearily get up off the loo. I pull the little cord under the mirror that turns its lights on and cautiously look at my reflection. I expect to see the usual Medusa. But actually, my skin looks clear. Ish. The whites and the rims of my eyes are a little red from crying (but this is good – makes the coloured bit – the iris? – look green instead of the normal battleship-grey). And something the builders put in actually works! Momentarily buoyed by this, I go downstairs to the kitchen.

'She's crying,' he says. 'Has she been fed?'

I shoot daggers at him.

'All right! Only asking,' he says, his face losing the boyish, jolly look it'd had only seconds before, as he hands Joey a cheese and onion crisp from the packet in his pocket.

And then I smell it. The unmistakeably sweet, sickly smell of beer and cigarettes on breath. And I'm pretty sure it's not Joey. No wonder he got home so late, he's been out boozing. I check his eyes.

'You've been drinking,' I say, my own eyes squinting with suspicion.

'I had a swift one at The Swan on my way home, yeah.' He cannot tell a lie, my Jack.

'Right,' I say, almost pleasantly, surprising us all. 'Crack open the wine, then. I'll sort Joey out, put her to bed and we can have a drink outside.'

Of course, Jack's already thought of this and points a finger to the bottle on the benchtop and two glasses filled to the brim. I smile, amazed at how the promise of alcohol can really brighten a girl's day.

Joey and Jack play-fight over the rest of the crisps until I've made her dinner. Incredibly, she actually eats some of the steamed broccoli and poached salmon and after we've splashed around for five minutes in her baby bath, I organise a bottle of milk for her and take her upstairs. Once she starts fading into sleep, I press play on the CD player and out drifts the *Sensual Classics* CD – it's all we have in the way of classical music. Jack got it for me when Joey was three months old in the hopes it'd arouse my moribund libido. I check her breathing, turn the lights down to their lowest and tiptoe out to the strains of Ravel's *Boléro*.

Two hours later, the relaxing drink outside on the deck is in full swing.

'Think we'll ever have sex again?' I ask Jack, feeling warm from the wine. Warm from the wine? Who am I kidding? Let's call a spade a spade – I'm quite tipsy.

'What – with each other?' he smiles, and for a split second I think he looks cute. 'Hard to say. Although I think the way things are going, either one of us is ripe for an affair.'

'Are you having an affair?' I ask, as I take a sip of my wine. I'm sure I know the answer to this one – no, no, a thousand times no. I mean, there's no way Jack would – he's far too honourable, way too decent for that sort of caper.

'No, not yet,' he says, a little too casually for my liking. 'You've got to agree though, one of us could easily fall prey to an interested party's advances. I mean, we're like bickering brother and sister at the moment.'

Since when did he start talking like a solicitor – 'fall prey to an interested party's advances'?

'What do you mean "not yet"? Anyway, I'm too tired to even think about anyone else except Joey. And when I do think of you, it's not in any kind of saucy way.'

'I've noticed,' he nods.

We sit in silence. For two seconds.

'Do you think it's *my* fault?' I ask, wide-eyed.

'No, not *entirely* . . .'

'But mainly, right? Everything's my fault,' I sigh.

'Twinkle, twinkle Mummy's fault, everything is Mummy's fault,' he sings to the tune of 'Twinkle, Twinkle, Little Star'.

'She is such a moany old trout, why won't she –' I join in.

'– pull her finger out?'

We giggle at our reworking of Mozart's classic and Jack tops up our glasses.

'I don't know. I do feel particularly rubbish these days. Maybe I've got post-natal depression. Delayed PND,' I suggest.

'Maybe you should go and see the doctor,' Jack says.

'So you think I've got it, too?'

'No. I think you've got Crap At Making New Friends

Syndrome. Particularly rife among city dwellers with babies who downshift to the country.'

'Really?'

'Yeah,' he says. He strokes my hair and then looks at the palm of his hand, grimaces and wipes the imaginary grease on his jeans, making me laugh. 'But going to the doc's might make you feel better. And you never know, you might meet some other mothers in the waiting room.'

'Can't hurt,' I say, picturing myself as one of those old ladies who hangs around doctor's surgeries all day just for the company. I'll be able to get a prescription for Ventolin, too, I think, as I light up another cigarette.

'And you know, maybe it's time we put Joey in the nursery for one or two afternoons a week. Just to give you time to do some work, bring some money in,' he says, his eyes catching mine optimistically, cautiously.

Here we go, I think. Here comes the dreaded money chat.

'But we can't afford—'

'Let's just try it for a few weeks, see how we go. What do you think of that?'

I think it sounds brilliant, but I don't want to jump at it too quickly, give the game away that I'm fairly frothing at the mouth at the prospect of some time to myself. To do some work, that is, of course.

'Sounds OK . . .'

'I think it'll make you feel better, too. You know, start

14

freelancing, getting back to your old life a bit, feeling a bit more like your old self.'

'A little less of the old,' I say.

'You know what I mean,' he says, waving my vanity away.

'Hey! Maybe I could write some first-person stories for *Positive Parenting!* about post-natal depression—'

'But you don't have PND! You're just pissed off. *All the time.* Think you could sit around taking the mickey out of yourself, making up nursery rhymes if you were seriously depressed?'

'Lullabies. I think "Twinkle, Twinkle"'s a lullaby.'

'Whatever.'

'It just seems so hard for me at the moment.'

'Why? I mean, what do you *do* all day?'

'I don't know! Look after Joey.'

'Been to the mother and baby groups, yet?'

'No. Just because I've had a baby doesn't mean I'll have anything else remotely in common with those women. Professional mums – yuk.'

'Maybe they're just like you, struggling with a baby. You never know, you might even make some friends. You need to get out more, stop making it harder for yourself than it has to be.'

'But it *is* hard.'

'Not as hard as it is for me,' he wheels round and stares at me.

I know I should say, at this point, that yes, he is my

hero, noble, true and brave – what with shouldering the full burden of responsibility for me and Joey, being the sole bread-winner and all – but I want him to understand what it's like, trapped here all day out in the middle of nowhere with no one to talk to except a baby. Who, it feels like, doesn't even want to know me.

'You don't get it, do you? *Your* life hasn't changed at all! You still go off to work – *by yourself* – have a laugh with your workmates, go out for lunch, have beers after work and then have time on the train to read the paper or talk on the phone – *if* you're coming home and not staying the night at Mum and Dad's . . . You have *hours* every day just looking out for yourself. AND you get paid for it!'

I don't want to sound mean, but I'm insanely jealous that he still gets time to do his own thing – in London – without constantly having to worry about what Joey's eating or how she's sleeping. I know, I know – I know he needs the break from the travel, and it's great of my parents to let him stay there – but I wish it was me. And I wish I didn't miss him so much, wish I wasn't so lonely. I swear it makes me more fractious when we eventually do get to spend some time together.

'Work's full-on and stressful,' Jack counters. 'And commuting is a nightmare. I'm stuck on public transport for over three hours a day – *if* there are no delays or cancellations. *You're* the one who's got it easy, sitting at home all day, watching telly, banging on to Charlie and Alex. Got the phone bill today, by the way – forty quid!'

'But I always do the cheap code thingy first . . .'

'Just shows how much you witter on, then, doesn't it? Especially long-distance to Oz. Can't you axe the calls to your brother for a while? It's killing me!'

'But there's no one to talk to in this hell hole—'

'Why don't you go back to work, then? Plenty of people to talk to there. You go to work and I'll stay at home and look after Joey. Yeah! I'd *love* it!'

'Ha! I'd give you one week – one measly week and you'd be bored stiff. And twice as frustrated as me.'

'I doubt it,' he says, calming down. 'But at least I try to help you out – paying for the nursery and stuff. Why don't you try to help me out?'

Oh, God. Back to sex, are we?

'Like how? What do you mean?'

'Like maybe not being in a foul temper every night when I get home.'

'*If* you come home . . . But I'm not! Well, not now, I'm not.'

We both drain our glasses and then, before Jack has a chance to get in before me, I say:

'Maybe it's time you looked for a new job closer to Riverside. Started thinking about something else other than IT.'

'There *are* no jobs closer to here. There aren't any jobs going anywhere – doing anything. I count myself lucky to still have a job.'

Oh, yeah. The Recession.

17

He starts whiffling on about the tragic day he's had at work and I zone out. There's nothing I can do or say to make it better for him (except get a job, obviously), so I just let him get it all off his chest while I glaze over and make sympathetic noises at what I hope are the appropriate moments. Eventually I stand up, heave a huge sigh and say:

'I'm going upstairs for a bath.'

No applause, no cheers, no Mexican wave of joy. Just a splutter from Jack.

'What? Christmas already?' he grins.

He's sort of like a baby in that respect – things'll get a teensy bit tense, one or two unkind things are said and then, once he's offloaded and before you get too narked, he'll get distracted, act as though nothing's happened, everything's fine, totally forgotten. And then he'll make me laugh.

So I try to return the favour and twist my mouth into a sort of lopsided half-smile, in the hope that my facial contortions will somehow miraculously reveal razor-sharp, super-sexy cheekbones. And then I say:

'That's quite enough from the cheap seats,' as I waddle inside.

Now, I've never really been one for baths. Not that I'm a soap-dodger (well, actually, I am a bit of one these days – it's just impossible to a) find the time and b) take my eyes off a crawling Joey for five seconds, thus letting her loose amongst the rubble and rusty nails in the building site that is our house), I just prefer showers. I suppose that's another thing that makes me a not-so-girly girl. It's the same with lying on a beach for hours, or shopping, or *shoes*, for God's sake. Why all women are supposedly obsessed with shoes is beyond me. But tonight, I'm well keen. On the bath, that is.

Checking out my saucy cheekbone smile in the mirror, I'm briefly disappointed that I look more stroke victim than Sharon Stone. And, of course, the water isn't hot. But simply being on my own in an enclosed space is bliss. Even the sight of my bloated, naked form doesn't shock me, goldfish-memory style, as it usually does. I just lie there, staring at the mud-coloured ('Outback Sunset' my arse) wall tiles, letting the lukewarm water go cold around me as I think about what Jack said.

It *is* hard for him at the moment, for both of us, really. But mother and baby groups? Do I have to? I couldn't possibly make friends with a bunch of perfect, happy, rich country parents when I feel so pissed off. Could I?

Suddenly I'm aware of the so-nice-it's-almost-sinister next-door neighbours having a barbecue in their back garden – their baby-free, love's young dream, just married, first-home buyer's garden. And it's a real garden, too – a proper countrified green space with flowers scenting the air and everything – not a poxy bit of dirt out the back of the house, like ours. The smell of burning charcoal and sausage wafts in through our window, replacing for a moment the reek of paint and masonry dust, and I can hear them laughing and chinking glasses and talking with their friends (friends? They even have friends!). Clear as a bell. Crystal.

Oh, God, oh God – they must have heard Jack and I bickering on the deck. Now they'll know we never have sex, drink like fish, smoke like chimneys and have no cash. They'll definitely think we're bad parents. And what's the bet they've spread it all over the village by now, too – gossip's rife in the country, isn't it? Bush telegraph and all that . . . I'll see it on the local newspaper's front page in Sunny Farm Stores tomorrow:

ALKIE CITY SLICKERS CRACK UNDER STRAIN

I sink further down into the bath, wishing the water would wash away my shame.

2

I'm *really rather* looking forward to getting off my face on Prozac, I think to myself as I pass the Really Rather Good Cafe and battle with the buggy. Charlie says it's like you've guzzled twelve cans of Red Bull – you don't notice how knackered you are, you just whizz around cleaning the house, making fab meals, singing 'Head and Shoulders, Knees and Toes' and loving every minute of it. I really couldn't give much of a toss about the cooking and cleaning (quite clearly, Jack would say), but I'd love to feel *into* something again – even if it's just kids' songs.

I'm on my way to the GP's to have this depression (Post-natal or Regular? And do you want fries with that?) sorted out, so I can get on the 'zac and get back to my BJ state of mind (that's *Before Joey*, you understand, nothing to do with blow jobs – you have GOT to be joking me).

An officious-looking woman calls my name and I jump up, nearly breaking into a run and tripping over Joey and her buggy in an effort to get into her room. She looks a bit like Hermione Norris – you know, the posh, blonde one in *Cold Feet* – all cool, calm and collected. Cold, even. Except for when she's in her leggings, red-facedly huffing and puffing as she pushes her all-terrain, off-road three-wheeler buggy around the village (the doctor, that is, not Hermione Norris).

She's got the best deal, this GP and her bloke, according to the friendly receptionist. They've got two kids and they're both doctors, so they job-share at the surgery. When one's working and bringing home the bacon, the other's looking after the sprogs at home – and you just *know* it's one of those gorgeous, detached numbers on Cowslip Crescent. Talk about the perfect set-up. They probably have nannies and au pairs and family and friends to help, too. I wince for a second, hoping she hasn't ever clocked me from one of her original sash windows sucking on a ciggie and pushing Joey at the same time.

'Hi there,' I say. 'How are you?'

'How can we help you?' she replies.

Oh. OK. Just like the doctors in London, then – straight down to business, no time for any cosy little get-to-know-you chats. I'd hoped she was going to be like Nick Berry's wife in *Heartbeat* or one of the lovely GPs on *Peak Practice* – you know, all warm and welcoming, caring and sharing. Wrong again.

'Um . . . I feel rotten. Emotionally, though, not physically,' I begin.

'Mmm,' she murmurs, swivelling her chair away from me to face her computer screen.

'I cry at everything. Not just things about babies or families – anything, happy or sad – even cheap car insurance ads. I want to sleep all the time, but I can't because of *her* and her dad's no help but she clearly prefers him over me – and she won't eat anything I make for her, but she's huge and—'

'How long have you been feeling like this?' she asks curtly, not looking away from our file on her screen.

'I don't know – a couple of weeks? Ever since we got back from staying at my parents'. We moved here two months ago, but we've had the builders in, so me and Joey were shunted around the country to avoid the rubble. It's still a bomb site and the builders have mucked everything up and we don't have any cash left to fix it now and I resigned from my job in London – at *Positive Parenting!* magazine, so I should know how to deal with everything, but I *don't* – and I'm *stacking* the weight on and Jack thinks I'm doing a bad job—'

'How old is he?'

'Thirty-nine, same as me.'

'No, I meant the baby.'

'SHE is ten months old,' I say, perhaps a tad loudly. Even Hermione thinks Joey's a boy – and she's got our notes right in front of her face.

'Are you drinking more than usual?'

'Chance'd be a fine thing,' I say, trying a bit of levity for the first time in a million years. It doesn't work.

'How much do you drink a week?' she continues.

'No more than usual – couple of glasses of wine . . .'
Yeah. And the rest.

'Hmm. Well, sounds to me like you're a little depressed,' she says softly, cocking her head to one side and opening her eyes wider, doing her best Princess Di vulnerable fawn impression.

I suppose this is what passes for good bedside manner these days.

'It's totally normal. Having a baby is tough, very tough. But before we go down the medication route, why not try the mother and baby groups? Everyone's pretty friendly here, and they're all going through the same thing as you. Give that a go and if in a couple of weeks you're still feeling the same, come back here and we'll see what we can do.'

Bugger. No drugs, yet.

'Um, all right. I guess it can't hurt. Oh, and Joey's nose is streaming and she's got a bit of a fever, so no one's getting any sleep. I've seen these ads for Medised – should I give her some of that?'

'No. Nurofen or Calpol to bring the fever down, that's all you need.'

'OK. Oh! And I need a prescription for Ventolin.'

'You have asthma?'

'Well, yes and no, really. I probably wouldn't need anything if I hadn't started smoking again –' Eh? Did I just say that? Out loud?

'You *smoke*? Did you smoke when you were pregnant?'

24

'No! Of course not!'

We both look at Joey, slumped in the buggy. She's sticking her bottom lip out to catch the snot, making her look more like a giant cod than usual.

'I'll organise the health visitor, Liz, to come and see you tomorrow morning. Ask her about the mother and baby groups, after she's weighed it.'

Seriously – she said 'it'.

She prints out the prescription for me, gets up and starts wheeling the buggy backwards towards the door. I'm still sitting down.

'So that's it, then?' I'm surprised that our 'consultation' has been so brisk.

'We're very busy, you know. If there's anything more, you'll have to book another appointment.'

Back on Cowslip Crescent, I put the hood of the buggy down and furtively look up and down the footpaths for women pushing prams or walking with toddlers. I can't see any, the coast is clear. I light up and blow the smoke out over my right shoulder. We're walking into the wind, so the smoke goes behind me, not anywhere near Joey's face. I shake my head at the way having a cigarette in the street has turned into a covert operation for me.

And then I cringe slightly. Not, for once, because of the deep shame I feel about smoking – that's always there – no, I wince and hunch my shoulders up to my ears in embarrassment at the way the GP just ushered me out of her office – she couldn't get us out of there quick enough.

I'm so desperate to offload. If I could just *talk* about it, get it off my chest, I *know* I'd feel a lot better. And not to a doctor. It's like Crocodile Dundee says in the first one – something like 'Who needs therapy when you've got mates?' I can't *believe* I haven't struck up any friendships here yet – I still don't know anyone I'd feel OK about asking out for a drink. And I *really* can't believe I'm quoting Crocodile Dundee. To myself.

The next morning, I'm rushing about like crazy, cleaning up. I try to make the place look at least a *bit* baby-proofed (i.e. coppers, nails, screws, sandpaper, bits of splintery wood etc off the floor) and get as much milk into Joey as I can in the vain hope she'll be well and truly conked out before the health visitor, Liz, gets here. Considering Joey kept us (well, *me*) up all night, she should be totally knackered – but that sort of logic doesn't seem to work on her.

So I've got a headache and she's probably got a tummy ache because we're both as ratty as a London sewer.

I finally find *Annabel Karmel's Superfoods for Babies & Children* (under a pile of late self-assessment tax penalty notices and unopened bank statements) and strategically position it on the benchtop next to the range cooker.

'I know, I know,' I say to a perplexed-looking Joey, who's sitting in her high chair, fascinated by this uncharacteristic energy and movement going on around her. 'But Mummy wants the health visitor to think we've got it all under control, you see. Now. You're going to sleep like a baby when we go up to bed, aren't you, Joey? Hmm? You'll be a good girl for Mummy, won't you?'

And pigs might bloody fly, I think, as I struggle to free her bulk from the high chair. She's crying and whacking my face as I carry her upstairs.

'Tea? Coffee?' I chirp, as Liz settles herself at the kitchen table and I close the kitchen door in a pointless attempt to drown out the wailing coming from upstairs.

'Only if you're making,' she shouts, getting out sheets of printed paper from her portfolio.

'Tea it is, then. Two for tea and tea for two!' I sing, barely masking my excitement at having some adult company to talk to for a change. Better keep a lid on it, though, I think to myself – don't want to sound too mad.

Once I've made the teas and decided against asking Liz to come outside with me while I have a fag, I sit on my hands at the kitchen table and we begin.

'So,' she sighs heavily as she clasps her hands in front of her on top of the papers. 'How are you feeling?'

'Well, you know . . .' I say, my voice quavering, betraying my desire to appear as normal and contented as everyone else, while my eyes start welling up. 'I have good days and bad, I suppose.'

'As does every new mum.' She flashes me a quick, forced smile, as if to say she's heard this sort of thing a million times before and it's time we got down to business.

But then I notice her deep crows' feet framing her twinkling eyes and somehow she seems more sympathetic, warmer. So I carry on.

'Yeah, I know. It's just I didn't expect it would be so *hard*. I mean, I feel so ridiculously *guilty* and lonely. I think it all started when . . .'

Liz's eyes stop twinkling and dart down to her left wrist, where her watch is.

'. . . when we moved here,' I trail off. 'Um, are you in a hurry?'

'No, no, sorry, sweet. I do have to crack on, though. Got a few more visits today before the clinic this afternoon. So, listen, why don't we do the Moods and Feelings Questionnaire?'

She hands me a form and a pen.

'Ooh! A quiz!' I squeal, compounding the slightly demented vibe I'm giving off.

'Sort of,' she says. 'It's based on the Edinburgh Postnatal Depression Scale and it's to give us an idea of how you've been feeling about everything in the last seven days, not just today. Be honest and tick the box that most applies to you, whether you've felt like this all the time, most of the time, sometimes, hardly ever or not at all.'

My heart starts beating faster. This is it. This is the test that's going to determine whether I really am as on the edge as I feel.

Have I been able to laugh and see the funny side of things? I tick the 'sometimes' box. Well, Jack's version of 'Twinkle, Twinkle' made me giggle the other night. If I'm in a good mood, he often makes me laugh, now I think about it.

Have I blamed myself unnecessarily when things have gone wrong? I tick the 'no, never' box. Nope, I lay the blame for pretty much everything squarely on Jack's shoulders these days.

Have I felt scared or panicky for no very good reason? No, never.

And *has the thought of harming myself occurred to me?* No, never. Not if you don't count the tried and true 'me-time' spot-squeezing/hag-hair plucking sessions I indulge in. It can hurt, granted, but beauty is pain, after all. So, no.

Liz tots up my score and I expect her to say: 'Mostly Cs – you're barking!', but she doesn't. She smiles and says:

'You *are* a little low, dear, but I don't think you've got PNI.'

'What about PND, though?'

'Same thing – we call it post-natal *illness*, now. Because of the stigma of the "D" word,' she says, packing her things away. 'What you're feeling is very real and unpleasant, I'm sure, but not in the league of serious PNI. For example, you've never entertained thoughts of killing yourself or Baby – or both – have you?'

'No. Maybe Jack sometimes . . .'

'I'll take that as a joke,' she says, her eyes boring into mine.

I smile weakly.

'No, of course you haven't. Anyway, the best thing you can do for yourself and Baby is to get out there and meet some people. Go to the mother and baby groups, go to the playground, be friendly, chat.'

'Is there a group for mums who are feeling low? In Riverside?'

'No. I could maybe organise some counselling for you—'

'No, no. I just . . . it's common, then, what I'm feeling?'

'Oh! *Everyone* goes through this at some time or another, when they've had children! You've nothing to worry about, there – you're totally normal, love.'

'That's a relief . . . but what about Jack? Is there anything he should do?'

'Make him a nice dinner, with candles, just you and him. Talk about things you used to talk about before Baby came along. And don't be so hard on him – he's no doubt feeling the pressure of providing for a family, now.'

Cheers. Thanks a lot, Liz. What happened to being on *my* side?

'Things will be hard for *both* of you for a little while, but it will get easier. It will all be worth it in the end – you'll probably be wanting to have another one soon, yes?'

'No bloody way!' I groan as we both look up at the ceiling, hearing Joey flinging herself against the wooden bars in her cot like a pinball. Make that a big, fat wrecking ball.

'You'll get there, Roxane, just be patient. You're doing

well – Baby is healthy and happy – most of the time! And remember, a happy mum equals a happy baby, so try to be more upbeat around her and soon the pair of you will be having lots of fun together. And rest assured, your best *is* good enough.'

I thank her for coming round and stand at the front door, gazing out at the juggernauts hurtling down the main road (so much for quiet country lanes) long after she's gone. So who would have thought it? I'm not depressed, after all – post-natally or otherwise. Just, it would seem, permanently *pissed off*.

Bugger Edinburgh, I think, and devise my own little Riverside Post-natal Fucked-Offed-ness questionnaire:

Have you ever wondered why the hell you moved from your cosy love nest to this purportedly quaint English village? And wished you hadn't?

and

Do you feel the locals regard you with suspicion and swear you can hear them mumbling, as you push your baby past them in a crap buggy: 'Ooh-arr – she's not from round 'ere, is she?'

and

Are you exhausted, thanks to a baby that never sleeps and

a bloke who never helps? Are you miserable, lonely and desperate to get things off your chest, even though no one wants to listen?

Joey's wails drown out the cattle trucks rumbling down our road, rattling my reverie, so I close and lock the front door and go back, once more, into the breach.

The next day, I take Joey to the Riverside Mother and Toddler Group. There isn't one just for mothers and babies, so this will have to do. It's at the village hall at ten a.m. which is a bit of a pisser, really – because that's when Joey's supposed to have her two-hour morning nap (two-second morning blink, more like), so no doubt she'll be awake and cranky for the rest of the day. No change there, then.

Still, everyone says these groups are great for getting you out of the house, making new friends and swapping feeding and sleeping tips.

'It's a nuthouse in here!' I say, smiling at Annabel (so her name tag tells me), the woman taking money at the door.

'Yes,' she says, not looking up from her (rather full) cash box. 'Buggies outside, please. Now, there's drinks and biccies for the littlies and coffee and tea for the mummies at 11 and we all have a sing-along at a quarter past. That'll be one pound fifty. And who's this little fella?'

'Joey. Josephine. He's a she.'

But Annabel's already scooted off, fussing around a group of women and their two-year-olds.

The smell of poo hangs heavily in the air where the younger babies and toddlers are. And, after a few desultory attempts at conversation that go nowhere (Me: 'Is that your little one? She's beautiful! Now tell me, how do you get her to sleep when she's got a cold?' Other Mums: 'Medised.' Me, talking to the backs of the Other Mums who are walking away: 'Right. So. Do you come here often?'), I go over to the coffee bar, make myself a tea and survey the scene.

There are clusters of women – all younger, slimmer, taller and much wealthier-looking than me – chatting away animatedly as their hands hug steaming mugs of coffee. The mums, like the kids, all look as though they've known each other for years – they probably all went to the same public schools together or something – and for the life of me, I can't see anyone standing on their own. And I can't catch anyone's eye – not even Joey's.

She's crawling about on the floor happily, picking up building blocks and plastic Barbies and holding them for a few seconds before some other baby snatches them out of her chubby hands. She doesn't care, though – she can't get the grin off her face. In fact, she's the smiliest I've seen her since . . . since the last time she was in Jack's arms.

I'm just starting to feel like I've got a massive 'L' tattooed on my forehead (for 'Loser', not 'Learner' – even though both would be correct), when two women actually approach me. Well, when I say 'approach me', I mean they're heading to the coffee bar, but I'm in the way. I stand fast, holding my ground, and try not to appear as awkward as I feel, straining my ears to catch the tail-end of their conversation.

'. . . I know, I couldn't believe it. Eva's only six months. How could she do it?' says the taller one.

'Shocking,' says the shorter one. 'It's not as if Giles doesn't make enough for a nanny. He could probably even afford two, what with the size of his bonuses . . .'

They both laugh and I think this is it – my chance to jump in and join them.

'Do you know of any good nannies, then?' I ask, addressing them both.

'Oh, plenty,' says the taller one as she looks down at me. I've seen that look before, I think to myself. It's full of that upper-crust confidence bordering on arrogance. It's friendly enough, but just millimetres away from being the look she'd give something rather unpleasant that had stuck itself to the bottom of her Aquascutum wellies. 'Are you in the market?'

'Oh no, no,' I say, shaking my head.

'No,' she says, looking me and my distinctly non-designer black velvet maternity frock up and down and taking a step backwards. 'No, I don't imagine you are. I was just saying to Hannah here that this is the most precious time, the most important time to be with your babies. A friend of ours put her little girl in nursery last week. Can you fathom it?'

'No,' I say slowly, trying to figure out what she's getting at, where she's coming from. Apart from the upper echelons of Riverside society, that is. 'But the nursery here is very good, apparently. Ofsted registered. A bit expensive, but—'

'No, no – that's not the point,' sniffs Hannah, the shorter one. 'Now, I'm not criticising, not making any judgement, but . . .'

Here we go, I think. Not criticising or judging? No, not much! It's like when people say 'no offence' right before they hit you with some horribly hurtful, grossly offensive remark.

'. . . one always has a choice. And that choice should be to employ a nanny and stay with the children until they go to school – not leave them with total strangers.'

'Quite,' nods Lofty. 'There is no earthly reason why, in this day and age, a mother should abandon her children simply to go back to work.'

A-ha. Clearly money's no problem for these two, and I suddenly realise that they're probably the women or the wives of the men responsible for this, the biggest depression since the 1930s (in economic terms, I mean – not me and my mindset. I'm not that old).

Looking around for an escape route, my eyes lock on to the perfect one.

'Ooh, Joey! No! Put that baby down!' I race over to

where Joey's about to raise a baby over her head, like a barbell. I make my apologies to the baby's mother and quickly scoop a now-crying Joey up, making for the door. I finish fastening her into her buggy just as we hear hoots of laughter and 'Sleeping Bunnies, Hop, Hop, Hop'.

Back at home, I call Mum, Charlie and Jack one after the other, and tell them how crap the mother and baby group was, how it was in no way the life-changing experience I was hoping for. I suggest to them that perhaps it's because I'm a freak, after all. And maybe I'm so desperately unhappy, that's what the other mums can smell, which is why they just don't want to know.

'Give it time,' says Mum. 'And join Weight Watchers.'

'Make a wish list. And a nice meal for you and Jack to eat at the table together. With candles,' says Charlie.

'You need to have sex,' says Jack. 'With me. After you've had a bath, obviously.'

3

Jack stayed in Paddington last night. When he called at about a quarter to five yesterday afternoon, to tell me he wasn't coming home, my heart sank. And what's a girl to do when her other half deserts her? Eat herself stupid, that's what.

The scoffery really takes a hold of me whenever I get those calls from Jack. I'm like a puppy left at home alone all day – but instead of eating the couch from lack of attention and loneliness, I trough my way through toast dripping with butter and Marmite and anything Joey doesn't eat (which is pretty much anything I make for her) in a full-on feeding frenzy. As a result, the race is on between my boobs and my bum – which will head south so fast it'll hit the floor first? My money (if I had any) would be on the boobs.

Tummy uncomfortably full, and craving some adult, human contact this morning, I have an extra-long call with Mum in Sweden. I miss her company so much. Not that she's any good helping me out with Joey – she says it was so long ago that she had me and Alex, she can't remember what to do with a baby. And when she's in London, she feels so nervous around Joey on her own, she won't ever offer to babysit. And I respect that, I really do. Through gritted teeth, maybe, but I do understand that she's got better things to do with her time.

But on this occasion, on the particularly weighty matter of, um, my ballooning weight and taking the focus off Jack and my perception of his shortcomings, I feel she may have a point. I definitely need to do something about the excess baggage I'm (barely) hiding under my maternity frock. Yes, perhaps, in this instance, Mother does indeed know best.

So, after scoffing loads of toast – as well as Joey's virtually untouched scrambled eggs – I turn on the laptop to find out where and when our local Weight Watchers meeting is on.

But, naturally, they don't do Weight Watchers out here in the sticks. What they do have, though, is a similar sort of thing started up by locals, called Waist Management. And, as luck would have it, there's a meeting on at ten – in exactly half an hour's time – at the Riverside Working Men's Club. Which gives me just enough time to a) get Joey organised, cleaned up and buckled into the buggy, b) pack her nappy bag with milk and the de rigeur tonne of baby paraphernalia and c) scrape together enough loose change from the floor, the back of the couch and the bottom of my bag for the joining fee.

Of course, we get there late, and cause a commotion at the double doors trying to unstick the buggy's trapped wheels, but at least we make it – and now, finally, my wonderful journey into the world of weight loss can begin.

I scan the jolly group for a familiar face, but don't recognise anyone – they're all sixty-plus ladies (in both age and dress size, by the looks of it). And when I get weighed, I'm shocked. Eleven stone and six pounds! On my five foot-nothing frame, that's massive! I was fourteen-stone-six just before I had Joey and twelve-stone-six a week after. So, even though I'm really rubbish at maths, even I can work out that's a stone lost in ten months. Which, in the scheme of things, isn't bad going at all – but all the weight charts say I should range from seven and a half to eight and a half stone, which means I have . . . um . . . about three whole huge stone to shed.

I flop into the nearest chair, wondering whether my sitting down has registered on the Richter Scale, and pull Joey's buggy up next to me.

There's much animated chatter going on around me until The Leader, standing at the front next to a poster of herself when she was much heavier, yells: 'Can we have some shoosh now, please, ladies?'

The members swap stories of dieting disasters and much merriment ensues. But I feel detached from it all – it's like looking fifteen years into my future and it makes me shiver. I don't want to be sitting around necking Diet Coke and shoving sugar-, fat- and entirely taste-free carrot cake into my gob with a bunch of fat old ladies. Now, I know it sounds a little harsh and quite a bit unkind – but it's true. I want to be with people nearer my own age. And even though they're all having a great time, laughing up a storm, turkey necks wibble-wobbling all over the place, the whole experience fills me with absolutely no confidence whatsoever in this Waist Management malarkey.

When the meeting finishes, The Leader calls me over and checks out my registration card.

'What's your occupation, love?' she asks.

'Ah . . . I left that bit blank, because I don't really have one anymore,' I answer sadly.

'Since you had this bonnie wee fella?' She smiles and coos and tickles a much-appreciative Joey's chin.

'Yes. Girl, though. Bonnie wee girl,' I nod, growing inured to this common mistake. 'But I used to be a journalist. In London.'

'Ooh! Which newspaper?'

'Oh, no – not newspapers. Women's magazines, mostly. I even had a column once,' I say, retrospectively impressed by my own self.

'How glamorous! Like *Sex and the City*!'

'Ha! I wish!' I smile.

She then asks me whether I'm now committed to losing my 'mummy tummy' and, pretty sure I've stumbled upon a fellow sufferer of the post-pregnancy belly hang, I nod eagerly.

'Yes, yes,' I say, getting excited. 'It's not like I've ever had a completely flat stomach, but now—'

'Caesarean?' she asks, raising her eyebrows.

With an eye roll to the ceiling, a grimace and a groan thrown in for effect, I answer in the affirmative.

'Just tuck it into your knickers like the rest of us,' she chuckles as she waves goodbye to some of her members, making her bingo wings flap.

4

I feel a prick of guilt as I walk away from the nursery. Not that Joey was upset to see me go – she pretty much *leapt* into the arms of the woman who took her into the baby room. Poor kid – probably couldn't wait to see the back of me. And who can blame her? We don't have too much fun together, these days. But I feel bad about leaving her. I feel like I'm dumping her on someone else so they can look after her. Which, let's face it, I am. I mean, who are we kidding here? All that gumph about how it's great for your baby to be around other kids, getting used to other people, socialising with them, teaching them how to inter-act etc is all well and good. There may even be some truth in it. But what we're really doing, in all honesty, is offload-ing the little buggers. Having a *break*.

I walk the fast way home, deciding to save my first fag *sans* Joey for when I've got a big, hot sweet cup of Yorkshire Tea in my hand and I'm sitting in the back yard. Joy.

But suddenly, out of the blue, I start crying. No warning, no starting off with small sniffs and building to a crescendo, just straight into a face-collapsing wail. I get in, stagger to the kitchen and stand by the table. The tears won't stop. Staring out into the back yard, my shoulders start shimmying with the sheer force of the sobs. I can hear Joey's miserable, near-hysterical cries as though she's being tortured; as though her fingernails are being ripped out. And it takes me a few seconds to realise she's not here – it's me. It's *me* making that noise.

I walk over to the kettle, rubbing my eyes exactly like Joey when she's tired (i.e. constantly) and snort loudly. I go to put the sweeteners in my mug, but the canister's empty. *Jesus.* You can't get sweeteners in Riverside, for some reason. Probably because all the yummy mummies here don't need to diet – they get all the exercise they need by shagging their gardeners and climbing in and out of their four-wheel drives all the time. Superb for toning the thighs, apparently.

I brighten up a bit when I spot the jumbo-sized packet of sugar the builders have left at the top of the cupboard. Three teaspoons of sugar can't be too many Waist Management points, can they?

I go out to the back yard, head for the deck and put my mug down on our old kitchen table from Chiswick that Jack's varnished so we can have it outside (there was no room for it inside, anyway). He's good, really. Quite the handyman. He's really trying to make it feel like home for us.

See? I *can* be quite nice about him, even miss him sometimes – but the minute I see him, he pisses me off. Even if he *does* the washing up, he doesn't do it *properly*. Like, he lets the teaspoons dry on their backs, so there's a water mark at the bottom of the curved bit. How infuriating is that? Poor guy – he just can't do right for doing wrong around me. I seem to have become so *anal* about things since I had Joey – obsessed with things I never even noticed before. But he *has* varnished our two Bentwood kitchen chairs well, so I sit in the one facing the row of pine trees blocking our view of the estate at the end of our garden and begin making my wish list.

I WISH THAT . . .

1. I could lose the lard, then maybe I
2. wouldn't be so hard on myself and harsh about everyone else around me which might then help me . . .
3. make some friends, have someone to talk to – and imagine, then, if . . .
4. I wasn't so tetchy all the time – particularly with Jack – then he might show some outward signs of liking me, and then . . .
5. maybe Joey would too. And then. . .
6. we could all be happy in Riverside together!

'It's no Chiswick, though,' I sigh. Fewer SUVs down our way, for a start. And hardly any Bugaboos. And loads

44

more mums pushing buggies around who don't look remotely 'yummy'. Come to think of it, none of the mums I've seen in Riverside Downs were at the mother and baby group. Or the Waist Management meeting – where do they all go?

Surely I can't be alone in feeling so wretched about my lot. Surely I can't be the only one with no mum or mates around. I can't be the only new mum totally pissed off with life, can I? And even though I'm not so *new* any more (Joey'll be one soon, shortly after I turn forty), it's really still getting me down. And this place is *heaving* with babies – they can't *all* belong to perfect, happy families, can they?

I think of the old Waist Management girls and how much fun they were having – failing miserably at their diets, but doing it together, with like-minded souls, the support of the group helping them cope. And what about that health visitor, Liz? She said there wasn't a group for miserable mums here – but everyone feels hugely hacked-off at some time or another so . . . so . . .

So why don't I get proactive and set one up?

I smile, thinking of the hordes that would inevitably descend on our house for coffee/tea/gin in order to vent their spleens, get their gripes off their chests. Maybe we should meet at a pub, so we could have a drink and I could smoke and not feel embarrassed about it.

It'd be brilliant!

The truth about what it's like having a baby would

finally come out, break through all the fluffy, Pampers adverts bollocks about cute, biddable babies and young, unflusterable, glamorous mums.

I can't get the idea out of my head. If I organised a club for pissed-off parents – say, the Pissed-Off Parents Club – would anyone show up? Would anyone admit to being even slightly less than satisfied with their lot as a parent? In the notoriously conservative country? Or would I end up feeling even more alone than before, with no one to talk to and blacklisted from the cosy country set?

Only one way to find out, I suppose. And things can't get any worse. Can they?

I dial Charlie's number. I know she's at work, but she's seeing one of the partners (French guy, called, um, Guy) at the law firm she's working at, so maybe they'll go easy on her and she'll be able to talk.

Never a good idea to dip your nib in the office ink, I told her, but she's been so lonely for years, since she split up with her daughter Rose's dad, and she's having such a great time with her newfound confidence. She started her law degree when she was forty – no mean feat in itself – and she managed to pass with distinction at the same time as holding down a dead-end job in an estate agent's, as well as looking after Rose.

She thinks she's going to marry Guy – convinced he's going to propose to her any day now. He's been married before and Charlie's keen to throw off the Miss Havisham aura she's sure surrounds her. Maybe too keen.

Mind you, I moved in with Jack barely six months after we met, and he proposed after twelve months (six years ago), so I guess there's no time scale for these things. And, I suppose, you eventually get to *un certain age* where you figure what's the point in waiting, and dive right in.

I met Charlie when we both worked as writers at *TVText* in London, a million years ago. Bonding over a mutual hatred of the bosses there – and work in general – we formed the Monday Night Club, where a bunch of us would get together in a pub after work on Mondays and lament our lots. It kept the weekend going a bit longer, began the week as we meant to go on and was a real morale booster – the bosses should've subsidised it.

So she'll love the Pissed-Off Parents Club! She's fond of a glass or two, she's into clubs – and she knows how hard it can be, being a mum.

'Hey!' I say to her now, 'What if, when you had Rose, there'd been a group you could go to, a mother-*no-baby* group, where you could moan about everything and hear other parents' stories? If the group met at the pub in the evening? And you could smoke with impunity. Would you have gone?'

'Yeah, I did. I *do*. It's called going out with your mates.'

'But what if you didn't *have* any mates? What if you'd moved to a new town and didn't know anyone? If you'd seen a note in the post office for something called the Pissed-Off Parents Club, would you have gone to a meeting?'

'You mean like a Monday Night Club,' says Charlie 'but waffling on about kids instead of work?'

'Yup!'

'Oh-kaaay. No one'll show, though. No one'll admit they're pissed off with their kids – it's just not the done thing. Particularly in *the country*—'

'But they *must* be—'

'And no one wants to bang on as much as you – especially about their troubles. People want to be cheered up, not reminded of how shit their lives are. They want to escape.'

'Going to the pub's an escape, though. And just getting away from the kids and your house is an escape, isn't it? I'm going to do it. I'm going to put a card up in the post office and set it up for next week.'

'Yeah, well, good luck. Give us a ring from the pub when you've been sat there by yourself for two hours.'

I exhale air through my nose loudly into the receiver, to let Charlie know I'm laughing – just more on the inside than the outside. Finally, she registers my fragile state.

'Just messing, Rox. It sounds like a really good idea. Honest. You go get 'em, tiger!'

By the time I pick Joey up from the nursery (who bursts into tears when she sees me – now the old bag's back, the good times are officially over), I've written the notice for the Pissed-Off Parents Club. And even Joey's apparent dislike of me can't dampen my excitement at this very moment. The lady in the post office said I could stick it on the cork board in their window – between an odd-job man's card, a hypnotist's note and a posh-looking, gold-embossed card saying: WEDDINGS! PARTIES! ANYTHING! – if I put asterisks over the 's'es:

Are you PI**ED OFF with your

a)   Progeny?
b)   Partner?
c)   Poor, pathetic excuse for a life?

Maybe you're PI**ED OFF with all 3!?!

Well, why not get it off your chest at
the inaugural meeting of

THE PIED-OFF PARENTS CLUB?**

WHEN?:   Wednesday, May 5
WHAT TIME?:   8.15 p.m. (so you can catch
                         Corrie first)
WHERE?:   The Swan
WHY?:   Well, why not?

5

'I'm not *his* mother, too, for fu—!'

Ah, the dawn chorus. Joey and I got up late (well, I was unable to get up at all and Joey had the good grace not to bellow too loudly until eight) and the kitchen's a tip. There's a Wet Dog-encrusted saucepan and plate in the sink and a cheese grater on its side with dried shreds of cheese surrounding it on the benchtop. Then there's the empty wine bottle and several small beer bottles ('They're French,' he'd say. 'Very sophisticated.') by the laptop on the kitchen table. What a mess. I hope Jack's hangover's a belter.

I'm filling the kettle for a) Joey's water for the day and b) an outsized cup of tea for me when the phone rings.

'Rox? It's meeee!'

It's Charlie.

'Chuck-eee!' I screech back. She usually calls at this time for a quick chat on her way into work.

'How are you?' she asks quickly, eager to get the formalities out of the way, desperate to tell me something.

'Oh, you know. There's crap everywhere in the kitchen, Joey barely slept last night and we've only just got up, so her sleep's all out of kilter for another day and she's nearly as grumpy as me. You know, the usual . . .'

'Right,' she says.

'But it's the first Pissed-Off Parents Club meeting tonight, so I'm looking forward to that.'

She doesn't say anything, but I can positively *hear* her grinning.

'So?' I say, to remind her that she had something urgent to tell me.

'Yeah. So. I think Guy and I are engaged!'

'Eh? *What?*'

'I know, I know! But listen, right, there's no ring yet, we only just sort of discussed it, after he'd had a fair bit of wine – not too much, he is French, you know. But – and this is the bad bit – I think there was mention of us actually getting married in *two years*. I mean, what's *that* all about? If we're just engaged, we'll *never* get married, we'll be like you and Jack and then, after five years, we'll break up and I'll be a single mother all over again and—'

'Hang on! Do you think me and Jack will break up?' Because, let's face it, it *is* all about me.

'No, no – Jack's lovely! You've just got to have sex with him soon, that's all. You've got to put Joey to bed, put on some make-up, put on anything but that ridiculous black

51

velvet maternity tent, down some wine and when he walks through the door tonight, pounce on him.'

'Urgh. I'd rather drink nuclear waste,' I say, looking around the kitchen and the filthy state he's left it in. 'Or eat Wet Dog. And anyway, I've got Pissed-Off Parents tonight, so he'll be babysitting. I told you – doesn't *anyone* ever listen to me?'

'Well, you do go on a bit,' she says.

'What*ever*. So anyway, when's Guy going to propose properly?'

'Who knows? Maybe in the Maldives – he's taking me there in a couple of weeks. Look, I've got to go, I'm at work now.'

I put the phone down and look over at Joey. She's got her hand in the coal pile in the fireplace, scratching it with her far too long fingernails – a handy reminder of yet another of my failings as a mum. But she screams blue murder and kicks me like crazy if I come anywhere near her with the nail scissors – what's a girl to do?

Remember you're the boss, that's what *Positive Parenting!* would say. Never forget that you're the adult, the one in charge, here. And ask someone at the nursery to cut them.

'No, Josephine, don't touch that,' I say in my low, stern, Supernanny-would-approve voice. Joey ignores me and blows a particularly deep, man-fart of a raspberry. I pick her up and struggle with her feet to get her into the high chair.

'You're not pregnant, so why do you want to eat coal?'

As I'm saying this, an image of me in my fifties and Joey as a fourteen-year-old sitting on the *Jeremy Kyle* stage flashes into my head. I'm fat(ter), wearing a light blue T-shirt and beige leggings, my hair's shoulder-length brown and lank and I sound like Deirdre off *Coronation Street*, thanks to my sixty-fags-a-day habit. Joey's got her hand up to block my face from her view and she's wearing skinny stone-washed jeans on chubby legs that look like sausage links and a red singlet crop top revealing a huge six-months-preggers bump. Her top lip is pierced, her greasy hair is pulled back tight in a ponytail and she's got tonnes of black eyeliner on. The audience is shouting abuse at us. Jeremy himself is clearly appalled, shaking his head in disgust. My mind's eye zooms into a close-up of his face. His mouth's turned down, looking like he's just got a whiff of horrendous BO. And he's looking right at me.

'Good *God*, woman – you're hardly a candidate for Mother of the Year, are you?' he says slowly, deliberately. And then louder, faster, more indignant: 'You make me *SICK*, you're so selfish! People like you don't *deserve* to have kids! I'm sorry, but I'm actually a bit speechless . . . No, no, I'm not! You're a bloody dis-*grace*, excuse my French!'

Oh, God. Please, no. Anything but teenage pregnancy. Or Jeremy bloody Kyle.

'No, no, no – it's time for your proper breakfast,' I say, blinking the image out of my head. 'What do you fancy this morning? Scrambled eggs? Good. Now you just sit there and watch auntie Lorraine Kelly while I sort the kitchen and your breakfast out. Jose*PHINE*!' I'm losing it now.

I get absolutely no co-operation from Joey (*plus ça change*, as Mum would say, always keen to get her favourite phrase in) and no matter how sing-songy I am, trying to emit positive, safe, secure, loving, fun vibes, Joey's having none of it and starts screaming.

'All right, all right,' I snap. 'We'll put on *Jim Jam and Sunny*, then. Happy now?'

And as I point the remote at the telly, switching channels to CITV, we're just in time to catch the credits for *Jim Jam and Sunny*.

Joey's chin goes all dimply, the corners of her mouth drop down and even I let out a sigh at this, our first small – but not insignificant – disappointment of the day.

But thank God – quite literally – that the build-up to Joey's trademark air-raid siren wail is cut short by the *Christians of Riverside* magazine crashing loudly through the letter box.

Leaving her looking miserable in her high chair, even though I've now put *Fifi and the Flowertots* on, I go into the front room. I pick up the magazine (more a thick, photocopied pamphlet, really) and flick through it on my way back into the kitchen.

I stop mid-trudge, though, when I see, in bold letters, that everyone's welcome at the Riverside Christians'

Mother and Baby Group. I sit down next to Joey and read on. The group gathers in the Church hall every Wednesday. Today!

Maybe we should go. We've got nothing else to do, let's face it. And maybe – just maybe – I might make a vague connection with someone.

I'm excited by this prospect – even if I have to join a cult. And I've got the meeting tonight as back-up – if this, my last-ditch attempt to make friends in Riverside, doesn't work. And at least I'll be able to say to Hermione in all honesty that I really gave it my best shot with the local mother and baby groups. She'll have no other option but to write me out a prescription for a year's supply of Prozac. It's the perfect plan.

'Hold on to your Pampers, Joey,' I grin, 'we're going to Church!'

When we get there, the place is packed. Well turned-out, too, these Christians – good looking, well-dressed and young. Must be the meeting place for the Riverside Chapter of yummy mummies. Urgh. I'm quite *suspicious* of that term – sounds a bit porny to me, something predatory dads on the school run who regularly log on to *Mothers I'd Like to F**** sites would say. And no one's *ever* called me a yummy mummy *or* a MILF . . . maybe I'm just jealous. But anyway, there's not one familiar face among them – I've never seen any of these women round our way. Maybe God doesn't get to the crap end of town much.

There's no room in the semi-circle of chairs for Joey and me, so we stand at the side, looking on.

A young, blonde woman (twenty-five, tops) dressed head-to-toe in a pink and white silk blend, signature bouclé Chanel suit stands up at the front, next to an overhead projector. Well, I worked in women's magazines for years, so even though I can't afford it myself, I can recognise the clobber of the rich.

'First things first,' she says, 'the charity fête is on next Thursday and we'll need cakes, jams and the usual assortment of goodies to sell.'

In the middle of the semi-circle, an identical-looking woman with a perfect, shiny bob and a perfect, shiny baby on her lap says:

'How many muffins shall I make? Will a hundred be enough? I'll bring my own cake stands, of course.'

Cake stands? *Her own* cake stands?!

Ms Chanel dismisses her expertly, saying sweetly that a hundred is more than enough, and everyone else is very welcome to try their hand at baking, bringing whatever they can, regardless of what the results look like. The muffin-making mum shifts in her seat and crosses her arms over her (slim, so it's easy) baby and looks narked. The other women rattle their pearl necklaces in unison and talk excitedly among themselves about the prospect of having the chance to shine – for charity, naturally – in what is clearly going to be one big bunfight of a bake-off.

Then Coco starts droning on about some foolish guy

56

who built his house out of straw, and a wise man who plumped for bricks. But this is no *Three Little Pigs*-type yarn, there's a big boat and a flood involved. The semi-circle of women, babies sitting still in their laps, are transfixed. I must be missing something, here, because I'm unmoved and, quite frankly, bored. But judging by the faces of the faithful, this walking advert for Chanel is a story-telling genius.

And then the recorders come out and the singing starts. I have no idea what they're playing or singing – all I know is it isn't 'All Things Bright and Beautiful', the only vaguely religious song I know. The words are up on the OP and as I look around at the women singing, I hear my mobile ring. I put Joey on the eucharist-crumbed carpet (sweet relief for my aching arms) and rummage around in my handbag. When I finally find the phone, it stops ringing.

Seeing as Joey's now crawling to her buggy, voting with her hands and knees, I figure this is our chance. Our chance to get the hell out of here.

I bundle Joey in the buggy and mumble apologetically something about bottles and naps to the women blocking the doors to the outside world. When they eventually move aside, letting my people go, we head for the hills, for home – a wise choice of location for when that flood hits, if you believe the Stepford Wife's story.

'Thank God I'm off to the pub tonight,' I pant, pushing Joey towards more familiar territory.

*

'You're all gong and no dinner,' says Blanche to Ken Barlow at the end of yet another brilliant *Corrie*.

I raise a brief smile, thinking I must remember to use that line on Jack one of these days. Joey's still faffing around in her cot upstairs, but it's eight o'clock – the hooter has sounded in my head and now Joey's officially Jack's responsibility. Let my joy be unconfined – tonight's the first ever meeting of the Pissed-Off Parents Club at The Swan. And I am *gagging* to get there.

'Right! That's me off, then,' I say, as Joey lets out a particularly pained howl.

Jack shoots me a wounded, ever-so-slightly hang-dog look, but still manages a pleasant-enough, 'OK, then. Have a good time,' as he hauls himself up off the floor to go upstairs for another no doubt futile attempt to soothe the savage beast.

He hesitates slightly as though he's thinking about kissing me goodbye, but just as I catch his indecisive eye, I leap off the couch, scattering millions of now-homeless dust-mites as I go, grabbing my keys and jacket and bolt for the front door. I shut the door behind me with a tad more force than is absolutely necessary and feel a nano-second of guilt.

'Just stop it!' I say out loud. 'Stop with the guilt. You're going to enjoy yourself tonight – it's *your* turn!'

I wonder if I'll recognise any of the faces that show up tonight. Probably not. I mean, all the women I've seen at the mother and baby groups are so cheery, so competent, so contentedly *complete*, they'd find the whole concept of the POPC anathema.

'What's to be pissed off about?' they'd ask themselves as their little cherubs wolfed down every last morsel of the Annabel Karmel meal it'd taken them three hours to lovingly and uncomplainingly prepare. No, most likely it'll be a bunch of women I've never seen before – glamorous, interesting, gin-soaked vocal-chorded Fag Ash Lils. *Real* women, women who aren't afraid to admit to themselves and the world that their lives aren't text-book perfect. Women who'll be able to tell their own nightmare stories of bastard boyfriends/husbands and annoying kids. Women who'll have worse stories than mine! Now *that'd* make me feel better. Bugger weaning or sleeping tips – I want the good stuff, the nitty-gritty, real horrendous tales of woe. Delight in other people's misfortunes, that's what I'm after.

I stop in at the 6-Ten for cigarettes on the way to the pub. Yup, you're in the country now, no 7-Elevens here – it's early to rise and early to bed. It's just not the done thing to be out after ten p.m. – and if you're still awake at that ungodly hour, you should at least be in your floor-length nightgown and cap, supping your Horlicks and listening to *Book at Bedtime* on Radio 4.

Briefly annoyed by how boring it is out here, I feel a hot rush of anticipation.

I do my best saunter into The Swan, casually casting what I hope is an indifferent glance around the recently tarted-up, dark wood-benched, slate-floored and supposedly female-friendly front bar. But it's totally empty.

'I knew it,' I lie to myself out loud. I just *knew* no one would show up – they're all too busy being good little mums and dads, tucking their adorable bundles into bed, watching *Who Wants to be a Millionaire?* and then having a five-minute regulatory missionary position shag before falling into The Sleep of The Just. I knew it.

'What can I get you?' asks the barmaid, appearing out of nowhere. I've been standing at the bar feeling a little bit lost and, quite frankly, stupid for about five minutes.

'Um, pint of Fosters, please,' I say, forcing a smile through my embarrassment at ordering a watery Fosters. With my accent, too. I've kind of picked up Jack's Australian drawl and twang and it comes out, mingling with my English accent, from time to time. Alex says when I speak to him on the phone, it's like talking to Dame Edna Everage. Without the jokes.

Anyway, the only other choice of lager is Stella Artois and while it tastes a lot nicer than Fosters, it's not called Wife Beater for nothing. No, I need to take it easy tonight. Pace myself. Even if it's just me on my own for an hour or two.

'Business not too good tonight?'

'Beer garden,' she says, jerking her head in the direction of the door outside. 'Smoking,' she adds, by way of explanation.

'Ah, yes!' I nod, eyes widening. A-ha! I *knew* people'd

turn up. In their droves, no doubt. I just *knew* it.

The beer garden's positively *heaving*. And while not everyone's smoking, there's a heavy cloud of smoke hanging over us all on this still, balmy night. I look around – for what? A table of people wearing name tags saying: 'Hi! My name's Jane and I'm a Pissed-Off Parent!', I suppose. A *sign*.

There's a group of people – about seven or eight, both sexes, taking up two tables pushed together. Could they . . .? Nah, too young, in their twenties – and far too jolly. They don't look knackered enough or remotely pissed off. They look like they've known each other for yonks and are having a whale of a time. I sigh, remembering the good old days, and quickly look away.

Then I see an older lady – who looks a bit like Diana Rigg – sitting opposite a younger woman (judging by the long, grey-free ponytail) who has her back to me. They're talking to each other, but looking around quite a bit, so I make my way towards them. As I get closer, the older one looks up at me, squints and says:

'Are you here for the Pissed-Off Parents Club?'

She says 'orf' instead of 'off'.

'Yess!' I squeal.

I sit down on the bench, next to her, facing the younger woman. It's only bloody Slapped Arse herself.

'Hi! Hello! Um . . . are you two the only ones here? For the meeting, I mean?'

'As far as we know,' says the older one, looking me up

and down and smiling. 'My name's June and this is Olivia.'

She nods her head in Slapped Arse's direction.

'Hi, hi! I'm Roxy. I've seen you round the village heaps,' I say to Olivia, sounding more Australian than when I ordered my beer. I mean, 'heaps' (or 'hoips' as I've just said)? You only ever hear that on *Home and Away*, don't you? Must come out more when I'm nervous.

'Really?' she says, looking at me for a second and then straight back at her pint. Obviously she's never noticed me.

'I've seen you at the baby weigh-in thingy, too. Do you not recognise me?'

She looks up and I manage to hold her gaze for a full *two* seconds this time.

'Nup.'

Bloody hell. This is going to be fun. A regular laugh-riot by the look of things.

'Right!' June pipes up, saving the day as she takes a sip of her red wine. 'Were you the one who put up the notice in the post office?'

'Yes! That was me!' I can barely contain my enthusiasm, despite Olivia's deadpan presence. 'I thought it would be a good idea to start a club without babies or toddlers. You know, a club for people like me – people who are a bit pissed off with this whole parenting lark.'

'Too right,' says Olivia, sparking up a cigarette.

'I see,' nods June. 'Is there a man in your life?'

'Oh! Yes,' I suddenly remember Jack. 'Yes, he's at home looking after Joey. Joey's the baby.'

'Girl or boy?' June actually sounds interested.

'Boy,' says Olivia, suddenly coming to life. 'I *have* seen you before. I've seen you pushing a boy about in the same buggy as mine.'

'The crappest buggy in the world, yeah! But no, a lot of people think she's a boy, but she's just big for her age. Not much hair, wears a lot of navy blue. Well, *I* dress her in navy. I thought it might brighten her eyes up a bit, make them look more blue—'

'So,' June cuts me off, pointedly looking at her rather elegant watch, 'how are we going to do this, then?'

'I don't know,' Olivia and I chorus.

Silence. We all take a gulp of our respective drinks.

'Why don't we just *start*? Start by taking it in turns to get one thing off our chests each? One person, one issue. And then let's see how it goes,' suggests the brilliant June.

'OK,' says Olivia. 'Sounds like a plan . . .'

'Great! Good idea! Bags I go first!' I have to sit on my hands to hide the fact I'm absolutely *bursting* to get talking.

'All right,' says June, all calm, collected and in control. 'Orf you go.'

'Right! Um . . . My partner – no. Sorry. I hate that word, makes it sound like we're in business together. Urgh. No, my boyfriend, Joey's dad—'

'Not married?' June cuts me off again.

I shake my head.

'Me neither,' nods Olivia.

'Engaged, though – have been for years – just never really seem to get the chance to organise anything,' I explain, lamely.

'But the intention is there?' June raises her eyebrows.

'Yes. Well, I *think* so . . . It *was*. Before we moved, anyway,' I say.

Olivia speaks through the smoke she's exhaling out the left side of her mouth and asks me where we moved from.

I tell her London and June sternly tells Olivia to stop interrupting to let me speak.

'No, no it's OK. Actually, it's *great* – feels like a real conversation, if I remember correctly! You know, a real chat. With adults. About adult stuff,' I say quickly.

Olivia, getting less surly every time she says something, sighs: 'Yeah. Makes a change.'

'Yeah! So, right. Jack . . . he . . . ah, well, sometimes – most of the time, to be honest – he really . . . really annoys me,' I say, taking a big, hasty slurp.

I notice there's beer trickling down my chin, so I bring my hand up to wipe it, not missing a beat, and tell June and Olivia what's been getting me down lately.

After about five minutes, June waves her bony but perfectly-manicured hand dismissively at me.

'That's just how it is when you're the mother,' she says, screwing a ciggie into her ivory cigarette holder.

'I know, I know,' I nod. 'But it gets a bit much some-times. I feel like he's thinking: *"You're* the one who wanted the baby in the first place – it's your lookout." And I feel the burden of the responsibility all the time – even when I'm asleep—'

'Does she still sleep in your bedroom?' Olivia butts in.

'No, not any more,' I shake my head. 'The thing is, Jack'll plonk her in her high chair in the kitchen and—'

'What kind of high chair?' interrupts Olivia.

'One of those Stokke ones. Brilliant. Lifesaver,' I say. 'Now we've got that, the stair gates and a place for Joey in the nursery two afternoons a week, I feel a teensy bit more relaxed.'

'What brand of stair gates? Where'd you get them? How much?' asks Olivia.

'Lindam. Easy fit. John Lewis. Can't remember how much. Still, at least now I can have a bath,' I smile, trying to look on the bright side and not sound quite so whingey.

There's a lengthy pause while Olivia studies her bitten-down-to-the-quick nails and June thrusts her nose in the air, waving at someone she knows at the other end of the beer garden.

'It just seems to me,' I go on, trying to pique my audi-ence's fast-waning interest with a little quick-bond man-bashing, 'that if Jack's not at work or in Paddington or playing golf, he's at home reading or playing on his computer or sleeping or having long baths. Any displace-ment activity to avoid dealing with Joey.'

'Or you,' smiles June.

'Yeah,' giggles Olivia.

So much for my cunning conversational tactics.

'Well, what about you then, June? What's *your* beef?' I ask her graciously.

Without a second's hesitation, June says: 'My daughter.'

'How old?' Olivia and I say simultaneously.

Thirty-eight, June tells us.

I surprise myself by saying out loud what I thought I was only thinking quietly to myself: 'Jeez – the hellness goes on for *that* long?'

'Oh, for *ever*, darling. For the rest of your life,' sighs June wearily.

She shuffles her bum back on the bench a bit, as though she's settling in for a long time and launches in to her spiel.

'Well. Where *do* I begin? She's had a little girl, you see – her first – and she expects me to be there all the time helping her. Well, I say helping, but I think she'd rather I do *everything*, bring her baby up for her. She gets extremely uppity if I say I'm busy and can't look after Harriet, but really! I did all that child-rearing stuff years ago with her and her brother. And now I've got my own, rather exciting life to live. I've got so much to do. And I want to spend some quality time with my husband, now that we're both retired and we finally can.'

We all take a quick slurp at the thought of it.

'Now don't get me wrong,' June carries on, 'I adore

seeing her – but she's not my *responsibility*. And I really would like to spend some time with my daughter, Emma, too – not just babysit for her when she goes out.'

'At least you're married, June. And at least you, Roxy, at least your bloke stuck around,' says Olivia.

There's much quaffing by all three of us. Finally things are getting interesting. And, if I'm not mistaken, we're all bonding nicely – feeling quite pally.

'So what's the deal with you, Livvy?' I ask, opening my eyes wide, trying to look friendly and sound chirpy.

'It's the same old story, I suppose,' Olivia goes on, drawing deeply on her fag. 'I got knocked up – sorry, June.'

'That's quite all right, my dear, you carry on,' says June.

'So my boyfriend freaked out . . . and then he took off. I thought – stupidly – I'd be able to handle it on my own. My parents are both dead, his didn't want to know, and so we – that's me and my boy, Stuart – moved in with my sister and her husband. They love kids but can't have any of their own, so it suited. Now we all live in Oxford Road.'

'That's right near me!' I shriek, relieved to have found some common ground. 'Are they looking after the baby tonight?'

'Yeah,' Olivia sneers.

'At least you have live-in babysitters. For free! Help on tap. Sounds great,' I say, coming over all Mary Poppins.

'It's not,' Olivia mutters matter-of-factly.

Both June and I are silent – June no doubt because she's polite and it's Olivia's turn to take the floor, and me because I suspect I'm about to hear something that's going to put my misery in the shade.

Olivia slumps down in her seat and rounds her shoulders as though the weight of her crappy situation's giving her a dowager's hump.

'There's nothing for free in this world,' she says. 'I pay, believe me, I pay. They treat me like I'm the live-in help. Treat Stu like he's their own. They look down on me so much, I feel even more worthless than I did when I was living with my ex. They don't approve of single mothers. Kids out of wedlock is a sin, you know. They bark orders at me like I'm Cinderella or something and I have to put up with their comments day in, day out. It's unbearable.'

'Jeez. Nightmare,' I say, suddenly feeling mean and cursing myself for wishing such cruel, clear victory for Olivia in the who's-got-it-worse race. I imagine her living in the *Daily Mail* newsroom – permanently stuck, *Groundhog Day*-style, in an editorial meeting with cigar-chomping suits shouting down single mums, making up surveys about how unwed mothers are ripping off the State, neglecting their be-hoodie'd, gun-toting kids, while smoking crack and living in luxury on benefits in their Playboy-Mansion-on-the-inside, shithole-on-the-outside council flats.

June saves the day – again – and says just the right thing at the exact right time:

'You poor thing. How positively gruesome for you, Olivia. Now. Who's for another drink? My round.'

Both Olivia and I grin and shoot our hands up in the air in the universal symbol for 'Me! I'm parched!' and while June's inside, at the bar, I try to cheer poor old Olivia up by offering her a Marlboro Light.

'It's not so bad, really,' she says, taking a cigarette. 'Lots of single mums have it much harder than me. I just miss having a life that wasn't end-on drudgery.'

'Yeah. I miss having a *life*,' I say, thinking how good I've got it. Comparatively speaking.

'I wish I didn't feel so downtrodden all the time. I swear that makes it worse – for me *and* Stu.'

'Yeah, I know what you mean. Speaking of, what's he like? Little Stu?'

'Lovely. Really lovely – doesn't take after his father, thank God. What about yours?'

'My father?'

'No, your baby.'

'Oh. Joey. She hasn't got much of a personality yet. Before we moved I thought she was quite cute. I actually surprised myself with how much it mattered, how much I cared about whether I thought she was good looking or not. But now, I just wish she'd smile a bit more, look like she liked me or something. And I know it sounds weird, saying it about a baby, but I think it's high time she lost some weight.'

We both drain our pints as we ponder this – me looking down at my thighs, spreading across the pub bench, taking up far too much room. I already saw Olivia's arse on the way in – couldn't miss it. Massive. Huuuge. Thankfully, I think twice about mentioning it.

She tells me she's joined Weight Watchers online and lets me in on the points system. Which is brilliant. Because not only does it sound easy, but I can do it for free and won't have to go back to Waist Management.

'Not that you need it,' Olivia says, smiling at me.

June then returns with a tray full of drinks ('I'm not queuing up in there again, so I got two of everything') and we settle in for a couple of hours, swapping stories and genuinely starting to feel like old friends. Amazing what a little – OK, OK, a lot – of alcohol can do.

It turns out June's a retired teacher, sixty-five and quite possibly loaded – there's definitely a monied air about her. Of course, she never actually comes right out and says it, but rich people don't tend to do that, do they? Unless they're *nouveau riche*.

Olivia works at the 6-Ten on weekend evenings and is twenty-eight.

I tell them I'm trying to freelance for *Village Life* ('Never heard of it,' says Olivia. 'I've got a subscription!' says June) and I used to work at *Positive Parenting!* After banging on a bit more about Jack, June suggests (again, brilliantly) that I turn a negative into a positive and make our arguments the basis for a story for *PP*. She suggests I call it 'The Rows All New Parents Have'.

'But what if it's only me and Jack? What if no one rows as much as we do – or about the same things?' I ask her, keen for her to expand on her world-beating feature idea.

'Well,' June says, 'for a long time after I had Emma, my husband and I had many, shall we say, heated debates about why we didn't get intimate any more . . .'

'Ooh, yeah. That's a biggie,' I agree and fumble around in my bag for a pen.

'And what about who gets up at three a.m. to tend to Joey?' Olivia pipes up.

'Yep, that's a nightly one,' I say, scribbling furiously on a beer mat.

'Who works harder – him or you? And who needs a break more . . .' June goes on, repeating what I'd said earlier.

'Do you think all new parents bicker like this?'

'Absolutely,' laughs June knowingly. 'Even parents who've done it more than once . . . It's all part of a healthy relationship. Anyway, arguing is good for you – particularly when you're finding your feet with a new baby.'

'And bloody inevitable if you're a single parent living with your sister,' nods Olivia.

It's a really good idea if I can do it justice. If I can pitch it to *PP* well, make them go for it, the extra money'll really cheer Jack up.

We finally finish, half an hour or so after they call last orders and vow to do it again. Same time, same place, next week.

'But Roxy, dear, we must work on getting some more

members for the Club,' June says as she puts her gold cigarette case and lighter in her purse.

'I know! But how?'

'The Really Rather Good Cafe. Put the next notice up in their window as well as the post office,' she says.

'Yeah,' says Olivia. 'Make it shorter. Snappier. And make it sound more fun, less official.'

'It sounded *official*? The last one?'

'It's all in the name – it speaks for itself, dear. Just accentuate the positive,' sings June as she kisses me and Olivia on both cheeks and disappears up towards Riverside Heights.

'What positive?' Olivia and I ask each other and laugh. We lock arms and start walking home together, decidedly unsteady on our pins.

'And can we start every meeting with: "Hi, I'm Whoever and I'm a Pissed-Off Parent"?' asks Olivia.

'Yeah! And maybe we should get some name tags made up!' I offer.

'Don't be ridiculous.'

'Yeah. Silly.' I shake my head. 'So what should I say on the next notice, then?'

'How should I know? *You're* supposed to be the writer – *you* think of something! But make it good, Roxy. The Pished-Up Parents Club could be the best thing that's ever happened to us.'

'Pissed-*Off* Parents—'

'Joke.'

'Anyway – aren't we supposed to say *our kids* are the best things to ever happen to us?'

'Yeah – ha!' Olivia's arm slips out of the link and she veers off left down Oxford Road.

I close and lock the door behind me as quietly as I can, but it still wakes Joey up. I stand at the bottom of the stairs, wondering whether I should go to her. Maybe my boozy breath would be just the thing to knock her out, like ether. The house is dark and Joey settles herself quickly, for the first time ever, so I go outside for one last fag, to think about the night I've just had.

'Not bad,' I whisper to myself, beaming back at the bright moon. 'Not bad at all.'

6

GROAN.

It can't be. It *cannot* be morning already. *Urgh.* Joey's crying in her room and I can hear Jack banging doors downstairs. With a hammer, it sounds like. I lift my heavy, throbbing head off the pillow to see the alarm clock's neon numbers. They burn my retinas. And, adding insult to injury, it's seven o'bloody clock.

'Why me?' I half cry as I stub my toe on the bedside table and stagger into Joey's room.

She's standing up, gnawing on the cot rail and smiles broadly when she sees me. I pick her up – God, she's getting *heavier* – and bring her into our bedroom. I lie her on our bed and stand over her. Stand-over tactics – often the only course of action open to a desperate woman.

'Now please, Joey,' I say, trying to be sing-songy, but sounding more drill sergeant. The amount of cigarettes I smoked last night has made my voice all deep, raspy and croaky.

'Will you be nice for Mummy? Yes? Today, you'll be good for Mummy, won't you? Because silly Mummy's hung way-hay-hay the hell over and feels like sh— She feels terrible!'

Joey squeals in delight at this and starts to get that hysterical laughy thing that little kids get and it always makes me laugh, too – such unbridled joy at nothing at all whatsoever. Even I can't resist that sort of cuteness, despite the state I'm in. I tickle her and she goes even more berserk. I'm giggling away like a mad thing, too, and I bend down to plant a big wet raspberry on her tummy, when DOOF! She kicks me square on the nose.

'Owww, Joey!'

I bring my hands up to my nose and feel it start to throb harder than the rest of my head. Jack walks in.

'What's going on in here?' he grins, thinking he's stumbled upon some touching mother–daughter scene.

'She 'icked me i' the 'ucking nose!' I say, my hands muffling my words.

'Hoo-hoo-hoo-who's a naughty one, eh? Hoo-hoo-hee-hee ha ha ha!' Jack and Joey just about kill themselves laughing.

'Not funny!' I peer into the dressing table mirror and rub my nose.

'Yes it is. Yes it *is*, isn't it, little one? It *is* funny.' Jack ignores me and lies on the bed next to a near-hysterical Joey.

'Bay-bee,' says Joey.

What?

'Did you hear that?' Jack sits bolt upright. 'Did you say "baby", Joey? Did she just say "baby"?'

I forget the various bits of my head that are hurting and sit down on the other side of Joey.

'Bay-bee! Say it again, sweetie! Bay-bee!'

'Ah-ooh,' gurgles Joey.

'Oh,' we both sigh, disappointedly.

'Typical, though, isn't it?' I say, pushing myself off the bed and rummaging round in the clothes on the floor for something to dress Joey in.

'What? That you're hungover when your child says its first word?'

'No! It's typical that her first word isn't Mama or Dada – it's baby. It's all about *her*.'

'Takes after her mum, don't you, gorgeous?!'

All our clothes – mine, Jack's, Joey's – are in a huge pile on the floor. They're clean – I've managed to put them in the washing machine, dry them and bring them upstairs – but I haven't had the time to actually put them *away*.

I search for something for Joey to wear in said pile.

'Ah, this'll do. Actually, I really like this one,' I say, trying to get the pink- and white-striped Baby Gap all-in-one suit over Joey's head. 'It's from Auntie Charlie!'

Charlie gave it to Joey when she was six months old, but now I can barely even squeeze it over her head.

'Ooh, mind yer noggin,' says Jack as he tries to help. It's too much for Joey and she starts crying.

'I'll leave you to it, then – gotta go.' Jack jumps up and heads for the door.

I feel tears start to well up, but just before I let them burst forth, something catches my eye. Something spindly moves quickly, escaping from under the clothes pile.

'Ja—'

'Wo-oh-woah!' shouts Jack, just missing the biggest spider I've ever seen with his size nines.

'Eeek!' I actually shriek and throw myself at Joey on the bed. I grab her and hold her up, so she's standing on the bed while I quiver behind her.

'Quick! Get a glass! No. NO! It's too *big*! I'll have to kill it. Oh, God, no. I can't *bear* it!'

For a big, burly Australian bloke, Jack's super-girly when it comes to spiders. I'm not exactly in love with them, either, but Jack's worse than me. He says they really give him 'the willies'.

The spider whizzes past us all and jumps down the steps into the en suite.

'Jesus!' screeches Jack. 'Where did it go? WHERE'D IT FAAAARKING GO?!'

'Good luck, babe,' I half laugh as I hug Joey to me, a bit more protective and less defensive now the danger's in another room.

'Bay-bee,' she says.

'Maybe that's her word for "spider"! Maybe she was trying to tell us something before!' I yell out to Jack.

'Shut yer noise, will you? I'm trying ... to ...' THWACK!

'Did you get it?'

'Oh, GOD!' THWACK, THWACK, THWACK! 'Think so. Oh, I'm so sorry, Mr Spider!'

I hear the loo flushing – probably to drown out Jack's sobs as much as flush the squashed spider corpse away.

'You poor thing,' I say sweetly to Jack as he staggers back into the bedroom, ashen-faced. 'You OK?'

'Much as I hate spiders, I hate killing them more,' he says, wiping the sweat off his brow and sniffing. In a manly way.

'My hero,' I say, lips pursed, holding back a guffaw. 'I'll make sure I put the clothes away in future.'

'Don't *you* laugh, Rudolph,' he smiles, pointing at my red nose. 'Ah, bugger! I'm late for the train – gotta go!'

Joey and I stay huddled on the bed for a few seconds until Joey can take no more and tries to wriggle out of my embrace so she can crawl after Jack. I lower her on to the floor and giggle. Then I remember how rubbish I feel and breathe out heavily through my possibly broken nose. It whistles.

'Bloody country. Nothing but spiders. Spiders and trees. Whose dumb idea was it to move here?' Jack shouts.

'Right behind you on that one!' I call down to him,

puzzled momentarily by the fact that we actually agree on something.

And with that, he slams the door. I can hear him locking it from the outside and I look at Joey.

'Don't worry, sweetheart. We should be safe now. Safe as houses,' I say, unconvincingly and unconvinced.

Joey and I muck about with her stuff for a couple of hours (well, I sit on the couch with a cup of tea; one eye on her, the other on *Escape to the Country*, *Cash in the Attic* and *Pocoyo*) and then I put her to bed.

After half an hour or so, she's flat out and I can finally sit down at the kitchen table and try to write the pitch for that story for *Positive Parenting!* It's virtually impossible, though, considering I haven't thought or written in magazine-speak for ages.

I send an email to the Editor (who I've never met – a new one started after I left) outlining the idea, grovelling a bit (you know, saying the photograph of her with her brood on the Ed's letter looks great and her kids are stunning and the mag looks fab lately), and asking her to get back to me if she's interested.

Five seconds later, I check to see if she's replied. And she has! That was quick – she must love it, want me to get on to it as soon as possible. She's probably yelled 'STOP PRESS!' and got them to hold off printing, so they can get my fantastic story in the very next issue.

I click on her message.

It's an Out Of Office Reply.

Bugger this, I think. I used to work there! Surely they'll take an idea from me over the phone.

'Hiya, Melanie! It's Roxane, remember me?' Melanie was the Features Editor and when I went on maternity leave, she covered my position as Deputy Ed. She kind of does both jobs now, proving, if proof were needed, that I was always a bit on the redundant side.

'Oh, hiya,' she says, sounding totally indifferent. Just about everyone I know in magazines says hello like that. Maybe certain *métiers* come with their own phone vernacular – like people in moneyish jobs, like sales or accounting, will always say 'Bear with me' when they're pretending to look something up and need to fill the silence while they make a cup of coffee.

'How's it going?' I say, sounding Australian and, as a result, betraying my nerves. If she doesn't go for this story, I'm right up shit creek, as Jack would say, cash-wise.

'Good, good. Now, what can I do for you?'

'Um, I've got a story idea – thought you might be interested. It's called – provisionally, obviously – "The Six Rows All New Parents Have".' I pause to give her a chance to say: 'Brilliant! You're a genius! I love it – can we pay you a thousand pounds a word for such incredible stuff? *Please*?' but the silence is deafening.

'. . . And it does what it says on the tin, basically. I'll find six case studies to go with the six arguments.' I pause again. Think I hear her texting someone. '. . . Like a he said/she said brief description of the row, from both sides,

80

and then I'll get a relationship counsellor to offer some advice.'

Nothing.

'Hello?'

'Yeah, hiya. Sorry about that, just, ah, just fixing a bit of waffly copy. Delete. There. Go on,' she says.

'*And*,' I sigh, breaking out into a small sweat, 'I thought the rows, the arguments, could be the Who Works Harder Heated Debate, like he who goes out to work or she who stays at home looking after the baby, and then there's the Why Don't We Have Sex Any More War, which, I suppose, is self-explanatory and then, maybe, the Who Knows Best Barney, the Whose Turn Is It Tantrum, a bit of Who Deserves A Break More Biffo and, to finish it off, the old classic, the Who Gets Up In The Middle Of The Night Nark.'

Dead air.

'So what do you think?' I ask.

'Ah, yeah, yeah, sounds good. I'll check with Ed, but I'm sure she'll agree. Let's say . . . DPS, two thousand words, three hundred pounds, due in two weeks? All right?'

'Yes! Thanks, Mel – you're a star.'

'Not a problem. Gotta go. Sandwich man's here.'

Well, that was easier than I'd expected. What a result! I'll email Jack and tell him – that should cheer him up a bit.

I sit down at the kitchen table and stare disbelievingly

at the laptop. I've got a new message! It's from Vanessa, the Editor of *Village Life* magazine.

Sender: Vanessa Reece
To: Roxane Carmichael
CC:
Subject: Re: 25 days out in your village
Message:
Hi Rixy
Would you like to do another feature for me?
All best
Vanessa

Rixy? Suppose she's too busy to proofread her own emails to lowly freelancers like me. She hasn't even bothered to change the subject line, just replied to my email from a story I did for her a while ago. The only bit of freelance work I've done since Joey was born. I email her back to say I'd love to.

I resist the temptation to put the 'o' in Roxy in capitals, or call her Vinossa, and instead get up to make a celebratory cup of tea when my mobile rings. I nearly twist my ankle, lunging at the phone on the kitchen table – it may well be just chimes and birds tweeting, but it's bloody loud and I couldn't bear it if Joey woke up because of it. I see Vanessa's name on the screen, open it and scamper outside, saying:

'Hello, hello? Hang on a sec, just going outside . . .'

'Oh, I'm awfully sorry, Roxy, is the baby asleep? I do hope you haven't just got her orf and I've woken her—'

She's got the same posh accent as June.

'No, no, you're fine, Vanessa, fine! I'm outside now, I can speak properly. Phew! How are you?'

'Very well, thenk-yoh. And yourself?'

'Good, great!'

'Good, good. Now. I'm wondering whether you'd like to do a restaurant review for me.'

'I'd love to!'

'Right. It's a gastro pub in your village, in Riverside. Thought it might be easier for you that way. A place called The Swan. In to me as soon as you can. I'll email you the owner's number and you can liaise with him. How does that sound?'

'Fantastic!'

'Good. Oh, and I can pay you seventy-five pounds for it. I know it's not much, but—'

'No, no, that's fine.'

'Good-oh. Any problems, just call. Bye now.'

And there we are. Not even midday and I've got two commissions. TWO! Not a bad morning's work. And with a hangover, to boot. Not too shabby at all.

Once Joey's awake, we go for a walk and look in the post office window at the notice board. There's just cork, a Pissed-Off Parents Club note-sized hole in between the odd job man's note, the party planner's and the hypnotist's.

They've taken the old one down. I put my hands around the sides of my head to shield the sun's reflection, put my face closer up to the glass and read the hypnotist's note:

ALL ADDICTIONS CURED!

* Cigarettes
* Alcohol
* Phobias
* Drugs
* Food

Want to stop living in fear and just start *living*?
Give me a call today and we'll get you back to your
future – fear-free and fabulous!

I take down the number and sit on the park bench outside the hairdresser's. I just might give this hypnotist a call. You never know, maybe I could kick the fags for good with a little subliminal help. And maybe it's all a load of complete bollocks. But you never know until you give it a go. Just like the Pissed-Off Parents Club – look at what a success that's been.

I start making up the notice for the second meeting. After ten minutes or so, doodling flowers and stars, with Joey getting increasingly restless in her buggy, I settle on:

Due to the resounding success of the 1st PI**ED-
OFF PARENTS CLUB meeting last week, we're
going to do it all over again! And this time, YOU
should come along, too, if:

a) you're feeling fed up
b) you can fork out for a babysitter or
c) you just fancy a night out

Join us at The Swan, Wednesday the 11th at 8.15 p.m.
for the 2nd and even more fun
PI**ED-OFF PARENTS CLUB
meeting

BYO cash, cigarettes, issues
SEE YOU THERE

7

Saturday nights never used to be like this. Before we had Joey and moved out to the middle of nowhere, I mean. Normally, Jack and I would be either recovering from the depredations of the night before with a Chinese take-away in front of *You've Been Framed* or some other crap TV show, or we'd still be out, a lunchtime drink having turned into a mammoth session, leaving the take-away and hang-overs for Sunday afternoon, to make that dreadful night before the working week begins just that little bit more horrendous.

But tonight I've come up to bed early, to watch telly quietly in our bedroom. I'm feeling a little rough – and Jack looked so uncomfortable scrunched up on the front room floor, I thought I'd be magnanimous and let him be uncomfortable on the tiny two-seater sofa bed instead, while I spread out in the ridiculously huge super king size bed. We used to have that sofa and a massive three-seater in Chiswick that we'd lie on together – or he'd sit on it and I'd lie down, my legs resting on his lap in what we used to call The Love Belt position. We got rid of that couch when we moved and, along with it, any prospect of – or, indeed, desire for – a cuddle together on the small sofa. Come to think of it, I haven't seen any belts – love or otherwise – around here for ages. No need, I suppose, what with three rapidly-expanding girths on the go.

Joey's still kicking up a fuss in her cot, confounding the experts' controlled crying techniques. We've taken it in turns doing the trips upstairs – after five minutes (me), then seven (Jack), then nine (me again). But still Joey hasn't settled.

It's not entirely her fault this time, though. The people across the street are having some sort of shindig which involves, from what I can hear, blasting out Coldplay, Travis and/or Keane (all sound pretty much the same to me), rolling kegs up and down the road, laughing loudly, setting off fireworks and making Rottweilers bark rabidly. No wonder Joey's got the hump.

I wait for Jack to come upstairs and sort her out – her dummy's probably just fallen out and rolled underneath her cot. But after ten or so mithering minutes, I get up.

She's sweating up a storm, sucking furiously on her dummy. Poor thing. I take off her pyjama bottoms, but leave her in her summer sleeping bag, and bring her into our bedroom. It's a bit quieter in here and maybe she's sickening for her mummy. Yes, that's it – she just wants to be near me.

As preposterous a thought as that is, she does seem to calm down a bit, lying on top of our bed, but she's still as hot as buggery after an hour. I go downstairs to get some cold water for her, in the 'sippy' cup she's supposed to be learning to drink like an adult from. I come back upstairs, sit on the edge of the bed and try to wake her up. I sit her slumping form on my lap, trying to get some of the water into her.

'Joey? Wake up, sweetheart. Joey? Have a bit of water, Jo – Joey? Joey, wake up!' She's not responding. Her eyes are tight shut, she's dripping wet and even taking the dummy out of her mouth doesn't rouse her.

I bounce her up and down on my knee about three times and then BLEURGH! She chunders all over herself, me and my hair, our bedroom wall and floor – there's bucket-loads of sick, milk mainly – and then her eyes roll back in her head and she goes all floppy.

'Jesus!' I try sprinkling water from the pint glass on my bedside table over her face with my fingers and then fumble about with the zip on her sleeping bag to get her the hell out of it, so she can cool down. She's heavier than normal and limp in my arms.

'What's happening?' pants Jack, who's just run up the stairs.

'How should I know?' I'm panicking now, lugging the deadweight of Joey into the en suite to lie her on the cold, hard stone floor.

'Shall I call an ambulance?' he shouts.

'Yes!'

'She breathing? Shouldn't you lie her on her side? So she doesn't choke?'

'Call the ambulance!'

By the time the ambulance gets here, Joey's still hot to the touch and is fast asleep on Jack's shoulder while he sways gently and shushes softly.

One of the ambulance guys takes Joey's temperature. It feels like an eternity passes before anyone speaks.

'Forty point one,' the ambulance guy says flatly, pulling up Joey's eyelids and waving a mini torch at the whites of her eyes. 'Has he had anything like this before?'

'No, *she* hasn't,' Jack corrects him, shaking his head, ever cool in a crisis.

I, on the other hand – *never* cool in a crisis – start babbling.

'No, no – not that I know of. She's always been a bundle of heat, though, ever since she was born. She wasn't flailing about like she was having a fit or anything – maybe it's food poisoning. She *did* have some roast pepper salad that could've been sitting round all day in the Really Rather Good Cafe. *And* some salmon fishcakes—'

'We better take her in,' the other ambulance guy cuts me off and starts packing up quickly. 'Mum, grab what she'll need for a few days.'

A few days? *A few days?!*

And then I really start to freak out – it must be really serious if we've got to go to hospital. So I fling myself up the stairs, chuck on the first bra I see and nearly come thumping down on my arse, I'm trying to get back to poor little Joey so fast.

Funny, in a way, isn't it? I would've given anything for a break from Joey earlier today, for someone else to look after her for a few hours. But now I can't bear the thought of being without her. Even for a second – let alone a few days.

'Nappy bag! Bring the nappy bag and put some nappies in it, will you?' I gasp at Jack as I gingerly take Joey from him. 'And maybe her soft puppy teddy bear? No, no, the donkey. Hang on – get the donkey *and* the puppy. And maybe the little Jelly Cat lion?'

'Stop rabbiting on, babe,' soothes Jack, stroking Joey's tiny patch of hair. 'I'll be right behind you.'

I lie on the stretcher in the back of the ambulance and Joey snores away on my chest as we speed towards the hospital. It reminds me of when she was a newborn and used to sleep on me in the sweltering heat of last summer. She'd stick to me, her head in my cleavage, hands curled into tiny fists resting on my boobs, and I'd marvel at the wonder of new life – *my* new life – for hours while she dozed.

'Just hold the end of this tube near her mouth and nose, Mum. It's oxygen. She's getting a tiny bit of colour back and this'll help bring her round,' the ambulance guy sitting in the back with us says.

'OK,' I whimper, waving the tube in front of Joey's face.

'Saturday nights, eh?' he smiles. 'It's usually beaten-up drunks we're picking up at this time.'

'Yeah, I bet. You'll probably be back to across the road from us in an hour or two,' I reply, suspicious of his obvious attempt to take my mind off Joey. 'So anyway – do you think she has epilepsy? My mum has epilepsy now, brought on by a stroke, we think, so maybe it's in the genes and this is a sign Joey'll have it, too.'

'Look, try not to worry. The hospital's very thorough. They'll find out what's going on in no time. She needs Mum to be calm, though, so just breathe . . .'

Thanks to his distinct lack of real reassurance, I'm forced to steal a bit of Joey's oxygen in a bid to stop myself hyperventilating. And once we arrive at the hospital, Joey and I – both reeking of vomit, pretty much like all the other drunks there – are rushed straight through to the emergency ward just seconds before an out-of-breath Jack shows up.

'How is she?' he asks.

'I don't know. They've gone to get an x-ray machine for her. She still smells pretty bad, though – or is that me?'

He smiles and puts his hand on my back.

'Do you want to hold her? She's *really* heavy . . .'

'Yeah, yeah. Come here, little one,' he says, his deep, creamy voice enveloping us, making me feel safe, like everything's going to be all right. That gorgeous made-for-movie-trailer voice almost makes me wish it was me wrapped up in his arms, getting a cuddle.

Joey has an x-ray done on her chest and they pump her

full of Nurofen and put a sort of baby sanitary pad in her nappy to get a urine sample.

A nurse takes us up to the paediatric ward and hands us over to the night duty staff there. But no one will tell us what's wrong with Joey and she's still out cold.

It has to be said, though, that the nurses here are so lovely – particularly compared to our GP. So warm and friendly and *kind*. They tell us she's in good hands and the doctor will see us on his rounds tomorrow morning.

'Want me to stay with her?' Jack surprises me by asking.

Oh. And did I mention the nurses are all really young and good looking, too?

'No, a girl needs her mum at times like this.' I smile inside, thinking how nice it would be to think that Joey *did* want me.

'OK,' he says, disappointed that he won't get to be with her. 'I'll be here first thing in the morning, then.'

'These nurses'll be going off shift by then, you know,' I grin, trying to make light of the situation. I look at Joey and stroke her brow, making her grunt and scowl and turn her head away from my hand.

'So?'

'Well, it'll probably be the old matron-types for the day shift.'

'Are all these nurses unbelievably gorgeous? I hadn't noticed.' He winks at me and then tickles Joey's chin gently, making her smile.

I think better of asking him to stay with Joey while I duck out for a fag and shake my head at the reprehensibility of the thought. This is my chance to prove I'm a proper mum – a caring, Florence Nightingale-ish, strong, comforting, *good* mum. And so, strangely excited by that possibility, I say goodbye to Jack and try to hold Joey's recalcitrant hand while I lie on the pull-out bed next to hers, asphyxiating myself with the smell of sick on my hair.

'Shh, sweetheart, shh,' I whisper to Joey as I put her dummy in for the umpteenth time and try to lie her down. (After I've picked said dummy off the floor and run it under the hot water tap at the basin behind us, of course.) She's the happiest I've seen her in yonks, though, and isn't interested in sleeping in the slightest.

And nor am I, truth be told. It must be about three a.m. and a new patient is being wheeled into the bay next to ours on the right. Our curtains are closed, but I can just about make out what they're saying.

'. . . stomach pumped . . . should be fine . . . will have one hell of a hangover, though,' a calm, authoritative voice says.

'. . . never done anything like this before . . . so sorry to be a bother . . .' And then louder, more upset, 'What were you thinking?!'

Silence but for a sniffly 'Sorry' follows the rustling of sheets and a groan.

Indeed, I think. Poor kid in the next cubicle must be feeling absolutely awful – and now has to put up with her mum or whoever banging on about how stupid she's been.

'Now's not the time,' the authoritative voice says. 'Let her get some sleep and I'll give her a bit of a lecture in the morning, when she'll be able to take it in better.'

God. I wish I'd had my stomach pumped and some doctor had given *me* a lecture on the dangers of drinking when I first started my illustrious career as a bit of a booze-hound. Things would definitely have turned out differently for me.

I take Joey off to the play room and we muck about with all the great toys in there for what seems like a few hours but is actually only thirty minutes. I know this because it says 3.35 a.m. on the big digital clock over the fish tank that's at the entrance to our ward. We linger at the tank so Joey can watch, fascinated, the bubbles bloob-bloob-bloobing to the surface from the scary jaws of a plastic piranha. And then I carry her back to her bed where, finally, we both fall asleep for two hours.

'Hello, my gorgeousness!' I hear Jack say as Joey nearly takes a tumble off her bed, she's so excited to see him.

'Hey there,' I reply, knowing full well he was addressing Joey, not me.

'Yeah, hi,' he says, kissing my cheek. 'How is she?'

'The hot nurses have gone home,' I sneer, 'so you don't have to put on that perfect dad act any more.'

'Christ Almighty, Roxane – will you just for once stop your sniping? I didn't sleep a wink last night, worrying about Joey. But fuh— forget that, forget thinking about someone else other than yourself for a change – why not just have another go at me, eh? Why not really kick a man when he's down? If that's what makes you feel better, go for it. Lemme have it. Couldn't let *you* be miserable for longer than five minutes, could we?'

Bloody hell! Who's rattled *his* cage? Oh, yeah. Me. I did. Without even thinking about it, if you want the truth. Just slipped out. I was trying to be funny, though. Sort of. And point out that it's *me* who's been with Joey all night – *me* who hasn't had any sleep.

But I have actually missed him these past few hours, so I don't know why I'm so unpleasant as soon as I see him. Habit, I guess. Must be the tiredness taking its toll. Yeah – sleep deprivation to the enth degree. Nothing whatsoever to do with the fact that I can be a bit of a cow sometimes. All right, all right, *most* of the time these days.

'Um, we're waiting for the doctors to do their rounds and let us know what made her so sick,' I say quietly. 'She seems happy enough though, don't you think?'

Jack's face lights up just like Joey's as he picks her up off the bed.

'Hooo! Who had an exciting night at the hospital, eh? Who gave her daddy a fright? Hey, little one? Heh-heh-heh-hey?'

I consider myself well and truly blanked. Can't blame

him, either – I'd be annoyed with me, too. Unlike me, though, Jack can't keep up his pissed-offedness. Once he's said his piece, he'll revert right back to nice guy Jack soon enough.

He takes Joey to the nurses' station to find out when the doctor is likely to get to us. I stay in our little cubicle and almost fall through the curtain on the right, I've got my ear up to it so close, trying to hear what's going on with the poor girl next to us.

'It's a very dangerous thing, alcohol,' says the same authoritative voice I heard last night. 'One or two drinks when you're older is fine, as a social thing. But it's very easy to get carried away, go too far and drink to excess.'

Ain't *that* the truth. I thank my lucky stars neither Jack nor I had touched a drop last night. Imagine being a bit tiddly and hopeless at helping a convulsing Joey. Or worse, not even noticing, just sitting outside, oblivious to the sickness, knocking back beers and puffing away on cigarettes. I shiver at the thought.

'You're still so young, your body's still maturing – why poison it with alcohol? That's why you feel so terrible, now – because you've effectively *poisoned* yourself. You'll feel pretty awful for the next couple of days, too, I'm afraid.'

Jeez. I'm dying to get a good look at this girl, so I step out of our cubicle and pretend that I'm looking around for someone to ask where the loo is. The front of their cubicle's curtain is open when I come out of ours, so I stare straight in.

The girl lying on the bed looks about sixteen or so. The woman on a chair next to the bed must be her mum – they look the same, but the mum's done some hard living herself and it shows: all baggy skin, dark circles under her eyes and deeply-etched lines between her eyebrows. That's what a hard life does to you, or maybe that's what kids do to you – the endless worry and frustration can really wreak havoc with your looks.

The girl herself has eyeliner smudged all over her eyes and is obviously suffering, crying on her bed. But you can tell she's very pretty.

'What *were* you thinking?' asks her mum sternly, as the doctor walks away. 'Is that the first time you've ever drunk anything? Or do you do that all the time? Why? Why on earth would you *do* that to yourself?'

'I just didn't want to be seen as a goody-goody,' sniffs the girl.

I know how she feels. My heart goes out to her and I really want to say something to make her feel better, but just as I'm opening my mouth to speak, Jack grabs my arm and steers me back to our cubicle.

'Stop gawping,' he says.

I jerk my head towards the fast-closing curtains.

'She's had her stomach—'

'I don't give a toss! Concentrate on your own daughter for a second, will you?' He looks angry.

'Now,' he says quickly, before I can get a word in, 'we have to get a urine sample from Joey. They've found a tiny trace of infection there, but want to make sure, so we have to get a clean catch – let her crawl about without a nappy and when she wees, collect it in this.'

He holds up a blue papier mâché hat.

'Jesus,' I say, incredulous. 'Bags you do it!'

'Thought you'd say that,' he half laughs. Phew. I'm back from the dog house.

We go off into the play room and take Joey's nappy off. I try to get her to drink some water (doesn't really work) and after about fifteen minutes, just as Jack's looking at the DVDs they've got ('Can't wait till she's old enough to actually sit still and watch *The Jungle Book* with us'), I see a small yellow puddle forming underneath Joey.

'Quick! She's peeing! Get it, get it!' I shriek.

Jack throws *The Jungle Book* DVD in the air, lunges for the cardboard potty that he's put on top of the telly and dives towards Joey's bum.

'Ah! Bugger!' Thank God no one else is in here and can hear us. 'Missed it.'

Joey laughs heartily and crawls towards the play kitchen.

'Could we scoop some off the floor?' I say, trying to be helpful and not get annoyed with Jack for missing the wee.

'Nah, this floor'd be covered in bacteria. Hardly what you'd call a clean catch,' sighs Jack.

'You can't take your eyes off her for a second,' I tut. 'Now Joey? Sweetie pie? Have some more water.'

'How long is it between wees for a baby?' Jack asks.

'Like I'd know.' I smile at Joey, who's giggling as she opens the plastic door of the play oven.

'Didn't you learn anything from *Positive Parenting!*?'

'Get on your hands and knees and hold it under her, just in case,' I offer.

'What? With *my* back? Oh, thank you, Joey!' He opens his mouth wide, looking like a laughing clown, as Joey hands him a plastic saucepan.

'At least sit next to her then, and scoot after her on your bum.'

'Why don't you, if you're such an expert?'

'What? With *my* bum?'

'True,' he smiles up at me, 'You might go *through* the floor and crash through the ceiling of cardiology.'

'Yeah, all right. Enough jokes at my arse's expense, thank you very much!'

'You know I'm only kidding – I think you've got a beautif—'

'Quick! She's doing it again!'

'Fark!' he squeals and drops to the floor, chest-first, one hand pushing himself along the floor, the other holding the potty outstretched, like a pee-seeking luge. He slides magnificently – the piss propelling him – and nearly lodges his nose into Joey's bum crack, his positioning's so precise.

I slap both hands on my knees and nearly wet myself.

'Got it!' he beams, holding the potty aloft, triumphantly.

'Well, only a tiny bit, but hopefully enough. Take it to the nurse! Quick! Go, go, *GO!*'

Like the last leg of a highly-trained urinary relay team, I turn to face the door, holding my arm behind me for Jack to put the papier mâché potty in. Potty in hand, eyes on the prize, I hurl myself towards the door, my legs pumping like coiled springs, and in one fluid movement open the door, breeze through the gap and race down the corridor. Without spilling a drop, it takes me two seconds, tops, to bowl up to the elderly nurse who's been taking Joey's temperature, stirring a cup of tea at the nurses' station.

'Clean (pant, pant) catch for (pant, pant) Joey. Josephine (pant) Everingham (pant, pant). Her dad did it (pant) – should've seen it (pant), it was (cough) brilliant!'

'Great,' says the nurse, without looking up from her tea. 'I'll see to it in a minute.'

The doctor eventually comes to see us and says Joey had suffered febrile convulsions, which is usually a sign of infection. Turns out urinary infections are very common in baby girls, but they couldn't find anything in Joey's catch, so she tells us to keep an eye on her and be vigilant about cleanliness and wiping front to back when changing Joey's nappy. The doctor hands me a leaflet about what to do when your baby has a temperature and then she gives us the all-clear.

Just as we're about to leave, the mum from the next-door cubicle walks over to me and says: 'I hope your little boy gets better.'

'She's a girl, actually,' I say, not minding, for once, that someone's got it wrong.

'Oh, I'm so sorry,' she says, looking drained. 'At least she's still a baby – not a teenager, yet. Only thirteen, my girl, and already she's had her stomach pumped. I'm so embarrassed.'

'God, don't be! There are worse things to be embarrassed about,' I say. 'Like imagine if it were her coming in to see you after you'd had *your* stomach pumped! And now maybe she'll be put off for life. But only thirteen, eh? I thought she was at least sixteen!'

'I remember when mine was your baby's age. So sweet, so innocent,' she sighs. 'And then they turn ten years old and it's all downhill from there. Then you've got all this to look forward to . . .'

I think about the broken limbs, the broken hearts, the (possibly inevitable) stomach pumpings to come – Joey's rites of passage into her adult world – and I well up.

'Come on!' says Jack from the fish tank.

'Yes, yes, all *right*!' I snap.

In the car park, a striking figure in a shiny black mac and ridiculously oversized sunglasses catches my eye. She's so immaculately groomed, so glamorous-looking, I can't help but feel a stab of jealousy as I glance down at my trackie bottoms and spew-stained sweatshirt, smelling the piquancy still.

'Mustn't have kids,' I mumble to myself, wondering if they do plastic surgery on the NHS these days as I watch her carefully getting into the back of a chauffeur-driven BMW, a poster girl for WAGs in her leopard-skin-print sky-scraper stilettos and her lustrous, jet-black, poker-straight hair.

So while I'm now officially in the running for Mum of the Year, selflessly tending to my poorly daughter all night, I see our little hospital stay's done nothing for my envy problem. And did I just see Jack wave to her? No, must be seeing things – delirium's obviously set in. I let Jack do all the work, buckling Joey in, and flump down in the passenger seat of our car, unwittingly giving the suspension a really good workout.

8

It's been a shit summer so far. Now, I know the UK's not known for its blisteringly hot summers, but compared to this time last year, when I was massively pregnant with what looked like could have been twin whales, it's *particularly* bad.

Still, it's warm enough for the Pissed-Off Parents to congregate in the beer garden again at The Swan – and as I spot June's classy salt and pepper bob, I see there are two other people sitting there with her. One bloke, one woman. No Olivia.

The woman is very glam – big lips, big hair, big boobs that make it look like there's a small child's bum bursting out of her shirt. She looks familiar. And the guy's all spiky blond hair with big, blue eyes and very slim – your classic Swedish porn star look.

'Hi there,' I say to June, putting my pint down on the table and crawling on to the bench.

'Ah, Roxy,' she says, blowing her smoke into the

already-acrid air. 'This is Tim,' she nods her head to the bloke, 'and this is Carina. This is Roxy, our founder.'

'Hiya!' Old magazine habits die hard. 'No Olivia?'

'Not yet, but I'm sure she'll be here.'

Tim takes a sip of some hot pink cocktail thing, moving the mini umbrella out of the way with his straw. He grins impishly and says: 'I'm so excited! I wanted to come last week, but, as per, Muggins here was roped into babysitting. *Again*!'

'For your wife? Girlfriend?' I ask.

'Oh, no, no, *no*! Perish the thought! No!'

'Tim's gay, Roxy,' says June.

'Really? Never would've guessed—'

'I *know*! Mad, isn't it?' Tim turns his head to the side and puckers his lips into a perfect Frankie Howerd/Kenneth Williams pout.

'Are you somebody's dad, from, like, *before* you were gay?' I ask warily.

'Sweetie, you don't *become* gay, you're *born* happy. Least I was . . . one look at where I was coming from on the way out and, honey, I was *ecstatic* to know I'd never have to go back *there* again!' He elbows Carina, snorts like a donkey and takes another sip through his straw.

I laugh, embarrassed by my naivety.

'So what brings you to the Club, then?'

'Well,' he sits on his hands, looking around at us and hunching his shoulders so he's lower to the table, looking conspiratorial, 'I may not be their biological parent, but I definitely *feel* like the twins' parent. And I get no help from my sister, Lisa, bless her. She dumps them on me every day, so she can see her friends or whatever and more often than not, I have to look after them in the evening, too, while she goes out.'

He takes a breath. We all take a breath.

'Now don't get me wrong, I love Lisa and I love the kids to *bits* – wouldn't be without them – but I'm not their full-time, stay-at-home dad, surely – do we have a Shirley in the house?' He laughs nervously and then answers his own question as he carries on, 'No. And my father's made it clear he'll have nothing to do with Lisa or her kids because she's a single mum, bringing shame on the family, yada, yada, yada. He won't let my mum go anywhere near them, either. I want to have my own kids someday, you see – but while I'm busy running after the two adorable little terrors, my love life's looking more like the Gobi Desert. Now with added tumbleweeds!'

'Hmm,' hums June in her wise way, 'can you just say "no" to your sister every once in a while? Make your plans and organise something before she has a chance to take advantage of you?'

'Not that easy, June, love.'

I feel June bristle next to me.

'Just June will be fine, thank you, Tim,' she says.

'Right you are, duck,' he winks. 'Lisa and me, we sort of only have each other, really – Dad's not too fussed about me, either, you know, being gay and what have you.

We're really very close and she needs a life, too, and I work from home which makes me an obvious choice for babysitter. Which I don't really mind, it's actually good practice for when I meet Mr Fabulous and we adopt. And I guess that's why I'm here – to have a night off, get me out of the house, try to meet someone . . . Mind you, I'm probably the only gay in the village!' He puts on a Welsh accent for the last bit, like that character in *Little Britain*.

'Sorry – watch far too much telly, stuck at home all the time. I'm a freelance graphic designer, you see.'

He speaks so quickly, I can barely keep up.

'So anyway, I feel like a parent – and a pissed-off one at that!' He looks around at the three of us, smiling. 'So? Do I qualify? Can I be in the gang? Can I, can I, *can I*?!'

We all laugh. Even June.

'Well, let's see . . . do you smoke?' I mock-interrogate him.

'Not really, no.'

'All right. Drink?'

'Does the Pope shit in the woods?!'

'You getting the next round?'

'Ah, yeah?'

'You're in!'

'I'm in the Club! I'm in the Club!' he sings as he races off to the bar.

By the time Tim's back, Olivia turns up.

'Sorry I'm late!' she puffs. 'What've I missed?'

'Hello there! Not much,' I say.

'Actually, a fair bit!' June corrects me. 'Tim's now officially a member of the Club – he looks after his sister's twins all the time – and Carina here was just about to let us in on her reasons for joining.'

'Great. Hi, Tim, hi, Carina – can you hold on a minute so I can get a beer? Don't want to miss anything!'

We all take sips of our drinks and I take the opportunity to give Carina a good, solid – but brilliantly surreptitious – once-over.

She's tall – you can tell even though we're sitting down – and has recently coiffed hair. It's sort of a reddish burgundy and smells of Elnett. Her make-up's expertly applied, albeit a bit too thickly for me, and she may have had a bit of Botox here and there. She's definitely had her lips pumped up with collagen, but not too badly, not too troutily, and her fingers are fairly dripping in diamonds. She's wearing an expensive-looking long, fine-knit camel-coloured cardigan over a white, wide-collared, open-necked shirt which barely covers her obvious kid's bum boob job. On her slim, long legs, she's spray-painted on a pair of white Capri pants. They're so bloody tight, you can just about make out the individual hairs on her thighs. Leopard-skin-print peep-toe sling-backs swing from her pedicured to perfection toes and she sports a deep, even tan. It's your basic *Desperate Housewives* look. Say, late thirties, early forties? Maybe younger, but her skin looks older – it's the first thing to pay the price for too many sunbeds. She's sort of a cross between Sue Ellen in

Dallas and a young Sophia Loren. Good looking, for sure. I've definitely seen her before, but can't put my finger on where . . . She positively reeks of wealth, too. New money, maybe – but definitely money.

'Why don't you take a picture, it'll last longer,' she says, a little slurrily, taking a rather large gulp of her G&T.

'Oh sorry, I didn't mean to stare, sorry! It's just those rings! They're really quite dazzling.'

'They should be,' she says out of the side of her mouth, blowing the smoke out at the same time. 'Cost me enough. In lost youth, beauty – not to mention muscle tone.'

Blimey. We've got a right one here, I think as I look at Tim and June, who both raise their eyebrows back at me.

'What do you mean?' asks Tim.

'The old man. My husband. We struck a deal. If I produced an heir to his fortune – he's, ah, very into The Family, if you know what I mean – he'd keep me in diamonds and gin for the rest of my life. But I never see him, it's just me and the kids rattling around in the mansion all day.'

'What's happening? Wait, wait, wait!' says Olivia, spilling her pint in the rush to pull up a chair and sit at the end of the table. 'God! The day I've had! Carry on, carry on, don't mind me,' she says, more animated than I've ever seen her.

'He's always working, taking care of business, you see. He's in waste management—'

'The slimming club?' I ask, incredulously.

'No, rubbish disposal. He owns a couple of strip clubs, too, so he has to tend to them. And his crew. I just feel a bit lonely, is all. It's a bit of a joke, really,' Carina carries on. 'Only problem is, I'm not laughing.'

'Ooh, know what you mean – best avoided at all costs,' Tim pipes up. 'Plays merry hell with your wrinkles, does all that giggling!'

Thank God for Tim – light relief! Everything Carina's said so far has been so dramatic, like she's been reading from a script. And the way she looks around like she's bored, but stuck here, killing time with us losers before her gangster boyfriend shows up.

As though she can read my mind, Carina smiles, out of one side of her mouth only. She looks like the Joker in *Batman*. Yeah – maybe it's not even a smile. Maybe it's just an old slash scar from a knife – wielded in a jealous rage by some other woman, desperate to get her hands on Carina's man. Or, even more likely, the scar from an unfortunate slip of the plastic surgeon's scalpel. Ah! That's it! It was *her* I saw getting into that posh car in the hospital car park the other morning. Probably a regular out-patient for day plastic surgery.

'How many children do you have, Carina?' asks June.

None, I think to myself – she's only here for the beer. Or, rather, the triple G&Ts.

'Four. So far. Four girls. He wants us to try again, but I can't face any more morning sickness, backache . . . and anyway, they won't let me have another caesarean. Four's the limit. And there's no way I'm going to push anything bigger than a Deluxe Rampant Rabbit out of *my* box.'

'Atta girl,' says Olivia, raising her pint to Carina.

'Bloody hell – *four*?' I say. 'How on *earth* do you manage?'

'I don't,' she says, fixing me with her steely gaze. 'The nannies do.'

Of course! How dozy of me.

'Nannies *plural*? How many?' asks June.

'Two. One for days, one for nights,' Carina sniffs, as though it was obvious.

'So you do still work, then?' I ask her.

'No. Yes. Sort of.' She brightens up a bit. 'I used to do publicity for kids' TV shows, mainly.'

'Ooh!' I interrupt. 'I thought your voice sounded a bit familiar! I used to work at *Positive Parenting!* – we're bound to have spoken on the phone at some stage . . .'

'Hmm, maybe. Can't say you sound familiar, though. Sure I'd recognise your strange English/Australian accent.'

Thanks *hoips*, I think, but don't say anything.

'I'm trying to do my own thing, now, though – take more control,' she says. 'I've set up my own business. An events management company called Weddings! Parties! Anything! You've probably seen my card in the post office.'

'No,' I lie. 'Can't say it rings a bell.'

'So, Liv,' I turn to face Olivia, 'what's got you so cheery tonight?'

'What? Am I?' she asks, genuinely unaware that her face has lost its slapped arse appearance of yore.

'Yeah,' June and I say at the same time.

'Ooh, our second meeting? Um, *that* . . . and we've got a new manager at the 6-Ten. Met him on the weekend. Nice guy.'

'Love in the air?' I ask.

'Don't be silly,' Olivia blushes. 'Working with him on Saturday was a laugh, though, you know? Almost bordering on fun. Which is unheard of for an evening shift in that dump.'

'I think I've seen him! Twinkly, smiley eyes, right? Thick, black hair. Dimple in his chin, like an Asian George Clooney?' Tim's own eyes light up.

'Haven't checked him out that closely,' says Liv. 'Now listen. What are we going to do about the Club notices you keep putting up, Roxy?'

June nearly chokes on her Merlot, she can't get it out fast enough: 'Oh yes, dar-*ling*! This week's was even worse than the last one!'

Knew they'd hate it.

'Why? What was wrong with it?' I can't see the problem.

'You've got to be concise, my dear,' says June, putting her hand on my shoulder. 'Short, sharp and to the point.'

'Yeah, short. Think short,' says Liv. 'Shouldn't be too hard – you're what? Five foot?'

'Why don't you do the next one if you're so keen?' I answer.

'Done!' says Liv, sloshing her pint down. 'I'll put one up in the 6-Ten, too – we really need to spread the word. I fancy a big do for the next one.'

'So there *is* going to be another one?' squeaks Tim.

'Of course there's going to be another one – loads more,' I say. 'With loads more members and loads more fun to be had!' I'm waving my arms about, clearly getting a bit pissed.

'Super,' says June, smiling.

'Same time, same place?' Tim asks.

'Same whines, same face . . . *s*,' I counter.

'More wines, women and wrongs?' suggests June.

'For another wicked singe, binge and whinge session!' laughs Liv.

And I can't remember what happened after that.

Jack's had a few days off work. Brilliant, I'd thought when he told me, now *I* can have some time off and *he* can see first-hand how utterly exhausting and frustrating it is looking after Joey all day, every day. But no. He's only taken himself off somewhere in Gloucester to play golf for four days. And he's taken the laptop, too (so he can play *Civilisation* – a computer game he's mad on), so I have to make do with the old computer in The New Study.

The New Study is the old larder under the stairs. Great idea, I thought at the time, to create a room out of what is essentially a tiny, sloping-ceilinged narrow cupboard. At least it was a great idea when I thought *I* wouldn't have to sit in it, surrounded by mould and electricity and gas meters. Thought it'd be a good place for Jack when he was working from home.

Ah. Yes. Working From Home. I thought *that'd* be great for me, too: he could watch Joey while I went off and did my own thing – like, um, work, with the laptop. But here's the rub – he actually *does* work when he's here. He's not just skiving. Too bloody conscientious for his own good.

It can really get on my wick if I know he's in there – and he can hear me in the kitchen, cooking and cleaning and struggling with Joey – and he doesn't come out to help. If he's not in the house, fine – but if he's right there, only inches away, and he doesn't help me or play with Joey or something, it can really send me over the edge. Usually, when things are reaching fever pitch between me and Joey, he'll call out from behind the closed study door:

'Cup of tea? Ooh, yes please! When you're ready . . .'

And I'll nearly spontaneously combust with rage.

So anyway, I've just dropped Joey off at the nursery for the afternoon. And, for once, we were bang on time. Usually, we're *at least* an hour late, which can really get on your thirty-six Double Ds when you've got bugger-all cash and you *pay* for five hours of child-care, but actually only ever end up *getting* three and a half.

As I come out of Sunny Farm Stores (with some broccoli that cost a whopping £2.16 that I had to scrabble about in my cash-machine-receipt-stuffed bag for), my mobile goes off. I plunge my hand into my bag to find the phone, simultaneously quickening my pace and lowering my eyes in an effort to avoid a *contretemps* with the *Big Issue* guy. Sounds terrible, I know, but if I can barely afford a bunch of broccoli, the *Big Issue*'s got no chance.

'I've just nipped out to get some lunch,' Charlie says. 'I'm completely on my own in the office today.'

'Is that good or bad? Probably good, yeah? You get to look at music videos on YouTube and—'

'No! It's rubbish! I've got so much to do and I'm *shattered*. Guy's been staying over every night for the past three weeks – which is great, but blimey!'

'What?' I'm genuinely interested, considering I'm living my sex life vicariously through Charlie's. I light up, hoping this is going to be a long one.

'He has so much energy, he doesn't stop! He's like the Duracell bunny – but sexier! We work, get home, have a glass of wine, go to bed – and then he wakes me up at four in the morning for another go! That's how we roll these days, Rox.'

'GOD! I can't even *imagine*!'

'Not that I'm complaining – really – it's great and everything. I'm just so knackered. *And* he's taking me off to the Maldives soon. Hoo. Can't wait. But what about you? What you up to?'

'Not much. Jack's had a couple of days off – been away playing golf and *Civ* at some club in Gloucestershire.'

'*What*?'

'Yeah, I know.'

'Who's he gone with?'

'Himself.'

'Really?'

'Well, yeah. That's what he told me. Unless he's having an affair . . .'

'Oh, GOD. What kind of woman would have an affair with someone who took them off to a golf club for a romantic tryst, for chrissakes?'

'I dunno . . . the kind of woman who loved golf, could drink both her and Jack's body weight in beer, who could play him at *Civ* . . . and wake *him* up at four in the morning for another great porn-type shag. Jack's ideal woman, basically.'

'Yeah, but that woman doesn't exist, does she? And anyway, maybe he's not playing golf at all. I mean, maybe he's taken her to a spa or something.'

'Hadn't thought of that . . .' I say, starting to wonder whether he might be seeing someone else. He did say he was ripe for an affair, didn't he? God! Maybe he was trying to tell me something! 'Nah, he's too good for that sort of behaviour. He'd break up with me, first, tie up all loose ends before he embarked on an affair.'

'Yeah,' agrees Charlie. 'Too nice.'

'And he can do what he wants, you know,' I say, feeling relieved Charlie doesn't really think he's having it away with someone else. 'And actually, I'm nowhere *near* as

115

pissed off as I thought I'd be – about him going off without me and Joey, you know, as a family and stuff. He needs a break and we're getting on fine without him.'

'Hmm. But still, you need a break, too. When're *you* going to get away – without *them*? When're you coming up here?'

'Well, interesting you should say that! I was thinking . . . *as soon as I bloody-well can*! I'll work it out with Jack when he gets back and—'

'Nyurgh,' she clicks the roof of her mouth with her tongue. 'don't *work it out* with him – tell him! And make it soon – before we go to the Maldives.'

'Well, yeah, OK – but—'

'Look, I wish I could talk to you for, ooh, I dunno, at least another thirty seconds, but some of us've got work to do.'

9

When we get to the village hall, it's the same as last time – toddlers tooling about like crazy, mums dressed to the nines competing with each other about every little thing. I'm sure I hear one say: 'Yes, well, Tallulah *is* awfully advanced for her age – your Harrison was at least *two* before he started picking his nose, wasn't he?' So when I spot Olivia, my heart leaps. A friendly (ish) face!

And get this. *She* actually bombs over to *me* and says, 'Thank God you're here!'

'Hi, Liv,' I say, looking up from my crouched position on the floor, where I've just put Joey down.

'Listen! I can't bear it in here. Wanna break out and go for a coffee at the Really Rather Good Cafe?'

Music to my ears. *Adult* music, that is – not that baby rubbish they play here that sticks in your head and wakes you up in a cold sweat in the middle of the night.

'Let's go!'

I run after Joey, who's not impressed when I pick her

up and plonk her back in her buggy outside. I put my right shoulder out in the process – but it hasn't been right since Joey was born. That and my right wrist, from tension and fear and holding her, I think – it's like I've got RSI or arthritis. Must be an age thing.

Liv turns up seconds later with Stuart, and we take off towards the village square – the bit of the road that has the most shops on either side of it, that is, not some easy walk-through quaint cobble-stoned actual square or anything.

I'm fairly beaming with pride as we walk along the street together – I must look like a real, proper, bona fide mum. I mean, this is what's supposed to happen when you have a baby, isn't it? You meet other mums and go for coffees all day, telling each other how beautiful your respective babies are and feeling – for a while, at least – as though you're back in the real world, something akin to your old world, where you'd meet up with friends and bang on about . . . um . . . work and men and how crap they can be, mainly.

'Hang on,' says Liv, just as we're nearly there. 'Shall we get a cheeky fag in before we go inside?'

We both look around furtively.

'Not here, not out the front,' I say.

'No! Are you crazy? Let's go round the back. I know just the place.'

She takes us down a little side road I've never noticed before, past some businesses and we stop. Right next to a stinking skip out the back of the cafe.

'Nice,' I say, lighting up.

'I know. Take you to all the best places, me,' Liv giggles. 'Oh, look! Joey's really checking my Stu out.'

I bend down, holding my fag far away, to see a totally uninterested baby boy looking sleepy in his pram. Joey's fascinated by him – she's grinning and trying to wriggle free of the buggy straps to get a better look at him.

'So how've you been?' I venture.

'Not so bad,' she says, blowing the smoke out. 'Not so good, either. But, you know, swings and roundabouts.'

'The POP Club's good though, isn't it? I always feel extremely rough the next day, mind.'

'Yeah? Lightweight. Must be an age thing.'

'Yeah,' I say, rubbing my right shoulder. 'Thanks.'

When we get inside, I go for a pot of Earl Grey with semi-skimmed and Liv plumps for a cappuccino. Even though I'm at a cafe with a fellow mum, and as I understand it you're supposed to go mad scoffing cake all day as well as coffee, I avert my gaze from the really rather tasty-looking cake section and head for the couches in the corner, away from all the tables and mums with prams on the other side.

'Gor,' says Liv when she joins us, 'clock the face on that one over there.'

I look over her shoulder at the sea of generic mums on the other side.

'Which one?'

'The one with a face like a slapped arse!'

I nearly say something, but think better of it and just smile and 'Hmm' a bit.

'Bet she could do with a night down The Swan – looks like a right pissed-off parent.'

We laugh and stir our drinks and then, after a few seconds, Liv suddenly looks me straight in the eye, puts her hand on my aching wrist and says, 'So anyway. My ex rang me two nights ago.'

'Really? What did *he* want, the bastard?'

'Well, he's been texting me for a while now, saying he'd been dumb and confused and didn't know what he was doing before. But now he's had time to think, he says he definitely wants to be a part of Stuart's life.'

'Whoa! What about *your* life?'

'*What* life?'

'You know what I mean. Does he want to get back with you, too – or just see Stu every now and again?'

'All he said was that he wanted to see Stu and I was to think about it and let him know. Says he doesn't want to muck us around, just wants to do the right thing.'

'Bit late for that, isn't it?'

'Hmm, I dunno. Maybe it's never too late. For him and Stu, anyway. A boy needs his dad.'

'No one needs an arsehole—'

'Think you'll find we all do, Rox.'

'No, no – you know what I mean! I'd far rather an absent father than one who's going to be part-time, unreliable and ultimately disappointing.'

'Yeah, I know. He sounds different, though. Sounds like he's changed.'

'Don't you watch *Jeremy Kyle*?' I ask.

'No, I don't actually. My sister's banned it from the house – says it's too near the knuckle. And anyway, I'm doing my Weight Watchers online when it's on. How are you going with that, by the way?'

'Good, good,' I say. 'I don't watch it, either . . . much . . . But anyway, the point is, leopards don't change their spots. And tigers don't change their stripes, either. And giraffes don't—'

'Wind their necks in? Hmm, reminds me of someone . . . You do go on a bit, Roxy. What exactly are you trying to say?'

'Sorry,' I say. 'Once an arse, always an arse, that's what I'm trying to say. In a nutshell.'

'Yeah . . . maybe,' murmurs Liv, softly, staring off wistfully at the mums on the other side. 'But having a bloke around, living away from my sister, Stu having his daddy on tap . . . it'd be nice, you know? Be like having a proper family.'

'Would you get back with him? Assuming that's what he's gunning for?'

'Don't know. He really dropped me in it when he left. Not sure I can forgive him. And I'm not sure he wants to.'

I look at Liv's face and see she's really quite pretty, when you think about it. She's got lovely, sparkling greeny-blue eyes and when she's not looking too pissed off, her mouth turns up at the ends. When she smiles, her teeth are so white, she looks like she could be in a Colgate ad – despite all the nicotine she sucks through them. And if she sorted her hair out – got some highlights and a decent cut, say, instead of scraping it back in a brown mess of a ponytail – she'd be quite the looker. Funny how someone's physical appearance can be radically changed, depending on their mood. And the mood of the beholder, too. She must be feeling a bit better – most likely down to the prospect of her ex coming back on the scene. Does wonders for a girl's face, I always think, that feeling of being wanted. And maybe that Weight Watchers is kicking in a bit, too.

'It's not all it's cracked up to be,' I say, thinking about Jack. 'Just means you've got to spread your resentments a bit thinner, that's all.'

'You resent Jack?'

'Sometimes, yes.'

'Yeah,' Liv breaks into her gleaming grin and I expect to hear the *Ping!* that used to accompany the ring of Colgate confidence in those old adverts. 'It's just *hellish* sitting in cafes all day and having drunken nights out every week!'

I smile and think that not only has she got great teeth, she's actually got a good point too. Things are definitely looking up lately.

And then her watch alarm bleeps.

'Urgh,' she grunts, the corners of her mouth turning

down again. 'Look, I've got to go – Big Sis'll be calling any minute to check on what I've fed Stu this morning and whether I'm keeping to his nap routine.'

'Righty-ho,' I say, finally remembering Joey's there, too, getting all antsy and tired. Hopefully.

'Honestly. You want to know what hell is? My sister. I'd swap places with you anytime.'

And so we wander off down the road together and when we're back in our house – just me and Joey – I realise it's not so small, after all. At the risk of turning into Goldilocks, I'd even go so far as to say it was *just right*.

Once I've put an exhausted Joey down for her sleep, I take a cup of tea outside.

And for once, it almost feels like a bit of a refuge, here – the rickety fence and small patch of dirt – almost private, a bit of sanctuary. Particularly after having been let in on Olivia's world for half an hour or so. What a nightmare.

At least we're free to do what we want, here – watch whatever crap we want to on TV, eat McDonald's every night if we want, drink, smoke and say whatever we want – without some old harridan breathing down our necks. No matter how bad I think I've got it, I definitely wouldn't want to be in Olivia's shoes.

And at least Jack hasn't left us. Yet. Despite his being a bit of a part-time dad, staying in Paddington and bleating on about being ripe for an affair, I don't think he'd ever entertain thoughts of buggering off entirely.

Although . . . now I think of it . . . When he came back

from golf, he had a massive bruise on his neck. He said a stray golf ball had whacked into him on the ninth hole. But I can't help wondering whether it wasn't some stray sexy lady golfer who gave him that huge hickey. On the nineteenth hole, probably. Definitely looks more like a love bite than a sports injury. But no, surely not. He's far too morally upstanding for those sorts of shenanigans.

And rarely more decent than when he lets me take a break and go up to Bath to see Charlie – which I'm doing tonight.

It's a monumental effort, though – I have to get Joey ready, meet him at Reading station, hand Joey over and then get the train up to Bath, in order to make it by seven p.m. And Jack's taken the next morning off work, meaning I'll never hear the end of his unselfishness – and no doubt I'll pay for it somewhere down the track, due to the tit-for-tat nature of time away when you're parents . . . But it's got to be worth it. Hasn't it?

As soon as I'm on the train, putting on make-up, I start missing Jack and Joey. More Joey than Jack, admittedly – despite the fact she's so delirious with joy to be in the company of her dad, she barely even notices I'm going – but it *is* nice of him to let me go away. On a week night to boot. Specially considering I know he'd love to come, too. He's always got on so well with Charlie; when the three of us used to go out together, I'd have to battle to get a word in. He's quite protective of her, too, when it comes to her boyfriends. They're never good enough for her (honestly, he's like a Victorian father), and one word from him about her latest suitor's unsuitability and it's over.

Charlie meets me at the station and we head straight for The Bell – one of Charlie's favourite big, ugly, patchouli-smelling, young student/old crusty-ridden Bath pubs. Bath's such a gorgeous city, but we only ever end up in the biggest dives there. We get our beers and go straight outside to smoke up.

'God! I don't understand your problem with Jack,' says Charlie, by way of cutting me off mid-rant.

'Apart from the fact he might be having an affair—'

'No, really. That wasn't an invitation for you to carry on,' she smiles. 'There's no way he's cheating on you. Unless,' she pauses for effect, 'unless he wanted you out of the way tonight, so he could have his fancy woman over . . .'

'He came back from golf with a massive hickey on his neck, you know. Well, *he* says a golf ball hit him really hard, but I don't believe it. So maybe he is . . . God! Maybe he's having sex with some woman in the front room while Joey sleeps upstairs?'

'You have GOT to stop this attention-seeking fantasy life of yours, Rox.'

'Yeah, but—'

'No, really.' She won't let me jump in. 'When I first had Rose, Jim never let me go out, couldn't understand anything about how I was feeling. We were stuck together at home alone. With a constantly crying baby.'

'Urgh,' I growl supportively.

'You've just got to get your sex life back – if you let this go on, he really will start having an affair, sleeping in a separate room every night until BANG! You're finished.'

'I know. It's kind of difficult—'

'Just do it,' she says, taking a gargantuan gulp of beer.

'So,' I say quickly, getting the words out before she's recovered from her drink and cuts me off again, 'how's it going with Guy?'

'Good, good,' she lights her roll-up again, 'except for his ex-wife causing a few problems.'

'Yeah? Like what?'

'Oh, you know.'

'No, what?'

'She still can't get over the break-up, so she's pulling all sorts of ridiculous stunts.'

'Like what?' I say, getting excited and impatient.

'Well,' she looks around and leans in, 'she sewed prawn shells into the curtain hems at his rented flat.'

'Not even original!' I squeal. 'And?'

'Cut off one sleeve of every Armani suit jacket . . .'

'Pathetic!'

'And is threatening to go to the Law Society, get him struck off, something to do with some dodgy deals they did as a couple. In France.'

'Ooh! What deals?'

'Don't know, can't get it out of Guy. But he's shit scared, so it must be bad. She says all he has to do is dump me and go back to her and everything'll be fine.'

'How long have they been broken up?'

'Seven years.'

'Seven years?! And she's still acting like a freak?'

'*And* she says she's going to stop him seeing their two kids, too.'

'Two pawns – or should that be prawns? – in her sick game,' I smile, impressed with my genius word play. Charlie, however, doesn't acknowledge my brilliance. Indeed, she appears completely unmoved, so I bring the conversation back to her. 'Jeez, you can really pick 'em, Chaz.'

'I know. I mean, do I walk now – when I'm not in too deep for my heart to be totally trashed – or stay with him?'

'What does he say?'

'Not much. Just that he'll sort it out and not for me to worry, it's over with her and he loves me.'

'Do you believe him?'

'I want to – I really, really want to. There's just something a bit fishy about it all.'

'Yeah – and not just in his curtains.'

'Yeah.' She ignores me, showing no signs that staying straight-faced and not bursting out laughing is in any way a struggle for her. 'He'll be here soon – you have GOT to tell me what you think about him later. Wish Jack was here to pass judgement.'

I do too, strangely enough. And it's a bit of a downer, I think, that I don't get a full night's banging on with Charlie on her own. But we'll have a chance later, I hope, back at her house, where we'll no doubt drink wine and listen to The Specials and The Beat till the early hours.

'Anyway, *you* can pick 'em.' She brightens up.

'Eh? Thought you said Jack was a good 'un.'

'He *is* – but what about the millions who came before him?'

'Hardly millions.' I feel my face reddening. 'I'll admit, I did go off the rails a bit when I broke up with The Ex. A bit berserk. And yes, I made some pretty poor choices, but—'

'Let's go through them,' she says, pulling out a pen and a small notepad from her bag.

'Do we have to?' I whine.

We did this once before, listed all the guys we'd ever slept with. And while I'm sure it cheered Charlie up, made her feel positively *chaste* in comparison to me, it merely made *me* feel like a rampaging tart. A desperate, sad, looking-for-love-in-all-the-wrong-places *tart*.

'Yes,' she smiles, 'it's fun!'

'For who?'

'Whom.'

'Whatever,' I sigh resignedly. 'But only if we do yours first.'

'OK,' she giggles, writing 'Charlie' on the left hand side of the pad, underlining her name. 'I've got a bigger pad in my bag for yours, so we'll just use this small one for mine,' she grins wickedly.

'Right,' she says, wriggling her bum on the seat, getting

comfortable for the long listing session ahead. 'Let's work backwards, from most recent to first shag ever. Won't take long.'

'Right. Guy, obviously, and then Scott, that guy from your law course.'

'Yeah. God – what did I ever see in him?'

'His keenness on you, I imagine.'

He really was nothing special – fifteen years younger than her, skinny and non-descript of face. Vaguely amusing, though, in a very studenty, *Monty Python*-reciting way.

'Remember that time he came with me down to yours in London?' She looks wistful.

'Yeah! You were like two hormone-charged teenagers, pawing each other all night, pissing yourselves laughing at your private jokes,' I say, happy for the heat to be off me for the time being. 'If you call The Parrot Sketch *private . . .*'

'Yeah, well . . . And then there was George – who I was engaged to, I might add,' she sniffs proudly.

'Yeah – whose heart you smashed to smithereens by breaking it off and getting the ring melted down.'

'Ah, it was doomed anyway.' She looks down and fiddles with a chunky gold modern art-ish ring that takes up half her left index finger. 'I should've known it'd never last – we proved that the first time round. Never ever *ever* get back with an ex.'

'You only did that, though, on the rebound from Jim,' I say.

'True. And what a nightmare he was.'

I nod emphatically. There's no getting away from it, he *was* a bit of an arsehole.

'But you get on OK with him now, don't you?'

'Yeah, fine. Not in a "Let's go out for a drink together, talk about old times" kind of way, but civil enough. Only because we have to, because of Rose.'

'Do you ever wish you'd stayed with him?'

'No. Used to, a bit, when I thought Rose might be lonely, being an only child. Which reminds me, Roxane,' she goes all stern on me – she knows I hate it when she uses my name, like a teacher telling me off, 'you've GOT to have sex with Jack at *least* until you're pregnant again. Can't have Joey being an only child.'

'Why not?'

'Imagine going on holiday! It'll be lonely and boring for her, with no one to play with – and you'll have to be Mummy all the time, you'll never get a break. Oh, you must do it. Only four more years and you'll be able to get your life back.'

'If not any stomach muscles.'

'That's another reason why I'm OK with never having any more kids,' she goes on. 'Can't bear the thought of my boobs scraping the ground, the sleepless nights and the endless rows . . . and just no life whatsoever.'

'You trying to talk me into it or out of it?'

'And that's why I'll go out every. Friday. Night. For the rest of my life. Because now, I *can*.'

'But what if the second one didn't like me much, either?' I pout, picturing Joey sitting in Jack's lap, gazing up at him adoringly, glad to have me out of the way.

'Don't be ridiculous,' Charlie pinches her tongue between her forefinger and thumb to get some tobacco off it, 'Joey loves you!'

'Doesn't look like it. Or feel like it sometimes . . . a lot of the time, actually.'

Charlie nods.

'When I first left Jim, when Rose was three, I'd ask her who she wanted to be with and she'd say: "Daddy. I don't even love you, Mummy."'

'Ooh, harsh.' I wince, holding on to the edge of the table and leaning back for effect, as if the force of Rose's remark was like a great gust of wind. 'God knows where she gets her sharp tongue from . . .'

'*Henn*-y-way,' Charlie straightens her back and looks down at her notepad, 'back to the list!'

We go through the rest – there are only three left – and we're laughing about her first serious boyfriend who was into wearing high heels and going to fetish clubs, when Guy rocks up.

He's good looking – very good looking, actually – in a distinctly Gallic way. And when he speaks, he sounds *divine*. The French have got it all over us with that accent.

'Ah 'ave a nice boddle of red in mah carr – shall we go 'ome and drink it therrre?' he says, sounding sexier than it looks on paper.

131

So we all go back to Charlie's, even though I really could've gone a few more hours in the pub, out and about. Thank God he showed up when he did, though – stopped us having to go through my miserable list of debauchery. Trust me – you don't want to know.

Back at Charlie's, Guy has a small glass and retires. They've both got work in the morning so, in an uncharacteristically mature move, Charlie follows Guy's lead and makes us a nice cup of tea.

'So what do you think?' Charlie whispers when Guy's been gone for ten minutes, figuring he'll be asleep.

'Nod bad ad orrl,' I say, trying to sound French.

'Think he's into me?'

'Defo!'

'Think it'll last? I mean, I don't want another failed relationship. I want to get married. And I'm going to introduce Rose to him soon.'

'I think,' I whisper, 'that he's very hot for you, but his missus will break you up.'

'Why do you say that?'

'Well, that's what she's trying to do, isn't it?'

'You think he's going to dump me?'

'No, no, no.' Oh God, I think. Here we go. Keep your snout out, don't mess with other people's affairs. 'I think you'll get bored of the dramas and dump *him*.'

Charlie looks shocked.

'And then you'll meet someone else who *is* the one, the real deal, the one you'll marry.'

'Right,' she says abruptly, looking pissed off, 'I'm off to bed, then. I'll be up at seven, leaving at eight.'

And with that, she stomps upstairs.

I haven't offended her, have I? Spoken out of turn? I know you shouldn't pass judgement (other than: 'He's great! Gorgeous! And so in love with you!') on a mate's boyfriend – but I thought I was being complimentary to her. Thought I was telling it straight, saying something she'd already know. I didn't say he was an arse or anything. Or even implied it. Did I? No, everything'll be fine. Charlie knows I've only got her best interests at heart.

'Yeah, right,' I say out loud as I pull down the sofa bed in the spare room. 'I'm for it.'

The next morning, the sound of the door slamming makes me groan underneath the duvet. I'd thought about venturing out into the kitchen, where I could hear Charlie and Guy chatting, but couldn't face the inevitable frosty reception I'd get. So I hid under the duvet, waiting for them to leave. Which they just did. *Loudly*.

And then my phone rings.

'Mornin', gorgeous!' It's Jack. Sweet, loving, know-where-you-stand-with-him-always Jack.

All I can manage is a heartfelt 'Oh, babe.'

'You all right?'

'I think Charlie's not speaking to me,' I sniff. 'And I wasn't even drunk!'

'Oh, God. Not again. What happened this time? What

did you say?' He laughs and I can hear Joey giggling in the background.

'Nothing! I think . . . I said I thought she'd get bored of Guy and move on . . .'

'You idiot!'

'But—'

'Why'd you have to say *anything*? Couldn't you just say he was a nice guy and talk about something else?'

'Well, she asked me—'

'You two are ridiculous!'

'I know, I know. How's my Joey?'

'Yeah, fine, fine. Missing you, though.'

'Really?'

'Nyeurgh, hard to tell. But probably. Now hurry up and get home.'

'Ah,' I sigh, hoping Joey's missing me – or has, at least, noticed I'm not there. 'You missing me too?'

'Of course I am! And I want to get a quick round of golf in before I go back to work this afternoon . . .'

'Oh. Right. Be home as soon as, then. Love you.'

'Yeah, love you too, you wally.'

God, I wish he was here right now. Or, rather, wish I was there. I could really do with one of his big, safe, warm bear hugs.

Eventually I get back to Riverside and schlep wearily back to our house. I've just closed the front door behind me, nearly tripping over a golf bag full of clubs, when Jack comes down the stairs carrying Joey.

'My family!' I nearly burst into tears.

'Hey! It's Mummy!' laughs Jack, putting a completely uninterested Joey on the floor.

He comes over and kisses me on the lips and when his arms surround me, I nearly swoon with the familiar, heady scent of Eau de Silk Cut mixed in with Lynx deodorant.

Joey starts to cry, so I leave Jack's embrace to go and pick her up. She makes a break for the kitchen, but I'm bigger (much) and faster (a bit).

'Nyargh-huh-huh,' she wails and reaches out over my shoulder for her dad when I pick her up.

I turn to Jack, but before I can get a word out, we see a waving hand and the tops of three golf clubs disappearing out the fast-closing door.

'So,' I say to Joey, as we walk into the kitchen, 'was it worth it? Hmm? A night away from you just so I could go up to Bath and fall out with my best friend. Was it worth it, sweet? Hmm?'

Joey answers with her bowels and lets rip the foulest, filthiest fart I've ever had the misfortune to smell.

'You're right, whifty,' I smile. 'Too bloody right.'

10

I tiptoe down the loud creaking stairs and pop outside to say goodbye to Jack. He's sitting on the deck, with the cold Corona he says he's been looking forward to all day, hooking himself up to his ipod's earphones.

'Just the one beer,' I say, shooting him a pleading look. 'And only one ear, too, please. You've got to listen out for Joey, remember, in case she wakes up.'

He salutes me, does as he's told and starts humming a happy tune, reading the paper.

He's so uncool with his music – but in an oddly endearing way. His favourite singer is . . . wait for it . . . Judy Garland. Now, I know what you're thinking – I've had many a moment thinking the exact same thing – but he's so *comfortable* with his straightness, he doesn't protest too much and I always end up believing him.

It's like guys in Speedos – they'll wear them if they're comfortable with, or even quite proud of their manhoods – and board shorts if a) they don't trust their members to not get aroused at an inopportune time or b) there's not much there to hide in the first place. Jack's a Speedos kind of guy.

And did I mention he loves musicals, too? All the old ones – *Meet Me In St Louis* and *The Wizard of Oz* (natch), *South Pacific* and *Oklahoma*. When I told Charlie about my worries re Jack's potential gayness, she totally allayed my fears by saying, 'Jesus Christ, Rox – he is so IN!' As opposed to being 'out'. Firmly locked in the closet, she reckons. But she's only joking . . . I hope.

I'm smiling about all this, thinking how sweet and thoughtful Jack can be as I buy cigarettes (a pack of ten – just for the meeting and then I'm off them for good) at the 6-Ten. And suddenly, I'm wrenched back to reality by the guy who takes my money at the till. Not because I'm parting with cash – although that *is* always a pisser – but because he is hot. Hot, hot, *hot*, as *Big Cook Little Cook* would say. He's Indian, about six-foot-a-million with the blackest eyes, the longest eyelashes, the thickest jet-black hair, the straightest, most perfect nose and the most strawberry-coloured, full lips I've ever seen outside a Bollywood movie. I've never noticed him before – where did he come from? Phwoar! I feel like a fifteen-year-old as I leave the shop, muttering 'He is *well* fit, man!' to myself.

When I get to The Swan's beer garden, Tim's there, sitting at a big table on his own. He waves frantically at me and shouts, 'Gorgeous girl for the Pissed-Off Parents meeting! Make way, make way, she's in the Club, you know!'

'Gor! Thought I was late – where's everybody else?'

'It's only just gone quarter past. Soon as the credits rolled on *Corrie*, I raced down here. Wednesday nights are now officially my nights off,' he says proudly.

'Oh, bugger, I missed it! Took me for ever to get Joey off to sleep tonight. What happened?'

Tim fills me in on a not that dramatic episode.

'Won't bother with the omnibus, then,' I say disappointedly.

'Oh, but you must! It was *brilliant*.' He's getting all excited.

'Why?'

'Well, it's not what happens in *Corrie* that makes it so fab, is it? It's what they *say*. And the way they say it.'

'True,' I agree. 'Whoever writes the scripts for it is a bloody genius!'

TIM: 'Exactly! Ever noticed how they'll just say something in passing? Something that's not relevant to any storyline, or anything, just normal character assassination or in-street chat?'

ME: 'Yeah! Particularly in the Rovers, it's so real, so everyday.'

TIM: 'And they never labour a point, hit you over the head with the fact that someone's

138

going to get killed by a psycho, they
build it up slowly, surreptitiously, just
bantering about like normal people do, in
the real world.'

ME: 'You mean it's *not* real?'

TIM: 'Thought it was a documentary of *oop
north*, did you?'

ME: 'Way *'Enders* carries on, you'd think
life in London was all about guns and
gangsters and gangster's molls—'

'You talking 'bout me?' Carina says as she sits down
next to me.

'Eh?' Tim and I chorus.

'Nothing.' She looks around the garden. 'Where's
everybody else?'

'Not here yet,' I say. 'Wonder if we'll get any new
members tonight.'

'Ah, who cares? If the same people turn up who were
here last week, it'll be just perfect,' Tim grins.

'Yeah, you're right,' I say. 'What *are* you drinking
anyway, Tim?'

'A Timblioni,' he says, pulling the straw up to his
mouth and taking a suck. 'It's two parts Parfait Amour,
four parts vodka and a dash of lemonade.'

'Sounds revolting,' sneers Carina.

'Urgh! Can I've a taste?' I ask.

I take a sip. Carina was right.

'That's dis-*gus*-ting!'

'Each to their own,' says Tim as his eyes are drawn skywards, falling on to a tall, dark stranger who stops at the end of our table.

'Is this, um, is this the ah . . .'

'Pissed-Off Parents Club?' smiles Tim, eyes wide.

'Yes!' says the stranger, looking relieved.

'At your service, sir.' Tim stands up, putting one arm around the guy's back and the other beckoning him to sit on the bench next to him.

'Great,' the guy says and sits down.

We all stare at him. God, first the bloke in the 6-Ten and now this guy – where are all these hot men coming from? Or maybe it's just me, finally noticing something pleasant and nice about Riverside. There's no getting away from it, though, I mean, he's bloody *gorgeous*!

'I ah . . . my name's Paul,' he says nervously.

'And you're a pissed-off parent!' Tim cuts him off.

'Well, yes, I suppose I am,' says Paul.

'What's your problem, Paul?' asks Carina, lighting up her umpteenth fag since she sat down. No wonder she's so trim – nothing like a million tabs a day to keep the scoffing at bay.

'Well, I—'

'Don't be so rude, Carina!' Tim cuts him off again. 'How about some introductions first?'

'Yeah,' I say slowly, still a little transfixed. 'That's Carina, that's Tim and I'm Roxy. June and Olivia should be here any minute.'

'Hi, hi, hi,' he says, nodding to each of us in turn.

Silence descends again.

'So go on, why are you so pissed off?' Carina cuts to the chase.

'Um, well, ah . . . My wife,' he starts, to audible, disappointed sighs from all of us. 'Well, my *ex*-wife, I should say.' We all sit up a little straighter.

'I set her up in a house, two years ago when we divorced – but now she wants to move to a bigger, more expensive one, further away from me. I can't afford any more money for her accommodation – and if she does move away, I'll never see my daughter, Tobi. We spell it with an i on the end, not a y.'

'Just caught the end of that,' says June, sitting down next to me. 'Hello there – I'm June.'

He takes her hand in his, brings it up to his lips and kisses it.

'Ooh!' blushes June. 'Wasn't expecting that!'

'Go on, Paul,' I say. 'Great name for a girl, Tobi, by the way. Why did you break up?'

'She says it's because I was unfaithful,' he shrugs sheepishly. 'But it was a drunken, big, big mistake of a one-nighter . . . And she'd been having a full-on, proper affair for months. My flingette was over before it began.'

'Must have been a very lonely time,' nods June sagely.

'Exactly!' exclaims Paul, pleased we all seem to be on his side. 'Everyone says having a baby can ruin relationships and that the man will probably have an affair. But I think she simply always felt she'd married the wrong guy and was desperate to get out, any way she could.'

'So who was this flingette with?' I ask.

'Someone in HR at work. But she didn't matter – she really did mean nothing to me. And it was one stupid night! The wife used it against me in the divorce settlement and I've been paying for that one, pathetic, pointless mistake ever since.'

'You were saying if she moves away, you'll never see—'

'Yeah. She's really got me over a barrel. I adore Tobi and love spending time with her,' he sighs. 'I feel so powerless, totally impotent.'

I sneak a peek at Tim and wonder if he's thinking what I'm thinking: bet there's nothing impotent about Paul.

'I'll get the drinks in,' announces Tim, standing up.

'I'll help you carry.' I get up, too.

Inside, while we're queueing up at the bar, I say to Tim, 'Fucking *hell*, where are all these stunning-looking guys coming from, eh?'

'Hmm?' he hums, staring off into space.

'Paul . . . I mean, he's *fit*, don't you think?'

'Suppose so, yeah,' he says, leaning over the bar to give the barmaid our drinks order.

'You fancy him?'

'Who?'

'Paul!'

'Not my type,' he says. 'Just because I'm gay doesn't

mean I want to rut with every stag who comes into my eyeline, you know.'

'No, no! I didn't mean that, I just thought—'

'It's not all glory holes and cottaging up Hampstead Heath when you're a poof, you know. We're not all into leather and chaps and—'

Bloody hell! Tetchy or what?

'I know, I know! I'm sorry, Tim, I—'

'No, I'm sorry, love – didn't mean to snap,' he sighs, putting his hand on my shoulder. 'It's not easy living round here, you know, with the intolerance. And the distinct lack of gay talent.'

'Are you all right? What's happened?'

'Older guy I've been seeing dumped me. For a fucking twelve-year-old fucking go-go dancer in London.' He starts giggling at his description. 'We'd only been together for a few weeks, but . . . another one bites the dust, as Freddie was so fond of saying. Oh, I'm just knackered, that's all. Need a good night out to take my mind off things.'

'Yeah, me too,' I mumble.

I look down at my saggy tummy, muffin-topping all over the shop, still obscuring the view of my feet, and wonder how many points there are in five pints of lager. Sod it, I think – liquid doesn't count.

Back at the table, Paul's got June, Carina and a recently-arrived Olivia in stitches.

'Stop, stop!' laughs June, wiping a tear from her eye.

'Hey Liv! What's this? What's so funny?'

143

'Haah, nothing.' June calms down a bit.

God, I hate it when that happens – always feel like I'm missing out on something.

'So!' says Tim, brightening up. 'How're *you*, Livvy?'

'Not bad,' she smiles. 'I've been rostered on for some more shifts at the 6-Ten. It's only a few evenings when Sis can look after Stu, but things might be looking up, finally.'

'Oh, that's good,' says June. 'More money?'

'Well, yeah, obviously,' says Liv. 'But more importantly, more time away from my sister.'

'Good for you,' says Carina.

'So,' says Liv, 'anyone watch *Corrie* tonight?'

'Ooh, I love that show – cracking one-liners,' Paul surprises us all by saying.

'I like Blanche, Deirdre's old mum. She has the best lines,' smiles June.

'And what top casting, eh? They really *do* look like mother and daughter, don't they?' Tim says.

Crikey! Am I at a *Corrie* Fan Club meeting or what?

'Like when Blanche comes out with her curmudgeonly remarks like "You're all gong and no dinner". Fabulous,' laughs June.

'Brilliant,' agrees Tim.

'Oh bugger!' I join in. 'I've been meaning to use that line for ages!'

'In what context?' asks Tim.

'Um, we're not . . . I'm not . . . Neither of us is . . .'

'Getting any?' suggests Tim.

'Mine's grown over,' sniffs Carina. 'My old man won't come anywhere near me unless I'm peeing on a fertility stick and it says I'm ovulating. Haven't done one for months. He'd kill me if he knew I'd had a hysterectomy a couple of weeks ago.'

So *that's* what she was doing at the hospital when I saw her. Not plastic surgery at all. God! She can't be that gorgeous *naturally*, can she?

'Maybe once you have kids, your sex life's over, too,' I wonder out loud.

'Well . . .' smiles Olivia.

'You? *You're* having sex with someone?' I splutter, dragging my eyes away from Carina.

'Not exactly. Not yet, anyway. Won't be long, though, if my calculations are correct!'

'Who is he?' asks June.

'Ah, no one. No one you'd know, anyway.'

'Spill! Spill! Spill!' shrieks Tim.

'Nah, nah – don't want to jinx it. And anyway, it's probably nothing.'

'Like my sex life,' I sigh, steering the conversation back in my direction. 'Jack's only ever interested in playing *Civ*. Talk about insulting . . .'

'*Civ*? What's that?' Tim asks.

'*Civilisation*,' I answer.

'Oh,' says Tim. 'And what's that?'

'Computer game,' says Paul. 'Particularly addictive.'

'Sounds hideous,' sneers Tim.

'It is – and so *nerdy*,' I add.

'Well, not *that* nerdy,' Paul begs to differ.

'Oh, come on! It's all trolls and hobbits and dungeons and dragons and—'

'No, actually, it's all about building villages, towns and cities through history. Montezuma, for example—'

'You in IT by any chance?' I ask.

'Yes . . . how did you know?'

'Lucky guess,' I say and get up to go to the loo.

While I'm washing my hands, Liv comes in.

'So? Who is he?' I grill her.

'Oh, nobody,' she grins.

'Well, what's going on, then?'

'Must be the Prozac kicking in, finally. I've got the health visitor coming round tomorrow for my final Moods and Feelings assessment.'

Poor Liv. She must've had a really high score on that post-natal depression – sorry, *illness* – questionnaire.

'Oh, Liv, I'm sorry – I had no idea things were that bad.'

'No big deal – I'm fine now.' She pauses and breaks into a cheeky grin. 'Oh, OK, I admit it – something else *has* happened.'

She hooks her arm into my elbow and brings her head in closer to mine, looking down at the bathroom basin and whispers conspiratorially:

'Remember that guy I told you about? The new manager at the 6-Ten? Well, I think he fancies me!'

'Yeah? Great! But how can you tell?'

'He flirts with me all the time and just about *begged* me to do more shifts. And the shifts he put me on are all just when there's me and him in the shop. At night. Alone!'

'Oh, I think I saw him on the way here tonight! He is *gorrrr*-geous!' I swoon, feeling like a school girl in the loos at an under-age disco. I look in the mirror above the basin, try to fluff my ever-thinning hair up and sing: 'Mirror in the bathroom, please talk free,' as Olivia looks at me quizzically and dashes into a cubicle.

When I get back to the table, there's peals of laughter and June's got a pad of paper in front of her, writing things down.

'What's this?' I say, expecting the whole lot of them to say 'Nothing' and swap knowing glances.

'We're making up rules. Club rules,' says Tim.

'Really? Like what?'

'Like "No member shall ever refer to their spawn as *Baby*. The definite article must be used at all times – or, preferably, just use the little bugger's name,"' reads June from her pad, over her glasses.

'Yes, yes,' I say, getting excited. 'I hate that, when people say: "So how is *Baby*?" Or worse, when they say: 'How's *Mum* doing?" and they're talking right at you, about you! I always feel like saying "My mum's doing fine – how's yours?"'

'And we've got another one about those Baby on Board signs,' June reads on. '"Baby on Board", "Little Person on Board", "Princess on Board" or "Nervous Mother Driving" signs for car rear windshields are strictly verboten. They are neither cute nor funny, and any member caught sporting one of these in their car will be suspended with immediate effect and denied admission to at least one meeting.'

'Ooh, that's a bit harsh, isn't it?' I frown, trying to remember whether the sunshield Jack got for the back sidewindow next to Joey's car seat says anything like that on it.

'Hmm, yes, it is a bit,' agrees June. 'What if we make the punishment that they have to buy all the drinks for an entire meeting?'

'Yeah, yeah – that's brilliant!' I say, thinking about cash – or, rather, my lack thereof.

'I know!' says Carina, clearing her throat. '"Certain woolly concepts like *bonding* may only be discussed if the speaker uses those quote-mark-thingamabobs and is essentially rubbishing the whole bollocks idea." How 'bout that?'

'Yes!' I jump up a little bit off the bench. 'And can we add: "Particularly when being spoken of in conjunction with breastfeeding"?'

June's writing it all down furiously.

'And,' Carina says, on a roll, '"Membership of the Pissed-Off Parents Club is dependent upon whether a proposed candidate has ever recorded their child talking on the answering machine and made it their outgoing message."'

'God, I hate that!' I slam my palm down on the table,

making the drinks spill a bit. 'You should try calling an *international* number and having to wait five bloody minutes for a four-year-old boy to say he and his sister and his parents aren't in! It's ridiculous!'

'It's worse when an old friend gives their unable-to-talk-yet, babbling grandchild the receiver and expects you to talk to them! Ludicrous!' grins June.

'Yeah – and they expect you to think it's really cute and adorable when it's just sooo annoying,' I say, wondering whether I've actually done that to Mum lately. Can't have – Mum's like June, she'd never *let* me do that.

Olivia, back from the loo, joins in: 'Hey, what about those stupid slogan T-shirts?'

'Like what?' asks Paul, fascinated, leaning into Liv.

'You know, for babies that say: "My mummy's a first-timer" or those ones with balloons on them, like party invitations which say: "Time: 2 a.m., Place: My cot, Bring a bottle"—'

'I think I've got that one,' I mutter, sheepishly. 'But work gave it to me and I never made her wear it, honest!'

'Yeah,' says Carina, rubbing her hands together, 'we should have a ritual burning of those things – I've got *thousands*.'

'Hmm – bit Nazi-ish, ritual burnings, don't you think?' says June, ever the voice of reason.

'Hey, why don't we get T-shirts made up for us? You know, Pissed-Off Parents Club T-shirts?' offers Paul, looking only at Olivia.

'Yeah!' she says, holding her pint glass up to cheer him.

'Who's for another?' I ask, standing up. I've got to get away for a sec, give myself a chance to think up some slogans.

I write down what everyone wants on a bit of paper June rips off her pad for me, and go inside to the relative calm of the front bar. I stand in there for ages, long after I've got all the drinks in, but I'm bereft of ideas.

I bring the drinks out on a large tray and distribute them to their thirsty owners.

'Shouldn't it be "says", not "say"?' Liv's asking June, looking puzzled.

'Well, technically yes, because the Pissed-Off Parents Club is a collective noun, so it's singular. But it's a rip-off of the old "Frankie Say Relax" T-shirts from the eighties. My daughter had one. Frankie Goes To Hollywood? The band. Remember?' June's well on form.

'No, not really,' Liv sighs.

'So, taking its cue from Frankie, it should read: "POPC *Say* Have a Beer and a Bitch",' June says slowly.

'Tim say it's brilliant!' says Tim.

'I've got one,' beams Liv, looking at me. 'It's for a bumper sticker. How about, in really big letters, maybe capitals, "Honk if You're a Pissed-off Parent".' She takes a gulp of her pint.

'Yeah—' shouts Paul.

'No, wait!' she splutters. 'And then, underneath that, in smaller letters, "I Know I Do!"'

June points at me and laughs. Liv looks round at all of us giggling and takes another decidedly-chuffed-with-herself glug.

'Ah, you bugger! It's not just me, is it? Please say I'm not the only cleanlinessly-ly-ly-challenged one in the Club!'

If this keeps up, I'm going to have to nip to the loos for a quick puff of the old Ventolin. I get all wheezy when I laugh a lot. Nothing at all to do with the five fags I've smoked since I got here. Honest.

'I know, I know,' says Tim, flapping his hands about. "My dad went to the POPC and all I got was this lousy T-shirt!"

'Or: And all I got was a lousy babysitter!' adds Paul.

'Or: And all I got was Granny to babysit!' chirps June.

'Or: My mum went to the POPC and all she got was a lousy hangover!' That was me.

'Actually,' says Olivia, her smile fading fast, 'I'd better knock it on the head soon. I've got the health visitor coming round tomorrow and I don't want to make her pass out with my boozy breath.'

'Mints,' says June.

'You called?' trills Tim.

'Trebor Extra Strong,' laughs Paul. 'Sure you won't stay?'

'I'd love to, but I've got to go. Got an early shift tomorrow, too – and I *defo* need my beauty sleep!'

As Tim's eyes follow Olivia walking to the beer garden door, his whole face suddenly falls.

'I'd better go, too,' he says, solemnly. His eyes are fixed on the door and when he jumps up out of his seat, he knocks his Timblioni over in the process.

I turn around and see an old guy standing there, shooting daggers at Tim, his arms crossed over his chest while his right foot taps the ground impatiently. Must be the older guy who dumped him, I think. If it is, Tim must like his men mean and moody – he looks so angry.

'What's that all about?' June asks, sliding up to me.

'Boyfriend of Tim's,' I say, as if I know.

She squints, looking at Tim and the old guy in the distance, putting her hand on my back as though she's trying to steady herself.

And then a flash of lightning and a scarily loud crack of thunder signal the start of a particularly heavy downpour. So we break the meeting up and all go home. Well, if you can't drink and smoke at the same time, what's the point?

11

Luckily, Joey's going to the nursery this afternoon, so I'll be able to get an hour's kip in, before I make a start on that story for *Positive Parenting!* It's not due for another week, but when you've got a baby, there's no guarantee they'll sleep when you want them to or won't get sick. And if they *do* get sick, or don't sleep for long, you'll never get anything else done.

I have to organise that restaurant review for Vanessa, too. Typical that out of all the fantastic restaurants in the countryside, Vanessa gives me my local to review. Still, at least it's a free night out for me and Jack.

'Bloody hell, Joey,' I say, rubbing my eyes. 'That club's going to be the death of me, you know.'

'Shuck-abee, shuck-abee,' she dribbles.

'You're singing to the choir on that one,' I sigh, and we go into the front room to watch *In the Night Garden*.

The phone ringing brings us back to earth.

'Roxy?' Charlie says, sounding far away. She must be in the Maldives.

'Chuckie?' I grin at Joey, trying to let her know that her mum is paying attention to her, even though she's on the phone. But she still goes berserk, so I hand her one of Jack's old, defunct, non-nuclear mobiles to play with.

'I'm fucking pissed off.' Charlie sounds livid. She can't still be upset about the other night, can she?

'Why? Is it raining out there or something? No chance to show off your bikini?'

'I'm back. *We're* back. In sodding *Bath*.'

'Eh? Why?'

'Guy's ex, Mignon, was there when we got out there. Wouldn't leave us alone.'

More drama than an ITV winter schedule, Charlie's life.

'But—'

'Yeah, she's a lunatic. In the room right next to ours – right up in our *grills*! We had to flee. No other choice, really.'

'Bloody hell! What's going on? He doesn't want to get back with her, does he?

'Don't know. He says he's finally met his soulmate with me, I'm the love of his life blah-de-blah-de-blah. But there goes my week in the sun.'

'And the proposal?'

'Nothing.'

'Jeez. What a pisser! What are you going to do?'

'What *can* I do? Just wait and see what happens, I suppose.'

'It'll be difficult, working together—'

'Yeah, whatever. I don't know whether it's wise to stick at this one. I *really* like him, Rox – haven't felt like this about anyone since . . .'

'Since the last one, yeah, yeah. I know.'

'No, really. I really think this is The One.'

'So where's Filet Mignon now?'

'Don't know, don't care.'

'She won't stop being a nutcase, you know. This'll go on and on and on—'

'Like somebody else I know—'

'And on – until she splits you two up. That's what she wants, and she sounds crazy enough to keep at it.'

'I know. *God!* Why's it so hard?'

'What does Guy say? It's up to him to put a stop to it, you know, it's up to him to tell her it's over and to leave him alone.'

'I know. I'm just *disappointed*, you know? Disappointed that nothing in my life can ever be easy. And if this one doesn't work out, I'll be doomed to be a single mum for the rest of my crocheting, cat-loving life. What if I never have sex again? Oh *God*!'

She lights up and blows the smoke out as she says:

'Talking of a sexless life, what's happening with you? Are you ever going to sort out your wedding?'

'Why don't you organise it for me, if you're so set on it?'

'Maybe I will. Look, I've got to go and pick Rose up from her dad's now.' She heaves a huge sigh. 'What a debacle.'

When I hang up, I feel dizzy and sit on the couch. I can't be sure whether I just had that conversation – or whether it was a part of this particularly trippy *In the Night Garden* episode.

I try to focus on Joey and see that she's beaming.

'What's that, sweet? What's so funny?'

And then I hear it – she's downloaded some tinny tune on my mobile and is well-chuffed with herself.

'How did you do that? Who's a smartie, eh? Eh? How did you do that?!' I prise it out of her hands and she starts bawling.

'Oh, please, Joey. Not this morning, *no*. Mummy can't afford downloads, sweetie, *please*.'

I take her off for a walk around Cowslip Crescent, and then get her into nursery. At home, I crash out on the couch, seconds after I close and lock the front door.

Normally, with Joey at nursery, I'd be outside gasping my way to a painful and untimely death. But my mouth feels as scratchy as a coconut husk and as dry as my bath towel, so smoking's not an option today. I gulp down loads of water – the hardest in the country, according to the guy at the hardware shop who sold me the water filter – and sit at the kitchen table. I would try to get some more sleep, but my heart's racing and I feel a bit panicky. This smoking has GOT to stop.

And then I remember I've got that hypnotist's number in my bag somewhere. No time like the present. And while I'm feeling so anti-fags and heavy of chest, I might as well give it a go.

'Yeh-lo?' the voice says.

'Hi there.' I try to sound friendly.

'Hi there!' he says back.

'Yep, hi there—'

'Yep, hi *there*!' Oh God.

'I'm calling about the hypnotism.'

'Well, you've called the right number!'

'Yeah – and, um, I'd like to, ah, just find out whether it'll stop me smoking.'

'Look into my eyes, look into my eyes . . . not around the eyes, just look into my eyes,' he laughs. What *is* it with the *Little Britain* obsession in this village?

'No, no, seriously.' He stops laughing. 'I'm not *that* kind of hypnotist – that's entertainment. Hey! That's en-ter-*tain*-ment, that's en-ter-*tain*-ment . . .' He starts singing that old Jam song. Paul Weller'd be turning in his grave – if he was dead. Which, thank God, he's not – but he might do himself in if he could hear this.

'I jus—'

'Right. No. Just playing. Now. With hypnotism, I can point you in the right direction. I can give you the tools, the devices, the *techniques*, shall we say, that you can draw upon to stop you smoking. But ultimately, it's up to you. Ultimately, only you can make the decision to

157

smoke or not to smoke. And that, my friend, really *is* the question.'

'OK. So how much does it cost?'

'Can I ask your name?'

'Roxane.'

'RAAAAH-ksanne!'

I nearly hang up.

'It's "ahn", actually, not "ann" – Rox-*ahn*,' I sigh.

'Hello there! I'm Barry. So, well . . . Put it this way, Roxanne, you won't have to put on the red light to be able to afford me! Ha! See what I did there? Ha! D'yersee?'

'Very good.'

'Look, Roxanne, the way I see it is, you pay what you *can*. An amount that won't break the bank, but is large enough to hurt you a little bit if you don't quit. *Comprende*? Oh, and first top-up's free.'

'Sounds all right. So when can I book in a session?'

'You can do it right now!'

'I meant— OK, so when are you free?'

'Ooh, let me see . . . just opening the old Filofax . . . ah . . . why don't you just tell me when you're available and I'll see if I can fit in with you?'

'OK. Monday? This Monday?'

'Yup. What time?'

'Oh, hang on – no. I'll have Joey all day . . . what about Thursday arvo, say two o'clock?'

'Do you come from a land down under?' He's singing again. 'Ooh yeah, yeah!'

'Two o'clock? Thursday?'

'Done!'

Even more exhausted after talking to Barry, the frustrated showman/hypnotist, I lie down on the couch for a while. There's so much stuff running about in my head, making me panicky. I've got next to no money and won't be able to afford *fags* soon, let alone the hypnosis and poor Jack pays for everything and . . .

'Just get ON with it!' I shriek to myself and lug my weary bones into the kitchen.

I call the head chef/part-owner of The Swan. He says Wednesday nights are the only slow-ish nights the pub has, so it's best if we go then. And he says if I want to bring some friends, make it a party of four, that'd be fine with him. Charlie's forlorn face pops up in my mind's eye. I'll get her and Guy to come along, Jack's mum can babysit and we'll all spend the night at ours. Jack and I will have to sleep in the kitchen, but that's OK. God. Imagine. Getting paid to eat and drink at a Pissed-Off Parents Club meeting – it doesn't get much better than that. People might even mistake me for someone who has some mates and a bit of a social life!

I ring Charlie – she's well up for it. Then I ring Jack and ask him to call his mum. She tells him she'll come up in the morning and look after Joey in the afternoon while I do some work, if I want. Now *that's* how a grandmother should be, I think. Keen to help out and available at short notice. So finally, it's all set up.

All this flurry of activity, organising things, has made me forget how much my head hurts. I'm on a roll. Making hay while the sun shines, I start planning out the *Positive Parenting!* story. I've got the six arguments, I'll get the case studies later (they're all mine and Jack's fights, anyway, but I'll use false names for four of them and get maybe an old photo of Charlie and her ex, and that'll be the photos sorted), so all I need to do now is set up an interview with a Relate counsellor.

I call the press office at Relate and they give me the number of one of their relationship experts, someone called Barbara Rand. She's an old hand at talking to magazines, giving them quotes, apparently.

'Baah baah baah, baah, bah, bra rand,' I sing to myself while I make a tea. Whatever Barry's got is catching.

'Hiya Barbara, my name's Roxane and I'm calling from *Positive Parenting!* magazine.'

'Oh, hello!' She sounds nice.

'I'm doing a story about the arguments couples have when they become parents, and I'd like to organise a time with you that would be convenient to get your advice.'

'I can do it now, if you'd like.'

'Ummm, yeah! OK.' I wasn't expecting to do it right now, was going to wait until I felt a bit more compos mentis. But what the hell.

'Shall we start with the big one? The Why Don't We Ever Have Sex Any More War. Basically, he's up for it, but she isn't. The baby takes up all her energy, her man

160

annoys her and she doesn't feel remotely sexy. What would your advice to this couple be?'

'Ah, yes, that old chestnut,' she says in her kind, I've-heard-it-all-before voice. 'I would say it's *imperative* they sort their sex life out. It's a central part of any adult, loving relationship and if that part dies, it's virtually impossible to resurrect it. He must try to understand that she's exhausted and thinking about the baby all the time and, at the same time, she must respect his needs and wants and desires.'

Oh here we go, I think. Same old stuff about how they need to talk, communicate with each other's largest sexual organ (the brain, apparently) and they'll be shagging, swinging from chandeliers, in no time.

'They just have to force themselves to *do* it, I'm afraid.'

'But how? How are they going to go from bickering with hardly any physical contact to, you know, being *at it*?'

'As new parents, their organisational skills have been pulled sharply into focus. And sex is another part of their busy day, so they have to treat it like everything else – make time for it and schedule it in. Even if they're dog-tired and wound-up and they just want to collapse on opposite ends of the bed and pass out, they have to do it. Sounds bonkers – excuse the pun – but *schedule* it in. Say to each other: "Right. Next Thursday night, we're going to have dinner together, after the baby's in bed, have some wine and then we're going to have sex." And follow through. Otherwise, things will start to look pretty grim for their relationship.'

'So schedule it in, then . . .' I say slowly, writing it down on my notepad in capital letters.

'They have to do whatever it takes, really. I can't stress it enough. Without it, they'll start having affairs and eventually fighting for custody of the child in the divorce courts.'

Bloody hell.

When he gets home that night, after 'a swift one' with his work mate whose wife's just left him, Jack finds me already in bed. I tell him about my conversation with the counsellor about sex as he gets undressed.

'Nooooo! I'm too knackered, now! Sorry, Rox, but I need to sleep!'

'No, I don't mean *now*. God knows, I can't remember the last time I had a bath. And *you're* hardly, well . . . No, I mean let's *schedule it in*, now. When would you be up for it, do you reckon?'

'I'm always up for it.' He falls on the bed, grinning, and gives me a big wet kiss on my cheek. I push him off me and he rolls over to his side.

'How about next Thursday? Next Thursday night when Joey's asleep? Maybe I'll even make us something nice to eat and we'll get the candles out and – oh! And we won't be going outside for fags all the time, because I'll have stopped by then – I'm going for hypnosis on Thursday afternoon. That's got to make us sexier to each other, surely. Come to think of it, why don't we stop

smoking, together on Thursday? We've got more chance
if the pair of us do it at the same time and . . . Jack? *Jack*?'

He's out like a light.

Bloody typical.

12

I'm such a hoarder, I hold on to so much rubbish. And not just the emotional type, either. I'm trying to clear out my purse – bugger the bag, that's too big a job – and there's receipts and cash machine advice slips and God knows what else lying in a big pile on the front room floor.

It's not like I can just chuck them all into the bin, you know. Well, I would have – before Jack got me all paranoid about identity theft and stuff, saying that people rifle through bins to get a couple of digits of your card and then bang! They've cleared out your bank account faster than you can say INSUFFICIENT FUNDS SEE YOUR CARD ISSUER.

So I have to go through each and every one, looking at it to see what it was for (just out of interest – and yes, out here, that's about as interesting as it gets) and then ripping it up into tiny pieces. Jack wants to get a shredder, but surely we could spend his hard-earned on something much more fun. Or romantic. Still, we are talking about the guy who, when one of his old friends got married, left it so late to get a present, the only thing left on the wedding list *was* a shredder, so he got them that. And they say romance is dead.

Anita, Jack's mum, gets to our place at ten. *Five to*, to be exact.

'God, you're early!' I say, relieved she's here.

Joey's being a right little pain in the arse – eating my receipts and being all whiney and whingey. Must get it from her dad.

'I'm prompt, yes. Like to be prompt,' she says. 'And I know you've got things to do, and I didn't want to spend all day on the trains trying to get here and anyway, I was in a hurry to see my little granddaughter!' And the award for Best Gran of the Year goes to . . .

'You're a lifesaver!' I say, picking Joey up and handing her over.

'Do you recognise your nanna? Do you?' Joey's clapping her hands together with glee.

'Cup of tea?' I ask.

'Ooh, yes, love one. Only if it's herbal, mind.'

Anita lives in Sydney, near her daughter (Jack's sister) and her four grandkids, and she's a real greenie. You know, saving rainforests, trying to get fluoride out of the water and eschewing caffeine at every turn. I haven't seen her this trip – she comes out every year and stays with her other son who lives in London – and the last time I saw her, when Joey had just been born, she'd grabbed my breast in front of everyone, trying to get me to feed Joey.

Joey and I'd come home from the hospital and it was *boiling*. The steamiest summer they'd had for forty years, they said. And up in our top-floor flat in Chiswick, it was as hot as buggery. And still. I had the fan on all day, every day. And even though I have really fond memories of that time – Joey, naked except for a nappy, falling asleep on my bare tummy and chest; me dribbling on her head, fast asleep, too, and every love song on the radio being about *her* now, not some unrequited love or even Jack – it's still a bit marred by my total and utter dismal failure at breast-feeding.

I'd been to the breastfeeding class and must've nodded off at the important bits, because when it came to it, when Joey was one day old and Charlie and Jack were at the hospital, I was clueless. Everyone bangs on about it being the most natural thing in the world, so I figured it'd be easy. I had absolutely no idea there was a knack to it.

I held Joey gingerly and pressed her poor, bruised face into my boob.

'No, you kind of have to put your nipple in her mouth, let her get a real gob-full of it,' Charlie said, trying to help.

After what felt like ten minutes, but was probably only about two, Joey started crying. I tried to soothe her, shush-ing her and rocking her. All in vain. And then she started to sound hysterical.

'Jack? Will you go and get one of those little formula bottles from the nurse's station? Please? *Now?*'

Joey took to the bottle immediately (definitely gets *that*

from her dad) and I promised everyone I'd keep trying (honestly – the number of times I heard 'Breast is best' bandied about by the midwife mafia), but I never got the hang of it. And poor old Joey hated it. Maybe that's when the obsession with getting something, everything – anything I haven't made – down her neck began. For the both of us.

So anyway, once we were back at home, the health visitor came round one afternoon and actually showed me how to do it. I was lying on my side, Joey lying next to me, her face turned in to my chest – and it worked! Felt a bit strange at first, her sucking on my boob – but it worked. For about five minutes, that is. I managed it once more, totally alone with Joey, later on that day, but never again.

In my panic about vitamins and minerals and fats and immunities – not to mention bonding – I sent Jack off one night to get a breast pump. He came back with this tiny, hand-held thing that actually did quite a good job. In twenty minutes, I nearly had 250ml of milk! If I could keep this up, Joey'd never have to drink that vile-smelling, vomitesque formula milk, she could drink mine! Halle-*bloody*-lujah!

As the days went by, the hand-held thing lost all its pull, so I ordered a super-duper, top of the range, double breast pump off the internet. For two hundred and fifty pounds, I might add – money being no object when your baby's health is at stake.

'You've never looked more attractive,' Jack'd say as I sat sweating on the couch, both boobs being pummelled and vacuum-pumped by this strong and probably very good – but ultimately ineffectual, for me, electric milking machine. I looked and felt like a cow. I'd put all my faith in this gadget, so you can imagine my dismay when no matter how hard it sucked, or how high I turned it up, I had no more milk left to give. I completely dried up within three weeks.

Just as I was about to drop from the exhaustion of being up all night with Joey, then all day pumping milk, washing and sterilising pumps and bottles – anything that went near our precious little girl's mouth – Anita came to visit. She brought Jack's dad (her ex-husband), Jack's brother, Steve, and Steve's girlfriend, Natasha, with her, too. Mum was already there, sitting next to me, with Joey on my lap, on the couch in our front room.

'You know, you really should give it a try,' Anita said, when I told her about my lack of success with breastfeed-ing.

'I have! I did!'

'Takes time,' says Natasha, who I'd met, like, once before in my whole life.

'It's just not going to work for me and Joey,' I said, getting a little antsy at the barrage of pressure to breast-feed – from virtual strangers. In my own house! Flat, whatever.

'And anyway, it's too hot. *She* gets all flustered and

upset and so do I and we both start crying and it's not worth it! Formula stuff's just as good.'

'That's what you and your brother had,' said Mum. 'And you two are fine.'

'You just have to persevere – it takes some doing to get it right. And look! She *wants* to feed from your breast!'

Anita was standing above us while Joey started pawing at my boob through my strapless maternity frock and gasping like a grouper out of water.

'I know, I know.' I felt like a teenager getting coaxed by my peer group to take drugs.

'Do you mind if I . . .?'

Before I could figure out what she was asking, Anita bent down and pulled my breast out. She pushed the back of Joey's head towards my nipple and said:

'She just needs to get some purchase, get a good latch-on going . . .'

I was so mortified I couldn't speak. They were all there, watching me and my sagging, drying-up old boobs. Fail.

'Steady on, Anita,' said Mum. 'Maybe she could do with some privacy for this.'

'Nearly there, just hold her head, let her get the whole nipple in her mouth . . .'

I looked at Mum and burst into tears. Joey joined me.

'That's enough!' said Mum, her voice slightly quavering. 'Let go, Anita – and everybody else, out! Just leave her alone!'

My hero.

'Sorry, love, sorry!' said Anita, backing away. 'I just want to help, that's all.'

'It's OK,' I sniffed, shoving my boob back in, hoiking Joey up on to my shoulder and disappearing into our bedroom for a good cry.

I shudder at the memory, shaking the horrible images out of my head, and make Anita a chamomile tea. I then make me an ordinary one (though there's nowt ordinary about that great Yorkshire Tea) and give Joey a Marmite-covered rice cake.

'I've got to sort out these receipts and I'll be right with you,' I say, darting into the front room and stuffing them all back into my bag. Don't want her to think I'm a crap housekeeper, as well as an unsuccessful breastfeeder.

'Look, love, why don't you have a bath? I'll look after Joey, you go on. And relax,' she calls after me.

I poke my head back round the door frame into the kitchen.

'Are you sure?'

'Positive! I've looked after so many babies in my time . . . I am a nurse, remember. We'll have a nice play about while Mummy's having a bath, won't we, Joey?'

God knows how long it's been since I last had a bath. Honestly, baths are such a rare thing for me these days, real momentous occasions – and who knows when we'll be able to afford to get a shower put in.

But who cares? How unbelievably *glorious* is this?

Maybe I'm finally starting to get why people are so mad about baths – uninterrupted, peaceful time to yourself. How great is that?

I put some of Joey's lavender baby bath in the running water and strip off. I study myself sideways in the mirror and pull my stomach in. It doesn't move, just hangs there. I don't think I have any stomach muscles left to suck in. I put my hands flat on the fold of skin that used to be my stomach and imagine what I'll look like once I've lost a bit of weight. Might need liposuction. Will *definitely* need liposuction. Better start making some serious money.

I ruffle my hair – my blonde highlights have long grown out, so I'm now left with my natural colour (brown) to my chin, followed by wispy straw-coloured split ends. I'm in desperate need of a cut and colour. Maybe that'll have to come first, before the lipo, when my freelancing money starts rolling in.

I then move in close and study my face in the mirror. After some badly needed deforestation around my chin and top lip with the tweezers, I'm ready to clamber into the tub.

Lying in the bath, I start thinking about the POP Club. I hope Liv's put up a new notice. Just imagine if it really took off. It could be like Weight Watchers – but with cigarettes and booze instead of cottage cheese and scales. You could Google it and find out where your nearest meeting was. And we could charge for membership – might get me closer to that haircut and lipo . . .

I close my eyes and start thinking about what I'm going to say when Richard and Judy have me on their show.

'Well, you know, Richard,' I say, looking impossibly glam (like Kate Winslet only glammer) and crossing my endless, slender legs, 'everyone gets a little *pee-ohd* every now and again—'

'Yes, yes, I *do* know as a matter of fact, yes! Indeed, just last night while we were talking about you coming on the show today, I said to Judy—'

'Oh, let her speak, will you, Richard?' says an exasperated Judy.

'I *am* letting her speak! Honestly, Judy, it's called a con-ver-*sa*-tion? You know? Where two people talk – sometimes over the top of each other, that's just how it goes, it's called *passion* . . . when you're talking about something that gets your gander up—'

'Oh, for Christ's sake! Do ignore him, Roxane, and tell us how you got the idea for the Pee-Ohd Parents Club. I mean, it's a real phenomenon – clubs are springing up all over the country. Did you have any idea, when it first started, that it would ever get this big?'

'Actually, Judy, yes. I knew we were on to a winner because, let's face it, everyone gets a little frustrated and annoyed and overwhelmed by life with a baby or kids—'

I hear Joey and Anita laughing downstairs. I sit up with a start, thinking I'd better get down there, quick – and then I slide back down again. There's no rush – she's in safe hands. Probably safer than mine, really, Anita having had three of her own and being a nurse and everything.

I wallow in the water for a bit longer, making the most of the luxury of being able to have a bath while Joey's awake and not worrying that she's falling face-first into one of the wide-screen tellies downstairs.

When Jack suggested we get a TV for the kitchen, I was incensed.

'But we've got one in the front room – one that takes *over* the whole front room *and* one in our bedroom . . . Should we get one for the loo, too? One on the banister going up the stairs? Have one on a mobile, hanging from the ceiling over Joey's cot?!'

'I'm just saying—'

'I don't want her to be watching telly wherever she goes in the house! She needs Early Learning Centre wooden toys, not digital flat-screen whatevers!'

'Just one in the kitchen/dining room in the corner, so I can watch it while I'm cooking.'

'Why don't you listen to the radio? Have music on – classical, preferably; we've got that Greatest Classic FM Hits for Babies somewhere . . .'

'But what if I want to watch the cricket or football or *The Wire* or *MythBusters* or *Police! Stop! Action! –*'

'Oh GOD!'

'– in the unlikely event you don't want to watch them with me, I could come and see them in the kitchen. I'll let you have the couch.'

'But what about Joey?'

'She'll have CBeebies.'

'But I don't want her watching telly at all! I don't want her to be tainted by TV! There's always some new study out saying how damaging it is for babies' brains—'

'It doesn't have to be *on* all the time, Rox – you *can* turn it off, you know.'

'I know, but –' and I gave in. Well, what would you do if the only comfortable seat in the house was being offered to you on a plate? And you could lie on it by *yourself*? And you could watch whatever you wanted without ever having to be bored to death by *Lost* (interest) ever again?

He was right, in the end. The more we've become house-bound and friendless, the more we've come to rely on the telly. The *three* tellies, I should say. Now they're our lifelines, our links to the outside world.

In fact, I'd say our happiest times these days are when he's lying on the floor and I'm lying on the couch and we're both slagging off whatever we're watching, or who-ever we're watching. Honestly, we're like two old ladies:

'Look at her *hair*!'

'I can't – can't get past the size of her *arse*!'

It's your average, cosy picture of house-bound new parents in apparent domestic bliss.

But not tonight, I think to myself, turning on the blow dryer (I'm not going to end it all, by the way – I'm out of the bath now and in the bedroom, about to dry my hair).

Tonight we'll knowingly and willingly miss *Corrie* and actually indulge in a bit of *real* real life, for a change.

'About fucking time,' I mutter and turn the telly on.

'You two have *GOT* to stop swearing!' says Charlie, mock-offended by something Jack's just said. 'I don't know whether it's because you're Australian, Jack – but Rox, you haven't even got an excuse. Just stop it, for Joey's sake if not your own bloody self-respect. I mean, there's nothing worse than hearing a two-year-old say "fuck". And any minute now she'll start talking, copying what you say.'

We're sitting in the restaurant bit of The Swan, having just hoovered up the entrée – some tiny, *nouvelle cuisine*-y, indeterminate green-brown blob on an oversized plate.

'Let's go outside for a cig,' says Jack, and we all take our huge wine glasses out into the beer garden, nearly getting whiplash in our haste.

'Feel bad, doing this,' I say, sitting down and sparking up. 'I'm supposed to be inside, drinking in the ambience and thinking about the taste, the subtle nuances of the food—'

'Bud you arre,' says Guy, sucking on his Gitane. 'Zis is all a part of zuh rist-orrr-on eggs-bear-ee-onze, uh?'

'Too right,' says Jack. 'Now what are we going to have for the next bottle of wine?'

We've only been here for half an hour and already Jack's had one pint and we've all gone through two bottles of wine.

175

'Just go easy there, tiger,' I say, that inner school marm surfacing. 'Let's not get hammered and embarrass ourselves just because it's free—'

'Nah, let's do it just because we can!' laughs Charlie.

'I *am* here in a professional capacity, you know.' I take a restrained, ladylike sip of my wine.

They all smirk.

As long as the restaurant takes out an ad in *Village Life*, they get a review – a bit of an advertorial. It's not totally fixed, but if you thought the food was crap, you definitely couldn't say so in print. You'd have to say something like: 'My dining partner could not stop raving about his salmon mousse and with such an extensive and – please excuse my gushing, but it *is* warranted – simply *wonderful* wine cellar, our experience at The Weeping Willow was one that we will definitely be repeating over the coming months.' Now, the cellar *itself* might've been large and wonderful – not actually any of the wines it housed; your dining partner might be raving about the salmon mousse because he got some nasty food poisoning from it and is delirious; and their *experience* means they *ate* – and no doubt they will eat again, thus repeating the experience, at some time over the next few months – just not necessarily at The Weeping Willow. It's all in the way you phrase it – as much what you *don't* say as what you *do*.

Speaking of repeating, Charlie's already got hiccups, she's knocking the wine back so fast. The waitress recognises me from the POP Club and comes over:

176

'All right, sweetheart?'

'Good, thanks,' I say, pleased that, for once, I have witnesses to prove I know someone in this village.

'You not with the others tonight?' She nods to the table
where June, Paul, Olivia, Tim and Carina are all sitting,
laughing.

'We might join them later,' I reply, trying to sound professional and not too desperate to hook up with the POP
Club.

'Right, right. Look, your main courses are ready now.
D'you want me to bring them out here?'

'That'd be great!' says Jack.

'No, no, I think we should have them inside if that's
OK,' I counter, shooting Jack a dirty look. I don't want the
owner of The Swan to grass me up to Vanessa, saying all I
was interested in was the free booze and smoking. Even if
it's true.

So we go in and out, in and out, in and out a-bloody-
gain for about a million times over the next hour and a
half until I finally say:

'Oh, bugger it. Let's stay out here.'

We join the POP Club table, much to the delight of June
and Olivia, who must think our numbers are swelling.

'A restaurant review? That's great,' says June, nodding
to Jack. 'More money for the family coffers . . .'

Good old June, I think, fighting my corner, putting a
good word in for me. It's a pity, then, that her words are

totally wasted, because Jack doesn't take a blind bit of notice – he's too busy excitedly swapping *Civilisation* tips with Paul.

'See? Now you two can afford a babysitter,' June goes on, 'you can go out together, spend some quality time—'

'No, we can't!' Jack shouts. 'We can't afford a babysitter! My mum's looking after Joey tonight!'

So he *did* hear.

'Still, at least you're out together. At a POP Club meeting to boot,' June placates him, accentuating the positive.

Jack grunts and turns back to Paul, resuming their computer-game-freaks chat. I tune into Tim and Olivia, who are moaning on to each other about how they never meet any eligible men.

'It's just too small here – not big enough for the likes of me,' sighs Tim.

'Maybe,' says Liv. 'But you've got to keep your eyes open, he might be right under your nose.'

We all look around the pub at the fat beer-bellied old men supping their real ales and smoking their cigars and turn back to each other.

'Hmm. Maybe not,' smiles Tim.

'Well, maybe not *here*,' laughs Liv. 'But in Riverside. There's bound to be someone out there who's made for you – you've got to keep upbeat. And when you least expect it, expect it.'

'Yeah, but the boxes he has to tick on my list are a little different to yours.' Tim sighs again, playing with a coaster sodden with the condensation from his Timblioni. 'You try being gay in Riverside.'

'Try being a single mum anywhere,' sniffs Olivia.

'Hey Tim!' I squeal. 'Who was that guy you went off with last week?'

'No one,' he says, suddenly looking all dark and serious. 'No one at all. *Persona non grata.*'

'Was he an ex of yours?' I go on.

Tim glares at me.

'Look, I don't want to talk about it. OK?'

'I bet they're exactly the same,' says June, changing the subject. 'I mean these *boxes* you speak of ticking.'

'Yeah – we're all after the same thing in the end. Something nice, tall, dark and handsome,' grins Olivia, looking at Jack and Paul who are nearly falling off their respective chairs, they're laughing so hard.

'What's so funny?' I ask Jack.

'Ah, nothing,' Jack titters. His voice has gone all high, his eyes are watering and he actually *titters*. 'It's just that Paul's Montezuma, right, well, his army attacked the Romans when, *obviously*, it's the Greeks who . . .'

And I zone out as I often do when Jack's talking about *Civ* (or work or money), only to focus on Guy, Charlie and Carina.

Guy's pawing Charlie while she admires Carina's chunky silver rings and mules – scarlet patent leather and treacherously high, of course.

'Yeah, well, they certainly get you noticed,' says Carina, blowing the smoke out of her mouth over Charlie's head.

Typical Carina, I think – everything she says, does or even wears is all designed to get attention. She's no shrinking violet, that's for sure.

'Think *Village Life* will subsidise the POP Club for tonight, doll?' Carina asks me. 'I don't mind drinking wine if you don't think they'd stretch to G&Ts. You know, all a part of getting a feel for the ambience of The Swan on a Wednesday night . . .'

'Course it will! The Pissed-Off Parents Club's a crucial part of village life, isn't it? I knew it'd take off, didn't I, Rox? Practically had to *force* her into organising it,' winks Charlie as she disengages herself from a drooling, nuzzling, leg-draping Guy and gets up to go to the bar.

We drink The Swan's cellar dry over the course of the next couple of hours, and the last thing I remember is shaking the chef's hand in the front bar, congratulating him on his fine food.

'YOU are a shocker,' says Jack into my face.

'*Me*?' I try to open my eyes. Which would be a hell of a lot easier if someone hadn't superglued my eyelids together while I slept. 'YOU'RE the shocker!' and I turn over to face the legs of the kitchen table, hoping Jack'll take the hint and eat a whole packet of Tic Tacs before he speaks to me again, so close up.

'Actually,' he whispers into my ear, 'Charlie and *Guy* are the real shockers. Did you hear them *at it* last night?'

'No—'

'That Guy must be a mechanic in the sack, way Charlie was moaning and groaning and carrying on!'

'Least *someone's* seeing some action,' I murmur as I sit up and try to get my bearings.

Right. Now I remember. Jack and I slept on the kitchen floor on the blow-up bed that Charlie brought down for us; Charlie and Guy slept on the sofa bed in the front room – if, indeed, they got any sleep at all – and Anita was in our bed upstairs. My mouth feels like I've eaten The Swan's chef's CV and half the sandpaper that's lying around on the kitchen floor, I'm so thirsty.

'Water,' I rasp.

Only good thing about a hangover is you really get to catch up on all those glasses of water you're supposed to drink every day, but completely forget about or just can't be arsed to drink. You can get a whole week's worth down in one day, sometimes. Which is great, really. Healthy, even.

And my right shoulder hurts. It's actually throbbing.

'My right shoulder's killing me,' I whine, never one to let a stonking hangover get in the way of complaining. 'Must be this bloody bed.'

'Yeah,' smiles Jack. 'That and the pub floor. You didn't half take a tumble down those steps!'

Oh God, oh God, oh *GOD*. It all starts coming back to me in slow motion. I wince at the vague memory of falling over, shortly after I'd clumsily given my compliments to the chef. Which was not long after I'd got Tim's back up by asking him about that old guy . . .

Oh God. When will the mortification ever end?

'And I think you better apologise to Mum,' says Jack.

'Why?'

'When we got home, Mum was sitting up watching telly and you said something about the breastfeeding thing.'

'Did I?'

'Yes. You only mentioned it, but I think she's quite embarrassed about it.'

Oh God, oh God, oh GOD! *Will* this mortification ever end?

13

I haven't had any cigarettes since last night – the farrago that's probably

a) ruined any friendships I'd been building in Riverside

b) turned Anita against me and made her unwilling to babysit for us ever again and

c) pole-axed my chances of getting any more work at *Village Life*.

It's no wonder I haven't smoked – must've puffed my way through at least fifty million. We probably totally depleted Riverside's stocks – couldn't get my hands on any even if I wanted to.

Which is a bit of a bonus, really, because I've just dropped Joey off at the nursery (only forty-five minutes late – definitely getting better) and I'm walking down to the hypnotist's house.

Big day today – hypnosis to knock the smoking on the head once and for all, and a scheduled-in sex date with

Jack tonight. Bit nervous about that, actually. I just can't even imagine going from a cup of tea and a HobNob one minute to a snog and a real, actual shag the next. I mean, how does it happen? What are the steps?

Speaking of steps, once I'm in the back of the hypnotist's house, in his study (a lean-to), sitting in a battered old leather chair, I'm completely taken aback to see him rolling a cigarette. This fills me with less than zero faith in him and his smoking cessation techniques, but I'm so muzzy-headed, I haven't got the energy to enter into a full-on discussion about it – all I do is ask him why he, of all people, smokes. He tells me he's actually a recovering alcoholic.

'Yeah, the good old twelve steps. Works for me – it's not for everyone, granted, but it's kept me sober for eight years,' he says, adjusting his John Lennon glasses. 'I'm also an actor, you see, when 'er indoors lets me. Need to keep a clear head for remembering lines and emoting and stuff.'

'But why smoke?'

'Lesser of two evils,' he says and takes a long, lusty look at his roll-up. The sight of which is just about enough to make anyone bag the fags on the spot.

'But listen, this isn't about me, it's about you. So tell me – why do you want to stop smoking?'

I look around the room and read some of the newspaper and magazine headlines he's wallpapered the walls with. There's SEIZE THE DAY! and FEEL THE FEAR AND DO

IT ANYWAY (with a big, fat capital 'L' angrily and heavily scrawled over the 'f' in 'fear') and ONE GIANT STEP FOR MAN – ONE BIG LOAD OF LAUNDRY FOR WOMAN! It's like my room when I was fourteen – except the only headlines I had were 'Woking Class Hero' (about Paul Weller) and 'Jam split!' and 'Why did Joe disappear?' when Joe Strummer took off to Paris in the middle of a UK tour. All the posters and pictures I had on my walls were of my favourite bands, not meaningless clichés. And I was fourteen! Not forty-five, like this guy.

'Um, lots of reasons. I'm coming up to forty, I've just had – well, nearly a year ago – a baby—'

'Aah. Kids. Gotta love 'em.'

'Yeah. And—'

'Got four nippers of my own – well, they're the missus', too! Three lads, one baby girl. They're at school right now, but don't worry, they know I'm working this afternoon, so they won't make any noise when they get back. Missus'll take 'em up to the park.'

'Great. So, yeah, I want to stop for her sake, the baby's – don't want to contract some horrendous cancer and die and leave her alone. And I feel like such a bad mum, pushing her in the buggy and having a cigarette at the same time. I can *feel* other people – other mums, especially – shooting daggers at me as we walk down the street.'

'The humiliation, the embarrassment, the shame,' he says, taking notes. 'Go on.'

'And . . . my husband – boyfriend – well, fiancé – he smokes and it drives me mad. I know it's hypocritical, but if he didn't, it wouldn't occur to me to, either. It's a great source of tension between us.'

'Your boyfriend's name?'

'Jack.'

'Little ditty – 'bout Jack and Roxanne . . .' he sings quietly.

'Eh?'

He coughs and strokes his goatee, sitting up straighter in his swivel chair.

'Um . . . Tell me about your parents.'

'They used to smoke. Dad stopped when he was forty and Mum had to stop when she was fifty-six – she had heart failure and they wouldn't do a quadruple bypass unless she gave up.'

'Mmm-hmm.' He doesn't look up, just scribbles furiously.

'And my brother'd kill me if he knew I was still smoking. He's always said he doesn't want to be visiting me in hospital, watching me fight for breath in an iron lung . . . I didn't when I was pregnant, obviously, and it wasn't such a hardship. And,' I pause, wondering whether to mention this final and intensely private reason to a virtual stranger, '. . . I've had two miscarriages. I smoked, because I didn't even know I was pregnant – but I was determined not to let this one, our Joey, go.'

'Miscarriages, blamed on smoking . . .'

186

'And I want to be able to run around with Joey, get fit, not be one of those mums you see on *Supernanny*, all fat and angry and smoking while their kids beat them up and throw horrific tantrums.'

'You do know that smoking is not necessarily why you had the miscarriages, don't you?'

'I know, I know – can't have helped, though.'

'Yup. So how long you been smoking for?'

'Since I was fourteen, I suppose.' I screw my nose up. Mentally, I take fourteen from forty. This is difficult for me and takes quite a while. I remember once, when I was in Grade Four at primary school in Adelaide, I got caught cheating, looking at someone else's exercise book for the answers, when we used to do 'mental' quizzes at the beginning of maths lessons. Must've only been things like *six plus ten minus four and a half* and *what's seventy-six divided by four?*, but I was *rubbish*. Totally clueless. The teacher made me and the girl I was cheating off sit on the floor, cross-legged, underneath the massive chalkboard for every maths lesson after that. For a whole term. No wonder I've got a block on figures. And now, if anyone ever says to me: 'You do the maths', I break into a sweat.

'Twenty-six years,' he says, stroking his goatee and looking at his notes.

'Bloody hell,' I sigh, thankful he put me out of my maths misery, but shocked by the serious number of years I've clocked up puffing away. That's, hang on – over half my life spent smoking!

'You grew up in Australia?'

'For a few years, when Mum and Dad were there on secondment, yes. I did two years at uni there, too, and went backpacking afterwards. But I am English.'

'Where's your favourite place in the whole world?'

'London.'

'A tranquil, peaceful place . . .'

'Oh, the bush, I suppose. In autumn or winter – it's too hot in Australia in the spring and summer. Mum and Dad built a kit home in the country – middle of nowhere. And it's beautiful. Why?'

'You'll find out,' he says, looking up. 'Now it sounds to me like you're over it, over smoking. You've done all that adolescent rebellion thing with cigarettes, you've got your own child to think about now and you're nearly forty – the same age as your father when he stopped. It's time to *move on*.'

'I have a bit of a problem moving on,' I say.

'Well, you won't have when I'm finished with you. Because, Rox-*ahn* – did I say that right?' He doesn't wait for an answer. 'Because, Rox-*ahn*, hypnosis will give you the tools to check yourself, think about it and, hopefully, not do it.'

'So it's not guaranteed?'

'Nothing in this life is guaranteed.' He points to a headline on the wall that says DEATH AND DEATH TAX – GUARANTEED.

'Hmm.'

188

'So, if you want to settle back in the chair, put up the leg rest and close your eyes, we'll get started.'

I must admit, it is relaxing, lying here, listening to him witter on about rainbows and climbing them and getting to the other side, but I can't help thinking his tone's a bit, I don't know, *porny*. Like he's talking dirty.

'So you see the rainbow, Rox-*ahn*, and it's beautiful. Red, orange, yellow, green, blue, indigo and violet . . .' he says softly, slowly. All I can think is Roy G. Biv – we learnt that at school, a mnemonic to help you remember all the colours of the rainbow in sequence.

'. . . and as you're effortlessly climbing up that rainbow, you can see for miles and miles. *Yeah*, Rox-*ahn*, miles and miles. And it's beautiful. The sun is shining – but it's not too hot, just right, ooh *yeah*, and the sky is blue and you're breathing in the clean, pure air, *hmm yeah*, *feels so good*, and your chest rises up and down, up and down, up and down . . . *hmmm* . . . and as you breathe out, you look around you and see what you want at the other end of the rainbow. *Yeah*. And you want it, Rox-ahn, *ooh yeah*, you want it *bad* . . .'

Crikey. I checked for exits when I first got here, so if I have to, should be able to run away reasonably easily.

'. . . and so, at the end of the rainbow, at the end of your journey, you look back and you realise, what you did before, you don't need to do any more. *Yeah*. You've done it. It was good – *really* good sometimes – but it's over now. You take a deep breath, filling your lungs with the sweet, tangy air of eucalyptus trees and you look around you, at the *bush – ooh, hmm, yeah –* and you breathe it all in, *yeah, it's beautiful. Feels so good.* You see kangaroos hopping by, wombats coming out of their nests—'

'Burrows.' I can't help myself and correct him.

''Kay, burrows . . . um . . . and *relax*, concentrate on your breathing, *yeah*, good girl, *ooh yeah* . . .'

His kids must have just got back from school or the park or wherever, because I can suddenly hear them shouting at each other in the next room, turning the telly up loud and thumping about on the floor.

'You see the sand and the koala bears in the trees and in the distance –'

'OW! Gerroff! MUH-*UM*!'

'You watch the aboriginal kids playing – the very *noisy* aboriginal kids –'

I smile. So does Barry, I can hear it in his voice.

'Now when I get to one, Rox-*ahn*, you'll come back from the bush, back to England, back to beautiful Riverside, where the air is pure and you can breathe easy, safe in the knowledge you will never smoke again. Ten, nine, eight . . .'

And I'm back.

'Hooh,' I say, opening my eyes and sitting up slowly. 'Very relaxing. But I'm not sure I was completely "under", you know?'

'You looked pretty relaxed to me – and that's the main thing, relaxing; leaving your mind open to suggestion.'

I hand over forty quid – though it pains me to do so – and he walks too closely behind me to the front door.

'Well, thanks for that and . . . see ya,' I say, not daring to turn around.

'Not if I see you first! Or you come and see me in the play. *Midsummer Night's Dream* – hence the goatee,' he says, stroking it again. 'You like The Bard?'

'I'm not really a fan of facial hair—'

'Not the *beard* – The *Bard*!'

'Oh. Yes, I suppose . . .'

'Should come and see us, then. Riverside Theatre, Wednesday nights—'

'Can't on Wednesdays – that's the Pissed-Off Parents Club night. Hey! Maybe you should come, if you get a night off—'

'We do Saturday nights, too – and matinees—'

'Right-o. Look, I've gotta go, got to pick the baby up.'

'Good girl,' he says and kisses me on the cheek.

'Bye, then.' I nearly trip over the doorstep, I'm trying to get away so fast.

'Good luck – although you won't need *luck*,' he shouts after me. 'If you want to talk, say you're having a weak moment, give me a call. And don't beat yourself up if you slip up once or twice – just come back here, first top up's free, remember!'

I have *absolutely* no faith in this hypnotherapy whatsoever, but what the hell – you've got to support local business out here in the country. And even if he was a teensy bit creepy, you never know, it might work – he might've expertly subliminally cured me.

I take deep breaths walking home. And despite the fumes from a couple of lorries which thunder past, I feel pretty good. Cleansed, even. And then it occurs to me. Maybe I'm looking forward to tonight's shag so much, I heard sex in Barry's voice where there actually was none. Maybe Barry was only doing his job, being professional – maybe I'm the horny one – fully *in the mood*. It's been so long, I'm bound to not immediately recognise the signs.

Luckily, I've got time for a quick bath and beautifying session before I have to pick Joey up. God. Imagine if we actually *did* have sex tonight! I'm not on the Pill and he's too well-endowed for condoms – or so he says: 'They don't make horse size, do they?' – so what if I got pregnant? Oh God, no. Couldn't bear it. There is *no way* I'm doing any of this all over again. *No way*. The chances of getting pregnant are slim at the best of times at my age, anyway.

And it took so long for me to get pregnant with Joey – we were just about to have our first appointment for IUI when I found out I was with child.

Jack had to go into the clinic to produce a sample, so they could see whether he was making enough sperm.

'There was only the tiniest drop in the sample jar – microscopic! It's going to say I haven't got *any* sperm!' he'd said when he got back from the clinic.

I reassured him, told him they only need a minute bit, that's all it takes. But he wouldn't let it go.

'But what's a man to do when all they give you is *National Geographic* to read, Rox?! It's not fair!'

A couple of days later, the result was in.

One hundred and thirty-seven million. 137,000,000 of the tiny little buggers swimming about in there.

Jack couldn't have been more proud. We told Charlie one night when all three of us were up in Bath. She was so impressed, she changed his name in her mobile contacts to 137 mill.

'What a waste of time and money,' Jack says when I tell him I went to see Barry.

'And then his kids made a racket and he said "noisy aboriginal kids" because I was supposed to be imagining I was in the bush, and it was really quite funny,' I say.

Jack's not laughing.

'D'you think it worked?'

'Haven't had any ciggies. Don't want one, either.'

'How much did you pay him?'

'Forty.'

'*Forty quid*?! Could have used that for the bloody phone bill. What a rip-off!'

'Yeah, probably. So anyway . . . ta-night's the night . . .' I start singing that Rod Stewart song.

'Hmm?'

'It's scheduled in.'

Blank.

'Sex, you wally! Tonight?'

'Ummm . . .'

'Don't you remember?' I say accusingly.

'No, no,' he laughs and grabs my waist, pulling me close to his body, 'of course I remember!' He kisses me. And it's quite nice. He's got these luscious, big soft lips that are really rather sexy when you think about it.

'Hmm. Juicy!' I say.

'Juicy!' he repeats in a cute, baby-talk voice.

'Oh, yeah,' I come back to real life, 'Joey. How's about I put her to bed and you sort out some wine?'

'Hmm, sounds great! I'll just have a quick game of *Civ* while you put her to bed and then I'm all yours, gorgeous.'

'OK. See you in a bit.' I raise my eyebrows at him and try to look seductive with Joey's bottle in one hand and her dummy in the other. He blows me a kiss and disappears into the study under the stairs.

Two hours later, I'm still waiting for Jack to make a move. A move into the front room would be a start, a move away from the study.

I go into the kitchen to make a cup of tea. I call out to Jack: 'You all right in there?'

Silence, save for the kettle boiling.

I walk over to the study door and peer in. He's got headphones on.

'You all right?' I say tetchily. I poke the back of his shoulder, noticing for the first time in yonks that it's very firm. And manly. I'm amazed he can fit in this minute room with shoulders that broad.

He pulls one ear of the headphones away, turns around to look at me and says: 'With you in a sec, babe – nearly finished.' He flashes me his sweet smile and I think he really is quite handsome.

'Don't be long, lover,' I say, and leave him to it.

Two more teas, a quick doze, a look at *every single channel* on the telly (twice) later, and I'm furious.

I get my bag from the kitchen, stomping about and harrumphing loudly. I go upstairs, check on Joey – she's looking lovely (but then again, she always does when she's asleep) – and I take my clothes off and get into bed.

I lie there, kaftan- and knicker-less, and wait. And wait. And – you guessed it – *wait*.

In the still, dark of the night, I start wondering why he's taking so long. Maybe his needs *are* being satisfied by somebody else. Maybe he's sated – totally and utterly spent after long nights of passion in Paddington. Or on the golf course. Maybe he's getting sick of sex, he's seeing so much action with *her* lately . . .

I nearly jump out of my skin when my mobile bleeps, breaking the silence. Someone's sent me a text.

A-ha! I knew it! I knew Jack wouldn't let this shag-op go by. Bet he's texted me something saucy from the study, something hot to get me going while he prepares to come upstairs and ravage me.

My fingers fumble with the phone. It's from an unknown number.

> Owzit goin?
> No cigs
> I hope!
> Baz xxx

14

'Rox? Roxy, wake up.' Jack's prodding me.

'You're too late, mate,' I grumble, not moving from my position under the duvet facing the wall.

'Pav's here. And there's some guys with him. In the kitchen.'

'Eh?' I roll over and look up. Jack's fully dressed, backpack on, standing over at his side of the bed.

'What time is it?'

'Quarter to seven. Look, I've gotta go.'

Morning already? And that ridiculous, poor excuse for a builder's here, too. Great.

'Is Joey awake?'

'Not yet,' he says as something crashes downstairs. Right on cue, she starts bawling.

'Bugger-*ation*!'

Joey and I are wandering aimlessly round the streets of Riverside, unable to go home.

The builders, supposedly fixing the kitchen ceiling, are making an almighty noise and mess in the kitchen and they're constantly traipsing in and out of the house, filthy work boots and all. Still, least we haven't got the new carpet in yet – better nag Jack about that.

It's impossible for me to make anything for Joey to eat – and it'll be even more impossible for her to get to sleep later on, so looks like we're out for as long as it takes for the builders to cock something else up in the house and leave. Makes it easier to diet, though, while I'm not stuck in the house, faced with bread and butter at every turn. And all this walking's got to be good for the ever-broadening beam, hasn't it?

It reminds me of when Joey and I first got back here after staying at Charlie's and Mum and Dad's – the house is a sty and we're forced to wander the streets, lonely as clouds again – but it also feels quite different. It's not freezing, for a start (now that we've got a completely new boiler – another mammoth expense we hadn't accounted for) and I don't feel so lost. I'm nowhere near as all-consumed with misery as I was back then, either. Maybe it's because it's summer, now – everything looks better in the sun. Or maybe it's because I've got the POP Club, something to look forward to. Which reminds me – I wonder if Liv's put up a notice for the meeting tonight.

I point the buggy in the direction of the Really Rather Good Cafe and call Jack. Straight to voicemail.

'Hey there. Me and Joey are out and about, just pootling around, and we thought we'd give you a call – well, *I* thought *I'd* give you a ring, see how you're faring.' I pause, as though I'm waiting for him to suddenly speak on the other end, as though I've called a landline and he's screening. 'Henn-y-way, gi's a call when you get a chance and . . . speak to you later. Bye.'

Probably too busy flirting with the woman he's having an affair with to answer my call, I think as I get to the big glass front door of the Really Rather Good Cafe. I'm stopped dead in my tracks by the fluorescent yellow, poster-sized sign sticky-taped on it that says:

THE PISSED-OFF PARENTS CLUB!
Every Wednesday, 8.15 p.m. at
The Swan

It's an eye-catcher, that's for sure. I smile and say:

'That looks like fun, doesn't it, Joey?' pointing at the sign. 'Mummy's definitely going there tonight, isn't she?'

I'm saying it loudly enough for the table of mums and babies sitting next to the front door to hear. One looks up at me and frowns. I take Joey inside.

I order a glass of full-fat milk for Joey and an English Breakfast with semi-skimmed for me. That's an English Breakfast *tea*, not a fry-up – if I have to be Riverside's biggest loser, I'd like it to be because of some serious lard loss, not because I've got no mates.

Joey and I chat amongst ourselves – nothing new there – and after, ooh, twelve minutes or so, I'm bored.

'What are we going to do with ourselves now, Joey? Any suggestions?'

She looks up at me from her pram and I study her face. She'd be quite the cutie if she wasn't so pudgy. Not that there's anything wrong with pudgy, God knows. I'm aware that there might be a *smidge* of transference going on here . . . and I know babies are *supposed* to be chubby, means they're healthy, apparently – but she just looks *fat* to me.

'I know! Let's go and get you weighed, eh? How about that? That'll be fun, won't it?'

We have to go back to the house for her red baby book. I leave Joey in her buggy at the front door and go in. I never thought I'd live in a house where the front door opens right on to the front room – you know, hallway-less – but here I am.

'How's it going?' I ask Pavel, who's sitting on the kitchen floor, smoking.

'Ah, eez OK, all OK.'

'Was it the bath or the loo or the basin that was leaking from upstairs?'

'No worry, eez all OK.'

I look up at the ceiling. There's a dirty great hole where it used to be.

'Right. We're off back out, then. See you later!' and I leave, muttering 'Eez all OK, my arzz' under my breath.

It's weird, though. If, say, five days ago, I'd walked in and someone had been smoking in the kitchen, I would have lost it on them. Totally. But now, ex-smoker that I am, I'm a *leetle* put out, but more in a calm, 'I'll open all the windows and doors later, let the smoke out – maybe even go round with some Oust' way, as opposed to an irate 'I'LL RIP YOUR BLOODY LIPS OFF IF YOU SMOKE INSIDE OR NEAR MY BABY EVER AGAIN!' way, as I might be if I was gagging for one myself. Which is a good thing, I think. Virtually grown-up.

At the weigh-in, I realise I forgot Joey's nappy bag, with spare nappies, so I leave her fully clothed and we weigh her as is.

'Twenty-eight pounds,' says the woman.

'Same as last time. Is that right for her age? She's nearly a year old now.'

'I just do the weighing, love. Do you want to talk to the health visitor?'

It's not Liz today, it's a different health visitor on duty. So I explain, while Joey's crawling around on the floor, cackling like a hyena, that I'm worried she's too fat.

'Well, we certainly don't want her to make any more fat cells,' she says, looking at the chart in the baby book.

'Am I feeding her too much? The wrong stuff? What—'

'How much milk does she have?'

'Only two bottles a day – 210ml each—'

'She should be off bottles entirely by one year, and there's no need for formula any more, either. Full-fat

201

cow's milk as a drink and cheese and yoghurt will give her all the calcium and vitamin D she needs.'

'But I just bought a huge tin of SMA Gold!'

'OK, OK. When do you give her her bottles?'

'One around ten in the morning, to get her off to sleep, and the other right before bed at seven, seven-thirty.'

'I suggest you start slowly. Drop the morning one completely and give her 80 or 110ml just before bed.'

'But I depend on the milk to get her to sleep! If she doesn't have it, I'll *never* get anything done!'

'She'll sleep. Look at her, she's moving about so much, that'll tire her out. And once she's up and walking, the fat'll really drop off her.'

'So you're saying she *is* fat?'

'No, no, no! Not at all! She's just . . . just a bit . . . fluffy.'

Fluffy?

'So when you've finished this tin, don't buy any more. She's no longer a baby – you need to *grow her up* a bit.'

So not only am I making my baby fat, I'm retarding her physical and emotional development by *treating* her like a baby. You can't bloody win!

'Grow her up?'

'Yes. Teach her to use a cup and get her off the bottles.'

'Do I need to sterilise the cups?'

'No.'

'Boil water for her to drink?'

'Nup.'

'So, no more sterilising?'

'That's right – once she's off the bottles.'

'Hmm. That doesn't sound too bad, you know. Thanks!' and off I trot to pick Joey up, who's terrorising some newborns round the partition wall. Imagine that! Liberation from the steriliser and the bottles. Joy!

'Joey's been a nightmare!' I say to Jack, by way of a greeting as he walks in the door later that evening.

'Hello to you too,' he says, and bends down to pick a tear-stained Joey up.

'She must be utterly knackered – no sleep *at all* today.'

'Aaah, poor thing! How are you, baby? You tired? You look tired to me! Early bed for you,' he says, kissing her as she throws her arms around his neck and puts her head on his shoulder. 'It's your turn to put her to bed tonight, isn't it, Rox?'

'I did it *last* night, remember? Or were the Orcs too busy monstering the Hobbits on *Civ* for you to notice?'

'That's *Lord of the Rings*,' he says softly as he sways from side to side, a subdued Joey in his arms.

'Whatever. Anyway, it's *Corrie* at seven-thirty and then I'm off to the POP Club.'

'Shh, shhhhh.'

'Maybe you should put her to bed right now,' I whisper.

'Yeah, think I will.'

He puts her to bed and he's back downstairs within ten minutes. Honestly, with Jack she's out cold in ten minutes max – with me, she usually takes well over an hour.

'Gotcha a present,' he says, pulling a small black HMV plastic bag out of his backpack.

Guilt gifts, now, is it? Feeling bad for having a hot affair while the little woman slaves away at home?

'But it's not my birthday,' I say suspiciously.

'I know – not yet, anyway. But soon, *forty*-year-old,' says Jack, wandering into the kitchen.

'Kate Bush's first album! It's got "Wuthering Heights" on it . . . And Olivia Newton-John's Greatest Hits . . . with the *Grease* songs . . . brilliant! Oh, thanks, babe – these are excellent.'

Jack checks out Pavel's 'handiwork' on the kitchen ceiling and winces.

'We're not paying for that, you know,' I sniff.

'No, I know – he was really sorry and said straight up he didn't want paying for it. Will you call the insurance people and see if our policy will cover them fixing it up?'

Jack flips the top off a bottle of beer and I've just made a hot mug of Yorkshire. We go outside. I tell him what the health visitor said and he gets a little misty.

'She's growing up,' he says, looking off into the middle-distance.

'Yeah. Growing up *slim*, hopefully.'

'Ah, she's lovely however much she weighs.'

'She's particularly lovely when she's asleep—'

'But even lovelier when she's awake.'

Bloody hell – who's this?

'You know, I've been thinking,' he says.

204

'I'll alert the press,' I reply.

'What would you say to another one?' he asks.

'No, I'm all right – haven't finished this one yet. And anyway, want to leave some room for later on.'

'Not tea . . . Another *baby*.'

'I'd say: "Are you *kidding* me?"'

'It hasn't been that bad,' he smiles.

'Not for you, maybe.'

'For Joey's sake, if not mine. I don't want her to be a lonely, only child.'

'I don't want her to be lonely, either. I think that's a myth about only kids being lonely, anyway. She's got me and you and she's so friendly, she'll never be short of friends.'

'Not the same, though, is it? I mean, I've got a brother and sister – and you, look how close you are to Alex. Wouldn't you want the same thing for Joey? The same relationship you and Alex have, I mean?'

'I suppose so, but there's no guarantees they'd get on – they might fight like cat and dog and before you know it, we'll be on *The House of Tiny Tearaways* with uncontrollable kids and getting divorced!'

'We'd have to get married first.'

'Yeah, well . . . what's brought all this on, anyway?'

'I dunno, just thinking.'

'Well, *I* kind of think we've been so lucky with Joey – she's healthy. And I'm getting on, more things can go wrong when you're over forty . . .'

'I know. But you'd have the amniocentesis and all the tests. We'd keep a really close eye on it . . .'

'And I'd have to have a caesarean – there is *no way* I ever want to feel contractions again . . .'

'So . . . you want to?'

'No! Oh, I don't know!'

I put a stop to this conversation. I mean, what if I get pregnant and Jack runs off with his affair lady? Charlie and Liv say being a single mum's a hundred times harder than when there's two of you to share the load. And I quite like Jack these days, even find him sexy. I don't want him to leave me!

'Can I have one of your cigs?' I ask him.

'No! You don't smoke any more, hypno girl!'

'Yeah, well,' and he hands me one.

'You're not on the Pill, are you?'

'No need,' I sneer, and remind him of last night's scheduled-in-sex/*Civ* debacle.

'Best contraception there is, that *Civ*,' I sigh.

We sit there for a while not saying anything. My head's spinning – and not just because I've smoked a cigarette. I'm reeling because while I thought about it a lot before we had Joey – thought: 'Yeah, easy – we'll have two. A girl and a boy and they'll be great mates and we'll all live happily ever after' – since Joey, the thought hasn't really crossed my mind – not counting those 'never again' moments, obviously.

'I'm too old for another baby,' I say. 'I can remember

when Dad threw Mum a surprise party at our house for her fortieth, you know.'

'Is that what you want? A party?'

'Nah, nah – who'd we invite, anyway? No, what I'm saying is, I was *fifteen* when Mum was forty. Fif-bloody-*teen*! We'll be lucky if Joey remembers my *fiftieth* birthday!'

We ponder the horrendousness of getting old, sipping our respective beverages.

'Jeez that commute's pissing me off,' he says eventually.

'Yeah, must be awful,' I agree, still thinking about being pregnant again.

'The job bores me to tears and I feel undervalued and unappreciated – and everyone's feeling the pressure; we've got a book going on who'll be made redundant first. But it's those *farking* trains that are really getting to me. And then the tube on top of that . . .'

'I know, I know—'

'. . . and when one's late or cancelled, it mucks the whole thing up. I'm dreading it in winter,' he says, looking up at the weak sun.

'Told you we never should've left London.'

'Yes we should! Should've left *years* ago.'

We'll never agree on that one.

'Actually, I reckon we should move to Australia,' he says casually.

'What?'

'Yeah,' he says, still looking at the sun, avoiding my stunned gaze. 'The Blue Mountains.'

I'm speechless.

He's been talking to his mum, that's it! She's always wanted him to move back to Australia and now that her other grandkids are getting older, she wants some new ones to take care of! A-ha!

'You've been talking to your mum, haven't you?'

'Yes, but that's not what this is about. I just want us to start living. England is great in your twenties and thirties, but now we've got Joey – and maybe another one – I think it's time for a really big change.'

Sometimes I forget that Jack's got things he wants to do with his life, too. I get so caught up in my own dramas and dissatisfactions that I take him for granted and think that whatever *I* want, he'll automatically want, too. But he doesn't.

Which, in turn, makes me worry we're just too *different*, me and Jack.

'I say brocc'lee, he says brocc-ol-eye; he loves summer, I love winter . . .' I say this out loud.

'What's that got to do with anything?' he asks.

'Only everything,' I say, exasperated that he can't see the deeper meaning.

'I love coats and jumpers and thick, woolly socks.'

'So? So do I. When it's chilly.'

'Yeah – but it's summer now, the sun's beating down on us and I feel like going inside, closing the curtains, putting a roast on and cuddling up on the couch.' My mouth starts watering at the thought of roast potatoes and gravy. I haven't eaten much today – I'm really getting into the whole Weight Watchers points thing.

'Yeah, well, chubsie – you're just a freak.'

'But that's why I don't want to go back to Oz – too bloody hot!'

'It'd be great! Think how good the outdoorsy life'd be for Joey—'

'She can do all that outdoors stuff here! So she'll have to wear a few more layers when it gets cold, but kids here do everything Aussie kids do . . . Look out by the river in winter, they're all out there in their canoes and kayaks—'

'The *rich* kids are. The ones whose parents can afford private schools. Everyone else's are hanging round the 6-Ten at night.'

'Oh, rollocks! Anyway, Joey's big and blokey enough already, without subjecting her to the roughness of Aussie kids.'

And I should know – I used to be one of them.

'She'll love it! She's going to make a great prop forward.'

My stomach starts rumbling loudly.

'The food's a lot better out there,' he says, looking at my tummy. 'More variety; fresher, cheaper – and the fish! Even *I* might get into fish more out there. Your dad's always banging on about how warm water fish tastes so much better than poor old cold water cod or haddock.'

'Anything tastes better than that Captain Birds Eye stuff *you* call fish – and insist on feeding to Joey.'

'Hey! Don't diss the Captain,' he says and salutes. 'And get some Febreze next time you're out, will you? After all that broccoli and salmon *you* insist on feeding her, the house stinks!'

How he always manages to lighten things up when I'm getting all heavy and serious is beyond me. He's so upbeat and positive.

'But the telly's so crap out there!' I say.

'We won't *need* telly when we're out there – we'll be too busy *doing* things.'

'The kids' telly's a-*tro*-cious, too. Ever seen *The Wiggles*? Talk about creepy . . .'

'*All* kids' telly's creepy – what's that *Night Garden* thing all about?'

He's right, you know.

'Unfurrow that brow and come here,' he says.

I go over to the other side of the table and sit on his lap. Gingerly. Don't want to break his legs with the full force of me all at once.

'Just promise me you'll think about it,' he says, nuzzling my ear. 'I'd be so much happier back out there. Just the thought of it's cheered me up.'

Then he starts burbling on about work and I tune out, nodding here and there whenever I hear him pause.

Poor guy, I think. It's not like he has any friends out here. And at least I've got the POP Club. And I can't be easy to live with. Even at the best of times.

I think back to when we met and how we couldn't get enough of each other then. I suppose it's the same old story – the first, fine, careless rapture and all that. I remember thinking he looked like Ali G then. Not Ali G as such – the guy who plays him. Sacha Baron Cohen. Yes! *Gorgeous*. I think, anyway. I've got a real thing for heavy eyebrows and big lips, just like Sacha – uh, I mean Jack.

'So I'm going to go for the promotion, even though I won't get it. Just show willing, I suppose. You listening to me?'

Jack puts his hands around my waist and strains, doing his best to lift me up off his lap. 'Can you . . . get . . . up? My leg's gone to sleep, I think . . .'

'Hmm? Yeah, go on,' I say dreamily, standing up. 'No! Bugger! I'm late for the meeting!'

And then quickly, like it's no big deal, he says:

'Oh – and I'm going to stay up in Paddo tomorrow night and Friday night, if that's OK. Leaving do at work.'

My light mood suddenly darkens and all I see before me are endless tussles with Joey for the next couple of days – and a groaning, hungover Jack on the couch all day on Saturday, snoozing in front of the football. And if I say anything about going to the playground together, as a family, all I'll get from Jack are moans about 'his' weekend and how tired he is. Happens all the time.

I tell myself not to be mean or selfish – the commute is horrible for Jack and he deserves a rest. He needs to have some fun, see his friends, go out, have a laugh . . . I try to be accommodating and nice and bright and breezy – I want to say: 'Of course, that's fine! And you don't need to ask my permission, darling!' But what I end up coming out with is:

'A-bloody-*gain*? Jesus, Jack – you're in London more than you're here lately. What's going on?'

'Nothing,' he says, his smile fading.

My eyes narrow suspiciously as I make my way to leave. Maybe he's *rendez-vous*-ing with his girlfriend. But if he's having such a wonderful time with her, why would he want to move to Australia? And if he was so in love with her, wouldn't he want to have a baby with her, not me?

'Well, I won't get pregnant if you're never here . . .'

'I'm always here! Either here or at work . . . Bloody hell, Rox – why won't you ever give me a break?'

'What about me? Maybe I need a break!'

And then he drops the bombshell on me.

'Maybe I need a break,' he says softly. 'From you.'

15

'Think I'm in trouble with 'im indoors tonight,' I say to Paul, who's taking his backpack off the bench next to him to make room for Olivia.

'What have you done now?' he asks me and smiles up at Liv as she lowers her considerably smaller bum on to the seat. That Weight Watchers must really be working for her.

'Nothing! Sometimes I tune out and stop listening to him blathering on about work promotions, but really, nothing!'

'Maybe that's the problem,' he says, finally looking at me.

'Apart from look after Joey all day!' I add hastily.

'But can't you see it from his side?'

'Yes, I can! Far as I can see, he's got all the time in the world for himself – and he gets paid for it.'

'Bollocks,' says Paul, going a bit red in the face. 'I used to have the same argument with my ex-wife. While she'd be at home, I'd be slaving at work, stressing that I'd lose my job and worrying about how the hell I'd then pay our mortgage, the bills and Tobi's food and clothes . . .'

I listen, fascinated to hear the other side of the story, and sip my tomato juice. Well, I don't want to be tempted to have any cigarettes tonight, so I'm off the beers.

'And because I *hate* it,' Paul goes on. 'I only do it for the money. Sooo dull. I'm not technical, really, at all – I'm more like the office manager. Much rather be doing something creative – something fulfilling or fun or interesting with my time.'

I know Jack feels exactly the same way about IT. He's often said he'd like to be a full-time photographer or plumber – something that he could really get into, find some satisfaction in. And he'd much rather work for himself as opposed to a couple of twenty-five-year-old jumped-up kids making loads of money out of his hard labour.

'So he's probably got all that to contend with and then when he gets home, you give him a hard time, won't let him relax – the guy can't get a break.'

'Maybe we both need one,' I say, looking at Olivia. 'A trial separation or something.'

'Slippery slope,' she says. 'Once you start going down that road, it's pretty much over. And then what would you do? At least now you have someone to have rows with.'

'And at least you guys talk,' Carina adds. 'Even if it's arguing, at least you spend time together communicating.'

She swizzles the ice and lemon around in her empty G&T glass with her straw.

'My old man barely sees me as human, sometimes. Incapable of conversation. He comes home, well after the kids are in bed, we eat together at opposite ends of the long dining table, miles apart, and then he goes out again. Doesn't get back till three or four in the morning. I'm lucky if I even get a "Hi, honey, I'm home!"'

We all stare at Carina. This is the most she's let us in on her life ever. And suddenly she seems softer, more feminine – more likeable.

'You must be pretty lonely,' Liv says, speaking for us all.

'Sometimes,' Carina sniffs and straightens her back. 'I blame myself, really, for giving up work. Never should have given away the camaraderie, the stimulation, the money – the independence. Now I feel a bit worthless, useless. And I don't know if I can do it, make a go of my own business, you know? Zero confidence.'

You'd never think it to look at her. She always seems so together, so on top of it all, so stridently capable, so fairly *bursting* with confidence.

Tim puts his arm round Carina's shoulder and says:

'Course you can do it, love. You've got all the guts in the world to make it work. Brains, beauty . . . and we're all right behind you, aren't we?'

He raises his glass and we all follow suit.

'To Carina!' cheers Tim.

'To the bar for me, I'm all out,' smiles Carina. 'Anyone else for another one?'

And as she goes inside with our order, Tim asks June whether she can remember what it was like giving birth.

'Cheeky!' says June, secretly loving the attention.

'No, really, I'm not being rude about your age, it's just that everyone says you forget what it feels like, otherwise you'd never have another one. Obviously, I'll never know what it's like and I've always been curious.'

'Urgh. Not one of those men that says: "I wish I could experience the pain of childbirth", are you? My ex said that once,' says Liv.

'I can remember,' I say. '*Horrendous*.'

'Well, there's a surprise.' Tim winks at me. 'No, go on!'

'Seven hours of gut-wrenching terror – had my eyes shut tight the whole time, holding on to Jack's arms and kicking him in the shins.'

'Jack was there? Lucky old you,' says Liv. 'I was completely by myself. For days. As usual.'

Paul puts a tentative arm around Liv. She smiles and puts her head on his shoulder.

'We were at the hospital right next to Wormwood Scrubs in London,' I continue. 'Seven hours of violent, brutal murder in my belly.'

'Didn't you have an epidural?' asks Carina incredulously.

'I was screaming for it! But they wouldn't *give* me an

epi – said there were other emergencies, but I knew it was a midwife conspiracy to try to make me have a so-called natural birth—'

'Ha! Vastly over-rated,' laughs Carina. 'So my sister says, anyway. She expected to feel empowered and to want to roar like a lion afterwards, but all she wanted was to get a divorce immediately and sleep for six years.'

'So finally I get the epi,' I go on, 'and a doctor comes in and examines me for the first time since we got there and tells me to stop pushing because Joey is stuck – too big for my pelvis. Three hours later, I've had a caesarean, Joey's all battered and bruised and Jack tells me I outdid myself in the swearing stakes. Says they got complaints from the prisoners next door!'

'You know, I like the sound of Jack,' says June. 'I didn't talk to him much the other night, but he sounds solid to me. I know you two fight a lot, but that's just having kids, isn't it? The pressure can seem intolerable at times. I remember *that* well, Tim. And it doesn't let up, even when your kids have left home and had children of their own. If anything, it gets harder.'

'Nooooo!' Paul, Olivia, Carina and I chorus.

'But what did it feel like?'

'A tsunami in your tummy,' I offer. 'Wave after unstoppable, massive wave of crashing pain. And the backwash hurts like hell, too.'

'Friend of mine was in labour for twelve hours with her first and the worst she came out with was: "Oh my gosh!"

With her second, it was five hours and all she said was: "Oh!",' says Liv.

'Well maybe her babies weren't Space Hoppers in disguise,' I say, pinching one of Olivia's cigarettes (well, she gets a discount at the 6-Ten) and playing with it, unlit.

'Let me guess, Roxy, you didn't breastfeed. Am I right?' Tim asks.

'I tried,' I say, 'I really did. But I couldn't do it and it made me and Joey both so upset . . . particularly when Jack's mum grabbed my boob in front of everyone and tried to get Joey to latch on. It was hideous, just not worth the grief.'

'I would've slapped anyone who tried to do that to me,' snarls Carina. 'No one touches these bad boys for free. Apart from my surgeon, of course – and only then when we're in the consulting phase . . .'

No one bats an eyelid at this confession of boob-jobbery. Well, it's hardly a surprise, is it?

'Straight on to the bottle, my Stu,' smiles Liv. 'No one was around to force me to do otherwise.'

'Same with me and Emma,' says June. 'We didn't have all the haranguing that you girls have these days, all the value judgements placed on breastfeeding.'

Suddenly, we all turn to the beer garden door when we hear a shrill, ear-piercing:

'RAAAAH-ksanne!'

Barry.

'You don't have to smoke that fag tonight,' he grins

218

as he nears our table and grabs a chair from another one, turns its back and straddles it, tough seventies cop-style.

I put the cigarette back into Olivia's packet and introduce Barry as a hypnotist to the rest of the POP Clubbers.

'Actor, Rox-*ahn*, actor,' he says in his deepest, Brian Blessed-esque voice, putting his left hand on the right side of his chest and pulling himself up to his full height. Of approximately five-foot-nothing.

'What are you doing here?' I ask him.

He mumbles something about poor ticket sales resulting in a cancelled performance.

'No, no, no,' says June, putting a reassuring hand on Barry's shaking left hand, the one without a roll-up – or a drink – in it. 'Roxy means what are you doing here at the Pissed-Orf Parents Club, don't you, dear? She means what's your problem.'

'Oh, well,' he takes his hand out from under June's and strokes his goatee, 'that's easy. Endless verbals from the wife to get a *proper* job. She wants me to go back to accounting – even though I was made redundant and there aren't any jobs out there. She wants me to beg for my job back, so I can provide for her and the kids better. Throw away my acting dreams, just like that, all because she wants a bigger, nicer house and steak on the dinner table – instead of our place up your end, so to speak, Roxy, and chicken nuggets for tea on our laps in front of the goggle-box.'

'We were just talking about the pressure women put on men when they've had kids, weren't we?' Paul nods his head towards me and leans over to shake Barry's hand.

'Ah, issa noh so bad, issa nice-a place, ah shaddap-a-you face,' sings Barry.

Silence descends over the table.

'Ah, sorry, um, I, ah, old habits . . .' stutters Barry, eyeing up everyone's drinks.

'How rude of me,' says June. 'What would you like to drink, Barry?'

'Nothing, nothing. I'm fine, thanks. I'll get myself a Diet Coke in a minute. Just wanted to say hi first, let you know I was here. Can't afford to do rounds, though, soz about that. Cash flow probs at the mo – money too tight to mention . . . Cutbacks!' he shouts the last bit, doing quite a good impression of Mick Hucknall.

'Ooh, I loved Simply Red,' says June. 'Or, rather, my daughter did. Superb musicianship.'

'But Barry,' I butt in, 'you don't seem pissed off at all! You're always singing and smiling and—'

'Tears of a clown.' He cocks his head to one side and turns the sides of his mouth down with his yellow fingers.

'You like The Beat, too?' I raise my eyebrows.

'Smokey Robinson, sweetheart! The old soul greats knew a thing or two.'

'Oh yes!' June clasps her hands in front of her. 'Now you're talking!'

'It's not that the missus says as much to my face,

though,' Barry goes on, frowning and looking serious. 'What really gets me is she talks through the kids. She'll say stuff to them, knowing full-well I can hear. It's classic passive-aggressive behaviour.'

'Like what?' Olivia asks.

'Oh, well . . . This afternoon, *par example*, my sons were fighting over some toy and she said: "I know you hate sharing a room with your two brothers, but when Daddy goes back to his *PROPER ACCOUNTING JOB*, we'll move to a bigger house where we'll all have our own rooms and you'll have all your own toys, so you won't have to share anything. And then we'll all be happy, won't we?" Stuff like that, mainly.'

'Everyone does that, though, don't they?' I ask, thinking about mine and Jack's versions ('It's Daddy's turn to take you upstairs to brush your teeth and read you books and then try getting you to sleepy bye-byes tonight, isn't it . . . *Daddy?*' and 'If Mummy wasn't feeling so sick because she went to the POP Club last night, she would *love* to be playing with you right now, but she's leaving it all to Daddy because she's a selfish, bad mum who won't give me fifteen minutes to wind down even though I've been working hard all day. Ye-es!' or my other stock standard: 'Where's Daddy? I don't know, darling, probably playing on his computer or having a beer outside. Silly Daddy, eh? Silly Daddy not spending time with you!').

'Only if they're on the rocks,' says Paul. 'My ex used to

do that sort of thing all the time. Drove me mad. I think it's more a woman's thing.'

'Rubbish,' says Olivia.

'Yeah! Jack does it to me all the time,' I laugh.

'That's the *only* way my brother-in-law talks to me – indirectly, through Stu. In this ridiculous sing-song baby voice. Urgh!' adds Liv.

'My husband never did it. Not that he was around that much when my kids were young,' sighs June.

'My old man never talks to me – through the kids in a baby voice or otherwise,' shrugs Carina.

'I don't *talk* so much to the nippers as sing,' says Barry, throwing his arms out.

'No!' I say in mock surprise.

'I make up songs about them and what we're doing. The kids love it. Like last Christmas, I'd sing to my youngest, to the tune of "Santa Claus is Coming To Town": "Cream on bum and put nappy on . . . Trousers up, we're singing a song . . . Sally's ready to go in-to town!"'

'That's great,' says Tim. 'Know any songs about dads – or gay uncles – I can sing to my little 'uns?'

We rack our collective brains.

'"Daddy's Home"?' June raises her eyebrows. 'Cliff Richard?'

No one even dignifies that suggestion with a response.

'Nup, they're all about mums,' sighs Paul.

'Mama! Ooh-wooh-wooh-wooh!' Barry closes his eyes and does his best Freddie Mercury.

'Mama, I love you,' sings Olivia sweetly, doing a really good rendition of that Spice Girls song.

'Mama Mia! Here I go again!' scream Carina, Tim and June in unison, putting their arms around each other's shoulders like they're rugby boys singing victory songs after a match.

And then all the colour in Tim's face drains away, making him look albino. He's staring at the beer garden door, shaking.

'Jesus Christ,' he says slowly, angrily.

'Soo-per star!' shouts Barry, shutting his eyes tight again.

'No.' Tim drinks his Timblioni in one go and slams the glass back down, making the umbrella and a bit of ice fly out on to the table. 'He just thinks he is.'

We all turn to look at the old guy standing in the doorway.

'It's his ex.' I elbow June, chuffed with my insider knowledge.

'Is it, Tim?' asks June, peering at him as he grabs his man bag, clutches it to his chest and strides away towards the door.

'No it fucking isn't,' Tim says through gritted teeth over his shoulder. 'It's my *dad*.'

There's raised voices from Tim and his dad, lots of chest-poking and, eventually, they leave the beer garden together, shouting as they go, leaving everyone still there stunned into silence.

Except for Barry, of course, who can't help himself and says, in his best Shakespearean accent:

'Exeunt all!'

16

When I go into Joey's room on Sunday morning, I hold her, still in her sleeping bag, and we roll up the brightly-coloured black-out blind that's got the letters of the alphabet all over it.

'Shall we see what sort of day it is outside? Hmm? It was a bit wild and woolly last night, wasn't it? Now let's see if it's still raining. Rain, rain, go away, come again a— Bloody *HELL*!'

There's brown, muddy water flowing fast down what was the main road out the front of the house and it's come up to the front tyres of our car in the driveway.

'What's wrong?' Jack runs in, putting his bath robe on his (rather impressive, truth be told) naked form.

'She OK?' He's in a panic, holding his arms out to Joey.

'She's fine – but we're fuh . . . flooded in!'

We all stand there, looking out the window at the river running down our street.

'*Farking*—'

'Hey, hey, hey! Language in front of Joey,' I tell him off.

He looks at me and runs into our bedroom to dress. I get Joey into some clothes, chuck on my long-sleeved, black velvet maternity dress and we all go downstairs.

Jack's running about like a headless chicken.

'Calm down, will you?' I laugh. 'You'll freak Joey out.'

'My camera – where's my camera?' He's buried somewhere deep in the study and we can only faintly hear his muffled cry.

'Eh?' I shout out.

He emerges, expensive camera in one hand and its equally expensive carry-case in the other.

'Might need the long lens . . . and . . . wellies! Where are my fuh— wellies?!' he says, darting into the laundry.

'Daddy's losing it, isn't he? Yes! Daddy's lost the plot!' I say to Joey, who's opened up one of the kitchen cupboards and is throwing all the bits of the food processor on the floor.

'Right! I'm off to find out what's going on. If I'm not back in an hour, call for the coast guard!'

Joey crawls over to the telly and turns it on.

'Ooh, good idea,' I say. Beats the: 'No! Joey! Get away from that television!' she usually gets.

She looks surprised and smiles. A particularly toothy, cute smile.

'Good girl! No, no, get it off VH1 and put on the news.'

I hand her the remote. 'And while you're at it, make me a tea, will you?'

I pick her up and sit her on my lap after I've switched the channel to BBC News 24. Turns out the Thames has broken its banks and our whole area's flooded.

'Let's go upstairs and see if there are any camera crews or news teams in the street!'

I grab her and we go upstairs to look out her bedroom window again. But all I can see is some kids paddling down the street in a double kayak.

Joey fixes me with her steely gaze. She's hanging on to the seat of one of the kitchen chairs and I watch as her face goes a deeper shade of crimson with every second.

'It's OK, sweetie, you concentrate hard and it'll all be OK.'

I let her go to it and then finally, after five minutes of her stopping and starting, looking like she's about to explode, the unmistakeable smell of poo wafts over to me.

'But first, let's clean up your act, gorgey!' I pick her up – careful not to squish the contents of her nappy out – and we trudge upstairs again.

'Poooo-weeee!' Joey says when I undo her nappy.

'You got that right,' I say, inspecting her poo and fumbling about for a nappy sack.

Weird how Joey's bowel movements don't bother me at all any more – even if they seem to give her some grief.

Jack still finds it a bit hard to cope sometimes, though. But that's because he doesn't change nearly enough dirty nappies.

We hear Jack opening the front door and Joey wets herself when she hears him. All over the changing mat, just when I've finished wiping her down.

'What's it like? Are we going to get evacuated? What's happening?' I've got Joey on my hip and she's straining to get into her dad's arms.

Jack wriggles his feet out of his sodden wellies and comes inside.

'I dunno – there's not many people out there,' he says, looking into his camera. 'Someone said they're going to cut off the electricity if it looks like it might get worse.'

And slowly it dawns on me.

'Well, what will we do *then*? Electricity? That's the telly, isn't it?'

'We've got batteries – we can listen to the radio. But it's not definite and it's still on now, so what's for breakfast?'

'Bugger breakfast! We won't be able to make teas or sterilise Joey's bottles! Or heat up Weight Watchers one-point-per-can soup!'

I'm losing it now. I know Joey's supposed to be off the bottles, but I'm letting her down gently, slowly – we've still got that whole monster can of SMA to get through first. And how will I make her toast or pasta or scrambled eggs?

'We've got some jars of food for her, so she can eat that if worse comes to worst. But – oh!'

'What?'

'I was going to have a bath today! Was going to wash my hair and try to dry it in a new way. Buggeration – I was really looking forward to that . . .'

'It's not your birthday, is it?' he grins.

'We're watching the news – my God! Has the flood got to you? Are you all right?' Mum has phoned.

'Yeah, yeah, we're all fine,' I say, watching Joey try to get the whole light end of the big torch into her mouth. And nearly succeeding.

'They keep talking about Gloucestershire, but Riverside hardly rates a mention! Is it in your house? Thank *God* the new carpets aren't in yet!'

'No, no. It's pretty high in the driveway, but it hasn't got inside yet. Jack says it probably won't, either.'

'It's come a bit out of the blue, this flood, hasn't it?'

'It's been raining pretty heavily for a few days, but hardly anything to worry about, we thought.'

'What about Joey?'

'She's fine, but it's like there's a river running through the village.'

'A river runs through it, eh?' Dad's grabbed the phone from Mum. And not only does he think he's hilarious, he sounds as smug as hell, now he's found the perfect opportunity to bray about how he was right, his point has been

229

proven, and that moving to the country was a really dumb idea.

'Well, that's what you get when you leave the city,' he says.

'But they reckon London'll be underwater in a few years, don't they, Dad?'

'Ah, we'll be long gone by then,' he says.

I hate it when Dad talks about not being here, dying. Can't bear it.

'Don't say that!'

'Why? We're all going to die someday, sweetheart – it's hardly news to you, is it?'

And the line goes dead.

'Dad? Dad? You there? Hello?'

No sound. I look up and see the lights've gone out, too.

Everything's suddenly really dark. And then it starts bucketing down outside. I mean, it's really coming down hard. Lightning flashes and I drop the phone on the floor and run into the front room where Jack's sitting on the floor, leaning against the couch, trying to prise big, fat batteries out of Joey's big, fat fists and put them into the portable radio.

'Come on,' he laughs. 'You don't need two at a time! Just give me one, then.'

I scream as the thunder hits. Joey starts crying.

'Now you've done it,' says Jack and picks Joey up for a cuddle, immediately soothing her.

'What are we going to do? I'm scared now!' I jump on

the couch and pull my knees into my chest, as far as my tummy will allow.

'It's coming in! Jack! It's coming in!'

'Keep your hair on, Rox! You'll upset Joey again!'

The rain hammers at our house, getting louder and louder, threatening to smash the window panes.

'It's hail!' I shout. 'Look! They're nearly the size of Sydney hailstones! Look!'

'Yeah, all right. Calm *down*, though, will you?!'

My mobile rings and it winds me up even more, not being able to find it in my ridiculously over-stuffed handbag.

'What happened?'

It's Mum again.

'They've cut the electricity off!' I shout, barely able to hear myself. 'And it's hailing now – huge hailstones!'

'Are you OK?'

'Yeah! Jack's a bit scared, but Joey's trying to calm him down!' I smile at Jack rocking Joey in his arms. '*FARKING HELL*!'

'What?' asks Mum.

'Language!' shouts Jack.

'The hail's coming down the bloody chimney into the fireplace! Jesus!'

Big blobs of ice bounce off the coal in the fireplace and then smack on to the kitchen floor, skidding across it.

Joey's fixated and breaks free of Jack's embrace, crawling over to the nearest hailstone and shoving it in her mouth.

'No! Joey, no! Jack?!'

'Can you drive anywhere? Can you get out of Riverside?' That was Mum.

'I don't know! Why?!'

'Listen. Get out of there while you can – while you're not trapped. God knows what'll happen. Drive to a hotel and stay the night – we'll pay for it.'

I repeat this to Jack as he goes arse over tit, slipping on a hailstone.

I start laughing hysterically – you know, like when you're on a rollercoaster and scared stupid.

'I'll call you later!' I yell.

You don't have to tell me and Jack something like that twice – she'll pay for it? Absolute legend, my mum. So we hightail it out of there, once we've spent a good hour faffing around in the excitement and packing things that Joey might (but probably won't) need.

I knock on the neighbours' door and let them know we're leaving. Jules stands on the doorstep.

'So listen – the top of our cooker is gas, so if you need to cook anything, use ours. Here's a key,' I say as Jack loads the car, yelling: 'Come on!' every five seconds.

They've already got all their candles lit inside, I see when I look past Jules. Tom's in their front room with a chunky jumper on, pouring two big glasses of red wine. All they need is a roaring fire and the cosy scene'd be set. But even though it's lashing down and dark, it's not cold – it's June for God's sake!

'Isn't it exciting?' says Jules.

'Hmm – a bit, I suppose. But aren't you scared?' I ask her.

'No! It's so romantic!'

'Stop fannying about, will you?!' Jack shouts. 'I'm getting drenched!'

'All right, all right!' I holler back. 'It *would* be quite romantic, if I wasn't frightened. Um, for Joey, I mean. It's different when you have kids.'

'Aah,' she sighs. 'When are you going to have another one?' As she asks me this, she strokes the three strands of Joey's sopping wet fringe out of her eyes. I hadn't noticed before now, but her hair's getting quite long these days. Still baldy in bits, but quite long where there *is* hair.

Jack beeps our horn.

'Gotta go! Do ring me if it gets any more horrendous!'

And with that, we float out of Riverside, finally touching tarmac once we get to Riverside Heights, making it easier to drive into the country proper.

'We're never going to find anywhere!'

We've been driving around for what feels like hours, even though it's only been thirty minutes. Joey's snoozing happily in her car seat in the back, despite – or because of – the din going on in the front – it is what she's used to, after all. Apart from Jack and I shouting at each other – not fighting, just yelling to be heard – the rain's pelting the car and we've got the radio turned up loud.

'. . . not seen flooding like this since 1897 . . . parts of Gloucestershire hit worst . . . heavy rain and more flooding expected . . .'

We drive around for a while and eventually find ourselves in a quaint little village called Aldenham.

'Isn't it gorgeous?' I say, staring out the window at the old Tudor façades and cobble-stoned street.

'Fabulous,' says Jack, his eyes never leaving the road. 'So can we get a room somewhere here and get settled? I'm cream crackered.'

We drive to the nearest hotel and it's lovely. Their gazebo/summer house/bistro on the brook outside the main house has been knocked down by the rain and the decking's all flooded, but you can tell it'd be a nice place for a wedding. In a dry summer. Must remember the place if Jack and I ever do get around to tying the knot.

The receptionist helps us with all Joey's stuff and takes us to our room, complete with massive four-poster bed and, most importantly, huge, wide-screen TV on the wall.

'There's your cot and some bedding and there are DVDs in the cabinet next to the mini bar,' she explains.

'Great!' says Jack, flinging himself on to the bed and bashing his ankles against one of the posters. Sometimes even *he* forgets he's well over six foot.

'Great!' a pained Jack says again, sarcastically, getting up slowly from the bed.

'Ooh, nice bathroom,' I coo as I pick Joey up off the

234

white tiled floor and gaze at the roll-top bath. Above the bathroom sink, on a plain glass shelf, is a selection of Molton Brown bath and shower products: conditioner, shampoo, body wash – I put Joey down on the floor and open each bottle to take a sniff.

'Hmmm, I love this stuff!' I can't help but enthuse out loud.

'Hey look,' says Jack, rummaging about in the mini bar/DVD cabinet.

'Yeah, I know – I *have* seen a mini bar before, you know. Cute little bottles. But don't be fooled – they charge like wounded bulls for those.'

'No!' he says. 'They've got *South Pacific*! You've never seen it, have you?'

No, I haven't. The only musicals I've seen are *Annie*, when I was a kid, and *West Side Story*, which I loved. Well, I really like that bit where Rita Moreno and all the other Puerto Ricans sing 'America', at any rate.

'Bung it on, then,' I say, fluffing up the pillows against the wall at the top of the bed.

He does.

'That's got to be bad for her eyes,' I tut, nodding my head at Joey, who's sitting in the middle of the bed, staring at the TV screen.

'Relax,' whispers Jack. 'This is my favourite bit – this song always makes me cry.'

'You are so IN,' I say, as someone starts singing and looking wistfully into the distance.

'Bally Hi? Is that somewhere in Ireland? Like *Ballykissangel*?' I poke Jack's arm.

'Shh!' He puts his finger to his lips and then wipes a tear from his eye.

Joey wriggles up to the top of the bed and lies between us. Ten minutes later, we hear her snoring softly and swap a look that says: 'Oh, isn't she gorgeous?'

We slowly and quietly organise her into the cot and then lie down together on the big bed, spooning as we gaze at our sweet sleeper.

'Thought any more about the Blue Mountains?' Jack whispers in my ear.

'I suppose I just don't want to leave Mum,' I say.

'She lives in Sweden!'

'Shh! But she's also in London a lot. If I had my way, we'd move back to London.'

'Think of the weather, the great outdoors—'

'But it's sooo hot in Australia. And with global warming it's going to be unbearable—'

'And London'll be totally underwater in a couple of years because of it. You said so yourself, to your dad. Let's head for the hills, I say – the blue ones!'

'I'm really not sure I want to leave Mum.'

God, I sound like such a mummy's girl. I've got to come up with another argument . . .

'And if I feel isolated and out of it in Riverside, the Blue Mountains is going to be a *hundred* times worse!'

'But think of Joey.'

'I am. She needs to see her granny!'

'I don't see your mum breaking her neck to see Joey, coming up to Riverside every chance she gets.'

'That's not fair – she's got her own things to do. She's got a life apart from me and her grandkids.'

'And she'd want you to have a life apart from her! With me! And your *own* kids . . .'

Kids. Plural.

'I couldn't take another year like the one we've just had – couldn't *bear* it.'

'It'd be totally different – we'd know what to do, now, with a new baby.'

'We'd have to have sex for that to happen, anyway.'

'Forget it, then.' I hear him smile.

'You really ARE all gong and no dinner!' Ha! Got it in!

'And you're nearly as old as Blanche!' He puts one arm behind his head and rolls on to his back, looking at the ceiling.

'We really don't have the luxury of time if we're going to have any more nippers,' he goes on. '*Together*.'

'Yeah. You can have kids any time, can't you? When you're sixty-four, if you live that long. With some young popsie who takes your fetid old fancy.'

'I suppose so,' he says, putting his arm back around my waist and kissing my ear. 'Especially with my feisty one hundred (*kiss*) and thirty-seven (*kiss*) million.'

When I open my eyes the next morning, Jack and I are still

fully clothed, in the exact same position. I look at Joey, who's staring back at me, beaming. I smile broadly at her and extend my right arm to the cot, my finger stroking her cheek. Now this is what it should be like all the time, I think to myself: cosy and warm, safe and snug, all happy together.

So happy, in fact, that I bet Jack's forgotten all about the other night when he said he needed a break from me, in his typical baby-tantrum style. And even if he still remembers saying it, he wouldn't feel the same way now, would he? I mean, this is just so nice.

I don't want to move, don't want to break up the lovely scene. But when my mobile bleeps, letting me know I've got a text, I slowly and carefully extricate myself from Jack's arm and pick Joey up. I plant a big, wet kiss on her giggling mouth and while I bounce her on my hip, rummage through my handbag for the phone. The text is from Olivia:

> Where r u? U OK?
> Call if u can – am
> worried about you! XXX

Worried? About me? I'm touched. And immediately appalled by my selfishness. In all the excitement of yesterday, I completely forgot about her and her family across the road – they must have been totally submerged by the flood. And the thought of her welfare or whereabouts hasn't even crossed my mind.

I text her back as fast as I can (which is pretty slowly, truth be told – I'm rubbish at texting), and it takes approximately three seconds after I've sent my message for her reply to arrive.

> Nightmare! But all alive
> and well. See you on Wed!
> Stay safe XXX

17

When I get to The Swan the following Wednesday, it feels different – not as jolly as usual, even though I can hear Tim laughing.

'Thanks,' I say to the barmaid and scurry outside into the beer garden with my tomato juice.

It's pretty much empty, save for the POP Clubbers.

'And here she is!' says Tim as I approach the table. He stands up, thrusts his elbows out to the side, and points with both index fingers to his chest. He's wearing a white T-shirt and in big, black writing it says:

KIDS GETTING
ON YOUR
TITS?

I smile.

'No, wait, wait!' he says excitedly and turns his back to me.

GET 'EM OFF YOUR BACK
AT THE
PISSED-OFF
PARENT'S CLUB

'No need for an apostrophe there,' says June.

'What-*evah*, June,' he says, mock-annoyed. 'I'm a designer, darling, not a scribe. I have an eye for the fabulous. You like?'

'It's great!' I laugh.

And instantly I'm reminded of a slogan T-shirt I saw in Sydney once. There was this gorgeous surfie guy in a Bondi cafe at the next table. He had salty, sea-swept blond hair, a deeply tanned face and the most piercing aquamarine eyes I'd ever seen. But I took it as a personal affront when he left the cafe and the back of his T-shirt said:

FAT CHICKS
SHIT ME

'Made you one, too, Roxy,' Tim says, pulling a white bundle out of his bag. 'Thought you might like it.'

I unravel the shirt and hold it up in front of my face.

GET IT OFF YOUR
CHEST
AT THE
PISSED-OFF
PARENT'S CLUB

'It's brilliant!' I gush. 'But it's huuuuge! How fat do *you* think I am?' I look at the label – it's a size eighteen.

Tim's suspiciously silent.

'Barry told me to pass on his apologies, but he's got a performance on tonight, so he can't make it,' I say, sitting down.

'Oh! Shame,' sighs June.

'Livvy not here yet?' I ask her.

'Doesn't look like it,' says Paul. 'She *will* be here, though, won't she?'

'Yes, yes – but she was pretty badly hit by the flood,' I say. 'I'll give her a ring if she's not here soon.'

Paul nods eagerly.

'So Tim,' I grin. 'what's the deal with you and your dad?'

'He can't get his head round my sister being an unmarried mother and me being gay. Never has, never will,' he says, calmly sipping his Timblioni.

'But why did he turn up here and drag you away?'

'Well,' Tim starts a little reluctantly, 'he thinks the POP Club is responsible for the slow but sure erosion of decent family values in the village. Wants me to split the Club up, get it disbanded. But his opposition to it just makes me even more keen for it to be a success.'

'Bloody hell—'

'Yep, hell – that comes into it a lot,' he smiles.

'Let's leave that one, shall we?' says June, squeezing my knee.

Just then, Olivia comes running up to the table.

'Soz I'm late,' she pants, rifling through her bag for her cigarettes. 'We're still cleaning up – well, I say "we", but let's face it, I'm doing all the cleaning while my *evil sister* barks orders at me.'

'Just like Cinderella,' says Paul wistfully.

'Yeah? Well, where's my handsome prince then?'

Paul goes a bit red.

'It's total devastation back there, honestly,' she says. 'I was working and my sister was babysitting Stuart and water started rushing into the house.'

She lights up swiftly and goes on.

'Stu was asleep upstairs, thank God – he's totally fine.'

'Oh, that's good. What about your carpets?' Carina asks.

'Totally sodden. We've pulled them all out and now there's just a concrete floor.'

'How awful!' says June.

'Yeah. My sister managed to get the TV upstairs in time, so . . .'

'*That's* a relief!' Tim puts his hand camply on his chest.

'Yeah. Couches are a bit manky now, though.'

'Will your insurance sort everything out?' Paul asks.

'Haven't got any.'

'Really?' June can't hide the disbelief in her voice.

'They never got around to it. It's almost funny – *almost* – that their precious Berber carpet and stupidly expensive furnishings are ruined now . . .'

'Still, at least you and your family are all safe and sound,' offers Paul.

'Yeah,' sniffs Olivia. 'Every cloud . . .'

'On the news they kept saying there was a sort of spirit of the blitz thing going on in Gloucestershire,' says June. 'Community spirit at an all-time high, apparently. But they never really touched on Riverside. I didn't see much of the flood, I must say, being at the other end of town . . .'

'Our bit of the road is OK,' I offer.

'It's around the corner from you that's really taken the brunt of it all,' says Olivia sadly.

'Will there be any financial recompense from the government for you and your family, Liv?' June asks.

'It'll be a frosty Friday in hell before *that* ever happens,' she says.

'Or a floody Saturday in Riverside,' says Tim. 'Ooh, I wish there was something I could do to help out . . .'

'But what can you do?' asks Olivia.

'I don't know,' says Tim dejectedly. 'There must be a flood relief fund . . .'

'Hey!' Paul sits bolt upright. 'What if *we* did something to help? You know, as a club, the Pissed-Off Parents!'

And suddenly I feel transported to the pages of the Enid Blyton *Famous Five* books of my childhood. So much so that when Olivia opens her mouth to speak, I expect to hear her say: 'Let's have lashings of ginger beer!' but instead she says:

'Like what?'

'I dunno!' says Paul, slumping down again.

We all sit there, thinking. Drinking and thinking until . . .

'I've got it!' Carina slams her palm down on the table. 'What do we do best?'

'Moan,' I suggest.

'Yes, that. And?'

'Whinge?' asks Tim.

'Oh, for God's sake.' Carina's getting impatient. 'We drink! Like fish!'

'Speak for yourself,' says Tim quietly and then coughs. 'So?'

'So-oh,' Carina goes on slowly, 'we get sponsored for it. Every penny we make will go to the flood relief fund.'

'How would that work?' I wonder out loud.

'I know!' Paul's sitting up straight again. 'Every drink we buy, we double the price and donate it!'

'Jesus, calm down,' I say, thinking I must have about ten pounds left in my account. If I'm lucky.

'You finished with these, love?' The barmaid's come over to collect the empties. 'Hey, Liv, how're you, y'all right?'

'Not too bad, you?' smiles Liv.

'Ho, bearing up,' she sighs and walks away.

'Poor thing – she got flooded worse than us,' says Olivia. 'It's just her on her own with her little girl. Can't've been easy for them, without a man around.'

'Know how she feels,' says Tim.

'He died, apparently,' Liv goes on. 'When her daughter, Ella, was three. Cancer.'

She whispers the word 'cancer'.

Carina stubs her cigarette out while I put back the one I just stole out of Olivia's pack.

'So how are we going to do this?' asks Tim, crossing his arms on his lap, hugging himself.

'I know,' says Carina, eyes fixed on a spot just over my head.

I look around and see a blackboard. It says:

> TAPAS, FLAMENCO DANCING
>
> AND PAELLA!
>
> HERE EVERY THURSDAY
>
> 6-12 p.m.
>
> HALF PRICE SAN MIGUEL ALL NIGHT
>
> OLÉ!

'We ask them to put on a night, a big night dedicated to the flood victims. The whole village'll come out in support and the pub will donate all their takings for that night!' Carina yelps and motions for June to pass her the pad and pen and starts scribbling.

'Sounds like a plan,' says Olivia, impressed.

'Sounds like a *great* plan,' agrees Paul.

'Carina! You're an absolute champion,' I say.

'I'll design some posters,' says Tim. 'Some big, eye-catching posters, printed professionally. It will be morally incumbent on the good people of Riverside to attend said piss-up!'

'And it'll be such good PR for the pub – I'll go and have a word with the manager,' says Carina.

'I'll come with you.' I stand up. 'I've sort of met him before.'

We go into the front bar and the chef/owner is standing behind the bar, flicking through a copy of *Village Life*.

'Ah, the lovely Roxane,' he says.

'Hello there!' Can't for the life of me remember his name.

'How are you this evening?'

'Better than the last time I saw you,' I say sheepishly.

'Thank you so much for your wonderful review,' he says, holding the magazine up.

'We have a proposition for you,' says Carina, rather seductively if I'm not mistaken.

'I see,' says the chef, smiling saucily at her. 'How can I help you then, ladies?'

Carina pitches the event to him and he goes for it. She's so charming, who wouldn't do whatever she asked?

'In fact,' says the chef, 'we'll *double* the takings, from the pub's coffers. When would you like to do it?'

'As soon as possible,' says Carina.

'OK, what about July seventh, in three weeks' time?'

'Done!' Carina says and I follow her back outside to fill the others in.

'Bring everyone you know in Riverside – and beyond!' Carina says, like Buzz Lightyear.

'Floody hell!' says Tim. 'Ooh, I like that!'

'I'd better book the hairdresser for that afternoon, then,' says Carina, looking crossly at her perfect French manicured nails, as though she doesn't go every week anyway.

'And I'd better get going – we'll have to work fast on this one, people!' says Tim, putting his jacket on, draining his Timblioni and making for the door.

'Take my mobile number, Tim!' June calls out after him. 'Don't want any more embarrassing grammatical gaffes!'

'And let me see the posters before you put them up,' cries out Carina. 'This could be just the thing to seriously put the country arm of my business on the map!'

18

The next day, when I drop Joey off at the nursery, a huge sign on their front door says:

FLOODY HELL!

WHAT: A night of drinking, dancing and donating
WHEN: Saturday, July 7, 5–12 p.m.
WHERE: The Swan
WHY: To lend your support to and raise money for Riverside's flood victims

COME ALONG AND GET WET FOR A GOOD CAUSE!

Brought to you by
WEDDINGS! PARTIES! ANYTHING! EVENTS
MANAGEMENT
and
THE PISSED-OFF PARENTS CLUB
in association with
THE SWAN PUBLIC HOUSE

'Poor Liv,' I say, shaking my head as I study the poster. 'No contents insurance – imagine how horrendous that'd be.'

I untangle Joey from the sophisticated system of ropes and pulleys that has her fully harnessed and trussed up in her buggy, pick her up and let her push the button of the nursery's doorbell.

Joey jumps out of my embrace just as my lips are about to make contact with her cheek and I get a mouthful of sticky fingers and sharp nails instead. She crawls over to the baby room with not so much as a backward glance and the sweet sorrow of our parting is, once again, short-lived. And hopelessly one-sided.

'Have a good time, sweetie!' I call out to her and wave half-heartedly as one of the nursery ladies shoots me a pitying don't-they-just-break-your-heart glance. I reply with my standard yes-they-do-and-your-arms-too-if-they're-anywhere-as-beefy-as-this-one look and I step outside to scrutinise the poster some more.

I must say, I'm totally impressed by the fast work of Tim and, much as I hate to admit it, Carina. They've done the POP Club proud. I thrust my hand into my jacket pocket and finger my mobile phone. I would call Jack to tell him all about it, but he's playing golf this afternoon.

I call Olivia, instead, to see how she is.

'Roxy!' she shrieks.

'Hey!' I shout back. 'Just wondering what you were up to, whether you fancied a tea at the Really Rather Goo—'

250

'I'm up to my neck in floody water, if you must know – this cleaning up's taking aaaaa-ges!'

'You poor thing . . .'

'I've been at it all bloody day, I'm well due a break. Why don't you come over?'

'OK – see you in five.'

I've never seen Olivia's place. Her sister bought it from the council a few years ago, so even though it's in the poorer part of Riverside, it's all theirs. To hear Olivia describe her sister and brother-in-law, they're quite the aspirational couple – all designer labels and status symbols. And because they don't have kids, they've got money to burn. But not on boring things like insurance, as it turns out.

It's around the corner and up the street a bit from where I live, and when I get there, Olivia's standing in the front yard, right by a knocked-down, uprooted willow tree. She's got one leg up on the tree's trunk, rocking her pram.

'Thought you'd never get here!' She flicks her dog-end into the still-damp street and it hisses.

'Oh, Liv.' I lean my head to one side.

'Come and have a quick butcher's inside, then we'll go to the Really Rather Good, yeah?'

The whole street looks like the back paddocks at the end of a particularly rainy, muddy Glastonbury festival. There's the bedraggled remains of once-potted plants scattered about; a range cooker, just like ours, on its side by a tree and an overturned car on the neighbours' front garden.

Inside, there are soggy books piled high, lining the tide-marked walls next to sodden IKEA bookcases. Their kitchen benchtops are packed with food processors, a posh Dualit toaster and kettle, Wedgwood plates and various other expensive-looking kitchen-y bits and bobs. The concrete floor beneath our feet seems to squelch with every step. It sort of looks like our place – except we *asked* and *paid* for the privilege of the destruction.

'You poor thing! Where do you sleep?'

'Upstairs, same as always.'

'Where's your sister and brother-in-law?'

'At work, same as always.'

'Have you done all the cleaning up?'

'Actually, they did help in the end. And we've all got a bit closer, too – there's nothing like a bit of personal tragedy and trauma to humble you, knock you off your high and mighty pedestal for a while and make you see what's really important in this life.'

'So sorry,' I mumble. 'I had no idea it was this bad – what can I do to help?'

'Thanks – but nothing,' she says. 'We're nearly there now. And I'm quite enjoying the cleaning up – makes me feel useful. And needed.'

I look around and figure it's going to take weeks to clean all this up.

'So anyway – that's the grand tour done,' she says. 'I'm

out of fags. Mind stopping in at the 6-Ten before we go to the caff?'

And we tread warily through the house, stepping outside, careful not to slip into the mud bath.

Just as we get to the front door of the 6-Ten, Tim comes stumbling out, dragged by two tiny but obviously very strong kids in identical clothing.

'Timmy!' I cry, delighted to see him.

'Can't stop, Clubbers!' he says over his shoulder as the twins pull him away. 'We're off to Tumble Tots!'

We admire the massive fundraiser-night poster on the door and once inside, Liv chats away to the girl serving at the till while I get some supplies for dinner. I might as well try to make the hard-working, bacon-home-bringing Jack a meal tonight.

I'm feeling lucky, compared to Olivia, and you never know, the intimate atmosphere of dinner by candlelight might just help me rediscover my long-lost libido – if Jack comes back from golf without any love bites, that is.

But what with the flood and the electricity being cut off, there's no candles or wine left at the 6-Ten. Fortuitously, though, there's still lots of Weight Watchers bangers, mash and gravy ready meals left, so I grab three (two for Jack, one for me) and join Olivia at the counter.

'Soooo,' Olivia's saying, running a finger along the edge of the plywood countertop, 'Marcus in?'

'Yeah,' says the girl. 'In the stock room, sorting out the bulk order for Lady Muck.'

Olivia leans down to me and whispers: 'Carina.'

Just then the hot manager of the shop who must be Marcus, staggers over to the counter, overloaded with cases of Bombay Sapphire. He nearly drops them, but gently lowers them down and stacks them neatly on the floor.

'Olivia, honey!' he squeals, straightening up and putting one hand on his hip, the other to his collarbone. 'To what do we owe the unexpected pleasure of your company this fine afternoon?'

'Fags,' smiles Liv and looks up at him from under her distinctly fluttering eyelashes.

'Where?' He goes all wide-eyed in pretend fear and looks around as though he's in a panic. 'I'll get my shotgun!'

We all giggle.

'Tracey, will you get the Marly cartons from out back? Damn sight lighter than these boxes of booze.'

'Soooo,' Olivia says again, blushing. 'How's it been? Business, I mean.'

'Oh, you know. Up and down.' He looks over our heads and sees we're the only ones in the shop. Then he bends down a bit, leans into Olivia and says quietly: 'Hate to say it, really, but natural disasters are brilliant for business. No offence, Livvy.'

'No, no – none taken.' Liv puts her hand on his forearm and fixes him with an intense gaze.

We all jump back from our cosy huddle when we hear the front door bell tinkle. We look around and see a blur of pale pink and argyle, oversized sunnies and black, shiny hair coming towards us.

'Oh, thanks, doll,' purrs a winking Carina. 'You're a life-saver!'

Carina sweeps me and Olivia aside and slobbers all over both of Marcus' cheeks.

'And hello you two! Be a pair of loves and give us a hand with this little lot, will you, girls?'

Weirdly, I do as I'm asked as she leads the way out of the shop.

Olivia ignores her and stays inside chatting to Marcus, who's cooing over her sleeping baby in the pram.

'Phwoar!' I say once Olivia joins us and we're all standing outside.

'Who?' asks Carina, looking around.

'Never you mind,' Olivia leaps in.

'So what are you doing down here, on the scuzzy side of the village?' I ask Carina.

'It's ten times cheaper here than getting it all delivered from Ocado. And anyway, keeps me in touch with the real people, the real village. Real life, you know?'

'No,' Olivia and I say as one.

We help load the cases of Bombay Sapphire and cartons of Marlboro Lights into her tank of a car.

'Should keep me going for a couple of days.' Carina laughs her old-man-about-to-croak rasp.

It's just like an impromptu, spontaneous POPC meeting – all that booze and cigarettes – but without the feeling of camaraderie, without the fun.

'Can I give you girls a lift anywhere?' Carina asks as she climbs into the front seat of her four-wheel drive impossibly elegantly, knees locked together, as though she's had to do this a million times, making sure the paparazzi don't snap her knickerless.

She fits a cream sun visor to her head, pulls up her navy blue and pink argyle socks and then checks herself out in the rear-view mirror. She slicks on some lip gloss, says 'Mwah' to her reflection and then looks at us, eyebrows raised expectantly.

'Um, no,' I say, scratching some dried mud off the velvet on the forearm of my dress. 'We're going to the Really Rather Good Cafe.'

'Oh.' She looks a bit dejected.

'Want to join us?' I ask reluctantly as Olivia ever-so-surreptitiously elbows me in the ribs.

'Normally, ladies, I'd *lurve* to. But I've got to crack on. I'm teeing off in ten minutes. And I'm putting on a Disco Mama – And Baby! this weekend . . . it's an organisational nightmare.'

'A disco *what*?' Olivia and I chorus.

'It's a disco for parents during the day that they can bring their babies and kids to. It's new, first of its kind in the UK. I'm hoping it's going to really take off.'

'Sounds like fun,' I say.

'Hey! You two should come! This Saturday, in Clapham! Bring your babies and other halves and I'll put you on the door. Make you VIPs even! There's a bar selling alcohol there, you know . . . What do you say? Call me and let me know if you're interested!'

And with that, she slams the door and speeds off up towards Riverside Heights.

'Couldn't imagine anything worse,' sneers Olivia as we walk to the cafe.

'Oh, I don't know. Might be all right. Might be like the old days, dancing and stuff. For free! What's not to like?'

'Carina,' sniffs Liv and narrows her eyes, staring at the fast-disappearing SUV. 'You can still see her balls from here.'

In the Really Rather Good Cafe, I rock Olivia's pram while she nips out the back for a gasper. I congratulate myself for not having had a cigarette for what seems like ages and smile smugly up at Olivia when she eventually comes back in and flops on to her seat, putting her head in her hands.

'Oh, Roxy – what am I going to do?' she sobs.

'Hey, hey, don't cry.' I try to soothe her. 'What's brought all this on?'

'I've been trying to ignore it, but this insurance thing's totally knocked us! I'm going to have to move out. I feel like such a drain on my sister.'

'But you're helping them out!' I say, getting angry at

the thought of Olivia moving away from Riverside. 'They don't want you to move, do they?'

'They haven't said as much, but they've got enough on their plates without me and Stu,' she snorts.

We both look at Olivia's sleeping baby.

'Couldn't you get more work at the 6-Ten?' I suggest.

'Not really. Can't afford the childcare . . .'

I think about offering to look after Stu while she does some extra daytime shifts at the shop, but quickly remind myself I can barely cope with just Joey on her own.

'Would you be able to take Stu in to work with you? For the daytime shifts, I mean?'

'No, don't think so . . .'

'But he's as good as gold! He sleeps all the time – you could have him behind the counter in a bouncer or something – no one'd even know he was there!'

'But what about health and safety?'

'It's worth asking.'

'I suppose so . . . Marcus might be all right with that – he is lovely, after all. And he does seem to like Stu.'

'What's not to like?' I smile.

'Yeah, he is a little cutie.' Olivia reaches in to the pram and tickles Stu's chin. 'Hoo! Brilliant. Thanks, Rox – feel better already. Now, there's a whole load of cakes back there . . .'

She gets up and heads for the counter. I check in on Stu. Olivia's lucky in one respect – she's got a baby who actually sleeps, even when there's crying and tickling going on. Joey can't even manage to snooze through me sneezing in another part of the house. And when Jack and I are bickering – outside on the deck, a million miles from her cot – there's no chance.

Olivia comes back with a humungous slice of chocolate cake.

'So what do you think?' she grins.

'About sixty points per slice!' I grin back.

'No! Marcus!'

'Oh! Yeah, I reckon he'll go for it, seems a nice enough guy.' I take a slurp of tea.

'I know that. But what do you think of him and *me*? Think he likes me?'

'Definitely! Course he does!'

'*Like* like, though. As in boyfriend and girlfriend.' She raises her eyebrows and sits on her hands.

'Ooh, I dunno. Only saw him with you for a second.'

'And?'

'Well, doesn't he seem a bit . . . um . . . a tad . . .'

'*Luh*-vly?' she says dreamily.

'Yeah, but, well . . . gay?'

'No! Not at all! Do *you* think he's gay?'

'No, look, I wouldn't have a clue! Maybe he's just a bit . . . *camp* or something. Not necessarily gay—'

'You are *so* wrong! Just because he's friendly and flirty—'

'True, true.' I back pedal as I quickly remember what happened when I gave my honest opinion about Guy to

259

Charlie. Last thing Olivia needs right now is to have her crush outed. 'Must be because we just saw Tim. You know, he's kicked my gaydar into overdrive.'

'Well your stupid gaydar's bloody broken,' she huffs.

I shrug my shoulders apologetically. Bugger! I was doing so well, there, a second ago – how come my new best friendship's going pear-shaped so swiftly? How can I make it better?

'You know, Jack could easily be mistaken for being gay sometimes – and he isn't. It's his love of Judy Garland and musicals that does it. Have I ever told you, the minute they start playing 'Do They Know It's Christmas?' in the shops, in November, Jack insists on skipping round the house drinking nothing but snowballs.'

'Really? And if he's worried about his weight, too . . . isn't that a sure sign of gayness?'

'Eh?'

'The dinner you just bought him. The Weight Watchers meals. Only gay guys worry about their appearance once they've bagged a wife. The wife's usually just a front.'

'Girlfriend. We're not married.'

'Whatever.' She peevedly takes a chunk out of her chocolate cake.

The sound of Olivia masticating fills my ears. She looks crossly at the wall, like the Slapped Arse of old, and we sit in silence for a minute.

Why can't I keep my big mouth shut? Shut my noise, as

Jack would say. I look at her sadly and when I catch her eye, she softens.

'Sorry to snap,' she says finally. 'It's just . . . God! When I think I've finally met someone I fancy, someone who could take me away from all this, turns out he might be gay!'

'Oh, Liv! *I'm* sorry! What would I know? Nothing, that's what! I've probably got it all wrong – I only saw him for five seconds, and he *did* seem into you . . .'

'You think so?'

'Defo!'

'You're not just saying that . . .'

'No way! Would I lie to a fellow founder of the POP Club? And what about when he leaned into you, to say the flood had been great for business—'

'I know! He didn't *have* to get that close!'

'The guy's smitten – sooo obvious!'

'I knew it!' beams Liv.

19

The girls at *Positive Parenting!* must feel sorry for me. Well, the Editor might do, anyway. Or maybe she just wants me off her back.

After I handed in (sorry, there I go, showing my age again – *emailed*) the last story I did for them, I stupidly expected to be contacted by them immediately, begging me to do more stuff.

But that didn't happen. So when I emailed the Ed yesterday morning, 'just wondering' whether she might be interested in me writing a regular column, I got an email back from Melanie, the Features Ed, who was also 'just wondering' whether I might be up for doing a story. Never heard back from the Ed herself, so I take it I can wonder all I like, but the column's a no-go. Fair enough – at least I've got a commission which should keep the wolf from the door (or Joey in Pampers) for a week or two.

So. The story's all about how to give your baby a happy

start. Which they wouldn't be asking *me* to write if they knew the truth. But hey! What they don't know won't hurt them – even if it's damaged Joey (and Jack – and me) for life. It's a two-page feature and I'll get three hundred pounds for it.

If it were down to me, though, it'd be a half-page, ten-point story – still for three hundred pounds, mind – divided into two columns. The left-hand column would be DOs:

DO make sure you have loads of friends in your street who've just had a baby

DO have heaps of cash

DO have doting grandparents desperate to babysit constantly – preferably living a few streets away from you (well, you don't want them too close, do you?)

DO make sure you're twenty-five or younger – there's a reason your body is ready to make babies at thirteen/fourteen – wait till you're over thirty-five and you risk permanently aching bones and joints, terminal tiredness and the wrath of the *Daily Mail*, branding you selfish, career-obsessed, money-grabbing, probably single and a drain on the State

DO be in a secure relationship. A baby will test even the tightest of couples – and put a potentially intolerable strain on a weak one.

And the right-hand column would be DON'Ts:

DON'T move house!

DON'T move to a house in the country if you live in the city – especially a city where all your friends are

DON'T move house from the city to the country and then get builders in, expecting them to turn a pokey mid-terrace into a sprawling country pile. Particularly in a recession when you'll run out of funds before the work is even finished

DON'T move house from the city to the country if you're crap at making new friends and find talking to total strangers about their babies bum-numbingly boring

JUST DON'T bloody move, all right?

It'd be a short story, sure – but straight to the point. And yes, yes, all from the mother's perspective, yes. But happy mum = happy baby and all that.

Luckily, though, it isn't down to me.

I call Carina to get the lowdown on her disco day and sell it to Melanie as one of the ways to make a baby happy. I tell her it is, apparently, the latest parent/baby sensation that's sweeping the nation (or cashed-up parents with loads of leisure time in London, at any rate).

'Sounds fab,' says Melanie, sounding bored. 'Just meet the deadline. Two weeks from today, no extensions.'

Carina's over the moon that her event will be in *Positive Parenting!* and even Jack gets excited about the prospect of going out *en famille* on the weekend. Or is it the promise of the bar?

It starts at two and goes till five p.m. – but judging by the foul moods all three of us are in this morning, we'll be lucky if we can stick it out for ten minutes.

It's tipping it down as we finally leave Riverside (amid the usual frantic questioning: 'Have you packed her water/bananas/sandwich/nappies/change of clothes/cuddly toy she totally ignores?' 'No – thought you did.' 'GOD!') and by the time we get to Chiswick and park the car near our old place (we kept loads of parking permits), it's turned torrential.

A quick look up at the turret, a collective sigh, and we head for the high street. It's the first time we've been back since we left and it's all pretty much the same, but it feels different, somehow. It cheers us up a bit though, pointing out all our old favourite pubs and shops (Game, the computer game shop for Jack; Carluccio's for me, where I'm forced to buy two cheese and tomato pastries to take away, after looking longingly at the Chiswick yummy mummy/Bugaboo set that's taken over the restaurant) – and when Jack points out that Chiswick High Street actually looks just like any high street in England – same chain shops, same generic British bleak look about it, I can't help but agree.

Which is a bit sad, really. I'd held it so dear in my head and in my mind's eye it was so perfect, so full of life and joy, so, so . . .

'So bloody expensive!' says Jack, when I tell him the pastries cost £4.50 each.

As we walk down to Chiswick mainline station, getting soaked and even more pissed off in the process (except for Joey – she's dry underneath her rain cover, but still a bit cranky), it strikes me that I need to let go. I'm the one with the retrospective rose-coloured glasses and Jack's the forward-thinking, *progressive* rose-coloured-glasses wearer. But can the twain ever meet, I wonder. And if the twain *does* meet, can it get on well enough to be a partnership for life? I'm still thinking about the twain and, consequently, say: 'The twain station!' to a wide-eyed, excited Joey when we finally get there and head for the seats underneath the shelter.

Five dodgy-looking lads loiter about – the bums of their jeans trailing on the ground, next to their knuckles – and sit on the seats next to us, cans of Foster's and cigarettes in their hands. Just like their Riverside counterparts at the 6-Ten, I think. Or me and Jack out the back of ours in the 'garden', for that matter . . .

Joey's mesmerised by all the people. She's not used to so many and gets all excited when Jack takes her out of the buggy to have a somewhat freer look around while I go off to see if I can find the ticket machine.

'Out of order,' I grumble, sitting back down next to Jack.

'Excellent,' says he. 'Train fares are too bloody exorbitant in this town, anyway. And it's not our fault – we tried to do the right thing.'

He's right. And a man after my own heart when it

comes to public transport fare evasion. I'm always trying to think of ways I can get away without buying a ticket on trains, lately – 'I forgot to buy a ticket! Der! Sorry, it's my cotton-wool brain – just become a new mum, you see' or 'Sorry! We had to run for the train, and it's a nightmare running with this buggy – no time to get a ticket!' and my favourite – although I've never had the bottle to ever try it out: 'I thought mums and babies under one travelled First Class for free!'

'Yes, there's the tracks that the train will come down on,' Jack points and explains to Joey, who can't take her eyes off the boys on the next seat.

'Ack!' she shouts.

'Yes!' laughs Jack.

And just then, a policeman saunters over to the lads. He stands on the platform, checks them out and then gets on his walkie-talkie. It's illegal to smoke on train platforms – maybe that's what he's about to do them for. That and underage drinking, probably.

'Can I have that description again?' he says into the mouthpiece just like they do on *The Bill*.

'Grey hoodie, baggy blue jeans, diamond-stud earrings in both ears, dark skin, white trainers,' a voice crackles over the walkie-talkie.

'That's him for sure,' I whisper to Jack, jerking my head towards the boy closest to us.

Jack doesn't respond, except for bouncing Joey on his lap a little faster and elbowing me in the ribs.

'Can I have some back-up?' the copper asks.

'Let's just take Joey round to my side, shall we?' I say quietly, but starting to panic a bit. 'Don't want her caught in the cross-fire if they've got *shooters*.'

'You watch too much telly,' says Jack.

'Just in case,' I whisper and put a struggling Joey back in her buggy, wheeling it to my side of the seat, away from the possible perps and any potential fracas.

Two more police officers show up – one male, one female – and as they get closer to us, Jack can't resist.

'Ner ner ner ner,' he sings softly – *The Bill* theme tune.

'Don't antagonise the filth!' I say out of the corner of my mouth, standing up and shuffling away from the boys and the cops, ready to run like fury if it kicks off.

But it doesn't. They just cuff the lad who fit the description – who puts up no struggle whatsoever – and off they go. Once they've gone, one of the other boys left there says:

'Wicked! Thought they were gonna collar me for the beer and fags! Woar, man!' and flicks his wrist, clicking his fingers like young urban punks do.

'How was that, Joey?' grins Jack into the buggy, as the train slows to a stop in front of us. 'You've just witnessed your first arrest! Still wanna live here, Rox?'

'Not at this railway station, no. And I couldn't bear Joey getting caught up with the wrong crowd when she's older,' I say.

Jack sees his chance and doesn't hesitate.

'At least in Australia, kids are surfing or sailing or going on bush walks in the sunshine when they're not at school – not loitering around train stations in the rain, drinking, smoking and getting arrested,' he says smugly.

We finally get to Clapham Junction and make our way down the stairs and through the endless maze of shops to the front of the station. The Clapham Grand, where Disco Mama – and Baby! is on, is directly opposite.

I'm quite excited now. This is the first time we've been out, as a couple, to a nightclub, since Joey was born. Yes, it's two in the afternoon and yep, we've got to look after Joey . . . but still, we're out somewhere, together as a family – with not a tinny boombox blasting out 'The Wheels On The Bus' anywhere in sight.

Carina greets us at the door with a kiss on both cheeks for me, same for Jack and a ruffle of scalp/hair for Joey.

'How nice to see you! So glad you could make it,' she says. 'And not just because it's great PR for me . . . no, really!'

She's wearing spray-on black lycra pants like Olivia Newton-John did in *Grease* and one of her signature skin-tight off-the-shoulder leopard-skin-print tops, showing off her impossibly buoyant-looking breasts to great effect. She's nearly as tall as Jack, in her sky-high peep-toe stilettoes and, as I look up, I see Jack's got a face full of cleavage and an idiotic grin on his face. I nudge him and say:

'This is Jack, my *boyfriend*.'

'Of course! I remember you from the POP Club meeting. And I've heard so much about you!' gushes Carina and stretches her arms out in a welcome-to-the-family kind of gesture, putting her hands on his biceps.

'Ooh, firm! Do you work out?' she winks at Jack.

'Only by picking Joey up all the time,' he smiles and takes Joey from me and my aching, flabby arms.

'Dying for a pint, aren't you, babe?' I say and shuffle us away from Carina.

'I'll see you at the bar, then,' she calls out after us. 'And save a dance for me, will you, Jack, honey?'

As soon as we're inside, I check Joey's buggy in while Jack heads straight for the bar, Joey still in his apparently toned-to-perfection arms. When I find him, he's nearly finished a pint and Joey's desperate to get out on the floor, so I take her down the stairs, away from the bar and into the dark. It's not so dark that you can't see, but with running, crawling, jumping little buggers getting under your feet at every turn (and that's just the parents), I could do with a bit more illumination.

Not like the old days, I think, where a club couldn't be dark enough to hide whatever heinous spot I'd been aiding and abetting that week.

'You're itching to get on the floor, aren't you, sweet cheeks?' I say to Joey as the DJ starts playing 'Get On The Floor' by Michael Jackson.

I put her down on one of the lighted squares on the dance floor and she shoots off, darting between other parents' legs until SMACK! some eight-year-old boy doesn't see her and trips over her as he runs along. Joey keeps going, even though she probably got a reasonably nasty kick in the ribs, but I stop to pick the other kid up.

'Get OFF me,' he yells and whacks my arms away.

His mum (I imagine) comes running over, grabs the boy by the wrist and says to me: 'What do you think you're doing? Back off, will you?!'

'I was only trying to—'

'Leave us alone before I call security!' And she picks him up, cradling him in her arms like a baby and wanders off, swaying and twirling intermittently in time with the music.

'Sod you then,' I say, and look away in the direction I last saw Joey crawling in.

But all I see is a swarm of kids and parents, dancing badly, totally bereft of rhythm. Clearly no one's trying to pull at this disco, to try out any sexy, seductive moves – they're all just trying to look like the most uninhibited, crazy, I-don't-care-if-I-make-a-fool-of-myself, it's-for-the-kids kind of parents they can. Which is great – it's just that I feel like I make a right tit out of myself all day every day where Joey's concerned, and it's high time we all had a break.

A break for the border, in Joey's case. Where the hell is she? As the dancing around me gets more frenzied, so do I, dropping to my hands and knees in an effort to get on Joey's level, give me a better chance of spotting her. I do two rounds of the dance floor on all fours – there goes that break from embarrassing myself, then. Not that anyone notices, I'm sure. They're all too busy checking themselves out in the mirrorballs hanging from the ceiling.

And then I see her. Standing up at the snacks table, reaching out for the bowl of organic crisps.

'I thought I'd lost you!' I scoop her up, making her cry.

'No, no, you don't want the crisps – what about some . . . sultanas! There! I'll get you a box of them – would you like that?'

Joey grabs the box of sultanas out of my hand and shoves it in her mouth while I make a desultory attempt at swaying to some Girls Aloud song on the outskirts of a group of mums. They're all singing along, eyes shut tight, heads back, arms flailing . . . and then the bubbles begin.

'Ba-boo!' shrieks Joey, revealing a mouth full of soggy cardboard.

I put her down on the floor to see if she can pop any bubbles, but the mums have gone berserk. They're all laughing and falling over each other in an effort to be the first in their group to get to the bubbles. So Joey doesn't get a look in.

'Come on, sweetheart – let's check out the chillax area.'

Once we tire of chillaxing (after about two minutes), I can just about make out Jack standing in the bar bit, looking at his mobile phone. God, he's always texting someone or getting texts these days.

I pick Joey up and carry her over to see her dad. About

time they did some bonding. Well, that and to let *him* look after her for a bit, have a dance with her while I go out for a fag. Just the one. I know, I know. I'll go back to Barry for a top-up soon.

Someone keeping guard at the front doors, a friendly-looking mum-type says: 'Going outside for a cigarette, love?'

'Yes,' I say, hanging my head, my chin(s) resting on my chest.

'Just let me stamp your hand so you can get back in,' she says, holding my left hand and pressing the stamp on to the back of it. I look down to see I've been branded and my hand now says:

SMOKER

in big, fat, black capital letters.

I stand under an umbrella with CINZANO emblazoned across it, and don't even light the cigarette. I'm about to, but the sheer misery of the whole situation – all alone in the pouring rain outside a disco for babies – makes me feel ashamed of myself. I throw the cigarette into the ashtray full of dog-ends and water and go back inside.

Flashing the door person my **SMOKER** stamp, I see a guy holding a camera with a powerful light on it and what must be a presenter, interviewing an impossibly tall, young, gorgeous woman holding an equally cute baby.

Carina told me they were running a Yummy Mummy Competition this Saturday – they must've found one.

I walk past a couple of times, but no one makes a mad dash towards me, begging me to take part in the contest, so I leave the foyer and head straight for the bar. And as I stand there, having ordered a Diet Coke, I realise I feel exactly as I did in my late teens/early twenties when I used to go to clubs. Well, not *exactly* the same – Jack and I are here by ourselves, no mates to be seen. And we have a baby in tow. *And* it's about four in the afternoon and we're totally sober. At least *I* am. But it's still eerily familiar – feeling out of place, often left standing alone, too painfully self-conscious to have a dance, not even a really drunk guy trying to chat me up. Thank God those days are long gone, I think. Thank God for Jack.

I look around for him and see he's on the dance floor with Joey and Carina. They look quite the cosy couple, pretending to swing their respective golf clubs in front of each other. Then they grab a hold of one of Joey's hands each and start skipping about like they're doing 'Ring-a-Ring-o'-Roses'. Carina throws her head back and laughs and so does Jack and, eventually, so does Joey. Bloody hell – they look like they're in some bad seventies hairspray commercial.

It only lasts a few minutes, the torture of watching the three of them having such a good time together, and after Carina says something hilarious into Jack's ear – making him laugh like he's having a fit – she kisses Joey's head and makes her way off into the crowd. Jack picks Joey up and they both look longingly after Carina for a few seconds and then, when Jack spots me, he waves and weaves his way back to the bar.

'See that whirling dervish dad over there?' he pants as he props Joey on a bar stool and points at some men in the crowd. 'Nearly knocked Joey over, he was so desperate to dance in front of the camera.'

I look more closely and see this mad dad flinging about some poor three-year-old girl like he's jiving. One minute, she's flying over his head; the next, he's dragging her along the floor through his legs.

'Yeah – apparently, there's a camera crew here scouting for yummy mummies.'

'Not dishy dads or *demented* dads as well?'

'Not that I know of.'

'Then that guy's even more of a twat,' he says.

'They've found a yummy mummy, though, out in the foyer.'

'You?'

'Well, I walked past them a few times, but they mustn't have seen me. Too short, I expect.'

'Yeah, that's probably it,' says Jack, putting his arm around me and finishing off *another* pint.

'*And* my hair's gone curly in all the bloody rain,' I add.

'You look fine,' he says.

'*Fine*? Not ravishing? Not beautiful beyond compare?

Not *stunning*? You might as well come straight out and call me fugly, if you're going to say I look *fine*.'

He cannot tell a lie, so he doesn't say anything more. He looks like he's taken note, though, like he'll never say 'It's fine' about anything to do with me ever again.

'Is that your – what? – third pint?' I say accusingly.

'Second,' he says, smacking his lips. 'Just about to get my third, though. You right?'

I look down at my Diet Coke.

'Yeah, fine.' Well, someone's got to be responsible.

I take myself off to the loo and when I've finished, do a little reccy of the place, try to earwig on what parents and kids are saying to each other. Not just because I'm nosy, of course – it's for the story, too.

'Did you know,' I say, sidling up to Jack at the bar a few minutes later, 'that Ant and Dec do the voices in *Engie Benjy*?'

'Is that what your pick-up lines've come down to these days?' smiles Jack, looking up from his mobile phone and putting it in his jacket pocket.

'I just heard two dads talking about it at the side of the dance floor,' I smile back.

'Well, yes I *did* know that, as a matter of fact,' Jack says. 'And it really pisses me off.'

'I know, I know – they're everywhere these days, those two,' I giggle and stand behind Joey, who's jammed her mouth so full of sultanas, she looks even more like Marlon Brando in *The Godfather* than usual.

'But it's not just them,' he goes on, warming to his theme. 'Tom bloody Conti does *Andy Pandy*, Stephen Fry does *Pocoyo*, Derek Jacobi does *In the Night Garden* . . .'

'Jane Horrocks is *Fifi and the Flowertots*,' I chime in. 'But I like her . . .'

'Peter Kay's in *Roary the Racing Car* – I mean, haven't they all got enough money? The greedy bastards. Why don't they bloody well leave the kids' shows for the struggling out-of-work actors? The people who really need a gig and the money? It's not as if the kids give a rat's arse whose voice it is!'

A good point, well made, I think. Must remember to pass it off as my own observation at the next POP Club meeting, and suggest Barry go for some auditions. Carina might even be impressed by my knowledge on the subject, having done PR for kids' TV.

'All right, all right – calm down,' I say, looking around, hoping none of the perfect parents can hear his ranting.

'It just gets on my, ah, tits, that's all,' he says, obviously eyeing up the rack on the yummy mummy who's just walked past us.

'You were checking her out!' I elbow him in the groin, such is our height difference.

'No I wasn't!'

'Yes you were! You couldn't've *been* more obvious.'

'If I was, it was only to compare boob sizes.'

'What?!'

'With *mine*! I'm the only dad here with bigger boobs

277

than most of the mums! I have GOT to lose some weight,' he says, looking down at his tummy and rubbing his chest.

So . . . worried about how he looks, all of a sudden, is he? Olivia would say that was a dead giveaway he was gay. *Cosmo* would say that was a sure sign he was having an affair. Charlie would say it was probably a bit of both.

I'd say it was an affair. A straight one. And I bet I even know *who* he's having it with, now – that up-herself, man-eating, golf-playing, home-wrecking ex-kids' TV PR Ca-*bloody*-rina!

'How come you know so much about the stars of kids' TV shows, anyway?'

'Um . . . I dunno.' He looks a bit sheepish. 'Ah . . . some columnist bleating on about it in some newspaper, probably.'

That *could* be true, you know – Jack actually *does* get a chance to read newspapers these days, when he's relaxing – sorry, *chillaxing* – on the train, on his commute. Best I can do is get GMTV's take on what the *Sun* has to say.

Still, it's a bit of a coincidence, isn't it? Maybe they find time – when they're having their post-shag fags, most probably – to talk about kids' TV. I try to shake the image out of my head. Probably just a coincidence. A particularly Carina-shaped coincidence, yes, but probably no more than that.

'I heard one of the dads saying how funny Ant and Dec are, too. Says they're the new Morecambe and Wise,' I smile, fully aware of the incendiary nature of this remark.

'That does it! I'm getting another pint!'

Any excuse, I think, and try to hold Joey's hands, moving them in time to Earth Wind & Fire's 'Boogie Wonderland'.

My mobile's been missing for a few days – can't find it anywhere at home. But Jack's jacket is hanging on the back of his bar stool and I'm desperate to call Charlie – she loves Earth, Wind & Fire – so I grab his mobile out of the pocket.

Scrolling down his contacts list, I've gone through the As, the Bs, and when I'm nearly at Charlie, in the early Cs', my thumb lifts off the key in shock. I feel my eyes bulge and tiny prickles of heat spread over my top lip when I see the name.

Carina.

I stare at this for I don't know how long, but then I sense Jack's form approaching, so I stuff the phone back in his pocket.

'So. How many Carinas do you know?' I ask him.

'Two,' he says. 'Girl on my team at work and your mate from the POP Club. Why?'

'She is most definitely *not* my mate!'

He holds Joey and sways to the music.

'Jeez – imagine being one of those professional dads.' He nods towards the crowd. 'Boor-*ing*!'

'And having affairs is exciting, is it?' I say, trembling a bit as my lips get thinner.

'What?'

'And drinking doesn't make you interesting, either, you know.'

'Nope.' He holds his pint glass up, looks down into the bottom of it, swills the dregs about and then drains it before he says: 'But it does make other people interesting.'

And I wonder if by 'other people' he really means me.

20

I get to The Swan quite a bit later than usual – I had to have
the de rigeur mini row with Jack once he'd got home *after*
I'd already bathed and put Joey to bed, thus missing *Corrie*
entirely. I mean, I'm all for this take it in turns thing (sort
of), but Wednesday nights are my nights off – Wednesday
nights are officially *his* turn. He says the train was cancelled
so he had to wait around at Reading station blah, blah, blah.
But it's not just tonight. He seems to be staying in
Paddington, working late or missing trains a lot lately.

And anyway, it was only a small bicker – I had something to look forward to, coming out to the meeting, and
didn't want to hang around. Jack seemed more keen on
having it out than me, if you want the truth.

The usual suspects are there – June's laughing with
Barry, Tim and Carina are swapping fashion tips and
Paul's looking around like he's lost something.

'No Liv?' I ask him as I settle myself down with my
tomato juice.

'No,' he answers, sounding disappointed. 'Hope she's all right.'

'She's fine. She texted me earlier saying she might not be able to make it tonight,' I reassure him. 'Because she's working extra shifts at the 6-Ten for a while, trying to help her sister out, make some more money to help with the repairs to their house.'

Paul looks relieved.

'Yeah. She puts on a brave face, but after the flood, she feels even more like the unwanted one. She pretends not to get on that well with them – all that wicked brother-in-law and evil, older sister stuff – but they're all she has in this world,' I say.

'I can't believe they didn't have any insurance,' June half laughs, calming down from her giggling fit and dabbing the corners of her eyes with her handkerchief.

'Not everyone can afford it,' says Paul. 'For lots of people, just paying the rent or a mortgage and having a decent holiday once a year is breaking the bank enough.'

'Add a kid into the equation and what've you got?' Barry pipes up.

We all wait for an answer to be sung at us, but all he says is: 'A nightmare waiting to happen.'

'Like that shirt, Barry – honestly!' shrieks Tim.

It's true, Barry's blue/gold tie-dyed shirt's making everyone's eyes hurt.

'At least Liv's got the POP Club,' says Tim.

'Hear, hear.' Carina raises her glass.

'So,' says Paul, 'how's poor Jack?'

'Poor bloody Jack is fine. Thanks for asking,' I say, suddenly all snippy. 'How's Tobi and your ex?'

'She's met someone. Someone local. So she's actually being quite pleasant at the moment. Or nicer to me than usual, put it that way.'

'Probably because she knows she's pushing it, wanting you to look after Tobi more, am I right?' says Tim.

'Yeah, I suppose so. But that's great – I love being with Tobi. And now she's seeing someone from the village, it means she won't be moving away and I'll be able to see Tobi all the time. It's weird. I mean, I almost quite like the ex again.'

'That's great,' says June. 'Good for Tobi, too – not to have warring parents around her all the time.'

'Yeah. You should try being a bit nicer to Jack when he gets home of an evening, Roxy.' Paul nods at me as he takes a sip of his pint.

'I do – I *am* nice to him! *He's* the miserable old boot in our relationship these days.'

'So separation no longer on the cards?' Paul looks sceptical.

In all the excitement of the fundraiser, I'd nearly forgotten what Jack said to me a few weeks ago – about wanting a break from me. But now I remember quite clearly.

'Don't think so. Not from my side, anyway,' I frown, wondering why Jack has been particularly tetchy with me. Guilt, probably.

'You've been bringing in some money, haven't you, dear?' asks June, ever the calming influence.

'Yes. But I need a column – or something regular.'

The word 'regular' immediately makes me think of Joey and the problems she has in the poo department. And the thought of her cheers me up no end.

'You should've seen Joey today. She's not even one yet and she pulled herself up on the telly stand, swaying about, just like I was doing, to Kate Bush. She was actually dancing!'

And then we all start talking excitedly about our offspring, like we're at a mother and toddler group, like we're at the Proud Parents Club or something. Strange – that's never really happened before.

But it's not me or Carina or June doing most of the braying – it's the lads.

'She's so bright – smart as a whip,' says Paul with a gleam in his eye.

'And gorgeous! Honestly, I want to eat the twins with a spoon sometimes – way too cute,' trills Tim.

'Yeah, yeah – and the talent!' laughs Barry thinly, looking a little jealous. 'They're right little show-offs, my boys – always putting on impromptu plays, making up songs about their baby sister.'

'God knows where they get that from,' says Carina quietly out of the side of her treacherous Joker's mouth.

'Nice to hear you boys sounding so pleased with your kids,' smiles June.

'Hey, POP Clubbers!'

It's Olivia and Marcus, the 6-Ten manager.

'Thought we'd try to make it here for last orders,' she says, slightly out of breath. 'Marcus, this is everyone. Everyone, this is Marcus.'

'Hello,' says Paul cautiously, holding his hand out to Marcus.

'Hiya! Again!' says Tim, leaping out of his seat. 'Last orders already? I'll get them in – everyone's usual?'

'Hi, mate, I'm Barry,' says Barry, standing up. He immediately looks shocked at how short he is next to six-foot-massive Bollywood star material Marcus and reaches up to pat him on the back, willing him to sit down.

'Take a pew, take a pew. We don't stand on ceremony here. This is the lovely June, this here's our resident glamour puss, Carina, and on your right is the non-smoking founder of our club, RAAAAH-ksanne!'

Knew it was too good to last.

'What brings you here?' asks June, looking Marcus up and down over her half-moon specs.

'The fair maiden Olivia, actually,' smiles Marcus.

'Do you have kids?' June presses on.

'No. I'd like to one day, but it's not really an option for me right now.'

'Marcus is destined for great things,' beams Olivia. 'He's already the manager of our 6-Ten – and he's only twenty-five!'

'Well,' says Marcus, slightly embarrassed, 'it's a family franchise – no big deal, really.'

'We've met several times already, haven't we, Marcus?' Carina winks at Marcus and grabs her G&T off the tray Tim's holding. 'Quite the old friends, aren't we, my tall, dark, handsome Bombay Sapphire?'

'I do like a man with ambition,' says June approvingly.

'Don't we all, doll,' Tim says, passing everyone else's drinks to them. 'So, do you have kids, Marcus?'

'No, no, I was just telling the others—'

'Then why are you here?' Paul snaps, his eyes flashing dark.

'We thought we could catch a quick drink before closing. And Livvy says it's the best place to meet people, this club. I'm new to the village, you see—'

'And it won't be long before he has a string of franchises – all over Berkshire!' Olivia carries on.

'We've had a few chats already ourselves, haven't we, Marcus? Down at the 6-Ten,' Tim grins. 'I must say, though, you've never struck me as – how shall I put this? – *the breeding type*, if you don't mind me saying.'

Marcus laughs and I look at Olivia. She's resting her chin on the palm of her right hand, gazing at Marcus who, in turn, is looking at Tim. Everyone's eyes are sparkling.

So, I see, are Carina's, even though they're half closed. And she's giving the straw in her drink a right royal going over with her tongue as she fixes Marcus with her sultry stare through her thick, black (probably false, let's face it) lashes.

I picture her giving Jack the very same look when they're alone together.

'Listen, luvvies, I need an early night tonight – got rehearsals tomorrow morning – so I'm off,' says Barry. 'And I won't be able to make next week's session – crisis talks for Riverside Amdram, I'm afraid. But I'll be here in spirit. Think of me as the spirit in the sky. Goin' on up to the spirit in the sky . . .'

And off he saunters, singing his merry tune about dying.

'What's with Barry's dress sense?' says Olivia, screwing up her nose, once he's gone. 'That shirt was well shameful.'

'A real midsummer's nightmare,' June joins in.

'Well, he *is* an actor,' says Carina.

'I wouldn't be seen dead in a tragedy like that,' adds Tim. 'Which reminds me, people. Floody Hell night's in just over two weeks' time!'

'Oh, yes!' cries Olivia. 'My sister and brother-in-law are up for coming. They almost seem quite pleased with *me* about it. Finally I feel a bit more – I don't know – worthy of their respect.'

'I know what you mean,' says Carina. 'I feel more worthy of my own respect, sorting it all, getting invitations out and organising the PR . . .'

'I feel great, too, knowing it's going to wind my dad up something severe,' says Tim wickedly.

'You shouldn't let them make you feel bad,' whispers Paul, turning to face Olivia.

'No, no, they don't. They've been brilliant lately,' she says, shrugging off Paul's suggestion. 'And I think I have, too, to be honest – happier, more full of *joie de vie*—'

'*Vivre*,' June corrects her.

'Yeah, that's what I said. And I think it's all down to the POP Club. Well, work and the POP Club.' Olivia smiles at Marcus.

'Work and the POP Club – because you're worth it,' says Paul, holding his pint up to Olivia.

'Work and the POP Club.' Carina, Olivia and June tap their glasses against Paul's.

'Work and the POP Club – for life, not just for Christmas,' I shout.

'Group hug!' beams Tim, standing up and throwing his arms out wide.

We all stay seated.

'Miserable bloody lot,' Tim mumbles, sitting down.

21

Mum's come down for the day. She won't spend the night, of course – 'Too much to do, darling, *far* too much to do' – but at least she's down here early, so she can hang out with Joey for a good couple of hours – and take me to lunch at The Swan, when Joey goes off to the nursery.

'You know this was totally covered in water just the other day,' I say to Mum as we walk across the meadow right next to the river. 'You couldn't tell where the river ended and the grass began.'

'Really?' says Mum. 'Bet it didn't bother those mansions on that side, there.' She nods her head to the enormous houses on the other bank of the river, on much higher ground.

'Yeah – what water they *did* catch probably just helped their Chelsea Flower Show prize-winners grow.'

'It's always the way, isn't it? Those who can least afford the devastation of natural disasters – or indeed, unnatural ones, like this recession we're in at the moment – are the ones guaranteed to be affected the worst.'

I get Joey out of the buggy and put her behind it, so she can hold on to the buggy as she tries to walk.

'Ooh, just look at her go!' says Mum, as Joey pushes the buggy all by herself. 'Gosh, she really is moving!'

We walk behind Joey as she starts to run (sort of – with her bulging nappy and her bandy legs, it's more of a rapid waddle), getting carried along with the speed the buggy's picking up.

Joey looks around to us and starts laughing uproariously. But she can't co-ordinate the looking, the hilarity and the half-trotting and she falls flat on her face, hitting the edge of the undercarriage on her way down.

I run to her, scooping her up into my arms, and start rocking her, pushing the back of her head so that her nose is buried in my shoulder.

'Is she all right? *Mum?!* Is her face OK?' I can't bear to look.

'She's fine, she's fine!' Mum says, unfazed by the drama. 'She's not even crying, darling – it's a shock to her, that's all. Bit of mud on her cheek, nothing to worry about.'

'You're all right, gorgey,' I say, more to reassure myself than Joey. 'That buggy carried you away with it, there, didn't it? Hmm? You're all right, sweetie pie.'

I put her back in her buggy, strap her in – making her cry in the process – and say:

290

'Let's go home, babe. You must be *very* tired now, mustn't you, eh? Eh? Who's a tired one, eh?'

'Don't panic so much, sweetheart,' says Mum. 'A little mud won't hurt her. And she's got to learn how to walk soon, anyway.'

'Not if I can help it – not if it involves breaking her neck in the process,' I say, wiping the mud off her face.

'Mud's good for her,' she says, echoing Dad.

'You and Dad! He'd say mud was a perfectly-balanced nutrient-rich meal, wouldn't he?'

'Perhaps,' Mum smiles.

'FRESH FRUIT AND VEG!' we shout in unison.

Back at home, I put Joey to bed and she's flat out within minutes.

'Must be all the extra activity she's doing lately,' I say quietly to Mum, coming back into the kitchen.

'Hmm,' says Mum, not looking up from the *Big Issue* she bought on her way up to the house. 'Is the sun over the yardarm yet?'

'No! It's far too early for a drink, Mum! I thought we could go to the pub for lunch and you could have a wine there.'

'Yes, yes, you're right. I'll have a coffee, then.'

'Let's go outside, where we can talk properly, not wake Joey up,' I whisper.

'It's a gorgeous day,' says Mum, once we're seated on the old kitchen chairs on the deck. 'Perfect for line-drying. You should get a load on now, so you can hang it out before Joey wakes up.'

'In a minute. Let's just sit for a while, take in the fresh, country air, listen to the birdsong,' I suggest.

The second I've said 'birdsong', twenty pneumatic drills start hammering away at the new petrol station they're building a few houses up the road – right on the outskirts of the village.

Mum laughs.

God it's nice to have her here. The company of your *mum* – who knows you better than anyone – and still likes you (or does a passable impression of it) – is amazing. Even if you're talking about washing.

'SO DO YOU THINK I'VE LOST WEIGHT?' I shout, trying to be heard over the noise.

'No, no, why wait indeed? Get a load on now – Joey's bound to be woken up by the drills any minute.'

'Ah, forget it,' I mutter, getting up and going inside.

Despite the cacophony of drills, once inside I swear I hear a knock at the front door. Can't be. Can't be *our* front door – no one comes by unannounced these days. Who am I kidding? No one comes by *at all* these days.

I unlock the door, open it a crack and peer round.

'Hello?' I say to the old-ish man standing there.

'Oh, hello there!' he shouts. 'I'm Wilfred. Wilfred Marlow? The rector at St Jude's!' He raises his eyebrows, pointing at his dog collar.

He looks familiar, what I can see of him through the

crack in the door. Yes, it's . . . it's that guy who keeps dragging Tim out of POP Club meetings. It's Tim's dad!

'Oh! Hello, vicar!' I say.

'Rector, dear, rector,' he corrects me sternly.

So Tim's dad's the local rector – who knew? No wonder Tim kept that quiet. But what's he doing *here*?

'I wonder if I might come in for a minute, have a little chat.'

'Um, well, the baby's asleep and—'

'I won't take up much of your time . . .' He's insistent, his right foot jammed in the crack, prising the front door open.

'Er, OK, then. Come in,' and I pull the door open wide, making a sweeping gesture with my right arm.

'We're out the back, baby's asleep—'

'Right you are, this won't take long,' he says, stepping into the house and surveying the carnage.

One of Joey's more annoying toys goes off. *EE-orrr! EE-orrr!* – it's one of those puzzle things where you put the animals in their corresponding shape and it makes the animal's sound when you get it right. It also makes the animal's sound randomly at three in the morning when no one's gone anywhere near it.

'Oh, sorry about that.' I drop to my knees, looking for said puzzle piece and shoving all the other toys underneath the radiator. 'It's a puzzle with a donkey in it.'

The back door slams.

'Jesus *Christ*, it's loud out there – can barely hear myself think!' Mum's stomping through to the front room.

'Oh, hello,' she says, looking at Tim's dad.

'Please sit down,' I say to him, motioning to the couch, sweeping crumbs and God knows what else off it.

Joey starts bawling upstairs.

'Mum, this is Wilfred,' I say. 'The village vic . . . um, he's from the church up the road.'

'Pleased to meet you,' he says, holding his hand out for Mum to shake.

'Are you the rector?' Mum asks as she shakes his hand and then sits down on the couch.

'That's right,' he smiles smugly.

'Um, I'll go and get Joey – Mum? Would you make Wilf a cup of tea?'

'Wil-*fred*,' he says.

'Yes, yes of course,' Mum says, jumping up while I go upstairs.

Joey's inconsolable now she's heard voices, so I bring her downstairs with me.

'Ah, and there's the little one,' says Wilfred.

'Yep, here she is!'

'Oh! Little *girl*, is she? I was just about to congratulate you on your fine choice of name for a boy, Joseph,' he says, peering closely at Joey.

'No, no, she's a girl,' I say.

'Has she been Christened yet?'

'No.'

'We have a lot of christenings at St Jude's – you're more than welcome to put her name down on the roster—'

'No, it's all right,' I say, sitting on the floor with Joey. 'She's agnostic – undecided as yet.'

'I see,' he says, pursing his thin lips.

'Here you go.' Mum hands Wilf a cup of tea. 'I haven't put any sugar in it – couldn't find any.'

'That's fine, that's fine,' he says, putting it on the floor.

'Now, I've come here today,' he says, putting his fingertips together to form a steeple on his lap, 'to talk to you about your club. The one that meets at the public house across the road from St Jude's?'

'The Pi— The club at the pub . . . yes,' I say warily.

'Now, it's come to my attention that there's drinking to excess at the meetings of this club.'

'Well, it is in a pub, that's what people tend to do—'

'*Some* people, yes. Now, indulging in the odd glass of wine is all very well and good – in moderation, of course – blood of Christ, etc – but it's the sentiments that this club are expressing that has a number of members of my congregation a little . . . how shall I put this? *Concerned*.'

'Eh?'

'Riverside's a God-fearing village, Mrs Everingham,' he says.

'No, no. I'm *Carmichael* – Joey and her dad are Everinghams.'

'Not married either?'

'What seems to be the problem here?' Mum chimes in, coming to my rescue, as always.

'I'll come straight to the point,' he says. 'We're a little *concerned* that, well . . . In the eyes of God – and the Church – family is sacred. We like to promote family values wherever we can, and we feel that your little club is, well, negating all our good work.'

You *what*?!

'. . . going quite some way to encourage drunkenness and the disintegration of the family unit, promoting a wanton lust for all things *detrimental*—'

'Hang about!' I say, cutting him off. 'We just meet once a week to talk about stuff that's getting us down.'

'Well, my son is one of your number and his membership of your club is in no way encouraging him to see the error of his ways – quite the opposite, in fact.'

'But Tim's a great guy! You should be proud that he's so caring and thoughtful and talented . . . and . . . compassionate. He did the posters for—'

'Yes, yes, yes. I see you've set up an evening to help the members of our community afflicted by the recent floods—'

'Yeah, we have! And your son was instrumental in organising it! And how come you didn't see *that* flood coming, then, eh?'

Mum shoots me her appalled look. My religious education's somewhat lacking, to say the least, and she's often bemoaned the fact she didn't send me to a convent when we were living in Adelaide. For many reasons.

'Miss Carmichael, we're a *tolerant* community, but I—'

'Just because they annoy us from time to time doesn't mean we don't *love* our families. God!'

'I think we've all said enough,' says Mum, standing up. 'Maybe it's time you went.'

I resist the temptation to say 'More tea, vicar?' because a) I want him out of our house now, b) I bet he hears it all the time and c) he'll only tell me off for getting his title wrong again.

Wilfred stands up and heads for the door. He opens it and just as he's about to step outside, he says:

'And we object to the use of – I suppose you'd call it a pun – the *pun* "Floody Hell" on your posters.'

'Yeah? Well, *I* object to you coming round here,' I say under my breath.

'I'm sorry to hear that, rector. Good day,' says Mum, closing the door behind him. She sounds like a 1940s Ealing Comedy headmistress for this last bit – so brilliantly superior and dismissive.

'Can you *believe* that?' I ask Mum. 'I didn't think people like that existed! Well, only on TV, on *Midsomer Murders*.'

'How *fasc*inating,' says Mum – always interested, my mum. Well, she *is* a sociologist – this kind of thing, life in a small English village, life anywhere, any kind of social interaction really is her bag.

'Well, I don't see him and *his* flock doing much to help flood victims – except say a few prayers or whatever – and it's *their* boss who got everyone into this mess in the first place—'

'More likely it's the effects of global warming than an Act of God, darling—'

'Yeah, well . . . what an *arse*!'

'It's a pity he didn't want to join forces with the POP Club, really – would've done the Church no end of good, being seen to really help people out. Shame.'

I butter some hot toast for Joey.

'Interesting,' Mum goes on, 'I always thought it was the Methodists who didn't approve of drinking. Might lead to dancing, you know.'

'Well, fuck 'em if they can't take a joke,' I say, taking a gargantuan bite of Joey's toast.

'Don't look now,' Mum whispers, leaning into the table, 'but that man behind you – don't look, don't look! – that man behind you has been on his mobile phone ever since we got here!'

We've dropped Joey off at the nursery and hot-footed it down to The Swan for lunch.

'Yeah – ooh! The risotto's quite nice, had it the other night. Not too fattening, either, I don't think—'

'I mean, how *bored* must his wife – or girlfriend, or mistress – *be*, sitting there, listening to him drone on about his shares or whatever?'

'Mind you, there's probably cream in it – *and* loads of butter—'

'If I were her, I'd walk out on him right now. I mean, how rude!'

'. . . Of course salad's always the dieter's favoured option – but I feel like something hearty, something a bit more *substantial*—'

'Honestly, there's nothing more boring than being forced to listen to someone else's dull work conversation . . .'

'Yes there is,' I say, sighing deeply.

'Hmm?'

'Listening to someone *tell* you about someone else's boring conversation – *that's* even more borax than having to listen to it first-hand.'

'I'm only saying—'

'I know, I know. So what're you going to have?'

We fanny about, trying to work out what looks like the most satisfying meal for the least calories and, eventually, I go inside to order.

'Hiya,' I say to the barmaid.

'Oh hi there. What can I get you?'

'Two bangers and mash, please!' Well, you know, it's a treat. And Mum's paying.

'Okey dokey,' she says. 'Looking forward to the big night?' she asks me.

'You betcha!' says an excited voice behind me as I feel my ribs being tickled.

It's Tim.

'Timotei!' I say.

'Wotcha, cock!' he replies, planting himself on the bar stool next to me. 'Timblioni, please, sweetheart.'

'What are you doing here? POP Club's not till tomorrow night!'

'Just meeting someone . . .' He splays his hands out in front of him, studies his nails and then starts chewing on one.

'Anyone exciting?'

'No. Someone fabulously, fantastically, excruciatingly *thrilling*, actually!'

'Wowsers,' I say, remembering how exciting it was when Jack and I first started seeing each other.

'What are you doing here?'

'Lunch. With Mum. Joey's at nursery.'

'You don't need to explain yourself to me, sweetie.'

'No, I know – but I *do* have to explain myself to your *dad*, it would seem!'

Tim winces.

'I did try to warn you,' he says softly. 'Sent you a text this morning – didn't you get it?'

'The "Watch out – rector's about" message? Oh, now it makes sense! I thought you'd sent it to the wrong person and it was something to do with erections, an erector or someone's rectum or something!'

'You're an idiot,' he smiles.

'I know,' I agree.

'Oh, I'm sorry about that, Roxy. He thinks he has the moral majority – thinks he's right all the time about everything. Religious fanatics, eh? What can you do?'

'And you never said your dad was the local rector!'

'It's not something I like to broadcast.' He smiles wanly.

We both contemplate the hellness of Tim's situation. And then June's words about accentuating the positive jump into my head. Yes! That'll cheer Tim up.

'Hey! The posters are amazing, by the way. You're really very talented, Timmy. And it's going to be such a brilliant night—'

'All part of the service,' he says, watching the door nervously. 'Do I look all right?'

'*Gor*-geous,' I say, looking him up and down and spiking my hand on his way over-gelled hair when I touch it. 'And, ah, what aftershave have you got on?'

'Hugo Boss,' he says proudly, pulling up the collar on his shirt.

Thought I recognised it – it's Jack's favourite.

'It's his favourite,' Tim says, picking a bit of fluff off his shoulder.

'So who is he, this mystery fancy man of yours?'

'That's for me to know and you to find out,' he grins. 'I'll fill you in tomorrow night. If I'm not too busy getting filled in my own good self, that is!'

When I get back outside, Mum's staring at the couple at the table behind my chair.

'He's still on his phone!' she says, not quietly any more, probably wanting to be heard, to shake the guy up.

Mum's caught the woman's eye and pulls a 'What are you going to do?' kind of sympathy face, fanning her hands out in front of her.

'Let it go, Mum,' I say, embarrassed.

She's always like this at restaurants. Drives you mad.

'So, d'you think we should move to the Blue Mountains?'

Mum tears her eyes away from the other table and looks at me, finally.

'Well, of course I don't want you to go, sweetheart, but you have to do what you think is best for you and Jack as a couple. And for Josephine, too.'

'Wouldn't be for about eighteen months, anyway – we're locked into our mortgage for a certain amount of time. And there's no way we'd be able to sell our house – we'd have to rent it out . . . But you'd come out and visit us, wouldn't you?'

'I don't know, darling – that trip's terribly taxing on the old bones, these days—'

'But if Alex and Chrissie are there, too – and all your grandkids. Hey! Do you think I should have another baby? Maybe we should wait till we're out there to have it—'

'But you'll be a hundred years old, by then!'

'I'm only just coming up to forty! And women get pregnant right up to fifty these days!'

'I don't know,' she says softly. 'Are you and Jack getting along better, then?'

'Yes . . . Except for the nearly-a-hundred-per-cent fact he's having an affair.'

'Darling, don't be ridiculous. He *adores* you.'

'I think he's adoring someone else a bit more lately. Someone from the POP Club, as it turns out.'

'Really?'

'I don't know for sure, but he's acting weird with his mobile and seems awfully chummy with Carina, the glamorous-but-a-tad-tarty one from the Club. And he came back from golf with a love-bite on his neck. She's a golfer, too.'

'Really?'

'He says he got hit by a golf ball – but it looked like a hickey to me!'

'Suspicion. Sign of an idle mind,' says Mum. 'And darling, you do let your imagination carry you away sometimes, don't you? Living in a dream world a lot of the time, hmm?'

'Maybe . . .'

'What does Jack say?'

'I haven't put it to him yet.'

'Bound to be rubbish. How's your sex life?'

'Speaking of rubbish . . .'

'Why don't you make him dinner? Tonight. Once Joey's asleep, have some wine and make him feel special. Loved.' She looks off past my ear, staring at the guy on his mobile again.

'Worth another go, I suppose,' I say, thinking back to the lukewarm reception I got for the wine and candle-less Weight Watchers ready meals. And the fish and chips Jack eventually went out to get.

Just as our full-fat, gazillion-points bangers and mash arrives, my mobile chirps. I finally found it this morning – in the Bermuda Triangle of the house, the study.

'Better get it, Mum – might be the nursery.'

It's Charlie.

'Listen to *this*,' she says, panting. 'He's gone.'

'Who?'

'Guy! He's left the firm, got a job back in France and is moving back there to be with Mignon today!'

'No way!'

Mum gives me that appalled look again.

'Can you believe it?'

'What a prick!' I say.

Mum tuts loudly and gets the *Big Issue* out of her bag.

'Yeah. Should've known he was a twat,' Charlie puffs.

'Where are you? Are you running?'

'Just went to the hairdresser's, about to get back to the office – I'm late. Only good thing is it means my job at the firm's safe – they can afford to keep me on if they don't replace him.'

'Well, that's good,' I say encouragingly.

'Sort of . . .'

'Hey! What're you doing this Wednesday night? Want to come to Riverside for a Pissed-Off Parents Club meeting?'

'Yeah, right! I've got to work – can't get any more time off – can't do it. I'll probably be otherwise engaged, anyway.'

'Yeah?'

Mum heaves a huge sigh.

'Look, Chaz – can I ring you later? I'm having lunch with Mum at the mo.'

'Yeah – laters.'

'It's over, then? With Charlotte and the Frenchman?' asks Mum.

'Yeah. He's gone back to his wife in France.'

'Poor Charlotte,' says Mum, stuffing a forkful of bangers and mash into her mouth.

'So anyway – do *you* think the POP Club's unethical?'

'No, not at all, sweetheart!' she says, once she's swallowed her mouthful. 'I think it's *fabulous* – and fundraising for flood victims is a wonderful idea.'

'Giving something back,' I say, delighting in watching her roll her eyes skywards. She hates those sorts of clichés, as though people are talking like pamphlets. American, Disney pamphlets. *Pamphlet-ese*, she calls it.

'Do you want to come? Should be lots of fun,' I say, loving the idea of Mum at the do. 'You and June would get on like a house on fire!'

'Next Saturday?'

'Yup!'

'I'd love to, but I can't, darling.'

'Why?'

'Tosca.'

'Same to you!'

'Opera, darling. Covent Garden.'

305

I tell her how much I miss London and she suggests all of us, Jack included, stay in Paddington next week. She'll arrive back from Sweden first thing on Thursday morning, but before that we can have the whole place to ourselves.

'Did you ever know that you're my heeee-ro,' I sing to Mum, doing my best Bette Midler.

When I get home, I start making a spaghetti bolognaise. I've got some £3.59 vin rouge ordinaire, organic lean beef, bacon, two onions, two cloves of garlic, sun-dried tomatoes, still-on-the-vine tomatoes, a tube of tomato paste and some wholemeal spaghetti. Jack's going to faint with surprise that I'm a) cooking and b) being so considerate, after he's had such a long hard day. He'll sweep me into his arms and ravish me there and then – well, shortly after he's put Joey to bed, anyway. And then, once we've flirted with each other over flickering candlelight, he'll fall madly in love with me all over again and dump Carina. By text. And all because the lad loves a tomato-ey Wet Dog.

While said culinary masterpiece is simmering away on the range cooker and I'm on my way to pick up Joey, I call Charlie.

'Can't talk for long,' she says. 'I'm on my way into town.'

I can hear her walking, her high heels click-clacking on the cobblestones.

'Just wanted to find out a bit more about Guy, the arseho—'

'Old news, Rox,' she says quickly. 'Already over it.'

Jeez, she's a fast worker.

'Who you meeting, then?'

'My date. Can you believe it? I'm actually going on a date!'

'Who with?'

'Guy I met the other night at O'Flannery's. He's *gorgeous* – probably too gorgeous for me . . .'

'Don't be crazy! But how . . . what . . .'

'Keep it brief – haven't got all night, you know!'

'Did he ask you out?'

'Yes – exactly how it should happen. Our eyes met over the crowd, he bought me a drink, we had a quick chat, he asked for my number and then he waited outside with me till my taxi turned up.'

'Wow! It's like in the movies! A proper *date*!'

'I know! He's not my type or anything – he's an IT manager – but he's really nice. I'm so nervous!'

'Sounds perfect! Always go for the opposite of your type, I reckon – your "type" is just shorthand for the usual bastards who let you down and dump you in the end.'

'Thanks a lot!'

'No, I don't mean you, personally, I mean *one*!' I say, thinking she sounds a little tetchy. Must be the nerves.

'Oh, right. But listen, that's not the really big news . . .'

'No?'

'No.' She pauses to light her roll-up. 'I only went and had a fringe cut in this lunchtime.'

'Ooh! Fringes are excellent,' I say, getting excited.

'Think so?'

'Definitely! They take years off you, make you look so much younger.'

'So you're saying I look old, then?'

Oh, for God's sake. Here we go . . .

'Gotta go – I'm here. Wish me luck!'

'Good luck! And DON'T SHAG HIM, OK?'

I shout the last bit, just as I'm greeted at the nursery door by the manageress.

22

'First up on the agenda, ladies and gents, is sex,' says Tim once we're all gathered round the table at The Swan. 'Anyone?'

'Chance'd be a fine thing,' I mumble. 'I made a special dinner for him last night, had the candles ready and everything, but he claims he was having *a swift one* with the guys he works with. Didn't get home till eleven.'

'Maybe he was too busy *singing show tunes*,' says Olivia.

'Musical kinda guy, is he?' asks Tim, sucking in his cheeks and opening his eyes wide like he's on to something.

'Yes, he is,' I reply. 'But that's not the point. I don't think that's the problem. I think he's having an affair. With a *woman*.'

My eyes dart to Carina, who's taking a larger than usual slug of her G&T.

'Really?' she says, after swallowing hard.

'Yeah,' I say, like a hard-boiled detective, my eyes

boring into hers in anticipation of some pretty heavy guilty ocular activity.

'Who's the lucky guy?' asks Tim, giggling.

'Yeah! Who do you think he's having this affair with?' Carina chimes in, acting all innocent.

'I've got my suspicions,' I say slowly. 'So . . . what were you up to last night, Carina?'

'I was at home. Sorting out some PR for the fundraiser.'

'I can't wait!' jumps in Olivia.

'I've seen the posters everywhere – it's going to be massive!' says Paul, rubbing his hands together and beaming.

'Only two meetings, including this one, to go until the big night,' says June, as though she's a six-year-old, talking about how many sleeps till Christmas.

'Interesting,' I say, the only calm one here.

'Ooo-kay,' says Tim, clasping his hands in front of him and looking round the table. 'Let's bring it up, people. Now. Guess who's got a hot date for the fundraiser.'

'Me!' shrieks Olivia.

We all turn to look at her.

'Well, sort of. He said he'd be here, at any rate.'

'That's great, Liv,' I say measuredly, waiting for Carina to expose herself any minute now.

'Yeah,' says Paul softly, forcing a smile.

'Yup, you're definitely *in*, there,' I say to Liv.

'Is Jack coming?' Carina asks me casually.

'Well, you'd know.' I narrow my eyes at Carina.

'Eh?' grunts Carina and pushes her cigarette packet towards me.

'No, thanks. Given up,' I say, grasping my tomato juice with both white-knuckled hands.

Not only will staying off the beers keep me from having any cigarettes, it should also help me remember things – like anything incriminating Carina might say.

'Good for you!' June lights up a Sobranie.

'How long's it been?' Carina actually looks interested.

'I don't know precisely, but it feels like ages.' I unfurrow my brow. 'It's thirsty work, though – anyone for another one?'

'I could murder a triple,' says Carina, looking pleadingly at me. 'I'll come and help you.'

At the bar, I try to cajole Carina into a confession. Easy peasy, this detective work. I study her face, anticipating her teary breakdown when I say:

'I just can't get it out of my head that Jack's hiding something from me. He's definitely got a guilty secret.'

'How do you know it's a guilty one?' she asks, coming over all coquettish.

'What other kind is there?' comes my razor-sharp reply.

'Hmm.' She smiles her one-sided, cheekbone-revealing smile and places our order.

While we're carrying the trays outside, my mind starts racing. If he's not having an affair with Carina – which I'm not a hundred per cent convinced about yet – who is he having it with?

I get a whiff of Tim's aftershave and it immediately makes me think of Jack – he always wears it when he's going out. Tim did say it was his mystery man's favourite . . . Oh God! Maybe Olivia and Charlie are right – maybe Jack *is* gay . . . Stray golf ball, my arse – what if Jack's having a stray affair with a man? And what if that man is . . . *Tim*?

23

'Joey! Can't you jump on Mummy for a bit? SHE doesn't have to get up for work tomorrow,' Jack snaps as he picks Joey up off his belly and puts her on the floor.

I'm lying on the couch reading the paper and Jack's lying on the floor, trying to do the same. It's Sunday afternoon, Father's Day. And because I've got bugger-all cash, all he got was a card from Joey and a tube of Pringles – with money I borrowed from him.

But that's not what's got him all het up. He didn't get the promotion that he went for at work, so now he has to report to some alpha male-type who, Jack says, goes about pissing on people's desks (metaphorically), marking his territory, establishing dominance, beating his chest and braying at every available opportunity about his prowess in selling their IT system. So not Jack's style.

Neither's all this annoyance in front of Joey, either, though.

'Fuck's sake!'

'Hey! Don't take it out on her.' I pull the paper down and see Joey crawling over to me, her bottom lip jutting out, trembling.

'I'm NOT! ARGH! I'm going out for a cig.'

'And I DO have to get up for work tomorrow morning,' I call out after him. 'After having worked all through the pigging night trying to settle Joey down. It's hard work looking after her AND trying to earn some money at the same time, you know – are you ever going to understand that?'

'Change the fucking record,' I hear him mutter as the back door slams and Joey collapses into a teary heap on my lap.

I'm not having this. *I'm* the one who goes in for the histrionics in this relationship – why's he stealing my thunder?

He comes back in, reeking of smoke and says, measuredly:

'I can't bear it any more.'

'YOU can't?' I counter.

'If only you hadn't given up work—'

'Who would've looked after Joey? I think you mean: If only we hadn't moved to the country—'

'If you hadn't given up work, we'd be quids in now. I'd be able to buy new golf clubs and maybe even a motorbike—'

'God! It's not all about YOU and what you can buy for yourself! There's three of us in this relationship now – and Joey comes first!'

'Oh yeah? Is that why you go to the POP Club every week? It's for her benefit, is it?'

'It IS for her, actually! The POP Club makes me happy – about the only thing that does these days – and a happy mum makes for a happy baby—'

'And a thoroughly fucked-off father,' he says. 'If you could earn some money – or we were in Australia – we'd be fine.'

'Would we?'

Usually Jack would reassure me at this point, give me a hug and say there, there – make me feel safe again. But he doesn't. He just looks straight at me and says:

'I'm not sure, to be honest.'

Then his left eye starts to twitch, betraying his nerves. And suddenly we're plunged into a darker, scarier kind of sniping place.

'What are you saying?' I ask cautiously, clutching Joey to my chest.

'I dunno. Maybe we need a break.'

'We definitely need a break – like, the house could stop falling apart around our ears and I could get a column at *Positive Parenting!*—'

'No, no – I mean us. As a couple.'

And it's then that I start to feel the tiny pin pricks in the back of my neck. Just like you do when you're getting dumped.

He doesn't say anything for a bit, just looks at Joey, being careful not to meet my eye.

'Which is why this week couldn't've come at a better time,' he says mock-cheerily, slapping his palms on his thighs.

'Whoa!' I stand up and hand Joey to him. 'You mean this week is a break for us? Not just a week off from Riverside for all of us – but a . . . a . . . *trial separation*?'

'No, no. I just reckon we could both really do with some time. Time to think. And it's good timing. You go up to Paddo, I'll take the week off and my mum can come and stay here with me. I've got so much to do . . .'

'A-HA! You'll have your mum round for the whole week, looking after Joey while you play golf or *Civ*!'

'No I won't. I'm looking forward to spending some time with Joey alone, the two of us together. Beats work any day.'

I don't rise to the bait, just stand there, mouth open, trying to take it all in and figure out what it really means.

I make a mental list of pros and cons:

PROS:

1) I've got a week up in London all by myself. YAY! It'll be just like the old days, going out, having a great time, unfettered by bloke or baby. It'll be like I'm twenty-five again! Trial separation? Trial jubilation, more like!

2) I'll be able to write up that *Positive Parenting!* story, get more commissions – maybe even a column!

3) I'll be able to sleep without being woken up by Joey

or the loud thoughts crashing about in my head that shout our sex life and, as a result, our whole relationship is over.

Which makes me frown and catapults me into the

CONS:
1) Is this it? Is this the end for me and Jack?
2) No, really – is this trial separation a gentle, slow torture precursor to getting chucked?
3) What if it is and he runs off with Carina?

'Earth to Roxane.' Jack smiles at me for the first time today.

'Or worse, he runs off with *Tim*?'

'What?'

'Er, nothing. Look, is this a trial separation? Is this us breaking up, Jack? Because if it is, I wish you'd just come out and say it.'

'No, no, of course it isn't!'

'Are you sure? Because I think things have been so much better, really rather good with us lately.'

'They have! I'm in a bad mood, that's all. Sorry. Think of this week as a good thing, exactly as it was before I just lost it. Ignore all that stuff I said . . . you usually do.' He smiles, letting me know he's calmed down.

'I've neglected you a bit, haven't I?'

'No. Well, maybe a bit. But don't worry about it. This is

your chance to get away by yourself, figure out what it is you want from me and our life together. You'll have heaps of time to get some perspective. And some work, too – help with the family coffers, as June would say. And up in London, eh? How great is that?'

'Hadn't thought of it that way,' I lie, biting my lip.

'Better get packing, then. Ready for your adventure in the Big Smoke!'

'You seem awfully keen to get me out of the house. Very excited about a week on your own . . .'

'I am, actually, as it goes. But,' he says, balancing Joey on one hip and putting his other arm around me, steering me towards the stairs, 'it'll be good for us – all three of us. We just need a bit of time apart. Don't you think?'

'Yes,' I agree. 'Yes, I suppose I do. But—'

'So what are you waiting for? If it was me going away for the week to play golf, I'd be out the door by now!'

And he would, too.

He bounces a giggling Joey on to the bed and grabs a backpack off the floor, emptying out its contents and shoving my velvet maternity frock in it.

Much as it pains me to admit, I have been wrong before. Quite recently, in fact. About a lot of things. I was way off about Tim's dad, who I thought was his boyfriend. And I could be wrong about 6-Ten manager Marcus being gay . . . Jack, too, for that matter. I thought he was having an affair with Carina – but couldn't see any real dead give-aways from either of them. Maybe he isn't busy settling in his new girlfriend while I'm gone and this week doesn't constitute a trial separation at all. Yeah, that's it – I've let my fantasies take over from reality, and everything's fine. Just fine.

I'm trying hard to convince myself, but I can't help feeling that *something* fishy's going on. I mean, he was pretty anxious to get me out of the house, wasn't he? To make way for his affair? I just can't shake the nagging doubts in my head as I leave Paddington station and wander up the road to Mum and Dad's flat.

Right out the front of Mum and Dad's, taking up half the footpath, is a big, yellow steel sandwich board-type sign that says:

MURDER
APPEAL FOR WITNESSES
ON SUNDAY 26TH MAY A MAN WAS INJURED DURING A
DISTURBANCE OUTSIDE 30 PADDINGTON GARDENS. HE
LATER DIED IN HOSPITAL. IF YOU REMEMBER HEARING
OR SEEING ANYTHING PLEASE CONTACT US IN
STRICTEST CONFIDENCE AT THE NUMBER BELOW.

I scurry down the steps to the basement, fumble with the lock, get inside and slam the door shut behind me. On the coffee table in the front room is a copy of the *Evening Standard*. Its front page screams:

319

GUN SLAUGHTER
IN THE SUBURBS

I make a tea and call Jack.

'Jesus, what a shocker,' he says when I tell him about the police sign in the street.

'I know! Scary stuff, eh?'

'You still want to move back there?'

'Ah, dunno, just got here . . .'

'And already there's death and destruction on your doorstep. Literally! It's no place for Joey. Or me. Or you! You never see those sorts of signs up round here. Just posters for drinking clubs and flood appeals.'

'So you're missing me?'

'Yeah, look, I better go – Joey did a massive poo after about an hour of straining, and it spilled out on to her tights. I took them off and had them in the laundry to wash, but she's crawling through the kitchen now and she's got them on her head.'

'Oh! Poor thing! Give her a big kiss for me, will you?'

'Yeah – once I've cleaned her up and washed her hair, course I will.'

Hmm. No evidence of an affair there, then.

I finish the *Positive Parenting!* feature, send an idea off to Vanessa at *Village Life* and then sleep.

And sleep.

And sleep some more.

And when Olivia rings on Wednesday morning, I'm still lying in the sofa bed in Dad's study.

She tells me how she's seen her ex and even though he seems well into her again – and, obviously, desperate to see Stuart loads more – she's wary. She reckons once you make a break, it's broken and there's no going back.

I tell her about my and Jack's little contretemps and she goes all 'Oh, I'm sorry, how awful' on me. I say it's not that bad, nothing to worry about, it's just a bit of a break.

'Slippery slope,' she says sympathetically.

I wonder if she knows something I don't – about Jack or, indeed, relationships in general – and ask her to keep an eye on him for me at the POP Club meeting tonight. And then, as if on cue, Jack calls the landline. He's the cheeriest I've heard him in a long time. I can hear the television on in the background.

'If she HAS to watch telly, can you at least make sure it's something *educational*?' I nag.

'Yeah – I'll make sure she watches *Neighbours* later, get her Oz-tracised for the Blue-ies.'

'Ostracised is right – it's too far away!'

'From what?'

'The *action*.'

'Mum says she'd stay with us for a week once a month and help look after Joey if we lived there – now *that* would be amazing. And you'd be near Alex and Chrissie and their kids, Joey'd actually get to know her cousins – both sets, my sister's kids aren't that far away, either.'

'Yeah, true.'

'It'd make having another one so much easier . . .'

'Yeah, well, we'll see.'

'Just think – a whole week off, once a month!'

'What if I was breastfeeding?'

'Don't let's go into that whole nightmare again,' he says, probably thinking about how positively bovine my last attempt made me look, hooked up to the milking machine – while all I can picture is his mum grabbing my boob.

'Anyway, I'm off to get Joey some shoes now. I'm trying to teach her how to walk. Talk later. Mmmmwah!'

And in my mind, the image of his mum's grasping, bony hand is replaced with Jack's big, juicy lips blowing me a kiss down the line.

Before we had Joey, I used to love coming to the Cafe Rouge in Whiteley's Shopping Centre, having endless pots of Earl Grey and talking on the mobile to Charlie. And smoking like a chimney.

But you can't smoke anywhere in Whiteley's these days – and thank God, I think to myself as I sit down on the Paris-style red and white plastic weaved chair. I don't fancy a fag at all – particularly now there's no haze of smoke hanging over you as you chow down on your croque monsieur.

I call everyone I know in London – all those great old mates – and not one of them is free to come out with me for a just-like-old-times drink tonight. They all say they'll see me soon, but tonight they're either going out with other friends or recovering from hangovers. So much for the old days.

I order a pot of Earl Grey and call Charlie.

'So how'd The Date go?'

'The Date was fab. Great, in fact.'

'Yeah?'

'Yeah. We had dinner, talked loads and it turns out he's perfect. He's forty, he's got two kids . . . He ticks all my boxes – he's the right age, lush to look at, has this amazing body and, and . . . we just got on so well, I can't believe he hasn't called me!'

'Maybe he's doing the old three-day wait thing – you know, not calling in case he looks too keen . . .'

'But it's been four days now!'

'Maybe it's a four-day wait in Bath—'

'No, let's face it. It's different for guys, the whole single parent thing. Me having Rose probably put him right off. He's got enough kids to contend with.'

'Well, even if this one hasn't worked out, it doesn't mean the next one won't. Least you're back in the dating game.'

'But I don't want to be back in the dating game! I thought he might've been a contender for The One.'

'He still might call, though! Maybe he's traditional, likes to take it slow. And if he doesn't call, then it wasn't meant to be. Then you can move on to the next one – and thank God you didn't shag him.'

'But I did!'

'Eh?'

'We were getting on so well, it was like meeting my soulmate – which I know sounds corny, but that's what it was like! And the sex was *fan*-tastic, too. Not that you'd know anything about that . . .'

'But just because you're getting on well, it doesn't mean you have to shag him! Not on the first date, anyway. *And* I told you not to! Don't you *ever* listen to me?'

'Not if I can help it.'

'The first date! Honestly, Chuck—'

'First and last, obviously. Maybe that's why he hasn't called – he got what he wanted without having to wait, without having to work for it, woo me a little bit . . .'

'Don't be ridiculous! That's so old-fashioned! Guys aren't like that any more. Are they?'

'The ones I meet are. They're only after one thing and as soon as they get it . . .'

'Why don't you call him?'

'It's up to the guy to call! And anyway, I don't have his number.'

'Why didn't you get it?'

'Because I wanted to be chased.'

'As opposed to *chaste*.'

'What?'

'Nothing.'

'Well what about you and Jack?'

'Ah, not so good. We had a bit of a barney the other day

and he said we needed a break, so I'm up in Paddington on my own.'

'What? No way! Not you two, you're supposed to be the solid ones – all fixed up. For life!'

'We are, I think. It's only a bit of time on our own.'

'I'll be there as soon as I can. Don't panic – I'll bring the vodka.'

'I'm not panicked. And anyway, don't you have to work tomorrow?'

'Fuck work, I'll throw a sickie – this is serious.'

'It's not that serious,' I say optimistically. 'It's not like it's a trial separation or anything . . .'

'Trial separation, I know, I know, it's serious,' she sings. 'As Morrissey might say.'

As soon as she says that, I'm reminded of Barry.

'*And* I'm missing the POP Club tonight, to cap it all off.'

'Sod that – we'll have our own mini-meeting right there in Paddington. I'm on my way!'

24

I know it's Charlie nearly breaking down the basement door an hour and a half later, because I can hear bottles clinking outside.

'That was quick,' I say as she shoots past me, marching purposefully down the hallway into the kitchen.

'No time to waste – a friend in need's a friend in need of vodka,' she shouts back at me. 'And I can't believe you're still wearing that stupid velvet maternity frock, by the way. No wonder he's chucked you.'

We sit at the kitchen table and both watch her intently pour huge amounts of vodka into two wine glasses and add a splash of Diet Coke – 'just a soupçon,' she smiles, 'to taste.'

'Now. Tell. Me. *Everything.*' She clasps her hands in front of her. Charlie in agony aunt mode is a sight seldom seen – and a little unnerving, to tell the truth.

'Well, on Father's Day—'

'Succinctly, please.'

'I suppose it's been brewing, really. The move, Joey, Riverside, the lack of cash – it's all taken its toll on us.'

'Whose idea was it? This trial separation?'

'It's not a trial separation!'

'It was Jack, wasn't it? I knew it!' She looks pleased with herself and slaps her knees. 'You're on the slippery slope to splitsville, sister, if you don't sort your sex life out soon, as I keep telling you.'

I'm momentarily silent, impressed with her alliteration.

'It's true! You'll be single before you know it, Rox – and no one wants to be a single mum, lemme tell you. But you, you and Jack, you can save your relationship.'

'Well, you didn't manage to save yours!'

'Why do you think I'm talking to you like this? I know what I'm on about and I can see how it can be fixed. Just let the niggles go, suck it down. And be nice to him. What have you got to lose?'

'Only everything, I suppose.'

'That's right. Don't want to end up like me, do you? Only shorter and not quite as good looking, obviously . . .'

And once she's put it like that – so simply even I can understand it, like a verbal slap in the face – I think I'm beginning to see the light.

Good old straight-talking, tough-love Chazzer. I want to call Jack right then and there and tell him I love him and say sorry for being such an old boot for such a long time, but Charlie warns me against it, saying I've had too much vodka. I take her advice, and decide on going back

327

to Riverside first thing in the morning – to fight for my man.

'Well you seem to be all full of the joys of spring tonight – did The Date ring?' I ask hopefully.

'Nope,' she says, deadpan.

'Oh.'

We both take several more large gulps and make a move out the front, to the basement stairwell, for a fag. I know, I know – but what can you do? Desperate times do call for desperate measures, after all.

'Thanks for bringing that up, though,' Charlie sighs, shooting me daggers. 'I doubt I'll ever hear from him again. *Pfft* – another one disappears into the ether.'

'No word from Guy then, either?'

'What is this? Taking pleasure in my misfortunes, are you?'

'No, I—'

'I did hear from him today, as it happens. First time since he left. It was a curt email saying sorry, but "Wherever you go, there you are"—'

'He said *that*? Doesn't sound very French . . .'

'His English was always crap. And anyway, I'm paraphrasing.'

'Oh. S'pose it is a bit Eric Cantona, now I think about it . . .'

'He said although he'd *thought* we had a future together, he finally realised that his heart was too firmly entrenched in France and with Mig-bloody-non and his kids for it to ever really work out between us.'

'Ah,' I murmur, looking up at the feet of the passers-by on the footpath above us.

'Yeah. So. Yeah.'

'So how do you feel about that?'

'Fine. Whatever. You know.' She leaves her roll-up in the side of her mouth, squints, and makes a big 'W' with her thumbs and forefingers.

'Really?'

'*Pfft.*' She blows the smoke out and looks up at the endless array of suitcases on wheels going past.

'I don't believe you. I know you too well, Chuckie – you must feel something. I mean, you were going to *marry* this guy!'

'*Ghee,*' she sneers. 'Fucking French.'

'You loved him, though, didn't you?'

'Whatever that means.'

We contemplate this metaphysical minefield, studying the human traffic at the top of the steps until I slowly become aware of a sound I'd never usually associate with Charlie. I hear soft sniffs and the splash of – what? Tears? – on the concrete by our feet. She's crying! Hard-as-nails Charlie's actually crying.

'Hey, hey, hey,' I coo, reaching up and gently putting my arm around her heaving shoulders, using a tone of voice reserved solely for Joey these days.

'Ah, what would you know about it?' She shrugs my arm away.

'Hey, hey – come inside. Come on.'

I steer her inside whereupon she skulls her vodka and ploughs straight into another one.

'It's all right for you. You and your cosy little life in Riverside.'

'It's definitely *not* all right for me. Jack's about to bail out on me and Joey—'

'Still huge? Still ramming food down her throat?'

'Ah, not so much any more. She's quite cute, really, now – and very sweet.'

I resist the temptation to whip my camera out and show Charlie my latest photos of Joey. For once I sense it would be inappropriate.

'Yada, yada, yada – you sound like one of those mother and baby group mums,' she sniffs.

'But Jack's certainly weird. I know you say he isn't, but maybe he is having an—'

'Nyurgh. He's not having an affair. End of. And anyway, what about me? I'm having a breakdown, here – or hadn't you noticed?'

'Sorry!' I say, forgetting for a sec that Charlie's been blubbing like a baby.

'I'm too giving,' she sniffs again.

I nod, sagely and slowly, trying to at once stifle a guffaw and mirror the agony aunt face she had on before.

'Too generous with my heart. I give my love too freely, only to get it thrown back in my face. Every time. It's just that with Guy, I could really see into the future – with us, as a couple, maybe him adopting Rose . . .'

'Maybe you were too quick with all that. You know, had him frog-marched down the aisle before he could say—'

'But why? Why does it have to be down to me, down to a fault of mine? What's wrong with being romantic? What's wrong with getting excited about building a life with someone? Why does that have to be such a bad thing?'

'You're right, it doesn't. It isn't. He was just an arsehole in the end.'

'Too right he was. He led *me* on. He had no intention of marrying me and leaving Mignon for good. But why me? Time after fucking time. What's wrong with me?'

'Nothing! You're gorgeous, smart, funny . . .'

'And a single mum.'

'You just don't meet the right guys.'

'You think so? Oh, it's all so bloody *complicated*. What about you and Jack, then?'

'Yeah, complicated . . .'

'No! I don't mean what about you as a *couple* – don't you and Jack know anyone I could hook up with?'

'Oh! Well, no, no I don't, really,' I say quietly, racking my brains for someone good enough, brave enough to unleash on Charlie.

She's been nagging us for years to fix her up with some-one. But nerdy IT friends of Jack's never made the grade and all the guys I knew in magazines were far too young or gay. And, let's face it, Charlie's pretty demanding. Specially when it comes to men. He's got to be stunning to look at, round about her age, have kids of his own but be divorced, clever, witty, charming . . .

'Hang on!' I say, getting all excited. 'I might have one for you! His name's Paul, he's in IT—'

'Nyeurgh,' Charlie snarls.

'No, wait! He's gorgeous – *lush*, as you would say – about forty, he has a daughter and he's divorced—'

'When can I meet him?'

'This Saturday! In Riverside! The Pissed-Off Parents Club is putting on a benefit night for the flood victims. It's going to be a big night, so if The Date doesn't call, why don't you come along?'

'Let's face it, The Date ain't gonna call. I'm as good as there.'

'Brilliant!'

'He bloody well *better* be . . .' She wipes what's left of her tears away and straightens up, pulling her shoulders back and puffing out her chest like she's pulling herself together, ready to face the fight again.

Coughing, she waves an imaginary Guy from her head, like she's shooing away a fly.

'But enough of that,' she says quickly. 'Let's go to the King's Head. I always find this flat too dark and depressing. Do I look all right?'

'Panda eyes,' I say, wiping the skin under my own eye to illustrate my point. 'Hey! Remember being at the King's Head watching Euro '96? Fark! Nineteen-ninety-bloody-SIX! That's like – hang on – that's—'

'A million years ago,' Charlie whispers, flashing me a look that says keep your voice down, even though there's only the two of us in the room.

'Yeah! It was all Britpop and Oasis versus Blur and that great video of that tall, skinny guy walking down the street, bumping into everyone – who was that?'

'Richard Ashcroft,' she says. 'The Verve.'

'Brilliant,' I say, smiling at the memory.

'Time to move on, Rox,' Charlie says, fluffing up her hair. 'And you know, *you* could try wearing a bit of slap every now and again.'

She studies her face in her compact mirror. Lipstick on, a final nose-blow, a trowel-full of liquid foundation and pressed-powder in place, she stands up and says:

'Let's go get 'em, tiger.'

I don't know what wakes me up first – Mum tutting loudly, sounding like Skippy alerting the humans to some bush catastrophe, or the kettle bubbling to boiling point in the kitchen. I cautiously open one crusty eye and manage to eventually focus on Mum standing at the doorway to Dad's study, shaking her head disappointedly as she stares at Charlie and me, both star-fished on the sofa bed.

'*Plus ça change*, darling,' she says. '*Plus ça*-bloody-*change*.'

25

On the train home, I look down at my engagement ring and wonder whether Jack really is my Mr Right. And I'm erring on the side of 'Quite possibly, yes!' when my mobile twitters. It's a text from Olivia.

> What's ur problem?!?
> Jack is soooo lovely!!!
> And HOT!!!
> Not married, is he?!?!

It takes me a record time of only two minutes to send a text back:

> Hands off – he's mine!

I call Jack.
'Hey-ya! How was last night?'
'Brilliant. Great crowd, that lot. And you're right –

going out and getting things off your chest to a couple of like-minded souls over a few beers does you a world of good. I've got a T-shirt for you from Tim, by the way, for you to wear on Saturday night.'

'Nice one,' I say, imagining the size twenty-eight T-shirt.

'Bit of bad news, though,' he carries on. 'Paul's been made redundant.'

'No! How's he going to afford Tobi? And his wife?'

'Ex-wife,' Jack corrects me. 'I dunno, he's pretty cut up about it – as you would be. IT's really copping it these days – I hope I can keep my job . . .'

'You know, I've been thinking,' I say slowly.

'I'll alert the press,' he says.

'About Australia. It mightn't be such a bad idea, after all.'

'Well, it was mine . . .'

'But would you be up for a city, like Sydney – rather than the country?'

'Yup!'

'And I've been thinking about our wedding, too.'

'Well, we'll *have* to get married for you to be able to go out there—'

'But I don't want to do it as a green card thing – I think we should do it unrushed.'

'How much more unrushed could it be? We've been engaged for six bloody years!'

'So you do still want to get married, then? I mean, to me?'

'I do.'

'I'll start organising it, then.'

'The words *piss-up* and *brewery* come to mind,' he chortles.

'No – I want something a bit more romantic than that . . .'

'I meant I won't hold my breath, I'll believe it when I see it. But anyway, on to more important, *likely* things, I've called the insurance people and they *will* fix up Pavel's crap job on the house, so you can cross that one off your To Do list.'

'Oh, thanks.'

Oops. Not sure that one's ever made it to any of my endless lists.

I don't tell him I'm on my way home, figure I'll give them a surprise. I'm sure Charlie would approve of me adding a bit of mystery and spontaneity back into our lives.

When I get off the train at Riverside, the sun's shining, the sky is blue and the birdsong almost drowns out the sound of fast trains whizzing past – almost. And Riverside, in the sun, no water or flood damage to be seen, looks decidedly pretty – just as a small English village should. I rush to Sunny Farm Stores and chuck my remaining fags into the bin out the front with some force, thrusting my nose in the air and breathing in the sweet smell of jasmine and freshly cut grass.

'*Big Issue* today?' says the *Big Issue* guy, shoving one in my face.

'Yeah, go on.' I smile at him. 'Actually, I'll take two!'

I give him a fiver and practically *skip* across the road to the Really Rather Good Cafe. One last tea on my own before I go home and throw myself wholeheartedly into this good mum/wife thing once and for all can't hurt, can it?

I'm sitting at one of the tables outside, grinning at all the mums and their kids and thinking how *nice* it is here, when I see a familiar wonky buggy approaching. It's got an exceptionally gorgeous baby in it – all in pink, *obviously* a girl – and it's being pushed by a really rather fit, broad-shouldered hunk of veritable *spunk*.

But hang on . . . just wait a sec . . . who's that tall woman flicking her hair and walking a bit too closely to him? It's Carina. I knew it. Talk about *in flagrante*. Well, as good as.

'He-he-he-llo! Look! Look, Joey! It's Mummy!' Jack sings.

Joey looks unsure at first, but slowly her brilliant, big blue eyes start twinkling and she starts smiling, her grin getting wider and wider until she can bear it no more and shrieks:

'Da-*da*!'

Well, what are you going to do?

'Hello, sweetness!' I nearly start crying at the sight of *my family* – dad and daughter together, man and child. *My* man, *my* child. There's something adorable about that baby girl and definitely something very sexy about that man. Something Carina's clearly picked up on as well, no doubt.

'I've got some errands to run, better dash,' she says.

'See you on Saturday, then,' I say, not trying to stop her.

'Not if I see you first!' She looks back over her shoulder at Jack in the most wicked, wanton way I've ever seen someone do in real life – apart from Charlie last night in the King's Head, that is, when she was in full-flirt mode.

'Ah,' sighs Jack, pleased with himself as he sits down next to me. 'Aren't you supposed to be in London?'

'What's going on here, Jack?'

'I like to give her a bit of fresh air in the mornings, that's all, before she has a snooze. Makes her sleep better.'

'Not Joey, you *dick*! What's going on between you and Carina?'

'Watch your language, Rox – and in public, too.'

'So?'

'Nothing! Nothing at all. I bumped into her outside the post office. Why? You're not ... you're not *jealous*, are you?'

'What – of Carina? Ha-ha-*has if*!'

'Good.'

'Should I be?'

'No,' he sniffs. 'Awfully ugly, jealousy. Anyway, what are you doing back already?'

I remember (amazingly enough) the pep talk Charlie gave me in London and try to get on with making Jack happier.

'Came back early because I missed you guys far too much to stay away for a whole week . . .' I say cautiously, studying his face for any giveaway guilty signs.

'We missed you, too,' he says, leaning over to kiss me.

'Mah-ma! Mah-ma!' comes from Joey.

'No way! Did she just say Mama? Did you, clever girl?' Jack proudly asks. 'We've been practising while you've been gone.'

'Da-da!' Joey responds.

Not practising *enough*, obviously.

'So who's got their first pair of shoes, eh? Who's got new bright pink, fur-trimmed, big girl's boots?' I ask Joey.

'Yeah,' says Jack, looking down at her. 'Bit girly, not sure you'd approve, but these are the ones she liked most in the shop and we thought they were pretty cute—'

'Who's *we*?'

'Me and Mum,' he says wearily, pulling his beeping mobile out of his jeans pocket.

'Bloody work,' he sneers and flips the mobile shut, sliding it into his pocket. He pulls something out of his other pocket and secures a hot-pink clip in Joey's hair.

'Where'd you get that?'

'Mum got it for her.'

'Hmm.' I go all suspicious again.

'Ooh! Mummy's come home in a good mood, hasn't she? She should go up to London more often, shouldn't she, if it makes her like this, eh? Good mood Mummy!'

'Actually, you know, I *am* in a good mood. I think

you're right – a bit of time away really gave me a chance to think.'

'That's me, Mr Right,' he says, as Joey grabs him round the neck and plants a wet, snotty kiss on his lips.

'And I really do understand how awful it's been for you, lately – what with a job you hate, the fear of redundancy, the commute, the whole money situation—'

'It's not even the money so much, Rox – it's just after a long, hard day, I get home and you always have a go at me.'

'Well, things are going to be different from now on.'

'Look, I had a chance to think, too – when Joey was asleep,' Jack begins. 'And I can see how tough you've had it out here on your own with Joey demanding all your time and attention. It can't've been easy for you lately, either.'

'It hasn't been. But even if it *had*, I'd still have the right to get frustrated and annoyed and exhausted every now and again, you know,' I venture.

'And me! We just can't get narked with each other any more, that's all. It's not good for us and terrible for Joey.'

'Maybe we should take it in turns, going to the POP Club, then,' I suggest.

'Sounds like a plan,' he says, wiping Joey's nose with his sleeve. 'Sounds like a fuh – lamin' *brilliant* plan!'

My mobile chirrups and Jack jumps a bit, his hand darting to pat his jeans pocket.

'Keep your knickers on,' my top lip curls, 'it's mine.'

It's a text. From Charlie.

He rang! THE DATE rang!
Will bring with to R'side
for 137 mill's perusal. Will stay
at hotel. See you at pub! xxx

26

'Where are you?'

'The Swan,' says Jack.

'Golf finished, then?'

'Only just,' he says, loudly swallowing what sounds like lager.

'But I'm not ready yet—'

'Well, hurry up – it's rammed already!'

'Who's there?'

'Loads of people!'

'Carina?'

'Yeah! She's working the place like a mad woman.'

'Yeah, I *bet* she is . . .'

'Put your T-shirt on and get down here!' he shouts and hangs up just as I hear piercing laughter and glasses chinking and Carina's voice shrieking 'Hiya, doll!'

I managed to have a quick bath while Jack's mum looked after Joey this morning, but haven't put any make-up on yet. I want to take my time, savour the moment –

getting ready for a party. Must be about four years since I've done that . . .

I put on my pre-pregnancy khaki peasant skirt. The zip doesn't do all the way up, but never mind – the fundraiser poster POP Club T-shirt Tim gave me to wear is *massive* and swamps me, so I figure I'll be able to get away with it. It's a bit of a bugger, though – I was hoping I might've dropped a few pounds lately and be able to fit into some old clothes.

'Quick weigh-in, Joey?'

I grab the scales and try to find an even surface, but can't.

'What are you doing, Roxane?' asks Jack's mum.

'Um, thought I'd weigh Joey, see how she's going.'

'Ooh, I wouldn't do that if I were you. You don't want her to end up obese – or worse, anorexic or bulimic. You obsessing about her weight will only give her a nasty little complex about it.'

Normally, this sort of po-faced interference would really piss me off – especially coming from Jack's boob-grabbing mum. But I'm too excited about the fundraiser to let it bother me.

'OK then, Joey – let's slap up!'

Anita tuts and shakes her head while Joey gets to work totally destroying my favourite Guerlain lipstick from the Chiswick days.

I manage to put some foundation, powder, mascara and eyeliner on, even though I'm way out of practice. I'm still doing my eyeliner just like I did when I was fourteen – on the inside rim of my eye, convinced it makes my eyes look greener (despite the fact that it hurts, particularly when you haven't sharpened your eyeliner pencil for a thousand years). And we're ready to go.

It's just gone five o'clock by the time we get down to the pub. And it's *heaving*.

There are loads of other prams and babies and mums – I even recognise a couple of faces from those mother and baby groups – and toddlers running a-thorough-mok, in and out of the grown ups' legs. I'm startled by this party scene and I'm just trying to find Jack in the beer garden when I hear:

'Hello, Josephine's mum!' I turn around and it's the woman who runs the nursery. Cigarette in hand, she says, 'Wonderful idea, this. You should be very proud of yourself.'

'Oh, wasn't *my* idea!' I say, looking around.

'Really? I thought you set the whole thing up.' She points to my T-shirt.

'No – oh! The Club! Well, yeah, I suppose I did!'

'Why didn't you ever let us know at the nursery it was going on?' she says. 'Most of our parents could really do with this sort of thing.'

'Didn't occur to me . . . I just imagined everyone was happy with the existing mother and baby groups . . .'

'You've *got* to be kidding me – they're a nightmare,' she laughs as she slaps me on the arm and strides off to the bar.

I see Hermione, the doctor, who waves hello just as Rector Wilfred, Tim's dad, sidles up to me.

'Very impressive turn-out, Miss Carmichael,' he manages to say through his rictus smile. 'In no small part due to my boy's enthusiasm and flair for design, no doubt.'

I raise my eyebrows, surprised at this public praise for Tim.

'He is very talented,' I agree.

'It's not how I would have gone about it, of course, but a good result nonetheless,' he says, clasping his hands behind his back and rocking back and forth on his heels.

'That's pubs for you, eh? They can really bring a community together.'

'Not as well as a flood, or any other Act of God, my dear. That's His mysterious way – it looks like a tragedy on the face of it, but it's how one responds to hardship and suffering that maketh the man. Or woman, for that matter. And that's what people are here for tonight – to support those less fortunate than themselves – not to get drunk.'

I'm about to get into a debate about this, tell him how wrong he is in this instance, how the success of tonight *depends* on everyone getting pie-eyed when Olivia bombs over to us.

'And here she is, only the cutest little girl in Riverside,' she says, bending down and stroking Joey's cheek. 'She's the dead spit of Jack, isn't she? Or whoever her dad is . . . you any closer to finding out who that is, Rox?'

She grins at me, exposing her orange teeth as she

munches on a cheesy Wotsit. Wilfred gasps, looks up to the heavens and crosses himself. When he looks down again, he winks, smiling mischievously for a split-second and then makes a speedy exit.

'Ooh – where are the Wotsits, Liv? I'm starving!'

'Loadsa nibbles on the big table at the back there.' She turns around and points. 'All donated to the night by guess who?'

'Who?'

'Guess!'

'I haven't got a clue.'

'Marcus! *My* Marcus. He's brought loads of stuff for everyone to eat – mostly flood-damaged, but don't tell anyone else that! Isn't he wonderful?' She goes all dreamy, holds her hands in front of her and sways from side to side.

Only then do I notice she's wearing a dress. One of those floaty, flowery numbers. And she's had her hair highlighted. She's lost a tonne of weight and looks very, very pretty. Bound to score tonight, for sure.

'Is he here?'

'Yeah!' she giggles. 'Honestly, Rox – I think tonight could be the night. He is *sooooo* lovely!'

I look over at the big table with the Wotsits on it and see Tim's back. I know it's him because his white T-shirt says:

MEMBERS ONLY

Now, I don't know whether that's a reference to the POP Club or merely a statement of his sexual orientation, but it's definitely Tim. His laugh penetrates through the raucous crowd and I notice he's talking to Wilfred and Marcus, who is, it has to be said, looking particularly dishy tonight.

'Hey! There he is, talking to Tim over there,' I needlessly point out to Olivia, who's staring at him.

'Yeah. Isn't he *fit*?'

'God, yeah!'

Desperate to get a drink, I look around for Jack again so he can mind Joey for a second. Doesn't take long to spot him – he is six-foot-two, after all, and towers above even the tall, strapping country lads here.

I bump Joey's buggy gently into the back of his knees. He turns around.

'Hey, little one!'

He stamps his cigarette out on the ground, puts his pint on the nearest table, unstraps Joey and takes her out of the buggy.

'She's getting more and more adorable!' says Jules, our neighbour, who's standing there talking to Jack.

'You think so?' I look at Joey.

'No question! Can I have a hold?' she says, sticking her arms out. 'Anytime you two want to go out, just give us a shout and we'll babysit.'

'That's nice of you, Jules,' I say.

'Yeah, but careful what you say – we might take you up on it,' says Jack. 'Actually, Jules, in a couple of weeks . . .'

I make my way through the crowd and end up standing near Tim, Wilf and Marcus, leaning over the rail that's overlooking a little stream. The willow trees dangle in the water and the buzz of people having a good time around me makes me feel calm, almost relaxed. So much so, I figure I'm in no danger of smoking, so I can have a drink or two. And anyway, it's for charity!

I can hear the woman on the other side of me, talking to some bloke.

'Yairss, yairss, quaite the sun trap in summer – even the particularly rotten one wee-yah having.'

That horsey voice. Sounds familiar. I can only see the back of her head, but it looks like the perfectly coiffed and highlighted, neat blonde bob of . . .

'Vanessa?' I tap her shoulder.

'Hmm?' She looks at me.

'Are you Vanessa? From *Village Life*? I've only ever seen your photo on your Editor's letter.'

'Yairss – and you are?'

'Roxane. I did the restaurant review of this place for you.'

'Of course you did! Hair-*lair*!'

'How did you hear about this? You don't live in Riverside, do you?'

'Nair, nair – Langley Wootton, darling – Langley Wootton *Hates*,' she says.

'Langley Wootton hates what?'

'Hmm? Hates, dear, hates. The opposite of Langley Wootton *Downs*.'

'Oh. So how did you hear about this?'

'You can't move for posters in Langley. And the event organiser called me, last week, to hector me into coming. In the end, I felt it was my duty – both professional and civic – to be here.'

'Right, right,' I say, thinking how good Carina's been. PR-wise, that is.

'*Love* your T-shirt,' she says, reading my chest. 'Floody hell!'

'Oh. Yeah,' I say, embarrassed she's essentially staring at my boobs.

'We must do something on this, this *club*, don't you think? *Pear*-fect for *VL* – spirit of the community and awl that.'

'You're joking me! Really? The POP Club?'

'*Airb*-solutely. From what I can gather, it's *quaite* the local phenomenon. Branches are starting up in villages all over Berkshire.'

I'm gobsmacked.

'Would you do it for me, Roxane? Would you write a monthly run-down on the activities of the various clubs in the region? See what you can sniff out?'

'What, you mean like a column? A monthly column?'

'You could think of it like that, yes.'

'God, yeah! I'd love to!'

Wowsers, you come out to a party and you get a commission – a *column*, even! Never worked like this in London. When Charlie and I first left *TVText*, we'd go to all the magazine parties we heard about in a desperate bid to scare up freelance work. But all we got was a little bit trolleyed and, more often than not, scrubbed off Features Editors' freelance lists because of our shoddy behaviour.

'See that hypnosis worked a treat,' someone whispers loudly in my ear.

Barry.

'Barry! Hi!'

Vanessa looks down her nose at Barry and his orange, red and yellow tie-dyed POP Club fundraiser poster T-shirt, then looks up, pretending she's seen someone she knows in the crowd and scoots off.

'How's it going? How's Riverside Amdram? Crisis over?'

'Ah, you know. Not so good,' he says sadly, looking at his feet.

'It'll pick up,' I say unconvincingly.

One of his kids slams into his leg, just as he's lighting up.

'Hey! You little monkey! Gave me a shock, you did! Hey! Shock the monkey, hey hey!' He fairly *yodels* that ancient Peter Gabriel song.

'You can always fall back on your singing career,' I suggest.

'True, true.' He blows smoke out and grins, making the ginger bits in his goatee sparkle in the sun.

'Ooh, speaking of monkeys, I think this is mine.' I nod over Barry's shoulder and he turns to look at Jack helping

Joey to walk, holding her little hands up. She'll be walking on her own any day now.

'Mum's going to take Joey home now,' says Jack.

'Oh, good on her,' I say, picking Joey up and planting a big kiss on her soft cheek.

'Yeah, I better get my nippers off, too,' sighs Barry. Unfortunate choice of phrase for him to use, I think, imagining the way he must read those kids their bedtime stories: 'And so the three little pigs each built a house – *ooh yeah, a house* – one of out of straw, one out of bricks and one of sticks – *so good, yeah, sticks* . . .'

I smile as Barry walks off and think what a genuinely nice guy he is, though. And how he's really brightened up a couple of POP Club meetings, bursting into song when things were starting to get a bit too heavy and depressing.

'Wotcha, cock!' Tim turns Jack around by the elbow and they move into a big bear hug, slapping each other on the back twice, Tony Soprano-style. Once they separate, I see the front of Tim's T-shirt which says, simply:

THE
PISSED-OFF
PARENTS
CLUB

'Hey! How come you're not wearing the poster shirt?' I ask, thinking at least June'll be pleased: no apostrophe at all – grammatical gaffe averted this time.

351

'Wanted to stand out from the crowd,' Tim grins as he sips his Timblioni, looking surreptitiously over the top of his glass at the Wotsits table. 'I don't care what she says about you, Jack, I think you're an absolute dream. She's just a whingey old moo.'

'Charmed, I'm sure,' I say.

Jack laughs and says: 'Ah, she's not so bad, once you get to know her,' and puts his arm around my shoulders, kissing the top of my head.

Tim nudges Jack and whispers, conspiratorially: 'Never fear, Jackie-boy. Whatever's said at the POP Club, stays at the POP Club. Oh, so *this* must be your little boy.' He winks. 'She's a doll, Roxy – just beautiful!'

It really is a good turn-out. Loads of people I've never seen before are here – and there's some familiar faces, too, like one or two women I've seen about the village, pushing their prams. I don't know their names or anything, but one who I always exchange a smile and a 'Hiya' with as we pass each other in the street ambles over to me. She's hugely pregnant and sips on her orange juice as she says:

'I think I saw you at the church mother and baby group a while ago – how come you never came back?'

'Um – Joey, my daughter, sleeps – with any luck – when it's on, so I can't really get to that meeting,' I reply, lamely.

'I see,' she says, smiling. 'Nothing to do with the fact it's a crashing bore, then?'

'No! No – I—'

'Well, it is, let me tell you – I've been going for months now.'

'You should come to the POP Club! Wednesday nights, right here.'

'I will, I will – I had no idea such a club existed in Riverside, until last week when the rector gave us some big spiel about the evils of it. Must admit, though, it sounded like a lot of fun to me.'

'It is! Come next week, then, will you?'

'Great – I'll see you then, then!' and off she goes, waddling back to her group of mates.

As the night wears on, and the assembled throng gets rowdier, June strides up to me and Paul who are sitting by the stream, talking about his upcoming interview for some contract work and arguing about whether dads feel the same intensity as mums do about their offspring.

'Look, I don't mean to alarm you, but I sense trouble at mill,' she says, nodding her head in the direction of Tim and Olivia, who also seem to be arguing.

'Why? What's going on?' I ask.

'I'm not one hundred per cent sure, but I think I saw Tim kissing a man.'

'Good for him!' I raise my pint, by way of a cheer.

'And bad for Olivia, by the looks of it,' says June.

Olivia's crying and Tim's looking mystified.

'Maybe I can help,' says Paul, getting up and going over to them.

'Who was he kissing?' I ask June.

'Not sure. I only saw the back of his head. His rather lustrous, full head of hair. That's him, over there – oh! It's Marcus!'

She sits down next to me and we look on, watching the drama unfold.

Paul has his arm around a sobbing Olivia and Tim's got his hand on her shoulder. They all look distressed. Well, apart from Paul, who actually looks a tiny bit pleased.

'Olivia's had her eye on Marcus for a while now,' I say to June. 'But isn't Paul nice? Offering her his shoulder to cry on. What a gent.'

'Oh, Roxane – are you *blind*? There's more to Paul than chivalry. Haven't you noticed? Paul's *infatuated* with Olivia. Besotted!'

'He looks at her a lot, I've seen that, but—'

'How could you miss it? It's been so obvious!' June says, slapping my knee.

Paul walks Olivia over to us and says, 'I'm going to take Livvy home. I think she's had one too many. Time for bed, eh, Liv?'

June and I swap knowing glances. Olivia blows her nose.

'Gis a ring tomorrow, Rox, yeah?' she sniffs and off they go, Paul draping his jacket around her.

And then I see her, Carina herself, swanning through the doors like she owns the place. She flicks her hair and after she's handed a dodgy bloke in a suit a pint of beer, she lights a cigarette. Said dodgy-looking geezer stares after her and then turns back to his crowd of equally shifty-looking men in suits, most of them wearing sun-glasses. Looks like a mini Blues Brothers convention in that corner.

'Hiya, doll,' she says, bending down to kiss my cheek.

She looks a-*may*-zing. She's had her hair done jet-black and sleek again. Her make-up is thick, but perfect. Tonight she looks like Shania bloody Twain in her 'That Don't Impress Me Much' video, all floor-length, long-sleeved leopard-skin-print coat complete with hood and blood-red Angelina Jolie lips.

'How's it going?' I say, a little icily.

'Brilliantly. Of course.' She laughs as she says 'Of course', as though it's her event, she organised it all, so naturally it's going fabulously. She fixes her face into her whiter-than-white Hollywood smile and looks around, admiring her handiwork, making me even more self-conscious of my beige, gappy gnashers.

'Took for *ever* to get a drink in there – the queue's massive! Had to get a quadruple gin – just in case,' she says. 'So what's happening with you lot?'

'Well, Tim kissed Marcus, who Olivia's fancied for ages, apparently. She's distraught and Paul's taken her home,' June fills her in.

'No!' says Carina. 'Well, he did fancy her the minute he showed up to his first meeting. And Marcus wasn't interested in me, so, he *had* to be gay, didn't he?'

She takes a huge, lung-busting drag on her fag, making me cough.

'Well, anyway – it isn't a party till someone's heart gets broke. And if I know anything, it's how to throw a really good party!'

And how to break someone's heart, I think. I'm starting to get a little tipsy, now, and think I can see things more clearly.

'Honestly, it wasn't my fault – I didn't know!' says an exasperated Tim, running up to our little group.

'Sit down,' I say, pulling at his elbow. I always feel more comfortable when everybody's sitting down. More of a level playing field, I find.

'. . . And *he* asked *me* out! Weeks ago! I wouldn't have done anything if I'd known – I'd never piss on anyone's chips,' says Tim softly.

'Is that the same thing as cutting someone's lunch?' I wonder aloud.

'I've been having a word with your mother, Tim,' says June. 'And I think I may have convinced her to see more of you and your sister, regardless of what the rector says.'

'Really? He's actually being quite friendly to me tonight. Says he's really impressed with this whole benefit thing. Thanks, June,' says Tim, flashing a wan smile. 'But what about Olivia? Oh, it's all my fault!'

'It is not your fault, Tim!' says June sternly.

'Course it's not!' I chime in.

Then manager Marcus appears.

'I'm really sorry if I've caused any upset,' he says, looking really worried. 'I had no idea Olivia felt like that – and it certainly didn't occur to me to feel that way about her.'

'Sit down!' I say loudly, tugging at the sleeve of his Nehru-collared, cream cheesecloth shirt.

'I was just being friendly,' he says, looking nervously at Tim. '. . . Moving to a new village, starting a new job and all, I really wanted to get on well with my staff. I never meant to give her the wrong impression.'

'Course you didn't!' I shout.

'Honestly, I didn't mean to hurt her,' Marcus says, putting his hand on Tim's shoulder. 'Or *anyone*.'

'I know you didn't, Marcus.' Tim looks into the manager's eyes. 'So what are we going to do now?'

'Have another Timblioni and talk about it?' Marcus smiles.

'OK,' says Tim, brightening up a bit. 'Come to the bar with me?'

'Always ready to help a damsel in distress,' he says and they walk off together.

'You *go*, girl!' says Carina, looking after them.

Through the mass of people, I see a dishevelled, but deliriously happy-looking Charlie. She's looking up into the eyes of a very tall, very dark and *very* handsome man. He bends down to kiss her and when she manages to tear her eyes away from him, she spots me. She gently breaks away from his muscly embrace and walks, a little shakily, over to me.

I jump up to give her a hug. She positively *reeks* of sex.

'Sorry it took so long to get here,' she gurns. 'Got delayed in the hotel.'

'You dirty stop-out!' I grin at her.

'Yeah, I know. I can't keep my hands off him. Isn't he to die for?'

'Is that *The Date*?' I squint in his direction. He's standing on his own and waves briefly, before he's accosted by Carina.

'Ooh, yeah. Fit as,' I can't help but agree. 'I'd watch out for Carina, though. Man-eater extraordinaire. The one who's screwing Jack behind my back,' I frown.

'What?'

'Carina. You've met her, liked her rings and slutty shoes, remember? I've told you all about her – she's the one who's got her hooks into Jack. I even caught them together, walking along the street with Joey the other day, when I got back from London.'

'You're such a *dick*!' says Charlie forcefully.

'Being in love's softened you up, then,' I say, wondering what on earth I've said wrong this time.

'You just don't know how lucky you are, do you?'

'Eh?'

'Jack *adores* you. He'd never be unfaithful to you. And certainly not with the likes of her. Not his type.'

'Don't think *I'm* his type any more,' I pout.

'Oh, come on! He's more likely to go for one of those two over there than a footballer's wife like that.' She nods in the direction of Tim and Marcus, snogging by the Wotsits.

'You still think he's gay, then? So *IN*, as you always say?'

'No! That's a joke! Honestly, Rox, you are so *dim* sometimes.'

'But he's definitely playing away,' I say, searching Charlie's eyes for confirmation.

'No he isn't. Why do you always do this, Roxane? Why do you insist on sabotaging your own self? I mean, you live in this beautiful little village with the wonderful Jack and Joey – I'd kill to be in your situation. Why ruin it with your silly little made-up stories? Too much bloody time on your hands, that's what it is!'

'Maybe. But that doesn't explain why Jack's been so secretive lately. Doesn't explain why he gets all funny when I'm there and his phone rings. What's that all about, eh? Hmm? Answer me that, Chazzer!'

'Oh, God!' She's getting really frustrated with me.

'You can't, can you? Well, that's it. I'm going to have it out with the pair of them, right now!'

Maybe the alcohol's messing with my mind – or maybe I'm finally seeing things clearly. Either way, I need to know, need to find out once and for all.

'Stop!' Charlie grabs my arm and pulls me back down to my chair. 'Don't ruin the best night out you've had together for, like, ever! Look at him, he's having a great time!'

'Yeah – with *her*. *And* we haven't had sex for God knows how long! You've got to admit, Chuckie, it doesn't look good from where I'm standing.'

'Sit *down*, Roxane!' Charlie shouts. I do as I'm told and look around, embarrassed.

'Look. Jack's gonna kill me for telling you this, but the reason he's acting all weird with Carina is . . . oh God . . .'

'Spit it out!'

'They're organising a surprise party for your fortieth birthday!'

'Wha—'

'You let on that you know and I swear, I'll kill you!'

I'm speechless, so just stare at Charlie with my mouth open.

'It's going to be in some swanky bar in Reading. Carina owns it, apparently – it was a wedding gift from her husband. Anyway, she's letting Jack have it for free—'

'I *bet* she is—'

'Shut. The fuck. Up! She's been contacting all your old friends in London for him – that's why your mobile went missing. It's been hell getting a date everyone can make, but it's set now. It'll be in four weeks' time.'

'Oh.'

We sit in silence for what seems like five minutes, but is probably really only five seconds. I'm having trouble taking it all in. And I've been such a bitch about Carina. I feel hot and elated – but rotten at the same time.

'I better apologise to Carina, then. For thinking the worst of her . . .'

'No! Don't! She'll know you know.'

'Have you been speaking to her?'

'Yes, a few times. She's really nice. Nothing like the bitch on wheels you describe.'

'Well, I thought she was a home-wrecker!'

'You don't need her help.'

'I feel terrible! I've thought so badly of her. And Jack!'

'She thinks the world of you, you know. She's doing the whole thing for you for free. To say thanks.'

'For what?'

'The Pissed-Off Parents Club. Reckons it saved her sanity.'

'Her and me both.'

'Well, *her*, yeah. Oh, promise me you won't say anything to anyone? I can't believe I just sang like a canary!'

I look at Jack, The Date and Carina all bending backwards, laughing. Carina tosses her hair about and Jack strokes his own balding pate self-consciously. My man. My fabulous, loving, thoughtful man. I catch his eye and beckon him over to me and Charlie.

'Jeez, so it's all kicked off here, then,' he says, stooping to kiss Charlie's fast-reddening cheeks.

'What?' startles Charlie, nervously. 'No, no, everything's fine! Nothing to see here . . .'

'He means Marcus, Tim and Olivia,' I say, putting my hand on her forearm to calm her down. 'Couple of the POP Club members got their wires crossed. Liv wanted Marcus, but Marcus wanted Tim. So Livvy left with . . . Paul – the one I had in mind for you.'

'Thank God I wasn't depending on you two for my love

life, then,' she says and beams at The Date. She mouths the words 'Come here' and he jumps at the chance.

Charlie proudly introduces The Date. 'John, this is Roxy and Jack. Roxy, Jack – this is John.'

'Nice to meet you,' I say, stumbling into Jack's tummy as I stand up to shake John's hand.

'Whoa!' laughs Jack, catching my fall. 'Shall we go home, darl? Something tells me you've had enough.'

The walk home clears my head somewhat. It's like I'm seeing everything in a whole new light: Jack looks more gorgeous than ever and I feel more attached to him – not as scared or threatened, insecure or hateful. I feel a glow of – what? Contentment? – surrounding me, like a full-body halo and, as he tangles his fingers around mine, I look up at him, coming over all peculiar. My tummy feels tingly and ... Ah, yes – that's it! No wonder I didn't recognise this alien, unfamiliar feeling ...

His mum's asleep on the sofa bed, so we creep past her, giggling as Joey's donkey puzzle starts braying.

We've barely got upstairs and closed our bedroom door before we're at it. And we *really* go for it – like two starving weight watchers gobbling down an extra large pizza when they've just found out it has zero points.

It goes on for much longer than you'd expect, considering we haven't been intimate with each other for several aeons. But that's guys as they get older for you, isn't it? Especially if alcohol's involved.

Don't get me wrong – I'm not complaining. No way! It's fun. Really good fun. And as our arms and legs entwine, I feel the distance that has built up between us over the past few months melting away.

'Did you . . . you know?' he eventually nuzzles into my ear.

'No. But it was still nice.'

'Out of practice,' he says snoozily. 'Sorry.'

'Don't be,' I whisper, as Jack begins to snore.

Epilogue

Since the benefit (which raised £70,000 according to spin-queen Carina – more like £30,000 if you ask June), we've had four more Pissed-Off Parents Club meetings. Jack and I have been to two each – and I've neither drunk nor smoked at my two sessions. And they say miracles never happen.

Now Wednesday nights at The Swan may *look* like any normal popular pub night, but there's a certain buzz, an air of collective cynicism, stressed-out solidarity about the place. Relationship-specific splinter groups have formed and sit at separate tables – there's the Narked Nannas, the Angry Aunties and, Jack's favourite, the Fucked-Off Fathers. One or two tables aren't parents at all, aren't even remotely pissed off, they're just there for the beer and the now legendary good night out. But the hardcore, the founders, still all sit together every week, banging on about the various hardships and frustrations of being a parent.

June brings her daughter, Emma, with her now, and they're so alike it's uncanny. Not just the way they look, squinting and peering over their glasses, holding on to each other's shoulders and knees when they've had one too many, but the way they talk and think, too. They both sit there smoking their fags through ever more expensive-looking cigarette holders and correcting everyone's grammar. June finally got what she was pining for, I suppose – quality talking time with Emma.

Olivia was mortified she'd been so wrong about Marcus, but they talked, both falling over themselves with apologies and now we all laugh about it – well, we did once and it's never been mentioned since. She's moving in with Paul – just until her sister's house is fixed up, she says. She reckons their relationship is purely platonic at this stage, and she wants to enjoy being single for a little while longer.

Paul got the contract job he went for and is much happier and far richer than when he was a full-time wage slave. It's common knowledge that he's crazy about Olivia but he says he can wait. Wait for her to come to her senses and realise that he is, indeed, her handsome prince. Persistence and patience, Paul says, always pay off in the end. It's the same thing he says to Jack when he beats him at golf or *Civ*, much to Jack's annoyance. They've played golf together a lot, recently – with Carina – which has been great for Jack. And funnily enough, it hasn't bothered me in the slightest.

Tim and Marcus are a full-on item. Match made in heaven, that one. They sip their Timblionis, holding hands, finishing each other's sentences or saying the same things at exactly the same time. Which, with any other couple, might make you sick. But they're so funny and so *right* for each other, it makes you a bit, I don't know ... *envious* more than anything else.

Tim says he and his dad had something of a rapprochement at the fundraiser. They've agreed to disagree about Tim's sexuality and Mrs Wilf sees both Tim and his sister much more. She's even babysat the twins once so far, so Tim and Lisa could go to a POPC meeting together.

That night, actually, there was even talk about Lisa being a surrogate mother for Tim and Marcus, the latter doing the honours into the old turkey baster. But that was just a joke. Or at least I think it was.

Carina's become a bit of a local celebrity and official spokesperson for the POP Club. She's been on the news, talking about the Club, the fundraiser and her Disco Mama – And Baby! afternoons. They're even having her on *This Morning* next week. And she's helping me organise our wedding at that hotel in Aldenham. Well, when I say helping, what I mean is, she's doing everything. And she's right, she *is* brilliant. I never would have thought I'd say it, but she's really genuine (unlike her hair/tan/nails/teeth) and nowhere near as hard as I had her down as being. Soft as Camembert that's been left out in the sun, really.

Speaking of soft, Charlie came down for a meeting a week ago. With John. She says he's The One and can't describe what she feels for him, other than that it's 'immense'. He feels the same way too, judging by the way he mauls her every five minutes. She's still brutally honest – but she smiles more. It must be love. And that John's a brave, brave man. Not that I'd ever tell *her* that – I've finally learnt my lesson on that score.

Barry's got a part-time accounting job and still does his hypnosis, which, he says, makes more money than the accounting – seems Riverside's ridden with addicts and troubled souls. He's written a one-man musical, called *When Barry Went Doolally* – about a born entertainer who becomes a father of four and tries to leave 'the biz of show' behind, but can't. Not remotely autobiographical, obviously – and we're all going to see it in a couple of weeks.

'Good on you!' we all cheered when he told us his show had been booked by Riverside Theatre.

'Well, we are all of us in the gutter, but some of us are looking at the stars,' he sang.

'Chrissie Hynde, right? The Pretenders!' I said.

'Actually,' said Tim, smirking at Marcus.

'I think you'll find,' said Marcus, picking up the baton in their conversational relay.

'It was originally Oscar Wilde,' they said in unison, nodding smugly.

Come to think of it, I take back what I said earlier – sometimes those two really can get on your tits.

It's Friday night now – the night before my surprise for-tieth birthday party. I've managed to keep the secret to myself and not let on that I know what's in store for me. Well, apart from babbling on to Joey about how wonderful and fabulous her daddy is and wondering who's going to be there and asking her whether I should wear the black velvet maternity atrocity or not. Actually, it's been quite easy. When I think of it, I just look lovingly in Jack's direc-tion and get this sort of beatific, sickly smile on my face, thinking how lucky I am and how much I really do love him. It probably gives Jack the willies.

It's sort of like that feeling you get when you find out you're pregnant – there's butterflies in your stomach and you feel a bit dizzy. Just you, your little secret and the heart-popping excitement and anticipation of what's to come. Exactly like that, now I think about it.

While Joey holds on to the TV stand and watches the Bedtime Hour on CBeebies, I open the kitchen drawer and grab the pregnancy test I bought earlier today. My period was due two days ago – and considering it's run like clockwork, appearing every twenty-eight days since Joey was born, something's not right. Maybe if I do the test and it's negative, I'll stop worrying and it'll bring my period on.

'Just nipping to the loo, sweet,' I say to the back of Joey's head.

Five minutes later, I'm back in the rubble that is our kitchen, cuddling Joey on my lap. She can't take her eyes off the telly – and neither can I. But while she's transfixed by Upsy Daisy, I'm just stunned – catatonic with disbelief.

Eventually, I manage to pull myself together enough to give Joey a bath. I make her munch on her baby toothbrush for thirty seconds or so, get her into her pink, plaid pyjama top and rock her to sleep, her head resting on my shoulder, singing 'Yes, my name is Igglepiggle, Iggle, wiggle iggle iggle piggle' over and over, getting slower and quieter with every round. Her chubby arm hangs off mine, and I make it last as long as possible. In fact, I don't rush any of her bedtime routine these days – not like I used to, desperate to get outside and have a cigarette. And, as a result, she's flat out by the time I lower her into her cot and zip her up into her sleeping bag. Looking beautiful.

Jack's back from his hypnosis session with Barry, and I can hear him opening a bottle of beer and going outside. I turn Joey's dim bedroom light off and she stirs briefly as the floorboards creak, like a klaxon, signalling my exit.

Downstairs, I make a chamomile tea and look around me. Will it ever end – the constant work in progress on our house? I'm transported back to a few months ago, when all this started. The house looks the same – unfinished and barely habitable – and dark clouds are spreading themselves against the evening sky, threatening a deluge any minute now.

It feels the same – but totally different at the same time. Or maybe that's just me. I step over the dust and bricks and bits of plaster and go outside to see how Jack's going.

'We're missing double *Corrie* out here,' I announce.

'I couldn't give a rat's,' he sighs.

Without cigarettes, Jack can quickly become quite snippy. I'll have to tread carefully for the next few days, not take any outbursts personally.

'So, how'd it go?' I ask tentatively.

'Bit weird. But can we not talk about it? Please? I don't wanna – talk about it . . .' He sings the last bit like Rod Stewart. Quite impressively, if truth be told.

Seems the Barry Effect has really taken a hold of all of us.

We sit there on the rickety old kitchen chairs from Chiswick and look out at the pine trees barely concealing the estate at the back of our place, listening to the squealing kids jumping up and down on a trampoline.

'Picture us out in Australia,' says Jack wistfully. 'Sitting on our verandah in the cool of the evening, sharing a bottle of wine, Joey playing in our huge garden with—'

'Bushfires? Spiders and snakes?'

Jack bristles. Only slightly, but he definitely bristles.

'No! With her little brother or sister.'

'Interesting you should say that,' I venture, even more warily than when I'd asked about the hypnosis.

'It's just . . . winter's fast on its way and that commute into London's going to be dark and cold and wet and I'll freeze my nadgers off. It's going to *really* piss me off.' He looks cross at the thought.

'There's a club for people like you, you know – right here in Riverside!'

'Urgh.'

'Issa noh so bad . . .' I sing.

'Ah shaddap-a-you face,' he says flatly. 'Look, I'm really pleased that you're so happy these days, Rox, really I am. But what about me? Can we move to Oz soon? See if it makes me happy?'

'OK, then!'

'Really? How soon?'

I try to do my mental calculations. Let's see . . . some airlines won't let you fly when you're over seven months, and you wouldn't want to take any risks in the first three months, so that means we've got a window of opportunity to fly in, roughly . . .

'Um, sometime soon! Really soon. After we get married.'

'Really? That's a surprise . . .'

I see my chance and leap in.

'Speaking of surprises . . .'

He takes a long, slow slug of his beer and I wonder whether now's a good time to tell him or not. I could save it for tomorrow night – see his surprise and raise it . . .

'Ummmm . . . I'm pregnant, Jack.'

He splutters and coughs. 'What?'

'Yup. Pregnant. Me. I am.'

'Is it mine?' He recovers from his choking fit and an almost-smile starts to curl around the sides of his mouth.

'But . . . but we've only had sex *once*, in, like, the last hundred years!'

'It only takes one—'

'Or 137 million in my case . . .'

We both jump up and he hugs me tight. Then he breaks away slowly and guides me gently back down to my chair.

'You should watch it, in your condition.'

'Australia, here we come.' I let out a deep sigh.

'Atta girl!' he says.

It's getting a bit chilly, so Jack goes inside to get one of his extra-large, five-pound bargain-garage fleeces for me, a celebratory beer for himself and to quickly check on Joey. When he comes back out, his eyes have nearly disappeared, they're so hidden by his cheeks, bulging up into them with glee. He looks just like Joey when she first sees Jack of an evening. He puts his hand on my knee and says:

'I can't believe it!'

He gazes at me, misty-eyed.

'It's going to be a real adventure!' he says. 'As long as we're together and the bundle's healthy and Joey's happy, what more do we need? Love, I believe they say, is *all* you need.'

'Next thing you know, you'll be putting Baby on Board signs in the car. Since when did you come over all Hallmark-card cheesy?'

'Since I became a daddy, probably. But anyway, it's true!'

I look at him, all dewy-eyed with excitement and expectation and realise I barely recognise the two of us any more. A few months ago we were different people, constantly rowing, always at each other's throats – stressed out and miserable. But now Jack's got his old optimism back and it's catching. Just like Barry's song-aholism, it's contagious. Things have changed – we've changed. We've grown. Grown *up*, even.

'You're right, you're right,' I concede.

We both smile and sit back, relaxing and imagining all the good things to come. I close my eyes and let myself go with the positive flow. And when he speaks again, I can picture his handsome face fairly beaming with pride.

'It's going to be amazing. And that's *Mister* bloody Right to you!'

And you know what? He just might be.

Acknowledgements

Firstly I'd like to thank Jon for his love, warmth, generosity, wit, charm and critical eye; his wonderful SOH and general gorgeousness keep me going. Thanks, Roo! And thank you, Sammi – the most beautiful, smart, vivacious, funny, brilliantly un-self-conscious, fantastic daughter ever. Long may you look at the world with those stunning eyes – and keep on processing it through your marvellously nutty filter.

Tremendous, gigantic and *boundless* amounts of love and thanks go to: my beautiful mum for letting me read out reams of stuff over the phone to her – and actually staying awake long enough to offer invaluable criticism; my handsome hero of a dad for his incessant worrying about, nagging and badgering me to at least *try* to do something with my life; Rolls for always being so hardcore about *everything* – and never failing to offer the opposing view. With gusto. Reading really IS the answer!

Massive thanks to Rowan Lawton (my fab agent),

Rebecca Saunders (my amazing editor), Emma Stonex (copy-editor extraordinaire) and all at Little, Brown in the UK and Hachette in Australia.

Shedloads of thanks go to Aideen Clarke for her encouragement and loveliness in the face of me voicing my doubts and insecurities with such alarming yet borax regularity . . . and not dumping me as a result. And all while juggling one wilful wood sprite of a kid, with another one on the way. Talk about Supermum . . .

And to Emma Kelly (nee Wyatt) – who in no way, shape or form *ever* provided *any* inspiration for any of the characters – I am eternally grateful . . . mostly for making me laugh at life's endless disappointments and making herself go blind reading bits of The POPC late into the night when she could have been out largin' it at some muddy festival somewhere. Or sinking San Migs at the Volly.

Huge thanks to Jamie for not only his continuing friendship, but also his highly-trained legal eye – thanks for not charging me for either of them.

Bucketloads of thanks go to Anna, Julie, Chloe, Frankie and Charlotte at the PDN for saving my life on more than one occasion – get those gaspers in, girls!

Thank you, thank you, a thousand thank yous to Paul Weller for so many hours, years, decades . . . a lifetime of listening pleasure.

And finally, a big thanks to all pissed-off parents everywhere. I applaud your honesty and good taste.